CODE NAME:
Grand Guignol

Novels by Ib Melchior

Code Name: Grand Guignol
V-3
Eva
The Tombstone Cipher
The Marcus Device
The Watchdogs of Abaddon
The Haigerloch Project
Sleeper Agent
Order of Battle

CODE NAME:

Grand Guignol

A NOVEL

BY

Ib Melchior

DODD, MEAD & COMPANY
New York

Copyright © 1987 by Ib Melchior
All rights reserved
No part of this book may be reproduced in any form
without permission in writing from the publisher.
Published by Dodd, Mead & Company, Inc.,
71 Fifth Avenue, New York, N.Y. 10003
Manufactured in the United States of America
Designed by Mark Bergeron
First Edition

1   2   3   4   5   6   7   8   9   10

Library of Congress Cataloging-in-Publication Data

Melchior, Ib
    Code name, Grand Guignol.

    1. World War, 1939–1943—Fiction.   I. Title.
PS3563.E435C6   1987   813'.54   87-9261
ISBN 0-396-08817-1

To Cleo—whose contribution is
greater than she knows

12/17/87 $0.T

GRAND GUIGNOL: Term for a type of short gothic play emphasizing violence, horror, and terror. This macabre form of theater became popular in Parisian cabarets and theaters in the nineteenth century, especially at the Theatre du Grand Guignol. The gory tales of mayhem and carnage probably were named Grand Guignol because the violent plots of the bloody one-act plays, performed by actors on a legitimate stage, resembled those of the Punch-and-Judy-like puppet shows that featured a popular puppet named Guignol, whose name became synonymous with the kind of miniature theater commonplace in France at the time. Thus, Grand Guignol was a horror show for grown-ups instead of a rowdy puppet theater for tots. *Webster's* gives the phrase "grand-guignolism" as a synonym for horror.

CODE NAME: GRAND GUIGNOL is based on a fantastic, little-known scheme of the Nazis during World War II just before D-Day—a scheme that has been "forgotten" in the dramatic events that followed the invasion, but a scheme that, had it been successful, might drastically have altered those events.

Acknowledgements

The author wishes to express his appreciation for the valuable assistance given him in the research for this book by:

Militärarchiv, Bundesarchiv, Freiburg i. Br. West Germany
National Archives, Modern Military Headquarters Branch, Military Archives Division, Washington, D.C.
Directorate of History, National Defence Headquarters, Ottawa, Ontario, Canada
Public Archives, Canada, State & Military Records, Ottawa, Ontario, Canada

HDP GROSSBATTERIE WIESE

RF 11 Sb 2

<u>Geheim!</u>   29.3.1944

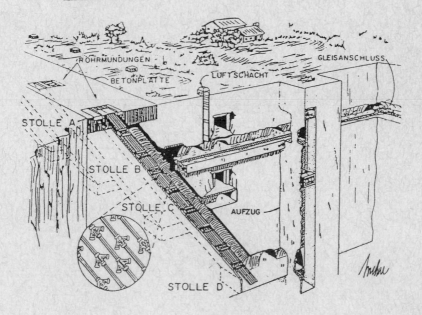

ROHRMÜNDUNGEN   GLEISANSCHLUSS
BETONPLATTE   LUFTSCHACHT

STOLLE A

STOLLE B

STOLLE C   AUFZUG

STOLLE D

"PROJEKT 51"
ANLAGE OST

Geheim

PROLOGUE

Berlin, December 1942

REICHSMINISTER Albert Speer, Armament and Munitions Minister of Adolf Hitler's Third Reich, stared at the sketches and plans, graphs and computations spread out on his desk before him. He knew he was looking at the work of a genius.

Or a madman.

He lifted his eyes to meet the steady, steel-blue gaze of the young SS officer who sat in stiff self-assurance before him. *Standartenführer* Dieter Haupt. He knew the colonel's reputation: a top-flight engineer, audacious and imaginative, who worked directly under August Cönders, the inventive Chief Engineer at the *Röchling Stahlwerke* (one of Germany's most important armament plants), where the effective Röchling fin-stabilized anti-concrete shell had been developed.

"Impressive," he acknowledged. "*Fast unglaublich*—almost unbelievable."

"But it will work, Herr Reichsminister," Dieter Haupt said earnestly. "It *will*."

Unconsciously he leaned forward in his chair, as if closeness would lend convincement to his words. Attentively he watched the expressionless face of the man sitting across from him. Despite himself, he felt awed. Speer was only thirty-seven—two years older than he, himself—and already he occupied the all-important position of Minister of Armament for the entire Reich and was a trusted friend of the Führer himself. And the man had been a mere thirty-six when the Führer had appointed him to the post. His predecessor, the brilliant engineer SS General Fritz Todt, head of the *Organisation Todt* that was in charge of constructing all the Reich's fortifications, had been killed when his plane crashed in taking off from the Führer's headquarters in Rastenburg. Speer was a man to be reckoned with. Exactly the kind of *Bonze*—big wheel—he wanted.

And needed.

Speer leaned back in his chair. Did it indicate disinterest? Haupt felt himself go tense.

"Why are you bringing this to me, Haupt?" Speer asked pointedly. "You have direct superiors—in your work at the Steelworks, in the SS. Why me?"

"Because, *Herr Reichsminister*, in your capacity of armament minister you are accountable only to the Führer directly. Doctor Cönders is, of course, involved in the development of the project, but he—procrastinates," the young officer said, his voice clipped with disdain. Like brittle ice crystals, his eyes fixed the older man. "There is no time for polite formalities, Herr Speer. No time for interdepartmental squabbles and jealousies. This project must go forward. Now."

"If your superiors learn you have violated demanded procedures so flagrantly," Speer warned, "you may well regret your actions."

"They will not learn," Haupt snapped. "Not from me." The hint of a smile stretched his lips. "And—with all due respect, *Herr Reichsminister*—I do not believe you will denounce me either."

"Why shouldn't I? You are supposed to be a loyal party member, *Standartenführer* Haupt. You are under orders to go through proper channels."

"Of course," Haupt acknowledged, impatience sharpening his voice. Brazenly he locked his disturbingly cold eyes on Speer. "I *am* deliberately going over the heads of my superiors—Doctor Cönders at Röchling, the SS hierarchy, *Reichsführer* Heinrich Himmler himself. Yes." The studied monotone of his voice bordered on insolence. "You are, as you point out, Herr Reichsminister," he continued, "fully aware of that fact. Yet you have consented to see me and to examine and discuss the project." He paused ever so briefly. "That, too, could be interpreted as, may I say, infringing upon the authority of others." Again the slight pause. "As it is, however, a priority order needs only come down from the Führer, through you, *Herr Reichsminister*, to proceed with the project. *You* will then place me in charge. *You* can allocate the necessary funds and provide a sufficient number of laborers. It will, needless to point out, take thousands. And they will, of course, have to be—expendable."

Speer stared at the young officer. The man's reputation for audacity had certainly not been exaggerated, he thought. There was a cold strength about him. He would be a difficult man to have as an ally. Far worse as an enemy. Speer was intrigued—both with the man and his incredible project.

"Why now, Haupt?" he asked softly. "Why is the urgency now so great that you elect to take such grave personal risks?"

For a brief moment Dieter Haupt sat silent, his face grim, his eyes hard. . . .

"*Herr Reichsminister*," he said finally. "It is now December 1942. Late December. The war is a little over a year old. We have had triumphs, unequaled triumphs, under the leadership of the Führer. But—that will not last. Our armies are even now being defeated in Russia. Stalingrad will not fall to us. Von Manstein and von Paulus are being beaten on the eastern front. The Sixth Army may well be lost. And, *Herr Reichsminister*, the Americans are not yet committed to the battlefields on the western front." He paused for emphasis. "Once they are, we shall not be able to prevail against the flood of men and materiel they will be able to hurl against us. Unless. Unless we have secured an undisputed, irreversible hold on the entire Continent. And on the British Isles. Unless we have made it *impossible* for the enemy to invade our territory." Without taking his eyes off Speer, he placed his hand on the papers on the desk. "With this!" he finished.

He sat back.

Speer contemplated him gravely. "You are playing with fire, Haupt," he observed quietly. "Dangerous fire. That is defeatist talk."

"But true, nevertheless, *Herr Reichsminister*."

"You know how the Führer deals with defeatism—and those who dare voice it."

"I am confident my remarks will remain in this office, *Herr Reichsminister*," Haupt said tautly. "But I stand by my words. I am willing to take the risk." His eyes were hard on Speer. "I *have* taken it."

Speer sat silent. There were risks. For him as well. But the young SS officer, with all his brash presumptuousness, had voiced what was in his own mind. Unless there was a drastic swing of power to the Third Reich, the war could not be won. Perhaps *Standartentührer* Haupt's project *was* the answer.

"One more thing to be considered, *Herr Reichsminister*," the officer broke in on his silence. "Unlike other superweapons, poison gases for instance, this weapon will in no possible way be able to inflict any kind of damage on the Reich or the German people. Only on the enemy." He smiled a strangely predatory smile, as if daring anyone to contest it. "That is another virtue of Lizzie."

Speer looked up questioningly.

"That is what I call the project, *Herr Reichsminister*," Haupt grinned. "*Fleissiges Lieschen*—Busy Lizzie."

"I admire your belief in your—Busy Lizzie, Haupt," Speer said, a caustic chill in his voice. "But—there apparently are several problems still to be dealt with before your project can become operational." He indicated the papers on the desk.

"Minor problems, *Herr Reichsminister*," Haupt said with a wave of his hand in dismissal. "They will be taken care of."

"How long will you need to do it?"

"Six months. By next summer Lizzie will be ready for the construction stage."

Speer stood up. "Report to me at that time," he said. He looked directly at the officer, who had risen when he did. "And Haupt," he said. "This conversation never took place. Understood?"

Dieter Haupt drew himself up smartly. He exulted. He was on his way. He—and Lizzie. "Understood, *Herr Reichsminister*." He threw his arm up in a stiff Nazi salute. "*Heil Hitler!*"

"*Heil Hitler*," Speer answered.

The young officer left.

Albert Speer stood for a moment in frowning thought. Perhaps. . . .

He walked to the window in his office in the imposing New Reich Chancellery—one of the great buildings he, himself, as the Führer's chief architect, had designed. Completed in 1939, it was part of the Führer's plan to rebuild Berlin in the image of the thousand-year Third Reich. He remembered well how proud he'd been when the Führer had appointed him Design/Architect in Chief for the Third Reich. He had been twenty-eight.

He sighed. Architecture. That was his life. Not armament. Not fortifications. Not the management of slave labor. But the Führer had appointed him to his present post. The Führer believed in him. And he would do everything in his power to carry out what the Führer demanded of him.

———

He gazed out the window. The hectic wartime traffic ground by on Wilhelmstrasse below.

Standartenführer Dieter Haupt had been correct, he thought. The war was going badly in Russia. But it was a temporary setback. He was certain of it. The Führer's leadership would bring ultimate victory. Haupt's Project Busy Lizzie might never have to be used—even if the young engineer and his co-workers could perfect it. Germany would still become the ruling nation in all of Europe. Perhaps in all of the world.

But as he briskly walked back to his desk, disturbing doubts rippled beneath the surface of confidence in his mind.

Busy Lizzie. An incredible, an astounding, and deadly weapon.

Perhaps she might after all be called upon to play a decisive role in the triumph of Adolf Hitler's Third Reich.

From all indications, she might well be equal to the task.

❆ **PART ONE** ❆

Paris, April–May 1944

❖ 1 ❖

KEVIN jabbed his gleaming screwdriver into Emile's eye socket as his fellow inmates pinned the terror-stricken victim down on the rough, wooden bench. Gleefully, he pried out the eye so it slid down the man's forehead in a spurt of gore to plop on the floor.

The German Wehrmacht officer front row center fainted dead away.

Even as he groped in the synthetic "gore" contained in the little rubber pouch hidden behind Emile's glass eye, Kevin grinned to himself with a glow of malicious satisfaction. When he'd forced Emile down on his back across the bench, the man's screaming head hanging over the end of it mere feet from the footlights and the front row of the audience, he'd noticed the German blanch. And as Emile's bloody eye plopped to the stage floor right in front of the man, he'd watched the Nazi officer go slack and slide down in his seat. Out cold.

The first-aid attendants who were always on duty during the performances at the Theatre du Grand Guignol hurried over to lift out the dead-to-the-world superman. Kevin noticed that one of them deliberately slammed the seat down on the major's limp fingers. He smiled to himself, as with the insane ravings demanded by his role in the play he found the eye, a gruesome object, lying in the crimson slime on the stage floor. The German would have a damned sore hand when he woke up, and wonder how the hell he got it. *Tant pis*—too bad.

The play was one of his favorites in the Grand Guignol repertoire. It took place in the ward of an asylum for the criminally insane somewhere around the turn of the century. Kevin played a child molester who had been blinded in rage by the father of a little girl he had killed. He'd gone insane, constantly seeking a pair of eyes as blue as those of the dead little girl to use for himself. When the other inmates in the asylum tell him that a young newcomer has bright-blue eyes, the result is inevitable at the Grand Guignol, which specialized in performing one-act plays of horror and violence—the bloodier, the better. He loved the part. A real set-chewer. He had the blind bit down pat. And Emile, with his empty eye socket (which had kept him safe from conscription and which could hold a bright-blue glass eye), was made for the part of his victim. That climactic scene on the bench never failed to reap at least a couple of dead faints.

As the curtain fell to the nervous applause of the audience, Kevin watched the limp German officer being carried away to the theater's little infirmary in the back of the auditorium, where a nurse was always in attendance. The evening had been a four-fainter, according to his count. But then, anything less than two patrons in the audience passing out cold at any given performance was considered a failure by the company.

Kevin peeked out at the emptying house through the dirt and grease-paint-ringed "house-counting peephole" in the curtain. He was always intrigued with the reaction of the audience. And its makeup. People from all walks of life and all ages came to the Grand Guignol—from sedate elderly matrons to wide-eyed sweet young things. And now, with Paris overrun by Nazi occupation troops, a great number of German officers and their mademoiselles. Even the Nazi big-shot Hermann Goering was a steady customer when he visited Paris. Kevin had often seen his fat bemedalled bulk sprawled in the front row. Horror and violence seemed to have a universal fascination.

He worked the hole around to sweep the little auditorium. In row four, stage right, an elderly couple remained in their seats. It often happened. A few people would stay behind for a while, replenishing their drained emotions, as it were, before braving the horrors and violence of the real world outside—a world torn by war and tortured by the subjugation of a brutal enemy.

The woman was staring at the program notes while collecting herself; perhaps even reading them, Kevin thought. If she were, he knew what she would read about the Theatre du Grand Guignol. It was an engrossing story.

She would learn that the Grand Guignol was one of the most unusual and best-known theaters in all of Europe, despite the fact that it was the smallest house in Paris; a theater so tiny that anyone in the audience who budged while the curtain was up was in danger of becoming part of the gruesome acts on the stage. The auditorium had only 280 seats, a maximum capacity of 302 patrons with standees, which, happily, was often the case. Fittingly located at the end of a gloomy alley off Rue Chaptal in the Montmartre area, it had originally been a chapel, where during the early nineteenth century, the fiery Dominican preacher Henri Gabriel Didon thundered his hellfire-and-brimstone sermons. Shades of things to come, Kevin had always thought. From him the place passed into the hands of the French painter George Antoine Rochegrosse, who used it as his studio and is said to have painted his famous painting "The Rape of the Sabine Women" there. Again, quite in keeping with what was to come, when in 1896 the building became a theater.

At first it was called Theatre Salon. It presented one-act plays in the new "realistic" style of the times, and it might well have stayed that way had it not been for one Edgar Allan Poe. Nearly six decades before, Poe had written a gothic story called *The Tell-Tale Heart*, which had been dramatized. It was presented at the little theater in 1901—and the Theatre du Grand Guignol was born, its fate sealed.

The theater prided itself on never closing its doors, performing plays seven days a week with matinees on Sundays, as was proudly pointed out in the program notes. The Grand Guignol had stayed open through depressions and wars. In fact, Kevin knew of only once that it had been closed. It had been the day of the funeral of the World War I hero Marshal Ferdinand Foch, in 1929.

Of the thousand to fifteen hundred plays submitted to the theater each year, only some twenty new ones were chosen for production. The oldies always seemed to draw bigger audiences. In the lobby and at the box office, pictures and posters of past performances were displayed—*The Mark of the Beast*, showing a leprous Hindu being horribly scorched with fire brands; *The Horrible Experiment*, with the proverbial mad scientist performing a bloody brain operation; and *The Lighthouse Keepers*, picturing a father whose face and hands had been mutilated by ferocious bites strangling his son who is seized with the maniacal fury of rabies—all in glorious color.

Some of the most prominent French playwrights submitted plays to the Grand Guignol, and a few of them were listed in the program: Octave Mirabeau, Sacha Guitry, Guy de Maupassant, and Henri René Lenormand. Many of the leading actors and actresses in Paris had had their start at the Theatre du Grand Guignol, and illustrious stars from foreign lands had performed there. The incomparable British actress Dame Sybil Thorndike, for example, acted in a horror play called *The Kill* in 1921, and it is said she was magnificent. But the unique aspect of the Grand Guignol ensemble were the regular company actors. Because of the special kind of plays the theater put on, several of the actors had special "endowments," as they chose to call them—a missing ear or eye like Emile, a missing limb, or other impairments. Such oddities were used to the fullest, most gruesome advantage.

This, too, was true of the two touring companies mounted by the Theatre du Grand Guignol. One that travelled throughout France, performing the most popular plays from the repertoire; the other that visited foreign theaters. Kevin, himself, had often gone on tour to other countries.

And there was more. Much more. Kevin knew it all. He had helped write the program notes.

The woman in row four finally got up from her seat. She let the program fall to the floor and followed her impatient husband to the exit.

In the back of the auditorium, the German major emerged from the infirmary looking dazed, nursing one of his hands. Shakily he made his way toward the door, steadying himself on the backs of the wooden church-pew-like theater seats. Uneasily his eyes roamed over the walls, paneled in old dark wood in a strangely forbidding combination of pseudo-gothic and baroque excesses. He seemed to shudder—and made a bee-line for the exit.

Couldn't have been a Gestapo man, Kevin thought as he left the peephole, or that bit with Emile wouldn't even have made him blink.

Kevin took a quick look around. The stage was deserted, only a work light was burning. The company manager was at the box office counting the evening's take, as he did every night, and the performers were in their dressing rooms, trying to get back to being normal.

He made his way to the stairs behind the pin rail that led down to the scenery and property docks under the stage and auditorium, the old chapel crypts.

The stairs leading down were worn and dark, the walls crisscrossed with scrapes by the set pieces carried up and down the narrow stairwell through the years. He turned on the light and started down. As he came to the basement level, he noted that the far end of the set storage area was in darkness. A bulb must have burned out, he thought idly. He peered across the angular shadows cast by the close scenery pieces toward the darkness beyond.

Suddenly his mind was flooded with the memory of the first time he'd gone down the stairs to the vaults below. It had been nine years before. A different, innocent time. Although he'd been sixteen years old, he'd just seen his first Grand Guignol horror play, and he'd clutched his father's arm, terrified at the forbidding place. Then, as now, the far bulb had been out. Then, as now, the looming, morguelike set pieces had stood leaning against one another at crazy angles, casting their jumble of sharp, jagged shadows across the docks like huge black knife blades.

What if, he thought. What if . . . ?

It was a mental game he played with himself. What if Poe's *Tell-Tale Heart* had never been written? Would the Grand Guignol *be* the Grand Guignol? Would it have survived as a theater at all? Or would it now be a bakery? Or a *maison de rendezvous*? . . .

What if Corporal Adolf Hitler had been killed in World War I on a messenger run? Would there have been a Nazi party? A Third Reich? A World War II? . . .

And now, as he stood staring into the gloom of the cellar storeroom, he thought: What if my father had not volunteered for the army in the First World War? Would I now be an actor at the Theatre du Grand Guignol? Would I even have been born? What if my father had not been a doughboy in World War I? What if . . . ?

But, he had . . . .

Michael Alistair Lavette was a minor league actor in Greenwich Village theaters in New York City when the United States entered the war in 1917. He was sent to France with the American Expeditionary Force under General "Black Jack" Pershing; fought at Chateau-Thierry; lost his left arm just below the elbow at the second battle of the Marne; and fell in love with a Parisian girl named Genevieve Lescault, whom he married in 1918 as soon as the armistice was signed.

Kevin was born the next year.

Mike stayed in France, and the first few years of Kevin's education took place in Paris before Mike decided to return to the

States with his French wife and little son. And while Mike appeared in off-Broadway plays, his parts severely limited by his handicap, Kevin continued his education in New York.

But when Kevin was in his first year of high school, Mike and Genevieve were called back to Paris, where the parents of Genevieve lay dying after a disastrous accident in the Paris Metro. Kevin went with them.

It took much longer than anticipated to clear up the estate of Genevieve's parents, and Kevin entered the American School in Paris to finish his education.

Mike, looking for work, found out about the Theatre du Grand Guignol, and his acting experience and "special endowment" quickly earned him a firm place in the permanent company of actors.

The year was 1935. The Saarland was incorporated into Germany, and the Luftwaffe was formed. Two years later, Kevin's mother succumbed to double pneumonia, and Kevin—having graduated from school—joined his father at the theater as a prop boy. He gradually advanced to assistant stage manager, stage manager, and to acting in bit parts. Because of his natural acting abilities, these minor parts soon turned into principal roles, and father and son often acted together, as in the revivals of *The Lighthouse Keepers*, the gruesome play in which a hydrophobic son tears his father apart before being strangled to death by him. Both Mike and Kevin loved the histrionics of it all. And no two performances ever seemed to be quite the same. Michael loved to ad-lib, both in words and action, anything that came into his mind. Kevin was often awed, if not a little put out, at his father's sometimes overenthusiastic impulsiveness. Though imaginative and possessed of a vigorously logical mind, Kevin tended to be more premeditative, more analytical, and less improvisational than his father. Somehow their different temperaments meshed perfectly, both on and off stage.

Yet Kevin was independent and prone to take charge. Someone at the Grand Guignol who was interested in things Oriental had once told him that 1919—the year Kevin had been born—was the Chinese Year of the Ram. Curious, he had gone to the library and looked up what that meant. He'd learned that, according to Chinese lore, people born in the Year of the Ram tended to look to others for guidance and were followers rather than leaders. He had been determined to prove the Chinese wrong. And he had . . . .

Kevin stood looking into the shadowy realm of make-believe.

It was all the result of his father's enlisting in the army, he thought. All of it. What if . . . ?

He walked to the far area of the storage room, feeling the gloom enveloping him as with a tangible black cloak. He looked up at the dark bulb.

Dead? Or merely loose? He started to reach up to test it. Suddenly he stiffened in shock as he felt himself grabbed from behind by two powerful arms that held him in a bear-hug grip, pinning his arms to his sides.

A hard, pointed object was jabbed into his back and a harsh voice rasped in his ear.

"*Ne bougez pas! Ne faites pas un bruit!*—Don't move! Do not make a sound!"

The French was spoken with a heavy accent.

❧ 2 ❧

"**Y**OU'VE got the wrong man, dammit!" Kevin protested. He spoke in English. The unseen assailant's accent had been unmistakably British. "My name is Lavette. Kevin Lavette. I'm an actor with the company here."

"*Kevin* Lavette, is it?" Switching to English, the voice hissed unpleasantly in his ear. "Try again, mate!"

"I don't have to," Kevin snapped angrily. "You heard me! He tried to wriggle loose, in vain. "Get your damned hands off me!"

But the iron grasp did not let up.

"Look," Kevin growled. "If you don't believe me, touch my face. I just got off the stage. I'm still wearing my damned makeup."

The tight hold did not slacken, but Kevin felt a finger rub hard across his cheek. So, there were two of them, he thought.

"Blimey!" another voice exclaimed. "He's right. He's got bloody goo all over his bloody face."

Kevin felt himself being pushed away roughly. He stumbled against a papier-mâché-stone archway and caught himself. He whirled on his assailants.

There were two of them, one a bear of a man with a fierce moustache. Both were clad in an all too obvious mixture of ill-fitting civilian clothes and parts of the uniforms issued to British airmen. One of them held a double-edged paratrooper dagger dangerously leveled at Kevin's gut.

"They told us to trust nobody," the big man growled, "and we bloody well don't." He watched Kevin warily, the dagger steady in his hand.

Kevin knew the man was right, but he had been taken by surprise. He was angry. "What idiot told you that?" he lashed out at the Britisher.

The airman watched him, narrow-eyed. Instead of answering, he said: "*Kevin* Lavette, is it?" Suspicion darkened his voice. He glanced quickly at his companion, who was covering Kevin from a spot slightly to his right. "And, *Michael* Lavette," he said slowly, "who is *Michael* Lavette?"

"I am!"

The voice boomed through the large basement storage room as a man came striding toward them.

He was a good six feet tall and built like a track-and-field athlete, neither too skinny nor too muscle-bound. In fact, at forty-eight he looked like a younger leading man who'd had to daub his full dark hair with talcum powder and paint makeup lines around his eyes and across his forehead to look old enough for Act Three. The fact that his left arm was missing just below his elbow was not noticeable at all. The prosthesis was perfect, and the way Michael wore it and manipulated it appeared quite normal.

He stopped at the group. He glared at the big airman, still holding the dagger on Kevin.

"I am Michael Lavette," he said steadily. "What the hell do you think you're doing? Put that damned thing away!"

The British airman stared at him. "You—you're a bloody *man*!" he exclaimed.

"What did you expect?" Mike snapped. "A gargoyle?"

"I thought—I thought when she said to mention *Michael La-*

vette, it was—it was some sort of a password," the airman stammered in confusion. He glanced at Kevin. "And that one, he got it wrong." He rallied. "How the bleeding hell was I to know you were a man?"

"Well, you know now," Mike said sourly. "And I think you'd better put that Kraut-skewer away."

The airman sheathed the dagger.

"How did you get *here*?" Kevin asked. "Who told you to look for my father? Who's *she*?"

The Britisher turned to him. He was again in full control of himself. "Your father, is it?" he grinned. "Sorry. But I couldn't be certain of you. I didn't know."

"Let's have your story," Mike said.

"It's a long one, chum, and not a very cheery one," the moustachioed airman answered soberly, "and I'm not going to fag you out with the ruddy details of it. I am Flight Sergeant Higgins, RAF, Alfred Higgins." Automatically, he drew himself up. He nodded toward his companion. "That's Corporal Burt Henshaw, our tail gunner. We are the only survivors of a Lancaster crew. The other five went down with the plane. Never saw the bloody chutes." He swallowed. "We were shot down near Chantilly, north of Paris, on our way back from a raid on Stuttgart. We had a rather dicey time of it. We were bloody well wrung out, so we kipped down in a barn and were doing the downey, when a bloke with a pitchfork poked us awake. He was a bit of all right, though. He gave us some clothes and fetched a mademoiselle he said could help us." He grinned at Kevin. "That's the *she*, chum. She concocted these bleeding get-ups." He indicated the strange assortment of clothing worn by his companion and himself.

"Did she tell you her name?" Kevin asked.

"She did," Higgins answered. "Suzanne. A real smasher, she was."

"How did you get here?" Michael wanted to know.

"We were piled into the back of an old lorry and deposited a few blocks from here, and—"

"Who drove the lorry?" Michael interrupted.

"Not the foggiest, Guv'nor. Never saw him. Suzanne sat with him in the cab. She's the only one we saw. Her and the farmer."

Michael frowned. "And she told you to come here and ask for me?"

"Not exactly like that. She told us to wait until the show was

19

done and the crowd had left." He shrugged. "We did. Last ones to come out was an old blighter and his missus and a Jerry officer who seemed all mops and brooms."

He had a sudden thought that obviously startled him.

"Gor blimey!" he exclaimed. "You do know the bird, don't you, Guv?"

"We do," Michael nodded.

"Good show," Higgins said, relieved. "So, anyway, the girl told us to go in a side door, told us where it was, and say *Michael Lavette* to anyone we saw." He frowned. "At least, that's what I thought she said. Her English was about as good as my French."

Soberly, Michael contemplated the man, sizing him up.

"Suzanne," he said. "Did you get a good look at her?"

"Abso-blooming-lutely, Guv'nor," the big flight sergeant grinned enthusiastically. "Who wouldn't?"

"Then you must have seen the little mole on her cheek," Michael continued. "On which cheek was it? Her right or her left?"

The airman frowned. "Mole?" he said, puzzled. "On—on her cheek?"

"If you got a good look at her," Michael said, his voice suddenly cold, "you couldn't have missed it." Narrow-eyed, he glared at the man. "Which cheek?"

Higgins stiffened. The air between them was suddenly tense.

"I—I don't remember seeing a mole, Guv'nor," he said slowly. "No mole." He turned to the tail gunner. "Burt," he asked, apprehension growing in his voice. "You see a—a mole on the bird?"

The man shook his head. He looked frightened. "No, Alf. I didn't."

Higgins turned to Michael.

"The girl we saw had no mole. At least we didn't see any." He stared at the grim Michael who stood facing him squarely. "No mole, Guv'nor," he said firmly. "Perhaps—perhaps we are not talking about the same girl."

"We are," Michael said.

He scowled at the two men. No one made a sound. Then Michael broke into a grin. "I'm glad you didn't see a mole," he said. "Suzanne has no mole."

The British flight sergeant looked blank. Suddenly he burst out laughing. "Lor' lumme!" he exclaimed. "You had me going a yard and a half!"

"As you said, chum, trust nobody," Kevin pointed out dryly.

He turned to his father. "Better get them out of sight. Choisy might be nosing around."

"Right," Michael agreed.

Higgins looked at him questioningly. "Choisy? Isn't her name on your poster out front? In big letters? Camille Choisy?"

Michael nodded. "Yes," he acknowledged, contempt in his voice. "But it's a he, not a she. And he's not part of our—our enterprise here."

"Doesn't know about it," Kevin added. "He's the theater manager. Placed in that position by the Nazis when the former owner, Madame Berkson, had to leave Paris in a hurry when the Nazis came here." He gave a crooked little smile. "She'd just put on a horror play to end them all. A real lulu. All about Nazi atrocities in Poland."

"Choisy is a damned collaborator," Michael spat. He reached up to tighten the light bulb.

"Hope you don't mind," Higgins said, nodding at the bulb. "We thought we were a little too much in the limelight with that thing blazing down on us."

"It's okay." Michael said. He started to walk toward the far end of the storage area. "Come on. We'll take you to your home away from home."

The back area of the cluttered cellar held a collection of major props used in the plays. Replicas of monstrous medieval instruments of torture lined the stone walls. Like ghoulish harbingers of terror waiting to lumber to life, they loomed ominously in the shadowy space: a rusty witches' dunking stool next to a branding brazier and a massive "iron boot"; a weathered pillory with a blood-soiled cat-o'-nine-tails and a set of thumb screws hanging from one of the holes; a guillotine, the slant-edged blade precariously poised above the half-moon-shaped neck rest stained and scarred, standing shoulder to shoulder with a hulking replica of an "Iron Maid," her peaked medieval headdress framing a rigid, cruel face above a large ruffed collar. Hinges on the sides of the forbidding figure made it obvious that the front could be opened up.

As the two British airmen eyed the chilling devices, Kevin grabbed hold of two heavy iron rings affixed to the front of the ferrous-looking cloak of the Iron Maid and pulled. With an appropriately creaking sound, the two halves swung open. The sharp points of the evil-looking spikes that studded the inside of the maid were discolored with brownish "fake" blood.

"What the bleeding hell is that?" Higgins exclaimed.

"She's called the *Eiserne Jungfrau*—the Iron Maid of Nürnberg," Kevin said cheerfully. "She's kind of our patron saint down here. The original stands in the dungeon torture chamber of the Burg in Nürnberg." He indicated the gruesome device. "The victims would be pushed inside her, and her embrace would impale them and slowly kill them."

"Blimey!" the airman said softly.

"Here she does double duty," Kevin went on, "in the play *The Secret of the Castle Dungeon* and in *The Inquisition*." He pulled the doors all the way open.

Higgins peered inside. He turned to Kevin. "After you!" he said.

Kevin reached into the maid and took hold of a spike that was bent at a slight angle, one of several misaligned in that manner, probably attesting to the violence of the victims' death throes. He pulled on it and the back opened up on a space beyond, so totally black that the darkness seemed to reach out to dim the light outside. Kevin reached in and flipped a switch.

The hidden room revealed beyond the maid was a fairly good-sized space. They all stepped through the opening in the device and through a hole in the wall behind.

"You'll be safe here," Kevin said, "until we can pass you on."

The two Britishers looked around, obviously awed. The room held four cots—French army issue—a table and three chairs. In a corner stood an army chemical toilet; a folding screen with a Japanese motif stood leaning against the wall, and—incongruously—a sledgehammer stood leaning into the corner across from it. On the table were several tattered and dog-eared old English-language magazines; a deck of cards so worn that each card had a distinctive look of its own, defeating its very purpose; and a few English books. One of them was an Agatha Christie mystery. Kevin had meant to remove it. No use adding torture to the danger and discomfort—some fiend had torn out the last three pages. Despite a vent to the scene dock above, the air in the room was stale and sour.

"There are candles and matches in the table drawer," Kevin told them, "in case you should need them. Go easy on them. They're worth their weight in gold."

Higgins glanced at the burning light bulb hanging from the ceiling. "Ta'," he said. "But you have electricity."

"Sure we have," Kevin said bitterly. "One hour a day, between eleven P.M. and midnight. The Germans take all our coal, and that's all Paris can afford. The City of Light has become a city of darkness." He shrugged. "We, that is the Grand Guignol, get extra power so we can put on our plays for the damned *Boche*. Courtesy of fat Goering, our number one fan."

Higgins looked around the bleak place. "You did say *home* away from home?" he said sardonically. "What *is* this place?"

"It was an old crypt," Kevin answered. "It connected to the maze of underground tunnels that runs under Paris. But the access has long been bricked up." He nodded toward the sledge-hammer. "In a pinch we can break through and escape that way."

"Tunnels?" Higgins queried.

Kevin nodded. "Almost two hundred miles of them. Abandoned rock quarries, some of them a thousand years old. Most of the stones used to build the city were quarried here."

"Blimey!"

"Some of the subterranean tunnels and galleries were once converted into catacombs," Michael added. "They say six million Parisians lie down here, their bones stacked six feet high like kindling wood. Some damned famous ones to boot. Racine. Rabelais. Descartes. Pascal."

"Blimey!" Higgins said again. It was obvious he'd never heard of any of Michael's celebrities.

"Right now the Resistance is using part of the tunnel network," Kevin said. "To hide fugitives. As clandestine command centers and safe meeting places. The Germans can't find their way around down there, so they don't try too hard to find them."

"The *Boche* keeps pretty much to the sections around Invalides," Mike added. "On the Left Bank. They've made the tunnels there into an air raid shelter for themselves, and they've got a telephone switchboard center down there. Their patrols rarely come up here."

"What happens to us now, mate?" Higgins asked.

"You'll stay here. We'll bring you some food, get you some clothes from our wardrobe department, and—"

"I mean, where do we go from here? How do we get back?"

"When the time comes, you will be escorted to the Pyrenees. To the Spanish border. From there you will be taken to Portugal. To Lisbon. And from there to England."

23

"Good show! When?"

"First things first," Michael said. "You'll have to have proper identification. You'll be on your own."

"I thought you said we'd have an escort?"

"You will. We call it a detached escort."

Higgins looked blank.

"It works like this," Kevin explained. "Your escort will take a train to a town near the border, and transportation will be afforded you from there. He will, however, have no contact with you whatsoever. You will simply follow him and do exactly as he does. If you are caught, he will not interfere. He will not even know you. It is for the protection of all of us." He looked soberly at the two airmen. "Escorts are hard to come by. Escapers are a dime a dozen. Those are the brutal facts."

Higgins nodded.

"We'll get you the proper ID papers, though," Kevin continued. "Only one thing is difficult."

"What?"

"Getting a photograph of the kind used on German permits. But we do have a way of getting them. There's a photobooth at the Gare St. Lazare, a railroad station only a few blocks from here, that takes the exact same kind of picture you'll need. You'll have to go there and have your photo taken. Both of you. You will follow a detached escort, a girl. Her name is Gaby. She is one of us. You will do exactly as she does."

"And if we are stopped?"

"You are on your own," Kevin said gravely. "You will have to get out of any confrontation yourselves. We can do nothing." He looked straight at Higgins. "And if you are taken away for questioning, Gaby will warn us. Because sooner or later, you will talk."

Higgins said nothing. It was obvious he did not agree. He looked around the room. "Quite an organization you have here, mate," he observed.

Kevin nodded. His mind leaped back to the beginning. It was August 11, 1942. He would never forget the day. The Gestapo had executed 99 hostages in retaliation for Resistance attacks on the Germans. One of them had been his father's best friend. They had decided then and there to fight the Nazi invaders until France was free once again. They *had* come a long way since. But a longer way lay ahead.

He looked soberly at the two men.

"Tomorrow, first thing," he said, "we'll find out if you're up to it."

❖ 3 ❖

IT was a raw, cold April day when Gaby Kerouac walked down Rue D'Amsterdam toward Gare St. Lazare. Bundled-up Parisians huddled in small groups over the iron grills in the sidewalk to take advantage of the warm air rising from the Metro below. Fuel for heating was all but impossible to obtain in Paris in 1944, and cutting firewood from the trees in the city park—the only alternative—was severely punished. Even so, many ran the risk.

Gaby drew her coat tighter around her. She glanced back. Her charge was following her faithfully, looking somewhat awkward in a large shop-worn overcoat from the *Fire and Ice* wardrobe. Flight Sergeant Alfred Higgins was his name. RAF.

She increased her pace. Partly to keep warm and partly because she wanted to get the trip over with. Acting as a detached escort was the duty she disliked the most. There was always the fear in her that she would be forced to abandon one of her helpless charges. Detached escort, she thought, a curiously paradoxical phrase. Certainly the furthest thing from her mind when she'd joined the company at the Grand Guignol as an actress five years—was it only five years ago? Paris had still been free, instead of cringing under the hob-nailed boots of the Nazis; submitting to having her homes arbitrarily searched; her citizens arrested; her valuables looted and carted off; her young men abducted to labor as slaves in foreign lands; her fuel and food rations impossibly minute. There was a gallows-humor story going around that a Parisian's meat ration was so small that it could be wrapped in a Metro ticket, provided the stub hadn't been punched. If it had, the meat would fall through the hole. Funny—if it weren't so close to the truth.

She was coming to the station. She tried to avert her eyes from the huge garish swastika flags that hung prominently from the main building, as they did from all public buildings in Paris, in what she was certain was a deliberate affront to the Parisians.

Feeling both humiliated and defiant, she crossed the street at Place de Budapest, weaving her way through bicyclists and velo-taxis, and making sure her charge was following her. She entered the station and headed straight for the three photo-automats in the waiting area.

Flight Sergeant Alfred Higgins watched the girl go up to one of the booths and disappear through the green curtain. He had enjoyed following her and watching her. She was a blooming looker, she was. He'd especially enjoyed the way her little firm ass moved as she walked. Those French birds had a way of wiggle-walking that would give any hot-blooded man a hard-on. When he saw her come out of the booth again and walk to a newsstand, he entered the booth and sat down in front of the camera.

The signs and instructions confronting him meant nothing to him, but he easily located the slot that would take the coin he had been given. All he had to do was put it in, sit still, and collect the strip of six photos as it was dispensed by the machine.

Automatically he wet his fingers on his tongue, slicked down his hair, and stroked his moustache. He reached toward the slot with his coin—and froze.

The camera had spoken to him. A low, urgent voice, heavily accented, had said:

"Be still, monsieur. I know you to be English!"

The thoughts exploded through Higgins's mind.

He was caught!

The voice was not coming from the camera. It was coming from a crack in the partition to the adjoining booth. Someone was in there. Someone who had found him out. The enemy? The Gestapo? He had been betrayed. How? By whom? He was trapped. Trapped in a dirty, cramped little photo-booth. And they *knew* who he was. When they questioned him, would he talk? As they had said he would? Or would he refuse? He did not know. He did not know. Would *he* betray his fellow crewman? Burt? And the Resistance members? The Lavettes? Gaby? . . . Gaby, who was waiting for him outside? He could not be sure. He would run. Lose his enemy in the crowds in the station. Make it on his own. The girl would be safe. He would—

"Listen on me, Englishman," the voice hissed through the crack. *"You stay—"*

He leaped to his feet and threw himself through the green curtain out of the booth. He began to run. Away. Away from the girl. Away from the threat in the booth. He caught himself. Careful! Don't run. Don't call attention to yourself. Just walk. Fast.

He did. He did not look back. Not at the booth. Not at Gaby. He just walked.

But the flesh on his back crawled. Any second he expected a cry to rise behind him and pursue him.

Or a bullet rip through his borrowed coat into his back.

He kept walking.

Gaby watched her charge rush from the photo-booth and rapidly walk away. She was startled. What was he doing? He was going the wrong way. Had he forgotten what he'd been told? In a moment he'd be out of her sight, lost. She started after him—and stopped.

Another man came rushing from the photo-automat. A man in a belted overcoat and a soft-brimmed hat. She saw him hurry after the sergeant, catch up with him, and grab his arm.

The chill of deep dismay coursed through her. Her deepest fear had come true. The charge entrusted to her had been caught. She would have to abandon him. . . .

Stricken, she watched the two men for a brief moment. She was about to walk away when she hesitated. Something was strange. Out of kilter. What? She stared at the men. The man who had accosted the big sergeant was talking to him insistently, but he didn't seem authoritative but afraid. She frowned. The Gestapo? Afraid? The big Englishman was listening, obviously not understanding, looking for a way to break off the encounter and not finding it.

Gaby bit her lip in indecision. It would not be long before the two men would attract attention to themselves. The wrong kind of attention. Resolutely she began to walk toward them. She would have to interfere. She would have to try to help. Perhaps she could explain why the big man had no papers. Who he was. A foreign technician? An imbecile? Something. She was grasping for straws, and she knew it.

She stopped. What she was about to do was totally against all the rules. Rules that were designed to save lives. Her clear duty was to return to the theater at once and report that her charge had been picked up. If, instead, she did go to the aid of the Englishman and was also detained, perhaps arrested, who would warn Kevin? And the others? She could not do it. She would have to leave the sergeant to fend for himself. He had not a chance in a million, but she had no choice.

Desolately she looked a last time toward the two men. The stranger seemed more insistent, the sergeant more desperate. The situation was coming to a head. She would *have* to do something. She could not help herself. Anyway, if both she and her charge were arrested and neither of them came back to the theater, Kevin would know. *That* would be warning enough to take safety measures. She would try to help. She would try to persuade the accoster to let the sergeant go.

Deliberately she suppressed the certain knowledge that she had no chance of succeeding. No chance at all. . . .

She walked up to the two men. Higgins gave her a bleak look, but he said nothing. She ignored him.

"Bitte," she said sweetly. *"Darf ich helfen? Ich spreche Deutsch* —May I help? I speak German."

Startled, the man turned to stare at her. Flustered, he answered her in French. *"Je regrette.* I—I do not speak German," he stammered. "I am French. *Excusez moi."* Abruptly he turned to go.

Gaby was momentarily taken aback. The stranger's action had been completely contrary to anything she had expected. Her mind whirled. Who *was* he? What did he want? What was going on?

"Monsieur!" she called. "Wait!" There was surprising authority in her voice.

The stranger stopped. He turned back to her. He looked frightened.

"What—what did you want with this gentleman?" Gaby asked.

"Nothing," the man answered evasively. "It was—a mistake. I was mistaken."

Again he turned to leave.

"He knows I am English!" Higgins suddenly whispered, just loud enough for the stranger to overhear. The man stopped dead in his tracks. He turned back to them, his face startled.

28

"Monsieur," Gaby said persuasively. "Please. Please stay. Who are you?"

"Nobody," the man answered. "I am just—" He let the sentence die.

"You think this gentleman is English?" Gaby nodded toward Higgins.

"Yes." It was barely audible.

"Why?"

The stranger looked up. "I—I was looking for an Englishman," he said. His eyes searched Gaby's. "You are from the Resistance, are you not?" he said. There was an unmistakable note of expectancy, of hope in his voice.

"Why are you looking for an Englishman?" Gaby asked, ignoring the man's question.

"Because—I need to establish contact with the Resistance," the man explained. He seemed surprised at his own audacity. He looked searchingly at Gaby. "Are you?" he asked again. "Are you from the Resistance?"

Again Gaby ignored his question. "Perhaps you had better tell us why you want to make contact with the Underground, monsieur," Gaby said quietly. "Why are you?"

For a moment the stranger studied her face, his head slightly cocked to one side. He seemed to make up his mind. He took a deep breath.

"I am a farmer, mademoiselle," he said. "I have a farm near Meaux on the Marne, about thirty kilometers east of here." He sounded on edge.

"I know Meaux," Gaby said pleasantly. It was not an earth-shaking piece of information, but she thought it would help put the man at ease.

The stranger nodded. "Many do." He paused. "We—we have a crisis." The words suddenly poured out. "There is a young woman. She has been grievously hurt, mademoiselle. Shot. By the Germans—the *sale Boche*! She is hiding on my farm. She is a—a spy, she says, an intelligence agent. From England. She was dropped by a parachute. She says she has vital information. Information that is of the gravest importance to France. It must get back to England. But she has no way. Her radio was lost. You see?"

Gaby nodded. "I understand. You want the Resistance to make contact with London for you?"

"Yes!" the man exclaimed. "That is it exactly!"

Gaby frowned. "But—what were you doing in the photo-automat?"

"I was looking for an Englishman."

"Looking for an Englishman?" Gaby was puzzled.

"Of course. I have friends, mademoiselle," the farmer said proudly. "I tried to learn how to find the Resistance, but it was not allowed me. I—I asked around. I learned only this. That photographs for permit papers were often taken at public photo-automats because they are like the ones the Germans use. On their papers. So, I thought, here, at the station, there is a photo-automat. And here, if I wait long enough, I will find an Englishman having his photograph taken." He looked at Higgins. "Like monsieur, who looks most English to me." He smiled. "And I would have him take me to the Resistance. I have been here two days. You see?"

Gaby nodded.

"You *are* Resistance!" the man said eagerly. "I am certain. You will help, will you not? It is of great importance. The woman— *l'espion*—she is dying."

Gravely Gaby contemplated the man. His beard stubble could easily be two days old. His manner could easily be that of a farmer. But his clothes—that belted coat—were not.

"Monsieur," she said. "Your coat. It is a city coat. Not a farmer's coat. Where did you get it?"

The man's face grew solemn. "It was my son's," he said quietly. "He worked in the city. Here, in a big store—Le Printemps. He was killed by the Germans. At Abbeville. Four years ago. It is for him I do this."

"I can do nothing for you, monsieur," Gaby said softly. "But I may know someone who can."

The farmer regarded her expectantly.

"You will wait here," Gaby went on. She pointed to a row of wooden benches in the waiting area. "Sit there," she instructed him. "On the bench farthest to the left. Read a newspaper. I will send someone to contact you."

"Merci, mademoiselle," the farmer beamed. He grasped her hand. "*Merci mille fois!*—Thank you a thousand times! I shall do exactly as you say."

Gaby turned to Higgins. "Sergeant," she said. "Go get your picture taken. Then follow me back. . . ."

Kevin and Gaby stopped at a spot near the photo-booths from where they could observe the benches in the waiting area. A man sat at the far left, apparently engrossed in a newspaper.

"That the man?" Kevin asked. His tone of voice came out harsher than he had intended. He was still disturbed. Gaby had placed them all in jeopardy. The whole thing could have been a trap set for her. It still could be. It still could be a trap to catch more than just one escaping Englishman and his escort. It could still be a trap to catch the whole Resistance ring. Dammit! He was angry, but he realized that his anger was really his reaction to Gaby's having placed herself in danger. He touched her arm.

"Stay here," he said softly. "Watch. If things go wrong, get back to my father. At once."

Gaby nodded earnestly. "I will." She looked up at him. "Be careful, cheri," she whispered.

He turned and walked toward the benches in the waiting area.

He stopped in front of the man whose face was hidden behind his newspaper. The man did not see him. Suddenly Kevin slapped the paper sharply with his hand. Startled, the reader dropped it and stared up at the man towering over him.

Kevin whipped a little leather folder from his pocket. He flipped it open, briefly exposing an identity card.

"Gestapo!" he barked. "Your papers!"

Apprehensively the farmer groped around in his pockets. Finally he came up with his ID. Kevin snatched it impatiently from his hand. Frowning, he studied it.

"You are François Marot?" he asked, his face grim.

"I am."

"Is this your current address?"

"It is."

"Meaux," Kevin snapped. "What are you doing here?"

"Life must go on, monsieur," the farmer shrugged. "There are things to be had in Paris that are not to be had in Meaux."

"Why are you *here*? At this station? The trains for Meaux depart from Gare de L'Est. Not from here."

"Ah, monsieur, I am here because of the photo-automats."

"There are photo-automats at Gare de L'Est."

"Out of order, monsieur," Marot shrugged regretfully. "All of them, more's the pity. And no one to fix them."

"What do you want with the photo-automats?"

"To take my picture," Marot answered ingenuously.

"Why?"

"My daughter," the farmer explained patiently. "She lives in

Epinac. Perhaps you have heard of it? It is beautiful in the mountains there. She wanted a photograph of me to show."

"Let me see it."

Again the farmer shrugged. "It is confusing," he said. "There are many instructions in the booth. They must be studied carefully." He ran his hand over the stubble on his chin. "I do not have such a photograph yet, monsieur. I must get my face cleaned up before I put my money in the machine to get my photograph."

"Then why are you sitting there?" Kevin asked sharply.

"I am waiting, monsieur."

"For what?"

"For the barber. He was busy. I saw it through the window. In a few minutes I will go there again, and he will give me a fine shave."

Kevin studied the man. What the hell else could he ask him? The fellow had answers, and damned sly ones at that, for everything he could throw at him. His gut feeling was that the man was what he said he was. A farmer. If he had been a Gestapo plant, he would probably have identified himself by now. He made up his mind.

"The woman hiding on your farm," he said quietly. "How badly is she hurt? Will she still be alive?"

The farmer stared open-mouthed at him.

"But you . . . you. . . ."

"I am the one you have been looking for," Kevin said quickly. "Just listen, and do what I tell you."

The farmer gulped, and listened.

"There is a train for Reims in forty minutes. From Gare de L'Est. It stops in Meaux. Go there. Get on it. We will be on it with you, but you will make no sign that you know us. Do you understand?"

Again the farmer nodded.

Kevin turned and walked away. He had just placed himself, and Gaby, in the hands of a stranger.

He hoped to God it had been the right thing to do.

The answer was to be found on a farm near Meaux. . . .

4

KEVIN was grateful that it was a cold, overcast day as they trudged past the dunghill piled up in a corner of the Marot farmyard. He knew the overpowering stench such manure heaps could produce on a warm day with the sun beating down on them. As a young man, he'd often lent a hand on a farm for a few days to make a little money when he'd been on bicycle tours through France, the Netherlands, and Germany during his summer vacations, usually with a friend, earning their way as they went. In fact, they prided themselves in coming back home with a little more money than they'd set out with. They'd clean barns, paint, do a little simple carpentry, even turn a dunghill or two—anything that needed doing. And they'd collected eggs the hens had been laying in favorite spots all over the farm. Sometimes hundreds of them, and some of them so big there were only ten to a dozen. He still remembered that in the summer of 1936, he'd watched a German farmer's wife put the eggs into storage in large barrels filled with water glass—a viscous, syrupy liquid that would preserve them—and with some astonishment had heard her say: *One for us* (as she put one egg in one of the barrels), *two for the war* (as she put two in the other). That had been in 1936. He'd learned a lot on those bicycle trips: about people, their land, and their customs, including an excellent knowledge of the German language.

Marot's farmhand, a sour-looking fellow named Gaspar, had picked them up at the railroad station with an uncomfortably hard-riding wagon. He was now leading the way with Marot toward a dilapidated barn.

Gray daylight seeped into the barn through a crisscross of cracks, daubing a spider's web of drab light-streaks across dusty-dry bales of hay, empty stalls, a couple of broken wagons, and an old canvas-covered truck without wheels that was propped up on heavy pieces of lumber.

Marot walked up to the truck and threw the canvas backing aside. A woman, lying in the gloom inside, resting on a stack of sacking and covered with a quilt of many once-bright colors, stirred, and with a gasp of pain rose on one elbow in apparent alarm as Marot climbed into the truck, followed by Kevin and Gaby.

"We could not keep her in the house," the farmer mumbled, a touch of guilt in his voice. "Neighbors can have prying eyes and loose tongues, no?" He stood aside as Kevin and Gaby squeezed past him and knelt beside the woman. Marot lit a sooty kerosene lamp hanging from a canvas strut.

It was impossible to tell the wounded woman's age. Her pale and drawn face was marred by deep scratches in which the blood had congealed in blackish welts. A blood-soaked bandage had inexpertly been placed on her temple over her left ear. Her lips were torn, and the caked blood that had trickled from the corners of her mouth gave her the exaggerated, grotesque appearance of the classic drama mask of tragedy. Her eyes, sunken deep in darkened sockets, stared at them in luminous terror.

"Don't be afraid," Gaby said. "We are friends."

The woman stared at her. The mad luminosity did not leave her eyes. Close up, Gaby could see she could be no older than her middle twenties. The girl tried to scramble away from her. She let out a sharp cry and fell back on her crude bedding. "Millipedes!" she rasped in delirious terror, staring unseeing into space. "An army. An army of millipedes . . . millipedes. . . ."

Kevin and Gaby exchanged glances. The girl was obviously raving. Gaby placed her hand on the girl's sweat-glistening forehead. The girl seemed not to notice.

"She's burning up," Gaby said, deeply concerned.

"She has been shot," Marot said under his breath. "Once in the belly. Once in the thigh. The right one." He shook his head slowly. "She has lost much blood. Her insides are torn. She will not last the day."

"Have you sent for a doctor?" Gaby asked.

Marot shook his head. "A doctor would have to come from Meaux," he explained. "I know no doctor in Meaux. How could I trust anyone?"

The girl groaned. She looked up at Kevin and Gaby bending

over her. The madness had gone from her eyes, leaving only agony. It was as if the pain had torn her back to lucidity.

"Who . . . who are you?" she whispered.

"Friends," Kevin said. "We are here to help you."

The girl shook her head. "Too late," she breathed. "Not me. You must—" She stopped. She closed her eyes tightly as a wave of pain swept over her. When she opened them again, they sought Marot.

The farmer nodded gravely. "They can be trusted, mademoiselle," he assured her. "They are from the Resistance. Of that I am certain."

"And I," the girl whispered. "How can *I* be certain?"

Gaby bent down to her. She nodded toward Marot. "This man," she said earnestly. "This man who has helped you. This man who is sheltering you at his own peril. Do you trust him?"

Slowly the girl nodded.

"He trusts us," Gaby said. "He has placed his life in our hands. Would he do that if he thought us his enemies?"

The girl closed her eyes as another spasm of pain racked her. Then she looked up at Kevin and Gaby.

"I am Nicole," she whispered. "I am . . . the only one alive." She winced in pain. "From a . . . a Jedburgh team. From England. . . ."

Kevin looked puzzled. "Jedburgh?" he asked.

"Not important," sighed Nicole. "You must . . . must contact London. It is of the greatest importance. Tell them—*Rebus* . . . understand? . . . *Rebus*—has been aborted. Entire team killed." Anxiously she tried to sit up, but the pain defeated her. "Do you understand?" she whispered urgently. "*Rebus* is no longer—operative. . . ."

"We understand, Nicole," Kevin said. "We'll get you help. We'll—"

"No!" Nicole exclaimed. "London. You must contact London. Tell them—*Mimoyecques* is impossible to penetrate. Remember *Mimoyecques*. Tell them—"

"Nicole," Kevin interrupted her. His voice was firm, yet soft. "We will help. We will carry out any instructions you give us. But, to be of the greatest help, we must know what we are doing. We cannot work in the dark." He paused. He looked gravely at the girl. "Tell us what you can of your mission, why you were sent here."

For a moment Nicole was silent, her feverish, pain-filled eyes locked on Kevin.

"Rebus," she whispered. "It was our code name. We were four. We were dropped near Saint Omer. South of Calais. Three days ago. On a mission of . . . of. . . ." She shuddered violently as a wave of pain knifed through her tortured body. Her eyes rolled back in her head, and apparently slipping into incoherence, she mumbled, "Millipedes . . . millipedes. . . ." She began to moan, a sound that wrenched their souls.

"Monsieur," Gaby said crisply to Marot. "Water. I need a pail of cold water. And a cloth. Please hurry."

Marot nodded. "Gaspar!" he called as he jumped from the truck.

Gaby turned back to Nicole. "Give me your handkerchief," she said to Kevin. He did. She wiped the sweat from Nicole's face as the girl tossed on her sackcloth bedding.

Presently Marot returned with a pail of water and an old piece of toweling. Gaby bathed the semiconscious girl's forehead. She opened her eyes.

"It is all right," Gaby said soothingly. "You are with friends." Feebly Nicole nodded.

"What did you find at—at Saint Omer?" Kevin asked. "What were you looking for? What happened?"

"Mimoyecques," Nicole breathed, almost inaudibly. "The site is impenetrable. No one can get near it. German soldiers everywhere. The Fifteenth Army. Tell London." She reached an imploring hand toward Kevin.

Kevin took it and held it. He nodded. "Mimoyecques." He asked, "What is it?"

"A village," Nicole answered. "A little village, southwest of Calais. But . . . but. . . ."

"What happened?" Gaby asked gently.

"It is a huge construction site," Nicole whispered. "There is something being built there. Something greatly important, greatly secret. There are . . . thousands of workers. They labor day and night. But . . . no one knows on what. No one knows what it is. . . . The locals think it is a secret ray to stop airplanes in flight. Photo Intelligence cannot find an answer. Only on one mission did they obtain a few aerial photographs. Only a few. Because of the heavy camouflage. And the many antiaircraft guns. It . . . it looked like, like a huge iron millipede hundreds of feet long! A . . . a gigantic round body with many, many iron legs creeping up

36

a hillside like an enormous iron millipede . . . ." She stopped, exhausted by her long speech.

Kevin frowned. "An iron millipede? Hundreds of feet long?" he said incredulously.

Nicole nodded wearily. "I know what you think," she whispered. "That I am . . . that I am out of my head." Her pain-ridden eyes flashed. "But I am not! Not now. It is true. There are many of them being built. And security is stricter there than anywhere else. What they are building is of the greatest importance to them. And therefore to us." She paused, her face contorted in pain. "That is why we were sent . . . but . . . we failed," she went on, her voice growing ever weaker. "We were discovered. My comrades—Larry, Claude, Jean. Killed. Our equipment—the radio—lost. I . . . I got away. Because the others covered for me. I headed for Paris. I knew there was an Underground Railroad there. We had been told in our briefing. And I thought, I thought I could get out. Back to England. But . . . the Germans discovered me. I was shot. And . . . and. . . ." Her voice died away.

Kevin and Gaby looked at one another bleakly. They knew there was nothing they could do for the girl.

"Nicole," Gaby asked gently. "Is there anything else you want us to tell London?"

Slowly, with an obvious effort, Nicole looked up at them. "We . . . we were sent to find out what . . . what they were. The millipedes. What purpose they have . . . and now," she breathed with evident difficulty, "now it is . . . too late. Too late to mount another mission. In time." Desperately, she tried to rally her ebbing strength. "But . . . tell London . . . the answer cannot be had at Mimoyecques. At . . . at another place. We . . . learned that much. . . ." Her eyes closed. Her breathing became labored and shallow.

"Where?" Kevin asked.

"On an island," Nicole whispered, her voice growing rapidly weaker. "A little island. In the Baltic Sea. Called Wollin." Her labored speech came in short staccato sentences. "Just north of Stettin. The German seaport. At . . . at Misdroy."

Suddenly she curled up in agony. Her breath was expelled from her in a sharp cry. She arched her back in convulsive pain—and went slack.

"An . . . iron . . . millipede," she breathed, "at Misdroy. . . ." They were her last words.

37

For a long moment Kevin looked down at the girl, at her lacerated face finally at rest. At the blood-soaked bandage on her head. It is real, he thought. Real blood. Not the fake Grand Guignol formula. Real . . . .

Somehow it looked different.

Gently he pulled the old soiled quilt up over the girl's face.

Marot turned the kerosene lamp down and blew it out.

"We will bury her," he said gruffly. "Here, on the farm of François Marot. And when the war is won and the *Boche* has left, we will honor her."

As they walked from the barn toward the wagon in which Gaspar would take them back to Meaux and the railroad station, Gaby looked at Kevin.

"Misdroy," she said quietly. "She said Misdroy. . . ."

She moved closer to him and took his hand.

Kevin nodded. "I remember, cheri," he said. "I remember. . . ."

It had been long ago. Four? Five years? Gaby had just joined the Grand Guignol company, and he had fallen for her from day one. She had gone with them on a tour of Germany that year—her first. They had been playing a three-week stand at the Schauspielhaus in the German seaport of Stettin. It had been 1939.

Their engagement had followed that of another Paris-based theatrical company, The English Players from Theatre de L'Oeuvre. They also toured Europe, performing their plays in English: George Bernard Shaw, Somerset Maugham, and Oscar Wilde—their witty sophistication a far cry from the horror plays of the Grand Guignol. The two companies often leapfrogged the same cities, the same theaters. And Kevin exchanged tips and pointers on the local stages with the stage manager of The English Players whenever they met on the road. A fact that often prevented unforeseen problems that otherwise might have cut into his limited time.

On their free days he and Gaby had taken trips through the countryside in a borrowed car—and they'd discovered the little island of Wollin and the charming village of Misdroy on the beach of the Baltic Sea. It had become a favorite spot. And it was there that he and Gaby, late one afternoon in a little secluded field newly mown, with the sun setting in a blaze of golden red, had made love for the first time.

He still remembered her intoxicating scent mingled with the fragrance of fresh-cut grass. He still remembered the excitement, the passion, when for the first time they joined as man and woman.

He still remembered the trembling desire when he held her soft, silken body close to his—and the rapture at the culmination of their love. The first time . . . At Misdroy.

And they had been there on September 1st, when Hitler's hordes invaded Poland, and the war began.

He remembered how the little company of French actors and actresses, who soon would find themselves enemy aliens in a hostile land, had opted to split up in order for each one to get back to France before war was declared, rather than staying together as a company, with the attending prominence that entailed.

And he remembered how he and Gaby, together, had set out to reach France before it was too late. At the time he had been surprised at the force of his need to get home. It had been more than simply reaching safety. With dangers dodging him, he had suddenly become aware of a strong attachment to the place where he had been born. Paris. And an overwhelming desire to return there. It was, he thought, a primeval vestige, an emotional or evolutionary appendix, much as the urge of so many wild creatures who return to the same place to spawn where they, themselves, were spawned. Seal and salmon. Turtles and birds.

And man?

They'd made it, he and Gaby. They nearly all had. Only one young man failed to return. They never knew what happened to him.

Misdroy. He would never forget the place.

Would the little sleepy village once again play a decisive role in his life?

He had an unsettling feeling it would.

As dismal as the overcast day was on the farm of François Marot, as beautiful it was at Misdroy on the Baltic island of Wollin. A clear blue sky flecked with a few high, fleecy clouds arched over the lush countryside, and there was the promise of a glorious spring in the air.

High above the ground, on the platform of Guard Tower No. 2 at the main gate to the inner test site, SS *Standartenführer* Dieter Haupt stood surveying through his field binoculars the gigantic test compound constructed for his Operation Busy Lizzie.

He felt proud of what he had accomplished; confident that he would succeed in his ultimate goal. Tomorrow was the day. Tomorrow, full-scale trials and tests would begin. Tomorrow, his

Busy Lizzie, jokingly daubed the *Tausendfüssler*—the millipede —by the technicians who worked on her, would finally come into her own.

Reichsminister Speer had been true to his word. He had to give him that. When he, Dieter Haupt, had returned to him with the final plans, Speer had personally approached the Führer, who immediately had seen and understood the tremendous possibilities of the audacious weapon. He had ordered work to begin at once on the further development of it and on the construction of operational sites. An area around the little French village of Mimoyecques on the Channel Coast had been selected. And Speer had, as promised, been instrumental in seeing to it that he, Dieter Haupt, had been placed in command of the entire project.

It had been a grueling two years. Two years and three months. Even before all the remaining design problems had been resolved, construction of a preliminary prototype of Lizzie—on a considerably smaller scale than the final weapon would be—had been undertaken. The initial trials of this Mini-Lizzie at Hillersleben had been successful enough to proceed with the project full speed. But because of the geographic location of the testing grounds at Hillersleben in the middle of Germany, only twenty kilometers from Magdeburg, a test site of far greater capacity had had to be found.

He had selected Misdroy.

Located on an island on the Baltic coast, it was out of the way, difficult to get to, easy to isolate, and had the entire Baltic Sea as a range. It had been the ideal answer.

The village of Misdroy was now a ghost town. It had been swallowed up by the Busy Lizzie test site, and its inhabitants spit out to work for the war effort elsewhere. Construction of the site itself and the full-scale prototype of Lizzie had progressed amazingly well and amazingly fast. Once again, Speer had come through, and a considerable foreign labor force had been made available for the project. Supplies had been on a top-priority basis, and worker deaths had been minimal, less than 12 percent. Haupt contributed that fact to his own efficiency.

And now—all was ready. Slowly he surveyed the huge compound. It had been brilliantly laid out. It consisted of three separate areas. The inner super-sensitive actual test site where the Lizzie—or the *Tausendfüssler*—prototype had been built bordered on the sea, which was constantly patrolled by gunboats, and it was surrounded on the land side by a double barrier of barbed wire under continuous observation by watchtowers and patrolled by SS guards with dogs. It was his own design. He'd gotten the idea when he visited Auschwitz, one of the more efficient concentration camps. After all, what can keep people in can keep them out as well.

The inner site was surrounded by a secondary area where all supporting activities took place. There were machine shops, laboratories, guards' quarters, and the like; and finally there was an outer area, again separated from the security areas with barbed-wire fences, where the housing for the labor force had been built, as well as their eating, sanitary, and hospital facilities. All most efficient.

Tomorrow, Haupt thought with prideful satisfaction, tomorrow the final test phase would begin. In another few months, if all went well—and it would—England would be brought to her knees. The installations at Mimoyecques were progressing rapidly and were nearly finished. *Alles war in Ordnung!*

Meanwhile, the newly completed vengeance weapon—the *Kirshkern*, an unmanned flying bomb the Führer had named the V-1, and other such possible weapons on the drawing boards—would soften up the Engländer for the knockout punch to be delivered by his Lizzie.

She would finish the job and bring undisputed victory to the Führer and the Third Reich.

It was only a matter of time.

Nothing could stop his *Tausendfüssler*—his iron millipede—now. . . .

❖ 5 ❖

"THERE you go again," Kevin snapped heatedly at his father. "Jumping in, both heads first. No thought for any rocks that may lie beneath the surface."

"What rocks?" Mike asked huffily. "The way you tell it, it's a piece of cake."

"I didn't say that, Dad," Kevin protested with exaggerated patience. "I said it would be possible. Quite possible. For us."

"And not for me?" Mike grumbled testily. "I can still take you over my knee, sonny-boy, and give you a good whaling!" He held out his arm on which he'd placed his special prosthesis. "Give me a hand with the straps," he said.

Kevin got up from his stool in front of the mirror in the little dressing room he shared with his father. He'd only applied his greasepaint base, a Leichner #2 Spot-Lite Klear, and looked strangely like an unfinished wax figure, even with a frown of exasperation on his face. He began to strap the prosthesis to his father's stump. As usual for this particular role, it felt heavy—filled as it was with fresh red horsemeat packed around part of a shank bone and little balloons full of the special Grand Guignol blood. The theater had had to get a special ration for that meat, even though it was mostly inedible waste.

Father and son were getting ready for a play called *The Lumberman's Revenge*, which climaxed with Mike's arm, held in a vise, slowly being sawed off by a buzz saw, with all the appropriate shrieks and screams and bloody chunks of meat and bone splinters spewing into the air. Very effective. Good for at least three faints.

"You might," Kevin commented dryly, "on a good day. But you might have a little trouble with the whole damned Nazi mob."

"And you and Gaby won't?" Mike asked archly.

"Okay, Dad," Kevin said. "Let's go over it again." He yanked one of the straps tight. "We know that a team of Allied agents sent out from London on a secret mission has been wiped out. We know that the information they were after is of vital importance to the Allies, and that there is not enough time for London to put together another special operation to get that information. We also know that it isn't possible to get near the place where they thought the information could be found. At Mimoyecques. The German Fifteenth Army is swarming all over the place. But it might be possible to find the information at Misdroy. Misdroy, Dad. Remember? The place Gaby and I were when the war broke out?"

"Of course I remember," Mike growled. "I'm not senile yet." He yanked the arm with the prosthesis away from Kevin, testing it. Kevin ignored the remark. "Misdroy," he pressed on. "Gaby and I know that place. And we know our way around. We both speak German; well enough to pass for foreign workers or something." He looked earnestly at his father. "Don't you see? We could make our way to Misdroy. That should not be too difficult. And we might be able to learn whatever it is London needs to know. And there'd be no time problem. We could start out right away. No need to put together a whole new team and all that."

"I agree with you," Michael said. "All the way. If there is half a chance to screw the *Boche* and get information that is vital to the Allies, go to it, you and Gaby. Fine. I'll help set it up." A note of obstinacy crept into his voice. "There's only one condition: I go along!"

"But, Dad—"

"I speak German, too," Mike said stubbornly.

"Yeah. With a Bavarian accent so thick you can cut it with a sausage."

"Can I help it if Hansi was from Bavaria?" Mike said defensively. "Bavarians are Germans, too. Or hadn't you heard?"

Kevin frowned. Hansi had been a stagehand at the theater for about a year. He and Mike had spent the long hours backstage teaching each other their native tongues. Hansi had stamped his distinctive Bavarian dialect indelibly on Mike, teaching him his language, including a string of swear words that would make a boiled lobster blush.

For a moment, father and son glared at one another. Then Kevin broke into a smile of surrender. He knew that tone of finality in his father's voice. "Okay, Dad," he grinned. "The three of us it is."

Michael brightened at once. He began to shrug into a colorful woodman's shirt that covered his prosthesis. "Now you're talking, my boy!" he beamed. "We'll play out the performance tonight, and tomorrow we'll be off." He waved his prosthesis triumphantly in front of him. "Rather than play-act for the damned *Boche* here for a few sous, I'd like to strut my hour on their home ground for a lot higher stakes!"

"Hold it," Kevin laughed. "Not so fast. There are a lot of things we've got to do first."

"Such as?"

"Well, first of all we have to make contact with London. Tell them what's happened and inform them of our plans. Find out if they'll go for it."

"Of course they will," Mike dismissed the thought.

"Perhaps. But we'll have to get instructions from them. What they want. What kind of time limit we'll have. Any help they can give us. Equipment. A radio. We'll need all that." He looked soberly at his father. "So the first thing we have to do is to make contact with a Resistance group that has the capabilities of reaching London. Easier said than done."

"We'll manage," Mike said confidently. "What else?"

"We've got to get the two British airmen on their way before we leave."

"Yeah. Forgot about them."

"We can't handle that ourselves. Any ideas for an escort?"

Mike thought for a moment. "Lisette," he suggested.

Kevin nodded. Lisette. She'd been an escort on two or three trips before. She was dependable, resourceful—as well as being one of the more unusual members of the Grand Guignol company. A remarkable woman, she'd joined the Lavettes and their little group in their "railroad operation" as soon as they'd sounded her out.

Now in her early thirties, Lisette in her childhood had had some kind of rare illness that left her bald. No hair, no eyebrows; in fact, she was completely hairless. She wore a wig, of course, and makeup brows, and no one was any the wiser. She played the horror lead in a play called *The Machine*, which took place during the early industrial revolution, a sort of one-act *Metropolis*. In the play, her long hair is caught in the gears of a machine that slowly rips it from her scalp—with strips of skin glowing bloodily in the stage lights. At times her screams were not entirely fake, she'd once confessed, when she suffered a certain discomfort in the process, especially if the gum that glued the wig to her pate had set a little more firmly than planned. Her name was Lisette Maynard. For a while everyone called her May, in honor of the popular European author of stories from the American Wild West, Karl May, whose characters more often than not ended up scalped. She didn't like it and made it known in no uncertain terms. So her colleagues, respecting her wishes, returned to calling her Lisette.

She was a forceful woman, the kind of female who'd cut the balls off a guy, throw them as far as she could and tell him to fetch. Kevin had thought she was a butch. He couldn't have been more wrong; a fact he found out when he personally verified that Lisette was indeed hairless. All over. It was a discovery he'd made before he met Gaby. After that, he'd had eyes—and other parts of his anatomy—for no one else. There had been no other girl in his life. Or in his bed.

Kevin nodded. "Agreed," he said. "Lisette will do fine."

"Lisette will do fine for what?" It was Gaby's voice that interrupted them as she entered the dressing room. Unnecessary formalities such as knocking on doors had long since been abandoned at the Grand Guignol. "Need any help with that mini-butcher shop of yours?" she asked Mike.

"All done."

"What about Lisette," Gaby asked again, turning to Kevin.

He filled her in.

Gaby was at once excited. She turned to Michael. "I'm so glad you agree with us that we should try," she burst out. "And I'm so glad you're coming with us!"

Kevin watched the two of them. Got my hands full, he thought. My father as irrepressibly impetuous as a twelve-year-old Little Leaguer; Gaby as spunky and generous as a Disney kiddie-film heroine. It wasn't a put-down. He rather liked her for it. He remembered what a difficult time they'd had with her when the Nazis had decreed that all Jews in Paris had to wear a yellow star with the word *Juif*—Jew—inscribed in the center. To protest and ridicule the German order, many non-Jewish Parisians took to wearing the yellow star with *Zulu* or *Martian* written on them. Gaby had wanted to join them, but Michael had vetoed it. And it was only by pointing out to her that they must do nothing to call attention to themselves and the Grand Guignol and perhaps jeopardize their operation that she had reluctantly refrained. But he *had* enjoyed her "innocent" put-down of a German officer who'd barrelled backstage after a performance and forced his unwanted attentions on her, complaining to her that Paris wasn't at all what he'd expected. Where was all the fun? he'd whined. All the gaity? The friendliness? The *joie de vivre*? Oh, Gaby had said sweetly, you should have been here before you came!

Three resounding thumps on the stage floor reverberated through the theater and interrupted his thoughts. The stage manager was giving the traditional signal with his staff that the curtain was about to go up.

Gaby turned to Kevin, her eyes aglow. "Tonight," she said, "after the performance can we start to look for a contact with the Resistance?" She looked from Kevin to Mike.

"I have an idea how to start."

6

"ESCORT?" Lisette said, arching one painted-on eyebrow. "Sounds fine to me." With hooded eyes, she looked at Higgins, the big British Flight Sergeant. "It's the 'detached' I may have trouble with." She looked admiringly at the man's dashing moustache and put her slender fingers on the biceps of his right arm. "I simply love your moustache," she cooed. Higgins's blush rose on his neck like the crimson liquid in a thermometer plunged into boiling water.

"Come off it, Lisette," Michael said, half amused, half annoyed. "You're not on stage now."

Lisette shrugged, an oddly seductive gesture. "Just being friendly," she said.

The little hiding place behind the Iron Maid was crowded. Besides the two British escapees and Lisette, Michael, Kevin, and Gaby were gathered in the room. It was past one o'clock in the morning, the play was long over, the theater dark—except for the activities of the Lavette Railroad.

"You'll leave tomorrow morning," Mike continued. "Everything has been prepared. You'll meet Six-Finger Santis in Tarbes. He'll take your charges off your hands. Evacuate them over the mountains through the village of Cervera de Buitrago."

Lisette nodded. She turned to Higgins. "Sergeant," she said, "you won't *believe* it. That little village is the *wildest* place on earth. Everyone, but everyone, has at *least* six fingers on each hand. The Mayor has *eighteen* altogether! You can't hold office unless you have at least twelve. It's the most—"

"Lisette!" Michael broke in sharply.

Lisette glanced at him. She smiled at Higgins. "I think he wants me to be quiet," she said conspiratorially. "Later, we'll—talk."

"If you are quite finished playing games, Lisette," Mike said stiffly, "we'll get on with it." He grabbed the big sledgehammer leaning against the wall in one corner. "Stand back," he said. "Here goes!"

He swung the hammer and whacked it against the wall.

It took twenty minutes with the men all taking turns with the sledgehammer before an opening large enough to crawl through had been pounded through the wall to the tunnel beyond.

Mike wiped the sweat from his brow. He pointed to a couple of small set pieces that had been brought into the room: contoured flats representing stone walls. "You know what to do," he said to Lisette. "Cut the flat that looks most like the tunnel wall outside down to size and plug the hole after we've gone through. There's only a chance in a million, but if a *Boche* patrol should happen by, they may not notice."

Lisette nodded. "It will be done," she said. She smiled at Higgins. "I am certain the Sergeant will help me."

"Very well," Mike said. He turned to Kevin and Gaby. Grab the flashlights and let's go."

Mike was the first one through. His light played across the rough tunnel walls. They glistened clammily in the beam. Kevin and Gaby followed him.

"Put out your flashlights," Mike said. Instinctively, he spoke in a near whisper. "Save the batteries. One light on at a time is enough."

Kevin and Gaby extinguished their flashlights. For a moment they stood in silence, feeling the depressing eerieness of the place creep through them. Then Mike aimed the beam of his torch up and down the tunnel they'd entered. It was quite narrow and ran straight in both directions as far as the light beam could penetrate the Stygian darkness. The air was musty and cool, the dampness almost tangible. The tunnel was obviously not a main gallery.

"Which way?" Gaby whispered.

They peered into the chill and dark in both directions. They knew that either way a labyrinth of galleries and tunnels, chambers and caves lay ahead of them, but they had no idea which way would be the quickest to lead them to a cavern used by the Resistance. They only knew that such centers did exist. And that they had to find one.

Kevin pointed down the tunnel to the left. "That way," he said. "As good as any. I think it leads west. Toward Place Clichy."

"Everyone got their chalk?" Mike asked.

They nodded.

Mike started down the corridor. "I'll make the first mark," he said. "On the opposite wall. Twenty paces. Remember that."

Kevin and Gaby followed him. Their footsteps on the rocky ground sounded hollow and dead.

Gaby shivered. She was conscious of the dull sound of her heart pounding in her ears. She suddenly remembered the sinister inscription that was written over the main entrance to the catacombs: *Stop! This is the Realm of the Dead!*, it warned. She fervently hoped it was not prophetic.

Mike shone his light on his watch. "We have four and a half hours," he said. "Then we have to be back here. Let's hope we make contact before then."

"Amen," said Kevin.

They walked down the gallery, trying to shake the feeling of oppression that enveloped them. Presently, they came to a side tunnel. On a rotted pole, a sodden sign pointing down the tunnel read: *Rue Blanche*. On the wall, a number had been painted in once-white paint.

"I know just where we are," Kevin said. "That's the house number on the corner of Rue Blanche and Rue Mansart."

"How do you know?" Gaby asked.

"The tunnels," Kevin explained to her. "Wherever they follow a street or avenue above, they marked them down here. Years ago. And they painted numbers on the walls corresponding to the house numbers on the streets above. Only the galleries down here are a hell of a lot more complex than the streets up there, so not all the tunnels are marked." He pointed to the left, down the corridor marked *Rue Blanche*. "Let's go that way," he suggested. "Toward Trinity."

"I'll make the mark," Mike said.

Hushed, they made their way through the dark, ghostly city beneath the city, passing deserted traffic circles and empty crossroads, walking through the subterranean streets and alleys in total silence and total solitude.

Where was the Resistance? . . .

Gaby took Kevin's arm. "It's—it's so eerie," she whispered.

At a place where a flight of worn stone steps blocked by debris led upward, they passed a large flat area filled with dirt and a pile of rotted wooden crates.

"Mushroom farm," Mike said. "Abandoned when the carriage trade was killed off by the automobile. The famous Champignon de Paris needed a lot of horseshit to thrive. I wonder where they grow them now."

"Vichy," Kevin suggested scornfully.

At another intersection they found a piece of soggy paper stuck to the base of the wall. A page from an old telephone directory.

"What's that doing there?" Gaby wondered.

"Chalk," Mike said. "Paper chalk marks. I've read about it. Years ago, people who ventured down into the tunnels took along a telephone book. They'd drop numbered pages from it as they went and checked the numbers when they retraced their steps, to make sure they were going in the right direction."

"Pretty clever."

"Even so, several of them got themselves lost," Mike said as he made a chalk mark on the wall. "They were never found."

They'd walked for about an hour through the bleak, soundless world of damp darkness. Kevin estimated they were somewhere under the Boulevard Haussmann area.

Suddenly they stopped. Ahead of them a tiny, steady sound intruded on the silence. A rustling, whispering sound.

Kevin, who was holding the lighted torch, at once turned it off.

Tensely they listened.

The sound continued. Unchanged.

Slowly, quietly, Kevin started to walk toward it. The others followed. The sound grew louder, until it seemed directly ahead of them.

Abruptly Kevin turned on the light and stared.

From the floor of the tunnel, a little natural fountain bubbled up and rippled down the rutted passageway, gurgling its eternal sound of rustling water.

"Unless you want to get your feet wet," Mike said, "I suggest we go the other way."

They retraced their steps and entered a side tunnel marker RU . . . . . IBE. The paint in the center had peeled off. Mike was again holding the working flashlight. The beam from it was yellowing, the batteries were running down.

Suddenly Gaby gave a sharp little cry. She grabbed hold of Kevin as she seemed to lose her footing and fall. Mike at once shot the feeble light beam on her.

Clinging to Kevin, she teetered on the jagged edge of a gaping hole in the middle of the tunnel floor. Yawning directly in their path, the pitch-black hole appeared bottomless.

Kevin quickly pulled Gaby to safety. Trembling, she held onto him. "What—what is that?" she whispered.

"A well," Mike said grimly. "An abandoned well—from God knows when."

He shone the light around. At the side of the tunnel the remnants of what appeared to be an old wooden bin formed a ledge.

"Sit down for a minute," he said to Gaby. "We'll take a break."

Gratefully Gaby walked over to the wooden bin and sank down on it. With the scrape of splintering wood, the bin collapsed. Gaby fell to the floor—and with a marrow-chilling, rattling clatter, an avalanche of whitened bones and tiny skulls poured from an opening in the tunnel wall, spilling out over the floor, swamping Gaby with the repugnant remains of death and decay.

She screamed.

At once Kevin threw on his light. He waded into the pile of bones, oblivious to the ear-grating, crunching sound under his feet and hauled the shaken Gaby to her feet. He held her.

Mike picked up one of the little skulls.

"Cats," he said. He looked around. "Cat skeletons. Hundreds

of them. What the hell? Someone trying to out-do the Grand Guignol?"

Kevin played his flashlight over the bones. "Well, I don't think its a feline counterpart of an elephant graveyard," he said. He let his light search the walls. He picked out a painted number. "Of course," he said. "That's it. *Rue Scribe*. That's what the street sign reads. There's a restaurant up there, I remember." He grinned at Gaby. "Specialized in rabbit stew and wild hare!"

"How awful," Gaby grimaced. She had regained her composure.

"They must have thrown the bones down an old shaft that led down here," Kevin concluded. "One good thing. I don't think I ever ate there!"

He and Gaby gingerly made their way out of the pile of cat bones.

Mike looked at his watch. "We'll go on for another forty-five minutes," he said. "Then we'll head back."

Skirting the well, he started down the tunnel. Kevin and Gaby followed.

Ten minutes later they came to a star where several narrow tunnels met, radiating from a high-domed cavern like spokes from the hub of a wheel. They selected one, and Mike marked it and the gallery from which they'd come. They started into the side tunnel. They'd walked a couple of minutes when they suddenly froze.

Kevin at once extinguished his flashlight—and they stood in utter darkness.

Ahead of them, the unmistakable sound of several heavy boots clanging on the rocky tunnel floor could be heard coming directly toward them.

Almost at once, where the tunnel made a slight bend, perhaps twenty yards in front of them, they saw the lights from several electric torches glisten on the dank wall, bobbing up and down in time with the marching steps.

"Boche!" Mike whispered urgently. "Quick! Back the way we came. Run!"

"They'll hear us."

"Take your shoes off! We've got to get out of this tunnel before they pick us up in their beams."

The rocky tunnel floor was hard and cold on their feet as they ran back toward the star in the darkness.

How far?

Mike was in the lead. Kevin, holding Gaby by the hand, followed closely behind. Totally blind, they raced through the gallery. They dared not use their lights.

Suddenly Kevin heard a soft thud and a choked-off oath.

"Watch it," he heard Mike hiss. "I just ran into the damned wall. On the right."

Kevin slowed down and shifted to the left, taking Gaby with him. They all kept on running. Behind them the flashlight beams were probing around the bend.

They more felt it than saw it. It was the soft, slapping sound of their shoeless feet on the rock that sounded different in tone. They had reached the star cavern.

"This way," Mike wheezed. "Right."

Away from the tunnel mouth he turned on his flashlight, holding his hand over it so only the barest glow escaped. It looked like an explosion of brilliance to them. Mike at once extinguished the torch.

"We can't risk running across the cavern," Kevin said in a quick whisper. "And we'd have to put on the light again to find the right tunnel. That would be sure to give us away. We'll stay here. Pick a tunnel that goes back pretty much in the same direction the patrol is coming from. Hurry!"

Mike risked another moment of light. The mouth of one of the side tunnels gaped quite close to the one from which the marching steps of the Nazi patrol reverberated ever louder.

They ran for it and dashed inside. A short distance into it, they stopped. Pressing themselves against the rough wall, they stood stock still, breathing their labored breath through their mouths to minimize the tell-tale sound of breathlessness.

And they saw the flashlight beams play on the ground of the cave outside as the patrol entered the star.

Motionless, they waited.

The first of the German soldiers, holding a lighted flashlight, came into view. He started across the expanse.

Suddenly a voice called out excitedly.

"Herr Feldwebel! Hierher!—Sergeant! Over here!"

There was a quick commotion and several voices speaking in agitation.

"Merde!" Kevin swore under his breath. "They found the mark

we made at the tunnel. They know it wasn't there before."

Tensely, they listened to the sergeant crisply issuing his orders. "Two men!" he shouted. "To each tunnel. See what you can find. *Los!*"

They heard the grating of hobnailed boots on rock as the soldiers spread out.

"On the ground," Kevin breathed. "Close to the wall. Cover your faces!"

Quickly they dropped, huddling close to the base of the tunnel wall.

Kevin buried his face in the crook of his arm. He was able to peek out toward the tunnel entrance only some fifty feet away. He saw the beam of a soldier's flashlight search the ground outside and the walls near the mouth of the tunnel. Slowly the shaft of light probed deeper and deeper into the tunnel toward them.

It was over. There was no possible way they would not be discovered.

Instinctively he reached for Gaby.

Suddenly a cry rang out from across the star.

"Hierher! Noch ein Zeichen! Alle hierher!—Over here! Another mark! Everyone, over here!"

At once the flashlight beam swung away.

Cautiously lifting their heads, they saw the German soldiers gather at the tunnel through which the three of them had entered the cavern, the tunnel that led back the way they'd come. Back to the Grand Guignol.

There were eight or nine of them, all armed with submachine guns carried at port arms, as they double-timed into the tunnel.

Slowly Kevin and his companions stood up. Soberly, they stood staring into the gloom, watching the rapidly dying flashlight glow coming from the tunnel mouth and listening to the fading footsteps. Finally Gaby spoke, her voice strained and bleak.

"Our marks," she said. "They'll—they'll follow our marks back the way we came. Back to the theater." She felt for Kevin and found him. Tightly she clutched his arm. "Oh, Kevin," she said miserably. "They'll—they'll find the others. Lisette. The Englishmen. Everyone. They'll take them away. And we led them to them. What can we do?"

"We don't have to do a damned thing," Mike said quietly.

"What do you mean?"

"The marks," Mike explained. "They don't go all the way back. There is a long stretch where I made no chalk marks at all. I'd rely on landmarks."

"What landmarks?"

"The cat skeletons." Mike said. "The fountain. The well. The mushroom farm. Remember? They would all lead us back. But the *Boche* will have a devil of a time trying to choose the right tunnels and galleries in that maze of excavations back there. There's not a chance in a million they'd ever pick up our marks close to the Grand Guignol. They'll be safe back there."

"But *we* have a hell of a problem." Kevin said gravely.

"Just one?"

"We can't go back the way we came or we might run into that damned patrol. To be safe, we can't even go in the general direction."

"Then how do we get back?" Gaby asked anxiously.

"We'll have to circle around," Kevin said. "Get back some other way."

"How? With no markings to follow?"

"I think I have a general idea where we are," Kevin said, "in relation to the streets above. At least judging from the last signs we saw. If we can keep our sense of direction, it should be possible to find our way back."

"A damned big *if*," Mike commented.

Kevin turned on his flashlight. He shone it into the tunnel. "If we keep going in that direction for a while," he said, "and then cut to the left, we should hit the area around the theater."

"It's our best bet," Mike agreed. "We might as well get going. Who knows how long it'll take."

They put their shoes back on, suddenly aware of their aching feet.

"We might even be lucky and find a way out," Gaby said hopefully. "A way to reach the surface, I mean. We could get back through the real streets up above. It'll soon be past five thirty. Curfew will be lifted."

"We might," Kevin conceded. But he was only trying not to be discouraging. He knew that the chances of that happening were close to nil.

His apprehension turned to despair when after more than an hour of walking, he realized they were hopelessly lost. In the eerie subterranean world, his sense of direction had been completely disoriented.

In silence they walked through the rocky labyrinth, searching for any familiar landmarks, each one of them trying to exorcise from his thoughts the dire horror stories of people lost in the tunnels that honeycombed the underground city only to be found as skeletons years or decades later.

Mike's flashlight was dead, the beams from both Gaby's and Kevin's already yellowing. Soon the pitch-black darkness would swallow them, rendering them utterly helpless.

They came to a spacious cavern and stopped. Their feeble light beams reached only a little distance into the cave.

"We'll have to cut across," Kevin said. "Find a gallery on the other side. Toward the left, I think. Perhaps there'll be a sign to tell us where we are."

They started into the cavern.

Suddenly a blazing white light exploded to life directly in front of them, instantly and totally blinding them. The cold metallic sound of several automatic weapons being cocked echoed through the cave, and a gruff voice cried out:

"*Arrêtez!*—Stop! Stay where you are!"

7

SHIELDING their eyes, they stood bathed in the blinding light.

"Who are you?" the voice snapped, its owner invisible behind the glare.

"I am Michael Lavette," Mike said. He took a step forward. "This is my—"

"Stay where you are!" the voice barked. "Don't move. Just tell me who you are." The voice was obviously French.

"My son, Kevin," Mike finished, stopping short. "And Mademoiselle Gaby Kerouac. We are actors from Theatre du Grand Guignol."

"Jacques! Maurice!" the voice ordered from behind the light.

Two grim men appeared through the glare. They walked up to Mike and the others. While one of them covered the three intruders with his gun—a British 9mm Sten Mark II submachine gun, Kevin noted—the other patted them down, efficiently and professionally. A gendarme gone underground, Kevin wondered? Even Gaby was thoroughly though dispassionately searched. Their identification papers were taken, and the men disappeared with them behind the impenetrable barrier of light.

For a moment there was silence. Then the strong light was turned toward the ground, and gradually they could make out a group of men, all armed with Stens. Four of them.

"What are you doing here?" one of the men asked coldly. It was the man whose voice had challenged them.

"We are looking for you," Mike said.

"Us?" The man's voice sounded startled.

"You are from a Resistance group, are you not?" Mike asked.

"Why?" the man demanded sharply. "What do you want?"

"Are you Resistance?" Mike insisted.

"I am Etienne," the man answered curtly. "Now. What do you want?"

"It is a long story," Mike said.

"Make it a short one."

Mike did. Briefly, to the point, he told about Nicole and her ill-fated team; about their own decision to take on her mission, and their need to make radio contact with London. A capability they did not have themselves, but one that the right command in the Resistance would have.

Etienne listened in silence. He made no comment. "Bring them along," he ordered his companions. He turned toward the wall of the cave. One of his three comrades motioned for Mike and the others to follow.

The light held by Etienne revealed a small opening in the rocky wall. They had to bend down to get through. They walked in a crouched position for several feet and suddenly found themselves in another high-domed cave, a large cavern lit by several electric light bulbs.

The place was roughly circular, perhaps fifty feet in diameter. Several men and women were busy with various tasks. Kevin noted a telephone switchboard attended by two women; and a small hand-operated printing press where three men in rolled-up shirt sleeves were engaged in turning out what appeared to be anti-Nazi propaganda leaflets. Crates and boxes—some opened, others still sealed—were stacked against one wall, and a row of cots protruded like the teeth of a comb from another. There were a few tables and chairs, a row of battered filing cabinets, and off by itself a generator powered by two bare-chested young men seated on a stationary tandem bicycle, pumping away at a steady pace. One large oil-spotted table apparently served as a machine shop for the repair of small arms, and another—stacked with pots and pans—for the preparation of food.

But most important, he also noted a radio transmitter manned by a woman wearing earphones that pushed down a headful of blonde curls in a strangely attractive manner.

Their guards held them at gunpoint while Etienne, carrying their ID papers, walked over to a man sitting at a table talking with a couple of other men.

They watched in silence as Etienne told their story to the man and showed him their papers. The man studied the documents and glanced toward them. He spoke to Etienne.

Etienne turned and motioned for the guards to bring the three strangers over.

The man seated at the table appeared to be in his middle fifties: graying hair, bushy eyebrows, and finely chiseled features—he could have been a lawyer or a doctor. He stood up as they approached. Gravely, he looked from one to the other, finally fixing his direct eyes on Kevin.

"The last time I saw you," he said dryly, "you were blind and wielding a screwdriver."

Kevin let out a sigh of relief. He surprised himself. He hadn't been aware of how tense he'd been.

"You know us!" he exclaimed. "Thank God! Will you help?"

"Not so fast, young man," the Resistance leader said soberly. "I know *who* you are. Not *what*."

"We are—like you," Kevin said. "Against the *Boche. Working* against them. Only we are not organized on the scale you are. That's why we need help. You must understand."

"I hear what you are saying, Monsieur Lavette," the man countered gravely. "But we have of necessity long since learned never to listen without also seeing and demanding proof that what we hear and see are to be believed. That you must understand." He looked searchingly at Kevin. "Can you give us such proof?"

"No more than we already have," Kevin said. "All we ask is that you contact London. Tell them what Nicole told us. Find out if we can take the place of the—the 'Jedburgh' team that was destroyed by the Germans. She said it was code-named Rebus. What risk is there in that for you? Why do you insist on more proof that we are what we say we are, monsieur . . . ?"

"I am Gerard," the leader said, "and I will tell you why. It is a matter of trust. Of reliability, which is carefully built up. It would not be possible for us to recommend you to London, not knowing. . . ."

"But—"

Gerard held up his hand. "—or even to tell London what you suggest we tell them without verification." He looked at Kevin. "Is it not possible that there was no Nicole?" he proffered. "Or, if there were, that you wish to find out her exact mission by taking her place, so you can divulge it to the enemy? Perhaps you *are* the enemy." He fixed Kevin with his direct eyes. "How are we to know?" he added. "How can we be certain that you are indeed, as you claim, working against the Boche? Proof, Monsieur Lavette. Proof."

Kevin stared at him. What the hell to say?

"Lisette," Gaby said quietly.

They all turned to her.

"Monsieur Gerard," she said. "Lisette is an actress at the theater. She is one of us. We all help Allied airmen to get back home to England. On a small scale we do this. We help get them out of France into Spain, to Lisbon, and home. That is the operation we are running." She looked straight at Gerard. "Even now, two British airmen are waiting in our hiding place at the theater. Waiting for Lisette to take them to the railroad station and follow her onto a train for Toulouse. This morning it will be done. Perhaps if you see this happen, you will believe us enough to make contact with London, no?"

Gerard stared at her. "What time?" he asked.

"The train is at eight forty-five this morning," Gaby said evenly. "Lisette will leave the theater with her charges one hour before."

58

Gerard looked at his watch. "Less than two hours," he said. He turned to Etienne. "Etienne," he said crisply. "Go with Monsieur Lavette and Mademoiselle Kerouac to observe this 'railroad operation.' I should like to know how it comes off." He called to one of the women at the switchboard. "Suzanne! Get me Jean-Pierre on the telephone." The girl acknowledged his request. He turned back to Mike. "You, monsieur, will stay here."

Affronted, Mike began to protest. Gerard stopped him. "It is not what you think, monsieur," he said. "You are not a, a hostage. I will contact London. Now. I will apprise them of the situation. I will convey to them my reservations. But if—when Etienne gets back—all is well, we can get you an answer from London at once. They will have had a chance to evaluate your proposition. It is, I think you will agree with me, highly unusual. You will therefore stay with me to answer any questions London may have about Nicole and about your plan." He gave Mike a searching look. "*D'accord?*—Agreed?"

" Agreed," Mike nodded.

Kevin and Gaby followed Etienne through a series of confining tunnels leading from the command cave. Finally they came to a flight of stairs. They ascended the stone steps and emerged through a trap door in the basement of a house. They made their way up to the ground floor and came into a kitchen, where an ample woman was boiling soup bones in a large kettle on a wood-burning stove. She barely looked up as Etienne led his charges to the back door. In a narrow alley, a small closed delivery truck converted to burning charcoal was waiting. A driver sat behind the wheel.

"In the back," Etienne said.

All three got in. Etienne closed the door, and they sat in silence in the dark interior of the van.

The ride took about twenty minutes. The truck came to a stop and they dismounted in another alley. On the wall of one of the houses was a prize example of Paris graffiti: *LES BOCHES AU POTEAU!—The Germans to the Stake!*; and on a fence, a poster with the portrait of a stalwart German soldier. The Star of David had been scrawled across his face.

Having no idea from where they started their ride, they emerged from the alley onto Rue D'Athenes, a stone's throw from Gare St. Lazare.

A little sidewalk cafe on Rue D'Amsterdam near the station

where they sat down to drink a watery-brown liquid masquerading as coffee was next to a bookstore, which—at its peril—displayed in the window large portraits of Hitler and Petain prominently placed next to two volumes of Victor Hugo's *Les Misérables*. After all, even a Gestapo officer might notice the subtlety.

At a table near them sat three "gray mice"—the Nazi women auxiliary of the Gestapo, thus named by the French because of the color of their uniforms and, perhaps, because of their propinquity to the "rats" for whom they worked. With a superior bearing, they watched the parade of Parisians go by.

Lisette and the two British airmen would pass the cafe on the other side of the boulevard.

It was 8:09.

They waited—and reluctantly sipped the unsavory beverage. Lisette and the Englishmen would soon come into view.

They were on their second cup of the brown liquid when they saw Lisette come walking purposefully down the street, neither too quickly nor too slowly, looking straight ahead. Fifteen feet behind her came Flight Sergeant Alfred Higgins, his magnificent moustache flying at full mast, and fifteen feet behind him, Corporal Henshaw.

There were not many people abroad. Ahead of Lisette, who was wearing a blue coat and a blue hat, walked a woman in a threadbare overcoat and an elderly couple, he carrying his umbrella over his shoulder like a rifle at shoulder arms and she lugging an oversized handbag. Behind Lisette were two nondescript women, and a little farther back, a couple of German Wehrmacht soldiers. It was an ordinary day.

Softly Kevin spoke to Etienne. "The woman in blue," he said, "Lisette."

They watched as Lisette and her charges came closer, on their way to the railroad station.

"The man with the moustache is a British sergeant," Kevin whispered to Etienne. "The man behind him, his companion."

They watched.

Suddenly Gaby gave Kevin a sharp nudge with her foot under the table. She nodded surreptitiously toward the table with the three "gray mice." Kevin followed her glance—and at once grew tense.

The German women were all looking in the direction of Sergeant Higgins. One of them touched her nose and giggled. The older of them said something to her, and she immediately grew sober. All three of them stared toward the approaching Higgins, curiosity on their faces. All at once they got up and started across the street.

Gaby felt her stomach knot. Stricken, she and Kevin exchanged glances. The three Gestapo auxiliaries were headed straight for the unsuspecting Higgins.

And there was nothing either Gaby or Kevin could do.

They watched with rapidly growing anxiety. They saw Lisette discover the three "gray mice" approach across the street, and they saw her realize that for reasons of their own, they were bent on accosting Higgins.

If they did, he would be lost.

Another few feet . . . .

Suddenly they saw Lisette speed up her steps. She caught up with the couple in front of her, and passing them she leaned slightly toward the man, lowering her head. When she straightened up, her blonde wig and blue hat were dangling from the tip of the man's umbrella!

With a shriek of outrage, Lisette tried to cover her totally hairless pate with her hands while screaming epithets at the man with the umbrella. Startled, the man turned—Lisette's hat-decorated wig fluttering from his umbrella like a battle standard. Yelling invectives at the top of her lungs, Lisette began to pummel the man, her bald head shaking in rage.

Immediately everyone on the street turned toward the commotion. The three "gray mice" stopped; pointing to the furious, hairless Lisette, they began to laugh derisively. The German soldiers came running to join the fun, and soon Lisette, her bald head bobbing up and down as she battled the bewildered man and his purse-swinging wife, was surrounded by a group of shouting, laughing, and gesticulating Parisians—and the three "gray mice."

Higgins and Henshaw had stopped. They stood in obvious indecision. It was apparent they had no idea what to do. What was happening was not according to script.

It would be only a matter of minutes before the three Gestapo auxiliaries would return their attention to Higgins.

"Dammit!" Gaby suddenly hissed. "Rules or no rules, I'm not going to sit here and let those two go to hell!"

And before Kevin could stop her, she leaped to her feet and ran across the street.

Under cover of the diversion caused by Lisette, they saw Gaby run to the two British airmen, speak to them quickly, and start to walk toward the station, with both of them following her.

When they were well past the group around Lisette, they saw the bald girl retrieve her wig, slap it on her head, hat and all, still screaming a stream of indignant outrage at the befuddled man, and finally stalk off after Gaby and the Englishmen, who were just disappearing into the railroad station.

With a mixture of astonishment and awe, Etienne looked at Kevin. Without a word he rose. Throwing a few coins on the table, he left the cafe and started to walk toward the station. Kevin followed.

They were headed for the track from which the train for Toulouse departed when they saw Gaby come striding toward them, a big smile on her face.

"They got on board all right," she announced. "Lisette, too." She took Kevin's arm. "Lisette," she laughed. "She is a woman to admire!"

"Mademoiselle," Etienne said quietly. "So are you."

"Now do you believe us?" Gaby asked.

Etienne looked at her.

"There is still a thing to be settled," he said.

❖ 8 ❖

COLONEL Dirk A. Baldon, United States Army, stood next to his jeep that was parked at the Main Gate to the Milton Hall Estate, some eighty miles north of London. His fingers drummed an impatient tattoo on the hood of the jeep, his lantern jaw thrust out angrily. He glanced at his watch. 0813 hours. Dammit! he thought, it had to be an American. The last Jed to reach the home roost from the exercise had to be an American. Not a Brit. Not a Frenchman. A damned American. One of *his* boys. He could already hear the ribbing.

The exercise was a good one. That wasn't it. He, himself, had helped lay it out. Take a group of Jeds in training, put them in a closed truck, take them twenty miles into unfamiliar countryside, and dump them in different places in the middle of the night, with instructions to report back to headquarters in eight hours. Shouldn't be too damned difficult, except the trainees would have no identification papers, no compass, and only a pencil flashlight and a map on which all the names of the English villages and small towns had been changed to French names. Empingham had become Castillou; Werrington, Entreveaux; and Little Bytham, Draguinan. Only the terrain contours and natural as well as man-made landmarks, all renamed, remained the same. The Jed trainee would have to orient himself solely from those features. Asking questions was, of course, strictly taboo. Anyway, there were few people abroad in the English countryside in the dead of night, and the foreign names on the maps would mean nothing to them, except arouse their suspicions. And that was risky business. The Brits were on their toes and saw Nazi parachutists behind every haystack. A fellow with no papers except a foreign map and a French or American accent would not get far in the helping-hand department. It was the kind of training exercise that offered real risk—the best kind there was.

And the Jeds would need just that. And then some.

He'd been with Operation Jedburgh for a few months, having joined shortly after General "Wild Bill" Donovan and his Office of Strategic Services—the OSS—joined forces with the British counterpart, Special Operations Executive—the SOE—and formed the Special Forces, headquartered in London. At SFHQ the Jedburgh concept had been formulated and put into action. Each Jedburgh team would consist of a British, a French, and an American officer, members of SOE or OSS, and an enlisted radio operator. In some cases, one of these Jeds would be a woman. The teams would be dropped in enemy-held territory in advance of the invasion, to collect intelligence and organize resistance. Since the inception of the operation, the members recruited for it had undergone basic training in Scotland near the little town of Jedburgh, which had lent its name to the operation and which was situated on the Jed Water, a tributary to the Teviot River just north of the English border. But some seven weeks earlier, with the invasion date drawing closer, the Jeds had arrived at Milton Hall for their final training and to form teams. In fact, a few early teams had already been sent into the field: Clover and Quatrain, Rebus and Mars.

Again he looked at his watch. 0816 hours. Where the hell was that idiot Hawkins?

Captain Edward "Ted" Hawkins, a West Point infantry officer who'd joined the OSS, had caught his eye from the word go. The man was a good six-two and so solidly built you could throw a tank at him without making a dent. Except perhaps on the gun turret. And with enough self-assurance to fill out his crossword puzzles in ink. So far he had formed no team alliance, perhaps because he was so exasperatingly self-contradictory. Capable of being imaginative and audacious, even brilliant, he'd let his early military training instill in him a strict by-the-book attitude. Hell, in the SF a little bending of the rules was expected. Even encouraged. Like stealing a bicycle to make better time on an orientation run, or matching up the name on a two-bit railroad station with the map and figuring out the other English names and where you were. But not Ted Hawkins when he was in his damned by-the-book mood. If he would only let himself, he could be one hell of a Jed, instead of a hamstrung also-ran. Like now, dammit! The bastard could have been the first one home. Instead, he was already over a quarter of an hour past the deadline.

A jeep came careening down the road from the manor house and came to a stop behind Baldon's jeep. A sergeant jumped from the vehicle.

"Sir," he said, saluting smartly. "You are wanted in the CO's office. Urgent, sir."

"Thank you, Sergeant," Baldon said. He at once got into his jeep. What the hell now? He gave one last look down the road before he started his jeep.

To the devil with Hawkins!

His SOE counterpart in the Special Forces, Lieutenant Colonel Clifton Hillsbotham Ramsey, was already present in the CO's office when Baldon entered, as well as another British officer, Major Howard Roberts, who ran the teams already in the field, and a French officer, Lieutenant Colonel Jean-Pierre Lamont.

Brigadier James Hindsmith Parnell, looking grim and drawn, sat behind his desk. A wiry, lean Leslie Howard look-alike, he was a man well liked and respected by both fellow officers and other ranks. The Jeds, especially the non-British ones, often affectionately referred to him as "Pips," because of his insignia of rank, which had three pips and a crown on it, the largest number of pips at Milton Hall. He looked up as Baldon entered.

"Ah! Baldon," he said, "have a seat." He looked at Major Roberts. "Howard, we are all here."

"Right, sir." Howard looked gravely at the other men. "Rebus has been burned," he said quietly.

There was a general reaction of startled dismay.

"All of them?" asked Ramsey, obviously shaken.

"All of them. Dead."

"Damn!" Baldon exclaimed. Somehow the one word conveyed all his shock, his grief, and anger. "They were good people."

"They are all good people," the brigadier said.

"How do we know?" Colonel Lamont wanted to know. "How was the intelligence transmitted to us?"

"Through London," Roberts said. "They had a signal from a Resistance group in Paris. Chap named Gerard has regular radio contact with London. They relayed the signal."

"Is Gerard dependable?" Ramsey asked.

"He has a top reliability rating."

"Rotten, bloody luck," Ramsey muttered.

"We have another serious problem," Brigadier Parnell said soberly. "The Rebus mission was vital. Perhaps more so than we realize. The entire Fifteenth German Army has been concentrated in the Rebus target area."

"Replacement?" Baldon asked.

"You are absolutely right, of course," the brigadier nodded. "Replacement." He looked around at the men. "How soon can we get a replacement team operational?"

"With the special training and briefing necessary," Ramsey said crisply, "we can have another team ready in two weeks, I should say." He looked at the others. They nodded assent.

"We may not have two weeks," the brigadier said quietly.

"The invasion?" Baldon asked eagerly. "Has a date been set?"

"Not yet. But it will not be far in the future, I should think. A matter of four to five weeks."

"So, if we are to put a replacement team in the field, give them time enough to find out what's going on at Mimoyecques, and act on their information, if indeed there *is* a threat to the invasion, perhaps a serious threat, we'd have to mount a new mission, a new team, day before yesterday," Baldon said.

The brigadier nodded slowly. "That is about the size of it, Colonel," he agreed. "And since that cannot be done, of course, we must consider other possibilities." He looked at the officers facing him. "That is why you are here. The signal from Gerard with the Rebus information contained a second part, a rather, eh, unorthodox proposition." He turned to Major Roberts. "Howard?"

Roberts cleared his throat. "Gerard, in his signal, informed us that the people who obtained the intelligence about the aborted mission from the last surviving member of Rebus, before—"

"Who was that?" Ramsey asked.

"Nicole," Roberts answered him. "Before she died, she told them that it would be quite impossible to find out anything about the nature of the secret project at Mimoyecques, at the construction site there. It is quite unapproachable. But she said that the information could be had at another place, a place called Misdroy."

"Where the hell is that?" Baldon asked.

"In Germany. On the Baltic coast. About fifty miles north of Stettin."

"What's there?"

"We do not know, actually," Brigadier Parnell interjected. "Presumably testing grounds of some sort. Like at Peenemünde, I shouldn't wonder."

"It seems the people who talked to Nicole," Roberts continued, "are suggesting that *they* take over the Rebus mission. They point out that they are already in the field and no time would be wasted. It seems they know the Misdroy area rather intimately."

"Who are they?" Ramsey asked. "A Resistance group? French Intelligence?"

"Yes—and no," Roberts answered. "They do run a minor operation, getting downed airmen out of France. Rather successful at it, actually. But they are not part of any organized resistance." He paused. "They are—they are actors, actually."

"Actors!" Ramsey exclaimed.

"From the Theatre du Grand Guignol."

"That horror thing?"

"Yes."

"My word!" Ramsey was shocked. "And *they* want to take on a Jedburgh mission?" he said incredulously. "Impossible!"

"So it would seem," Brigadier Parnell said. "At first glance, at least. But, in view of the, eh, rather pressing situation, let us not dismiss the possibility out of hand."

"But—*actors*, sir?" Ramsey protested. "Amateurs?"

"Some of our best Jeds are amateurs, Colonel," Parnell pointed out. "I shouldn't be surprised if there were an actor or two among them, what? Some of the most valuable intelligence has been supplied by rank amateurs more than once."

"Yes, but . . ." He let it hang.

"How much experience *do* they have," Colonel Lamont wanted to know. "How do we know they have even a chance of succeeding?"

"Gerard is checking them out, Colonel," Roberts answered. "He will transmit his evaluation and recommendation to us as soon as his assessment has been completed sometime today."

Lamont grunted.

"If they're caught," Ramsey said, "which seems bloody likely, they could conceivably give away more than they could possibly learn."

"What?" Baldon countered. "They know nothing about Operation Jedburgh. They know nothing about our methods or procedure. The Germans already know we are trying like hell to find out about that Mimoyecques project. Those actors couldn't tell them anything they don't already know. All they could give away, Cliff, would be their own "railroad operation," and that's small potatoes in the scheme of things."

Brigadier Parnell nodded. "I agree with that, Baldon," he said. "I do not think there could possibly be a security problem." He thought for a brief moment, then made up his mind. "I suggest," he said, "that we wait until we have had further word from Gerard before we make a final decision. I suggest that meanwhile we at once select an existing team of Jeds and begin to brief them."

"I agree, sir," Ramsey said. The others nodded assent.

"And if Gerard's recommendation is favorable?" Lamont asked.

"Then I suggest we let those, eh, volunteers have a go at it," Parnell said. "I do think the importance of finding out what is going on at Mimoyecques—what those deucedly mysterious installations actually are and what threat they constitute—warrants that we take advantage of every chance we have," he continued gravely. "Including using a, a group of people who have no special training. We must, in effect, take advantage of them—and consider them expendable." He thought for a while. "I want your individual evaluations and recommendations on how we can field this team, and I want them by 1200 hours. If we do use them, we must give them our best support. We must make the most careful decision possible. In our, eh, profession, even chance cannot be left to chance. I have only one condition myself. I shall want a trained Jed to accompany the chaps from the Grand Guignol. Someone who can be dropped in at once, whose first task will be to evaluate the feasibility of using them, and secondly, to go along with them on the mission to Misdroy." He looked around. "Any suggestions?" he asked. "I suppose it should be someone who is not already committed to a team. We should not want to break up anything, what?"

The men looked uncertainly at one another.

"I have a suggestion," Baldon finally ventured.

"Yes?"

"Ted Hawkins," Baldon said. "Captain Edward Hawkins. He is fluent in both French and German."

"Gentlemen?"

There were no objections.

"Right, then."

"We shall need a code name for the team," Ramsey said.

"Volunteer," Roberts suggested.

"Grand Guignol!" Baldon said. "What else?"

❈ 9 ❈

FAR from imposing, Etienne thought, as he and Kevin and Gaby walked down the alley from Rue Chaptal toward Theatre du Grand Guignol. He'd never been to the place before, probably one of the few Parisians who hadn't.

It was still before ten in the morning, and the theater was deserted. Theater people in Paris usually didn't stir until well after noon.

Kevin unlocked the stage door. He motioned for Gaby and Etienne to wait, and went inside. No use running the risk of bungling into that *canaille*—that bastard—Choisy or someone else not connected with the railroad operation, who might get curious.

No one was around, and Kevin and Gaby took Etienne to the stage, which like any stage stripped of its scenery and lights looked cold and barren, with only a naked work light on a stand providing illumination. They led him down the stairs to the gloomy scenery docks below.

Etienne looked around the eerie basement crowded with its ghastly props. "This is where you hide your escapers?" he asked, obviously skeptical.

"No," Kevin said pleasantly, "we hide them in here." He walked over and pulled open the front panels of the Iron Maid.

Etienne stared into the spiked interior. He frowned. Were they making fun of him? Did they play him for a fool? Angrily, he turned to them.

Kevin reached past him and took hold of one of the crooked spikes. "Allow me," he said, twisting the spike and pushing the back open. He stepped into the room beyond and switched on the light.

"Come on in," he said to Etienne. "We cannot provide luxury accommodations for our guests, of course, but this does the trick quite nicely."

Etienne gaped at the hidden chamber, taking in everything. He was obviously impressed. He turned to Kevin. "And the, the tunnel?" he asked.

"Over here," Kevin said. He pushed aside the Japanese screen. Behind it was the hole they had battered in the bricked-up wall. It was plugged with a piece of scenery that showed its unfinished side, with supporting battens and papier-mâché applied over contoured chicken wire.

Kevin removed the plug. "Shall we?" he said, motioning Etienne through the opening. He picked up a flashlight, and the two men entered the tunnel.

"Put the cover back," Kevin called to Gaby. She did.

Kevin played the beam of his flashlight over the set-piece wall plug. It looked quite real. The papier-mâché stonework had obviously been painted to match the tunnel wall. Lisette had done a good job, Kevin thought. Only direct examination would reveal the cover to be fake.

Kevin shone his light up and down the narrow tunnel. "This is where we entered the maze of excavations," he told Etienne. "It is, I believe, a seldom visited section."

They went back inside. Kevin replaced the wall plug. Gaby turned to Etienne.

"Now, monsieur?" she asked. "Now do you believe us?"

It was just before noon. Activities in the Resistance cave were somewhat less hectic than when Mike, Kevin, and Gaby had first been taken there. A few people were sleeping on the cots; there were two different young men pedalling the tandem hooked up to the generator, and the operators at both the telephone switchboard and the radio transmitter were different.

Kevin, Mike, and Gaby were watching Etienne and Gerard off by themselves in earnest conversation. Finally Gerard nodded and walked over to the radio transmitter. Etienne joined the three Grand Guignol actors.

"Well?" Mike asked.

"Gerard is going to recommend that you be allowed to carry

out your plan to take over the Rebus mission," Etienne said. "He is contacting London now. We shall see what they decide."

"He was impressed with Lisette, was he not?" Gaby said.

Etienne smiled at her. "He was, mademoiselle," he acknowledged. "But more so with you. I believe it was your reaction, your *action* at seeing the charges committed to your care in danger that impressed him most."

"What now?" Mike asked. "What happens now?"

"We will get instructions from London," Etienne said, "in due time." He shrugged. "We wait."

He had been waiting almost an hour. SS *Standartenführer* Dieter Haupt had consciously had to control his urge to fidget as he sat stiffly on one of the upholstered chairs in *Die Lange Halle* in the New Reich Chancellery, the imposing one-hundred-and-forty-six-meter-long marble gallery called The Long Hall. It was twice as long as the famous Gallery of Mirrors at Versailles, Haupt knew, and he was impressed. He sat just outside the fully eight-meter-tall marble doorway that led to the private office of Adolf Hitler, whose initials adorned a golden shield over the double doors. Looking straight ahead, the two SS guards from the SS *Leibstandarte* paid him no attention. Although it was sunny daylight, he noticed irrelevantly that the two ornate gold sconces on the wall flanking the doors were brightly lit.

Reichsminister Albert Speer had summoned him to Berlin on a moment's notice, informing him that he was to have an audience with the Führer. He wondered what it would be about. And why on so short notice? A whim of the Führer's? Trouble? Was it because of that accident two days ago? The accident that killed nine foreign workers? He thought not. Accidents were part of forced trials such as the ones being carried out at Misdroy. And real damages had been minimal. What then? He was not worried, but he knew the palms of his hands were moist. Unconsciously, he rubbed them on his sharply creased uniform trousers. It would not do to appear the slightest bit nervous.

Driving from the airport through Berlin, he had been shaken at seeing the destruction inflicted by the Allied terror air raids since their planes began to bomb the city only a short month before. Burned-out buildings. Bomb-cratered streets. Whole sectors demolished.

A deep rage welled in him when he thought of how the enemy

had wrought destruction on the Fatherland. And on its capital city. But one ray of solace burned brightly in his mind.

It would be nothing against what his *Tausendfüssler* would do to London. To England!

The door to the Führer's office opened and an Adjutant emerged. He beckoned to Dieter Haupt and stood aside as the young SS officer entered the office.

His first impression was one of spacious splendor. The huge room was panelled in rich woods, with a high ceiling of crossed wooden beams. A stern portrait of Bismarck hung over a fireplace mantelpiece at one end of the room; fine paintings adorned the walls; and a golden German eagle soared over the great doors. The furniture was sparse. A long sofa in a blue-patterned print stood before the fireplace, a massive marble table faced the doors, and the desk of Adolf Hitler dominated the end of the room opposite the fireplace. The desk was surrounded by three upholstered chairs. *Reichsminister* Speer, who—Haupt knew—had designed and built the magnificent building, sat in one of them. The Führer was seated behind the desk.

Dieter Haupt came to attention with a barely audible click of his heels. His arm shot out in a stiff Nazi salute.

"*Heil Hitler!*" he sang out.

Hitler rose, walked around his desk, and extended his hand to the young officer.

"*Mein lieber Haupt,*" he said cordially. "I am delighted to meet you at last."

Haupt took the Führer's hand. He felt the clutch of pride and patriotism tighten his chest. It was a landmark moment for him. He was shaking the hand of Adolf Hitler. The hand millions of people the world over had seen raised in the stirring salutation of the glorious Third Reich; the hand that had guided the fate of the Fatherland to peerless triumphs. And he, SS *Standartenführer* Dieter Haupt, was shaking it. Again he came to attention.

"*Mein Führer!*" he said.

Hitler walked back to his straight-backed leather chair behind his desk, which stood on a luxurious Oriental rug beneath a magnificent Gobelin. He motioned to a chair next to Speer.

"Sit down, Haupt," he said.

Haupt sat. He noticed the panel of inlaid wood on the front of the desk, facing whoever would be sitting across from the Führer. It was a sword half pulled from its scabbard.

Soon, Haupt thought. Soon it would be pulled out all the way.

"Speer has filled me in on the progress of your project," Hitler said. "But I want to know the details directly from you. Please give me your complete, in-depth account of the status of Operation Busy Lizzie."

With pride and enthusiasm SS *Standartenführer* Dieter Haupt began his report.

Gerard turned away from the radio transmitter and the message written out by the operator.

"London has authorized you to proceed with your plan," he told Mike and the others. "But there is one condition."

"What?"

"They want one of their trained agents to join you. He will be paradropped with instructions and equipment. We are to supply the coordinates for a drop zone. Organize a reception committee." He frowned. "We do not operate outside Paris," he said. "It will take a couple of days to set it up."

"A couple of days!" Mike exclaimed. "Why so long?"

"It is not that simple," Gerard said.

"It is." Kevin turned to Gerard. "I can show you a drop zone we can use right away. Do you have a map of the area around Paris?"

Someone produced a military map.

Kevin searched it. "Here," he said, putting his finger on the map. "Right there is your drop zone."

Gerard bent over the map. He turned to the radio operator.

"Send these coordinates," he said. "And tell them they can drop their agent tonight."

Gaspar expertly kept the wagon wheels in the deep ruts of the dirt road as he drove through the little grove to the secluded alfalfa field on the Marot farm near Meaux. The remote cultivated clearing was bordered on one side by the Marne River and on the others, by the woods. It was well past midnight, and the darkness was all but total among the trees.

Three people rode silently in the back of the wagon: Mike, Kevin, and Etienne. At their feet stood a can of kerosene and four old buckets packed with straw. All the men except Gaspar held a Sten gun across their knees.

"Once more," Etienne said, speaking in a low tone of voice.

73

"The drop will be at 0130 hours. By that time we must each be in position at one of the four corners of the field assigned to us. The straw in the buckets will have been soaked with kerosene, and—"

He suddenly stopped, remembering something. "You all have your matches?"

Kevin and Mike confirmed. Etienne turned to Gaspar.

"Gaspar?"

The man grunted.

"*Bon!* When we hear the plane," Etienne continued, "wait until you see my bucket lit, then light yours. Is it understood?"

"Yes," Mike and Kevin said.

"Gaspar?"

Another grunt.

Etienne looked at his watch in the light of a small flashlight. "We have better than an hour to set up—and to make certain that the drop zone is clear. We must all be in position fifteen minutes before the time. Agreed?"

"Agreed."

There was a sudden, violent bump and the wagon swayed as it left the ruts and came to a stop a short distance off the road. Gaspar dismounted and placed a canvas feed bag over the muzzles of the two horses. It would serve to keep them quiet. The men all peered into the darkness. Ahead of them lay the clearing, and the Marne. The stillness lay softly like a black shroud over the land.

"We will walk around the clearing," Etienne instructed them. "All the way." He suddenly talked in a whisper. "Michael, you and Kevin go to the right. Gaspar and I will take the left." He began to climb down from the wagon. "Don't forget your buckets," he reminded them. "I'll take the kerosene. We'll meet on the river bank on the opposite side and soak the straw, if all is well, yes?"

It was not a question that needed an answer. The four men set out in silence.

There was one hour and twelve minutes to the drop.

Damn that bastard, Baldon, Ted Hawkins thought for the umpteenth time. He'd wanted to get into action, sure, but not as a nursemaid for a bunch of lousy ham actors playing secret agent, flashing decoder rings. But he'd had no choice. Pips, himself, had leaned on him. His head still reeled with the mass of information they'd stuffed into it during the few hours he'd had to get ready. It could, of course, all be a crock of shit, but the mission *did* sound important; that mysterious construction site, and he *was* intrigued. Iron millipedes, for crissake! But, dammit!, what the hell was he going to do with a bunch of greasepaint monkeys?

The steady, deep-throated drone of the twin Rolls Royce Merlin 73 engines on the little De Haviland Mosquito XVI bomber made him drowsy as he sat in the hard seat near the hole in the floor of the aircraft fuselage through which he'd be dropped over the DZ. He eyed the lid covering the hole. He liked the way they did it in the good old US of A a hell of a lot better—out through the side door. Much more civilized. Being chucked out through a hole in the bottom made him feel like a bird-dropping from the asshole of a giant bird. Not a bad idea at that, he thought, if that shithead Baldon would be standing underneath.

He dozed off . . . .

He woke with a start. Someone was shaking him. It was the young jump master. Mitchell? Mitchum? What the hell. The Brit NCO.

"Fifteen minutes out, sir," the noncom shouted over the engine noise. "Time to get ready."

Hawkins glanced at the two jump lights above him. The red light was on. The pilot had begun his approach to the drop zone. He looked at his watch. Right on the button.

The NCO checked his chute and hooked the snap-on ring of the parachute static line firmly to the jump cable in the plane. He inspected the equipment package attached to the agent and uncovered the jump hole.

"Sit in the hole, sir," he shouted. "Watch the light."

Hawkins took his position on the edge of the hole, his legs dangling down into the black void beneath him. Instantly, the wind tore at him; the cold seemed to bite into his bones. He kept his eyes riveted on the lights. This was for real. Not a piddling training jump. His instructions tumbled through his mind: You'll be dropped from two thousand feet. "You'll be on the ground in two minutes. Your reception committee contact is named Etienne. . . .

Abruptly, the light turned to green. In the same instant, he heard the jump master behind him bellow, *go!*, and felt a sharp slap on his shoulder. With the heels of both hands, he pushed himself from the edge of the hole and plunged into the black void.

Instantly a jet of pure force gripped him and slammed him horizontal to the ground as he plummeted into the slip stream. With every possible sense, he waited the eternal seconds for the static cord to rip the parachute from his backpack and for the canopy to be filled with air. The jerk, when it came, was as violent as he remembered.

He reached up, grabbed hold of the risers, and began to check his oscillation, stabilizing his descent. He felt for his equipment package. It was still firmly attached. Already the drone of the plane was disappearing in the distance.

He was alone in the black void. And the silence.

He looked down.

Below, and a little in front of him, he could make out four yellow-red points of flickering light. The DZ. On his right, he could see a pale ribbon of gray convoluting its way through the black countryside. The Marne River.

His forward momentum carried him slowly toward the drop zone, which loomed ever closer. He felt himself drifting toward the river on his right. Shit! He wasn't about to be dunked. He corrected, pulling on the left risers, slipping to his left as that part of the canopy above him partly collapsed.

He was suddenly aware of the ground rushing up to meet him. Quickly he gave a sharp pull on all four risers, momentarily checking the speed of his descent—and he was on the ground. He rolled in the direction of his fall, came to his feet, and at once began to haul in the billowing chute as four figures came running toward him.

Jed agent Edward "Ted" Hawkins was committed.

He freed himself from the harness. Two of the men coming toward him ran to the chute and helped trim it. The other two came up to him.

"Ted?" one of them asked.

"Ted," Hawkins acknowledged.

The man broke into a smile. "Welcome to France," he said. "I am Etienne." He indicated the man with him. "This is Monsieur Michael Lavette. Mike. He will be on the team with you."

Mike stuck out his hand. He looked appraisingly at the Jed agent. "We shall be delighted to have you with us, Ted," he said. His tone of voice did not ring entirely sincere. It was not lost on

76

Ted. The feeling is mutual, chum, he thought. He shook Mike's hand.

"Mike," he said noncommittally.

"Come," Etienne said. "We must gather our light pots. And your parachute. We must take you to a safe place."

The wagon ride back to the Marot farm was silent. Ted had been introduced to Kevin and Gaspar, but—by mutual consent—any significant conversation would wait until they'd reached the farm.

Gaspar brought the wagon to a stop in the farmyard near the barn and began to unharness the horses as the four men, led by Kevin, walked toward the main house. It looked dark and deserted.

Kevin knocked on the door.

There was a short wait, and the door was flung open.

Ted stared into the room beyond, and his mouth dropped open in astonishment. . . .

❖ 10 ❖

THE room beyond blazed with light. Across the back of it, flanked by two huge green boughs and a frayed and faded Tricolour, a white sheet had been strung, with the words, *BIENVENU À LA FRANCE MONSIEUR TED!—Welcome to France, Mr. Ted!—* painted in uneven red and blue letters on it. An old windup gramophone began a scratchy rendition of the "Marseillaise"; a pretty girl holding a bouquet of flowers stood next to it; and from behind a table laden with bread and cheese and wine, a beaming man, with several World War I medals flopping on his chest as he ran, came rushing up to Ted.

"Welcome, welcome, Monsieur Ted!" he cried. He enfolded Hawkins in a bear hug and kissed him resoundingly on both cheeks. "I, François Marot, welcome you to my house. A great honor. A great honor!"

He rushed back to the table and began to pour wine into several large mugs.

Ted stared. He was slowly recovering from his astonishment. Crazy, he thought, horrified. They're totally, unequivocally crazy. Turning a serious mission into a three-ring circus, for crissake! And where the hell was the brass band? Heaven deliver him from these—amateurs! His eyes wandered to the equipment package with his radio. First order of business, he thought determinedly, an urgent report to Roberts. Cancel, cancel, cancel!

Cancel—Team Grand Guignol . . . .

The girl with the flowers came up to him. She gave him a radiant smile. "I am Gaby," she said. "Welcome! We are so very happy to see you." She handed him the flowers and kissed him on both cheeks. She smells a lot better than that farmer, Ted thought, but it wasn't enough to cheer him up.

He took the bouquet. Awkwardly, he stood holding it in front of him. He felt like a damned fool. Like a klutzy homecoming queen on the stage of a high school auditorium, he thought.

The gramophone wound down in a mournful, off-key finish as Mike came up to him. He took him by the arm. "Come, Ted," he said jovially. "Eat. Drink. We must get to know one another, yes? Tomorrow Gaspar will take us to Meaux and the first train for Paris."

Resignedly Ted let himself be propelled toward the food table. It'll be a long night, he thought glumly. A damned long night. . . .

He had been right, he thought, as the train rattled over the switch tracks leaving the railroad station at Meaux. It had been a long night. A damned long night. It had been more like a high school reunion than the beginning of a vital intelligence mission. First thing, he fervently vowed to himself, first thing in Paris, off goes a message to Roberts: Forget it!

The taciturn Gaspar had driven them to the station at first light, and they had boarded the early train for Paris, some fifty miles away; he, Mike, Kevin, Gaby, and Etienne, the Resistance fellow. Marot, the kissing farmer, had stayed behind.

Thank God, he thought.

Mike had examined his Milton Hall–manufactured ID minutely and pronounced it perfect. The photographs were the right format, the cards were acceptably dog-eared, and the stamps on them appropriately smudged. Etienne's Sten guns had been disassembled for the journey and packed in two bundles along with foodstuff provided by Marot: bread and cheese, potatoes, cabbages, and carrots. Apparently a lot of Parisians made sorties into the countryside whenever they could to forage for food to augment their own meager rations or to sell on the thriving black market. His own X-35 radio was packed with a pound of butter, a loaf of bread, and a bunch of beets. His Browning GP-35 9mm automatic was tucked into his belt at the small of his back. He had chosen the American X-35, on which he had been trained in the OSS, over the SOE Type B Mark II, which was built into a small weekend suitcase. Both had a more than adequate transmission range for the mission. But at thirty pounds, the Mark II was the heavier.

The train was fairly crowded, and they kept to themselves as they sat on the uncomfortable wooden seats in silence, watching the countryside roll by.

They had just left the station at the village of Esbly, about fifteen minutes out of Meaux, when a sudden explosion thundered over them from the distance. It came from behind them and was immediately followed by several even more violent explosions.

The passengers started uneasily. Mike opened a window and leaned out. In the distance, somewhere between Meaux and Esbly, a huge column of dense smoke tinted red at the base rose into the air.

"*Maquisard*," a corpulent man in an expensive though threadbare overcoat with a fur collar said sagely. "Sabotage."

"Mais non, monsieur," a small man with steel-rimmed glasses contradicted him. "I beg to differ with you. Not the *Maquis*. *Les Cheminots*—the rail workers. It is the *Resistance Fer*—the Railway Resistance. There is no doubt."

The corpulent gentleman looked down his ample nose at the contradictor. "And what, monsieur, makes you think so?" he asked haughtily.

The small man spread his hands. "But it is evident, monsieur," he said. "It is the *Bataille du Rail*—the Battle of the Rails—that goes on."

"It might as easily be the Maquis, no?"

"It might. But it is not."

"And may I ask, cher monsieur, how you know this?" the corpulent gentleman asked disdainfully.

"It is unmistakable. It is how they work, the Cheminots," the other man answered. "They know the schedules of the German trains, monsieur, from the dispatchers. They do not wish to wreck a French passenger train such as this one." He looked around at the passengers, all listening to him. "Back there," he said importantly, "it is where the main railroad line from the south joins this one. From Lyon. From Marseilles. It is then one of the most important lines for the trains to Germany. Many of them with troops going home on leave from their duties of occupation." He nodded pensively. "I should not be surprised," he ventured, "if such a train has been blown up." He looked pointedly at the man in the big overcoat. "By the Cheminots."

The corpulent gentleman, out-argued, fell silent.

For a while the train clattered on. No one spoke. Each was occupied with his own thoughts. What would the Germans do? An uneasy rustle whispered through them as the train sped past the scheduled stop at the Lagny station without slowing down. From the windows they glimpsed rows of armed Waffen SS troops grimly lining the track on both sides.

What was going on?

The answer came quickly.

At the village of Brou-sur-Chelles the train came to a wheezing halt. Everyone strained to peer out the windows. They were met by an alarming sight. The entire railroad station was surrounded by Waffen SS soldiers, their weapons held at the ready, their faces scowling angrily. They know about the troop train blown up by the Cheminots, Kevin thought bleakly. They know about their comrades. The little man had been right.

The platform where the train was coming to a stop was cordoned off and heavily guarded. At the forward end, a barrier checkpoint had been set up, manned by armed SS men and a few grim-looking civilians. Gestapo.

When the train had come to a full stop, an SS *Scharführer* stepped forward. Legs apart, arms aggressively akimbo, he shouted a command:

"*Raus! Alle raus! Schnell! Schnell!*—Out! Everyone out! Quickly! Quickly!*"

Instantly the apprehensive passengers began to collect their belongings. Fearfully they crowded at the doors, shoving, pushing, elbowing to obey, spilling out onto the platform. Roughly, they were gun-butted into groups by the SS troops and herded toward the checkpoint. The Germans were searching for the saboteurs. No one would be spared a thorough examination.

And at the feet of the team from the Grand Guignol lay two bundles with disassembled Sten guns and one with a clandestine radio transmitter the size of a small portable typewriter.

Hawkins glared out the window at the scene of chaos and confusion as the passengers milled about on the platform. Damn it to hell! he thought bitterly. Shot down before we even get off the ground.

Etienne suddenly spoke in a sharp, crisp staccato. "The bundles," he hissed under his breath, "with the Stens. Under the seat. Quickly. No one can connect them to us when they are found."

"The radio," Hawkins said. "What about the radio? It's vital. Irreplaceable."

"That too," Etienne said brusquely. "And your gun. London will have to make another drop."

"When, for crissake?" Hawkins blurted out.

"As soon as they can. There will be a delay. But you have no choice."

"Where? We sure can't use Marot's place. The Krauts will be swarming all over the damned place after this!"

Kevin looked at the Jed agent, his eyes bleak. "We'll think of something," he said. "Not now."

"We'll have to scrub the damned mission," Hawkins declared with the snap of finality.

They all stared at him.

Kevin's thoughts raced in his mind. If the mission were aborted even before it had started, London would most certainly be reluctant to reactivate it. They could not lose the radio. Not now. It was as simple as that. They *had* to find a way to save it. And the mission. They *had* to prove their mettle. Right now.

He thought furiously.

"Wait!" he suddenly cried. "There is a way."

"What?" Hawkins asked.

Outside, the SS *Scharführer* bellowed at the train passengers to get off the train. *"Schnell! Schnell! . . ."*

"No time to explain," Kevin shot back at Hawkins. "Just do as I tell you."

"Now wait—" Hawkins started to protest.

—

81

"No, Ted. Not now," Kevin hissed urgently. "No time. Just do as I say!"

Something in the actor's voice silenced Hawkins. He eyed him speculatively.

"Shoot!"

"We split up," Kevin snapped. "Meet later at the theater." He turned to Etienne. "Etienne, go. Now. You'll have no trouble."

Without a word Etienne left.

"Gaby, you take Ted. Don't lose him. Your papers will get you through the checkpoint." He turned to Ted. "Leave the gun. Give me the radio."

Hawkins hesitated only a split-moment, then he handed the bundle with the radio transmitter to Kevin.

"Now, go!"

Gaby and Ted took off. Kevin turned to his father, who had stood silently by.

"Dad," he said soberly. "Now it is up to you and me. . . ."

Holding on to one another, Ted and Gaby were being jostled toward the checkpoint along with the other passengers. Gaby looked back for Kevin and Mike. They were nowhere to be seen. Ahead of them Etienne reached the checkpoint. His identification papers were minutely inspected. He was thoroughly searched— and passed through. Everyone was searched. Every package and bundle ripped open; all the food was confiscated and thrown on a huge pile.

Again Gaby craned her neck to try to catch a glimpse of Kevin and Mike somewhere in the throng of people behind them. Everyone by now was off the train. Several soldiers began to go through the cars, heaving packages and bundles left behind out onto the platform.

There! Fleetingly, she caught sight of Kevin, clutching his bundle with the transmitter in his arms. It looked to be the size of a barn, she thought. How was he ever going to get it through? Oh, dear God, how? And she saw Mike. The two of them were among the last people on the platform. Had they stayed on the train all that time? What had they been doing? Where had they gone?

She was suddenly torn from her brooding by a hoarse cry. An SS man was shouting: *Halt! Halt!*

And she saw him.

A young man, desperately hurtling down the platform, racing

---

away from the checkpoint in headlong flight. The SS man raised his submachine gun. Once more he shouted: *HALT!*

But the young man kept running. Men and women passengers scrambled to get out of his way.

And the SS man opened fire.

A burst of 9mm bullets ripped into the man, disintegrating one of his legs at the hip. He spun around as if struck by an invisible fist and pitched heavily to the ground. A convulsive spasm wracked his body and a piteous scream tore from his throat.

Another soldier joined in the shooting. An elderly woman, clutching a package wrapped in newspaper and tied with string, was not able to get out of the line or fire quickly enough. Several of the bullets caught her in the chest, and with a look of utter astonishment she collapsed, her bundle splitting open as it hit the ground, spilling a hoard of new potatoes that rolled out onto the concrete, to be colored crimson by the blood that spurted from the woman and mingled with that of the youth.

An elderly man, with a cry of anguish, started to run toward the woman. SS men held him back.

One of the soldiers stalked up to the young man and turned him over with his booted foot.

The boy was dead.

So was the woman who had not been quick enough—or young enough—to get out of the way. . . .

Gaby stared in horror. She was deeply shaken. Her entire face felt numb. She had never seen violence before. Not like this. Only make-believe at the theater. She had never seen—death. She shuddered. It—it could have been Kevin. She felt the hot tears sting her eyes. She held onto Ted, digging her fingers into his arm—and they were at the checkpoint.

While an SS man gruffly patted them down, a Gestapo officer inspected their papers. He looked searchingly into their faces—and let them pass.

They joined Etienne, and together they stood on the platform beyond the barrier, watching with the other passengers who had passed inspection. Off to one side, held at gunpoint by Waffen SS troops, stood a small group of frightened people who had not been that lucky.

With all the passengers off the train and all the coaches searched, the train gave a jerk and slowly inched forward past the check-

point and stopped, ready to board the passengers for the contin-
uation of their interrupted journey as soon as all of them had
passed through the checkpoint.

Or had been taken away.

Gaby was worried. Where were Kevin and Mike? Had they
gotten away? Impossible. There was no way for them to get through
the cordon of soldiers ringing the station, standing almost shoulder to shoulder. She strained to see, but she could not find either
Kevin or Mike in the crush of people still apprehensively waiting
to be examined.

Two soldiers came up to the officer at the checkpoint. In their
hands they had two bundles. *Their* bundles, Gaby saw with sudden alarm. Ripped open, the disassembled Sten guns could be seen.
The officer pulled out a gun barrel and examined it. For a moment
he conferred with the Gestapo man. He pointed toward the dead
youth still lying on the platform—the passengers making as wide
a circle around him and the woman as they could.

The Gestapo man nodded slowly.

Gaby drew an inaudible sigh of relief. The Germans obviously
believed that the weapons had belonged to the dead youth. Reason
enough to try to flee. She felt a pang of part grief, part guilt. The
boy had been too young to die so horribly. But—is not everyone?,
she thought. At least suspicion that others not yet discovered
might have jettisoned the weapons had been allayed. For now.

Suddenly a man elbowing his way through the crowd came
hurrying up to the officer at the barrier. A couple of SS men at
once tried to stop him, but the officer waved them off.

In obvious agitation, the man began to talk to the German.

Startled, Gaby saw it was Mike.

Raptly, she and the others watched—unable to hear what Mike
was saying.

He was obviously distraught. Waving his arms animatedly, he
appeared to be pleading with the officer—gesturing back at the
crowd of passengers still waiting to pass through the checkpoint.

Suddenly he stopped and pointed excitedly.

The officer looked.

Far back on the platform, close to the abrupt drop down to the
track, Kevin could be seen stumbling awkwardly about, obviously
in trouble, still clutching the big bundle to him.

Gaby gave a startled gasp. She recognized Kevin's helpless motions as he fumbled about. He was playing at being blind! As in the insane asylum play at the Grand Guignol.

What on earth was he doing?

She saw Mike start to run back toward his son—and she saw him being roughly restrained by two SS men.

She saw two other soldiers walk back, take hold of Kevin, who started violently at their touch, and drag him back to the checkpoint. Trembling, his "blind" eyes searching without seeing, he appeared panic-stricken. She saw Mike talk to his son and take him by the shoulders, and she saw Kevin grab hold of his father in desperate need.

Once more Mike gesticulated his appeal to the officer. He pointed to Kevin's eyes; he rolled up his sleeve and showed the German his artificial limb. With both arms, he made a wide gesture, as if describing a big explosion, and he hugged his son in comfort.

The German officer listened grimly. He motioned to a couple of SS men, who searched both Mike and Kevin while the officer inspected their identification papers.

Finally he returned the papers to Mike and waved them through.

Gaby exulted. They'd done it!

Suddenly the officer barked a crisp command. Instantly an SS man tore the big bundle from Kevin's arms.

A chill of fear shot through Gaby. Mike's plan was going awry. He and Kevin were caught. In her mind's eye she suddenly saw them both lying dead on the platform in a pool of blood next to the ill-starred youth and the old woman.

In horror she watched as the SS man ripped open the bundle, spilling a profusion of vegetables and other foodstuff out on the concrete. Vegetables, a loaf of bread, a chunk of cheese. But there was no sign of the typewriter-sized X-35 radio transmitter.

Where was it? Had they hidden it somewhere, planning to return for it later? Bleakly Gaby knew that if they had, their plan would fail. The Germans would be going over the entire railroad station inch by inch. They would expect contraband to have been hidden. The radio was lost.

For a moment the Germans stood looking at the food, then one of them kicked it onto the steadily growing pile of confiscated provisions on the platform and gruffly pushed Mike and Kevin through the barrier.

Complaisantly Mike guided his son through the waiting crowd

toward the train standing by on the track, walking past his friends without a sign of recognition. He and Kevin, anxiously holding his father's arm, took up positions close to the door of one of the railroad cars and began to wait. . . .

It was almost noon when Kevin and Mike showed up at the Grand Guignol.

Gaby, Ted, and Etienne were sitting in Mike and Kevin's dressing room. They looked glum.

"What the hell kept you," Ted growled as they walked in.

"Just being careful," Kevin answered pleasantly. "We wanted to make absolutely certain that there was no one sticking around to see what we were up to before we came here."

Ted grunted, obviously not impressed.

"What on earth were you doing at the checkpoint?" Gaby asked Mike.

"Playacting," Ted grumbled disgustedly. "Grandstanding."

"What *did* you say to that officer, Mike?"

"I told him a fairy tale, cheri," Mike said cheerfully. "I told him that Kevin was my son. I told him he was blind, as he could see, and that we had become separated in the confusion. I told him I was afraid my son might not understand, might not react properly to a command, and perhaps be shot like that other young man. I told him we had both sacrificed much for the German cause. My son his eyes and I my arm. In an accident. An explosion when we were helping to build the fortifications on the English Channel coast." He chuckled delightedly. "I think he believed me."

"But why?" Gaby wanted to know.

"Simple, *ma petite chou-chou*. To draw suspicion away from us. People who have something to hide do not make spectacles of themselves. So, we did. As it were," he said gleefully. "We almost got the bundle through!"

"Bloody bully for you," Ted said acidly. "But you didn't. The damned radio is lost. I've already asked Etienne to send a message to London to scrap the mission." He glared at Mike. "What the hell did you do with the damned thing?"

"Do with it?" Mike asked innocently. He was enjoying himself. "Why, nothing. It's right here."

He rolled up his sleeve, unstrapped his prosthesis, and spilled a jumble of tubes and transistors, condensers and converters, partially assembled segments of circuitry, modulators and demodulators, resistors, amplifiers, and oscillators out on the table.

They all stared at it.

"It's all there," Kevin said. "All the special, irreplaceable parts. All the unique X-35 items. All there. The only parts missing are commonplace radio components. Etienne can easily replace them. And, of course, the housing. But it will be a simple job—a matter of a couple of hours—to reassemble and rebuild the transmitter into a new casing."

Ted leaned over the table. He fingered the radio parts.

"I'll be damned," he said. "I'll be triple damned!" He looked at Kevin and Mike, reluctant respect in his eyes.

He turned to Etienne.

"Etienne," he said. "Change that message to London. Send instead—*Grand Guignol is go!*"

Kevin grinned at his father. He felt great. They had proven their mettle. In spades.

There was a sudden knock on the door.

They all looked toward it.

Quickly Gaby threw a towel over the radio parts on the table. Kevin opened the door.

In the open doorway, frowning suspiciously, stood the theater manager, Camille Choisy.

Behind him stood two SS officers, their black uniforms immaculate and forbidding, the silver death heads gleaming ominously on their caps. . . .

❊ 11 ❊

"**A**H! Lavette," Choisy addressed Michael. "I see you have company." There was acrimonious disapproval in his dry voice. "It is, however, of some importance that I speak with you."

Kevin rose and took a step toward the theater manager.

"Monsieur le Directeur," he said expansively. "Please come in." He gestured toward Etienne and Ted. "My father and I were just discussing with these gentlemen the feasibility of making the replacement prostheses for *The Lumberman's Revenge* at a lesser price."

"I see," Choisy said, considerably mollified. He stood aside and nodded respectfully to the two SS officers who stood with him.

"May I present *Hauptsturmführer* Hildebrandt and *Obersturmführer* Schindler."

The two officers made a small bow, carefully calibrated to show only the minimum degree of courtesy.

"The Messieurs Lavette and Mademoiselle Kerouac are members of our Grand Guignol company," Choisy told the Germans. "They will be participating in the performance of the requested play."

The officers barely acknowledged the information.

"What can we do for you, Choisy," Mike asked, able to control his distaste only with difficulty.

"Ah!" Choisy said importantly. "The matter is as follows. The *Generalstabsarzt* of Army Group West, General Gerhardt Riekhoff, is on a visit to our city. He has done us the great honor of expressing his desire to see a performance of *The Lighthouse Keepers*. So we shall present it tomorrow instead of *The Asylum*, which, as you know, was scheduled. It will, of course, require some special attention."

"I see," Mike said. "There should be no problem."

"Ah. Well. I rather thought not," Choisy said. "The Captain and the Lieutenant will be in charge of, ah, special security in connection with the attendance of the *Generalstabsarzt*. They have requested that they be given a tour of inspection of the theater, and I thought, I thought you, Monsieur Lavette," he nodded to Mike, "would be so good as to show the gentlemen around."

"But of course, Monsieur le Directeur," Mike said. Inwardly, he seethed, but dammit! this was not the time to do any boat rocking.

"Excellent," Choisy exclaimed. He stepped back to give Mike room to join the Germans. He put his hand on the makeup table and got a smear of greasepaint on it. He reached for the towel that covered the radio parts on the table.

Quickly Gaby stepped in front of him. She reached for a clean towel on a shelf and handed it to the theater manager. "Please, Monsieur le Directeur," she said sweetly. "Use this clean one."

Choisy nodded, his attention on Mike and the SS officers. He took the towel, wiped his hand, and threw it on the table.

The tiny tinkle of glass went unnoticed by both Choisy and his visitors.

"Perhaps the gentlemen would like to begin with an inspection of our first-aid room?" Mike inquired of the officers. "I believe we have a bottle of quite excellent brandy there. For medicinal purposes, of course." Without waiting for a reply, he turned to Etienne and Ted. "You will excuse me, Messieurs. My son will continue our discussion. He is fully as knowledgeable in the matter as I am myself." He turned back to the officers. "This way, please."

With a glance at Kevin he walked off, followed by the two Germans and Camille Choisy.

For a moment after the unwelcome visitors had left the little dressing room, no one spoke.

"It will not interfere with any possible plans, is that not so?" Etienne asked worriedly.

"It will not," Kevin said. "It may be a little awkward to have to contend with a big-shot Nazi, but we'll manage."

"Riekhoff," Ted said pensively. "I know who he is. He's Chief Medical Officer of von Rundstedt's Army Group." He snorted. "I had to learn the whole damned TO [Table of Organization] of von Rundstedt's command in my training."

"What's he doing going to the Grand Guignol?" Kevin wondered sourly. "Busman's holiday? Doesn't he see enough blood and gore to satisfy his Nazi heart's desire?"

"Beats me," Ted said. "And I couldn't care less. But it gives me a hell of an idea." He looked at the others. "We have to come up with a way to infiltrate Germany and get to Misdroy as quickly as possible, right?" He paused. He nodded toward the door.

"Perhaps those two Nazi flunkies have handed us a solution on a silver bedpan!"

SS *Standartenführer* Dieter Haupt idly watched the two motorcycle outriders hurtling before him along the road from Calais to Antwerp. He was impressed with the skill of his driver—the distance between the outriders and his staff car never varied.

He stretched and sighed deeply. It was good to be able to relax. He had been driving himself too hard, and he knew it.

After his memorable meeting with the Führer, he had at once flown to Calais and Mimoyecques on a tour of inspection that had been interrupted by his summons to Berlin. He had decided to return to Misdroy from Mimoyecques via surface routes rather than by air. He needed the time to rest, and he knew that the moment he'd get back to the test site there would not be a minute he could call his own. He had opted to go by car. It was a long ride, some eight hundred kilometers, but he'd make it in one day. One long day. He preferred cars to trains. More control. And he liked to have control. He could stop wherever he wanted, whenever he wanted, and he could take whatever route he deemed the most expedient. And, best of all, he would be able to rest—he slept soundly in a car—and, of course, prepare his report to Reichsminister Speer, based on his inspection of the Mimoyecques installation, undisturbed.

He placed his briefcase across his knees to use as a makeshift desk. He started his notes.

Punkt—item: Foreign workers at Mimoyecques. At the present, 5,500 on a 24-hour shift. Request to be made for a weekly allotment of a minimum of an additional 10 percent of this number to make up for losses.

Punkt: Since the severe damage inflicted by the Allied air strikes of November last year on the construction site at Mimoyecques, only minimal air-raid damage has been experienced. The cover roofing of eight meters of concrete has proven impenetrable by enemy bombs. Vulnerable, however, is the system of railroad tracks that lead to the entrances at the base of the installation. Although the eight-meter-high, two-meter-thick sliding steel doors provide adequate protection for the site itself, the rail network is exposed to damage. Consequently, antiaircraft defenses must be kept at full strength, and railroad workers and materiel must be constantly available for repairs.

Punkt: As it is apparent that the enemy has mounted a concerted intelligence effort to both discover the purpose of the construction site at Mimoyecques and to penetrate it, it is imperative that the Fifteenth Army be kept in the area as security.

Punkt: For the same reason, security must be strengthened at Misdroy. Request must be made for additional *Waffen* SS troops.

Punkt: Progress at Mimoyecques is ahead of schedule. No problems foreseen. All three shafts have reached the depth of 160 meters and have been widened to 17 meters in diameter. The 70 by 30 meter *Betonplatte*—concrete platform—at Level A has been completed and camouflaged. Work on Level B is nearly completed, and work on levels C and D is progressing rapidly.

Punkt: Progress at Misdroy has experienced some unavoidable mishaps, all correctable and all leading to improvements. Perfection of the *Tausendfüssler* is expected within two to three weeks, at which time Mimoyecques should be ready to become operational.

Punkt: Project Busy Lizzie is proceeding as planned.

He sat back in his seat. What else?

He closed his eyes. The gentle swaying of the car lulled him. He pushed the briefcase off his lap and settled into a corner. Perhaps after a nap he'd think of something else. And he'd organize his notes and put them into proper language. Later.

He pulled his travel blanket over him, and within minutes he was asleep. . . .

Mike watched the two SS officers walk to their car, parked in the theater alley. A driver noncom, seeing them approach, jumped out. He gave a smart, stiff-armed salute and held the door open. The officers got in and the car drove off.

When Mike returned to his dressing room, the others were all still there, talking animatedly. They looked up as he entered.

"I feel like taking a bath in boiling water," Mike grumbled disgustedly. "Those two Nazi bloodhounds were all over the place. Even sniffed around the Maid."

"Any trouble?"

Mike shook his head. "They didn't know what the hell they were looking for. Just showing off their importance." He snorted disdainfully. "But *I* found out a few things."

"What?"

"There will be four SS guards here tomorrow. Two in the auditorium, one in the foyer, and one inside the stage door."

"Taking no chances, are they?" Kevin remarked.

"The general will be accompanied by four other officers in addition to the Bobbsey Twins, Hildebrandt and Schindler. There will be two cars with drivers parked in the alley."

"Great!" Kevin exclaimed. "Fits right in with the plan."

"Plan? What plan?" Mike asked, puzzled.

"Ted's plan," Kevin answered him. "To get us to Misdroy." He turned to Ted. "Tell him."

Ted did.

When he was finished, Mike looked at him, his mouth slightly agape.

"Holy shit!" he said. "It might work. It might damned well work!" He looked eagerly at the others. "Can it be done? Can we do it?"

Kevin nodded. "We are sure we can. It sure beats all the other ways that we could get there. Trains. Bikes. All that. Ted has already given Etienne a shopping list of what we'll need."

Etienne handed Mike a piece of paper. "Here," he said.

Mike read it, his eyes growing wide. "What?" he commented. "No kitchen sink?" He looked hard at Etienne. "Are you certain you can get all this stuff? And complete the necessary paper work?"

Etienne nodded. "I am certain."

"Lisette is due back later today," Gaby said. "I'm sure she'll do her part and do it well."

"So am I," Etienne affirmed. He was obviously a fan.

Gaby smiled at him. "Your faith is well placed, Monsieur Etienne," she said.

"Then, according to this," Mike said, waving the paper in the air, "we should be on our way in no more than forty-eight hours." He turned to Etienne. "How much time will you need after tomorrow's performance?"

"Twelve hours," Etienne answered, "at the most. But we must make certain the job is done as well as absolutely possible."

"Amen!" Kevin said.

"You have the right people?"

"We do. We will also have Monsieur Ted's radio rebuilt." He looked at Ted. "And to replace your lost gun, your Browning, I shall give you an Astra, if you wish me to. It is a Spanish-made, nine millimeter automatic. It is capable of accepting and firing almost every type of nine millimeter automatic rounds, including the Luger and the P-thirty-eight. It might be useful in Germany."

"Thanks. I accept," Ted said. "I am familiar with the Astra. It's a damned good little handgun." He looked at the others. "Under the circumstances, I don't think anyone else should carry a weapon on the mission. It would be a dead giveaway if we are detained and searched."

"Okay with me," Kevin said. "No arms."

"Speak for yourself, son," Mike grinned. "I plan on taking along an extra arm or two."

"It's settled, then," Ted said. "We jump off at noon day after tomorrow." He looked around at the others. Not such hayseeds as he'd thought at first. "Send the message to London, Eticnne," he said. "And include our time schedule. We are committed."

He grew sober.

"It all depends on what happens during the performance tomorrow night," he said.

❧ 12 ❧

*T*HUMP! *Thump! Thump!* The hollow thuds boomed through the theater as the stage manager banged his staff on the stage floor, signaling the curtain was going up. The houselights were dimmed down and out, and the curtain at the Grand Guignol went up to reveal a darkened, moody stage with a set representing the round living quarters in a lighthouse. Dim light was reflected in a rhythmic cycle on the "fog" produced by a smoke pot outside the windows, and a doleful fog horn wailed in the distance. From a spiral staircase leading to the stage from the basement below, Mike and Kevin, father and son in the play as well as in life, came up into the Spartan room. Mike went to a kerosene lamp and turned it up. *The Lighthouse Keepers* had begun.

As Mike turned from the lamp he glanced at the front row in the audience, now faintly bathed in the light from the lit stage. The row was resplendent with the dress uniforms of several high-ranking Nazi officers.

Jed agent Ted Hawkins's plan had also begun. . . .

Gaby and Lisette giggled coquettishly together as they walked from the theater toward the two German staff cars parked in the alley. Two noncom drivers stood talking at the first car, which flew the standard of the *Generalstabsarzt*. Each of the girls had a bottle and a glass in her hands. They exchanged glances. Lisette nodded. They walked up to the drivers.

"Bonsoir," Gaby said pleasantly.

"Bonsoir," the drivers said almost in unison, their German accents making the soft French word sound guttural.

"It is a long wait you will have out here," Gaby said. "We thought you might like a little something to warm you." She held up the bottle, but it was quite obvious that was not the only warmer-upper she had in mind.

Both the drivers grinned with anticipation.

"Merci, mademoiselle," one of them said. "That is very kind of you."

Lisette looked brazenly at the other driver. "Which car do you drive?" she asked.

The driver pointed to the second car. "That one," he said.

"It is chilly," Lisette said, putting her arms around her in a sensual gesture. She locked her bedroom eyes onto the German. "Perhaps we could go and—sit in your car while you warm yourself with—with a little drink?"

"*Bitte*," the driver said eagerly, all but licking his chops. "Please. After you." He motioned Lisette toward the car.

Lisette walked over to the car, her hips swinging provocatively. The driver followed. As Gaby saw them get into the car she turned to the driver of the general's staff car. She knew she need not worry about the other driver for quite a while. Lisette would keep him occupied as only she could.

"Can we sit in *your* car, *Herr Unteroffizier*?" Gaby asked, wide-eyed. "Is it permitted?"

"Of course," the driver said. "Climb in."

They both climbed into the back seat of the car. Almost at once the German grabbed for Gaby. Laughing teasingly, she drew back. "A little drink first," she said seductively. "You call it schnapps, yes?"

"Schnapps it is," the driver said. He seized the bottle and took a hefty swig. He shook his head vigorously. "*Ist gut.*" He smacked his lips and gave Gaby a lecherous grin. He put one arm around her and began to feel her breasts with the other.

Gaby did not fight him. She knew he would stay conscious for less than thirty seconds.

She was right.

She pushed the unconscious German away from her. Quickly she searched him, removing all papers and identification on him. Then she turned her attention to the car. In the front seat she found a clipboard with several papers and documents clamped onto it. German travel permits. Licenses. Authorizations. She removed them and stuffed everything into her dress.

She glanced back toward the other car. Neither Lisette nor the driver were to be seen. Quickly she stepped out of the car and hurried back toward the theater.

The storage basement was deserted and quiet except for the voices of the actors on the stage above, faintly heard. Quickly Gaby made her way to the Iron Maid. She entered the room beyond.

Etienne looked up. "You have it?" he asked urgently.

Gaby nodded. "I do." She pulled the papers from her dress. "You must be quick. The man will be out only twenty minutes."

"I will."

Etienne strode to the table. On it a camera had been mounted on a stand. He turned on a strong light, and one by one he photographed the papers Gaby had brought.

Fourteen minutes later Gaby stepped back into the general's car. Quickly she replaced all the papers she had taken. She sat down in the back seat next to the German driver and cradled his head in her lap.

It was only a few minutes later when he stirred.

"You are quite a bear, *Herr Unteroffizier*," Gaby said as he groggily sat up. "The girls must love you very much."

Uncomprehendingly, the man stared at her.

She smoothed her dress and her hair. "But I have been much too long, cheri," she worried, a pretty little frown creasing her forehead. "I will be missed if I do not return."

She gave the man a peck on the cheek and stepped out of the car, leaving a thoroughly perplexed German staring after her.

Outside, she stopped and waved at the second car. A few moments later Lisette, looking slightly dishevelled, came out from the car. She joined Gaby, and the two girls, carrying their bottles and glasses, sashayed back to the theater.

Stage one of the Hawkins plan had come off without a hitch. . . .

The jury-rigged directional antenna had been built in the attic of the house on the alley where Kevin and Gaby had emerged from the Resistance caves. Was that only three days ago? Gaby thought. It seemed like an eternity. It was the kind of antenna Ted would have to erect when he wanted to transmit from Germany. Quickly, crudely made. But effective.

In the attic, the Grand Guignol members and Etienne were anxiously gathered around Ted and his rebuilt X-35. It was a crucial moment. The radio had to work. It *had* to. Everything depended on it.

Using the double-transposition words given him at Milton Hall, Ted had encoded a short, to-the-point message for transmission. He wanted to be on the air the shortest time possible. There could be not the slightest chance of discovery by a mobile monitoring unit.

He placed his hand on the key. He was surprised to realize his palm was slightly clammy. It would be his first direct transmission to Milton Hall.

He began to tap the key.

First, three letters, RMH, the call letters, which stood for *Roberts Milton Hall*. Three times. Then the group, QSP, which meant *Accept my priority message*, followed by his brief message: TEST ACKNOWLEDGE, which came out to exactly three groups of five letters when encoded. And finally his own call letters, his signature: TGG—*Ted Grand Guignol*—and his security check, a special group of letters that if changed would tell the home station that the operative had been captured and was transmitting under duress.

His fingers operated the key with quick, crisp motions. The transmission was completed in less than forty-five seconds.

"Now what?" Gaby asked.

"We wait."

No one spoke. Everyone was staring at the X-35.

Ted looked intense as he strained to listen to the faint static in his earphones.

The seconds ticked by.

A watched phone never rings, Gaby thought. I wonder if that holds true for a watched X-35? "How do we know they're even listening?" Gaby whispered.

"Schedule of transmissions," Etienne answered her under his breath. "Ted has certain hours when his contact in England will have an open set. He has—"

Ted suddenly tensed. He bent over his writing pad. He wrote: QS5—QS5—QS5.

He looked up at the others, a broad grin on his face. "We're in!" he said. "Good job, Etienne."

"QS5?" Gaby asked. "What does it mean?"

"It means *We read you loud and clear*," Etienne said.

Ted was writing more letters on his pad. Then he sent a brief sign-off and closed down the set. He looked up at the others.

"We go," he said. "*D* has given his blessing!"

"Who the hell is *D*?" Mike asked.

"Code name for the Chief of SOE," Ted told him. "The Big Cheese himself." He stood up. "Okay," he said resolutely. "As you theater types say, 'Let's get the show on the road!' "

Thirty minutes later the four members of Special Jedburgh Team Grand Guignol had changed from their own clothes into those they would wear during their journey to Misdroy, supplied by Etienne's Resistance group.

Gaby adjusted her white cap with the Red Cross insignia on her head. Instinctively, she tried to make it look attractive, but her fetchy Parisian chic had effectively been replaced with the practical look of a *Krankenschwester*—a German nurse—in her light-blue, long-sleeved dress and big white apron.

She looked at her "patient." In his military hospital gown and robe, his bare feet stuck into brown ersatz leather slippers, Mike looked awkward and uncomfortable.

Ted, she decided, looked most the part, trim in the uniform of an *Unterarzt*—a Master Sergeant doctor—with Kevin a close second, wearing the uniform of an *Obergefreiter* in the *Sanitätsdienst*—a corporal in the German Medical Corps.

Enemy uniforms all, she thought, with a pang of discomfort. She felt on edge. And the irrefutable knowledge (which had remained unspoken by them all but lurked behind every word) that their unmasking would mean certain and unpleasant death did nothing to alleviate her apprehension.

Etienne, who somehow had assumed the role of local control for the team, held up his hand. "One last check," he said. "First, your papers. Your personal identification papers? Your tags? Your *Soldbuch*?"

Kevin felt for the military record book all German soldiers carried. It was there in his pocket. Automatically, they all checked. They nodded.

"Your ID for later is packed with your clothing," Etienne went on. "Now your travel papers. Permits? Special orders? Driver's license? Medical papers? Special authorizations?

Kevin flipped the papers on his clipboard. All there. He was again impressed with the super job Etienne's men had done—in record time. Forged from the documents they'd photographed, the papers all looked completely authentic, down to the signature of *Generalstabsarzt* Rietkoff, found on some of them. Even someone who might know the general's signature (and there weren't apt to be too many who did) would accept the forgery as being genuine. And several of the special permits, designed to get them out of the city as expediently as possible, were signed with a perfectly forged signature of General Hans von Boineburg-Lengsfeld, Commandant of Greater Paris. Couldn't be more official than that. As Etienne had said, a faked document must be more real than a real one.

"Now," Etienne continued, "once more. You are transporting a special high-ranking patient, *Genertalarzt* Ludwig Bauernweiss, an Army Corps Chief Medical Officer, from Ortslazarett Clamart, a military hospital in the southwest outskirts of Paris, to a general military hospital in Berlin. Your patient is—"

He was interrupted by a young man who came bursting into the room.

"It is here!" he shouted excitedly. "It is just outside."

"Tres bien," Etienne said. We shall look it over."

He strode to the door. The others followed.

The field ambulance was parked in the alley outside. It was a regular German military ambulance, marked with large Red Cross emblems on the sides, but a prominent sign had been stenciled on the back doors:

WARNUNG!
QUARANTÄNE
Ansteckende Krankheit
ZUTRITT VERBOTEN!

WARNING!
QUARANTINE
Contagious Disease
DO NOT ENTER!

Kevin went up and peered through the windows in the doors into the interior of the ambulance. There was a cot and a chair, both fastened to the walls; a small shelf-table, also attached to the side of the vehicle, with a few medicine bottles and sanitary gear, a metal container of drinking water with a screw-on top and two mugs; and a medicine cabinet with two doors, set into the space under the isolated driver's cab. In the ceiling, the rim of a filtered ventilation fan could be seen, and two large sealed metal

99

containers marked CONTAMINATED WASTE—HANDLE WITH EXTREME CARE were clamped with steel bands to one wall. That's where the X-35, Ted's gun, and our clothing are stored, he thought. Not bad.

"The license plates have been altered since we stole the vehicle last night," Etienne told them. "So you should have no trouble getting out of Paris, yes? Not with your papers."

He looked gravely at them.

"Goodbye, mes amis," he said. "Et bonne chance!" He nodded toward the ambulance. "The thing runs on real gasoline," he said. "Your papers will allow you to fill your tank at any military depot."

Solemnly they all embraced.

One by one they entered the ambulance. Mike and Gaby in the back, Kevin behind the wheel.

Ted gazed at the ambulance. Labeled and packed, he thought. A remembered report suddenly bubbled to the surface of his mind, a report about the clandestine German military operations prior to 1933, forbidden by the Versailles Treaty that ended World War I. Contrary to agreement, the Germans had trained military personnel in tank and air warfare on secret bases in Russia—and shipped the bodies of young men accidentally killed during the exercises back to Germany in wooden crates marked MACHINE PARTS. Labeled and packed . . . Labeled and packed.

At least he and his fellow team members were alive, he thought. For now.

Etienne put his hand on his shoulder and held him back for a moment.

"My friend," he said soberly, "a final word. Remember. If you *are* caught, do not be afraid to betray us. We shall have moved from the cave. Within the next few hours. But we shall leave enough evidence so the *Boche* will know you have spoken the truth."

"But—-"

"No, mon ami," Etienne interrupted him. "Do not protest. The Germans, they can make the walls talk. . . ."

When Lieutenant Colonel Ramsey hurriedly entered the office of Brigadier Parnell in the main building of Milton Hall, Colonel Baldon, Lieutenant Colonel Lamont, and Major Roberts were already there with the CO.

"I apologize for being late, sir," Ramsey said. "But I was in the field with a demolition exercise when I got the word."

Parnell waved at an empty chair. "Have a seat, Cliff," he said. "Roberts has had a signal from that Resistance chap in Paris. Gerard. Relayed from London. We are discussing it." He handed Ramsey a sheet of paper. "Read it," he said. "A bit of a grue, actually. It outlines the entire plan Grand Guignol has underway in order to get them to Misdroy as quickly as possible."

Ramsey read the decoded message. He looked up.

"Imaginative buggers, aren't they?" he commented.

"A bit—theatrical, I should say, what?" the brigadier said.

"Right up the Grand Guignol alley, I'd say," Baldon grinned. "Horrible contagious disease and all."

"Ah, yes," the CO said. He frowned. He turned to Ramsey. "If the team does reach Misdroy," he said, "is their local contact reliable? Kepper, is it?"

"Keppler, sir," Ramsey said. "Janusz Keppler."

"Capital. They cannot just arrive blind, what? Who is this Keppler?"

Ramsey looked uncomfortable. "The man is a canal barge captain in the area," he said. "He is of Polish descent." He hesitated. "We—we haven't actually a great deal of knowledge about his current activities. But several years ago he was of help to one of our agents, Jeff, on the Enigma matter. After that we placed him as a sleeper." He looked at the brigadier. "We haven't actually been in touch with him since that time. All we know is, he is still in the area."

"That's pretty damned thin," Baldon said. "The Enigma Machine caper, for crissake! That's almost five years ago."

"It is the best we can do," Ramsey said stiffly.

"Do better!"

"You have a suggestion, Dirk?" Ramsey looked archly at his OSS counterpart. "Keppler is a sleeper. We can reestablish contact with him only directly. Someone must go there in person to see him. That someone may as well be Grand Guignol."

"So, in essence, they *are* going in blind," Baldon said heatedly. "Or worse. That Keppler guy may have had a change of heart for all you know. He may work for the damned Nazis now. How can you be sure?"

"We can't. But there is no reason to believe that."

"And Grand Guignol. Do they know how—how dicey, as you say, their contact is?"

"Ted knows," Ramsey said. "I do not know if he has informed his teammates."

"They don't have much of a chance to pull it off, do they?" Dirk said bitterly. "We'd better bloody well cross our fingers on this one."

Parnell nodded slowly. "It was a difficult decision to make," he said, "sending in Grand Guignol. *D* is skeptical of the operation, too, but for different reasons. He unfortunately considers Grand Guignol a lame effort. Three of the four are completely without training, he pointed out. One is a girl, and one is a cripple. Missing one arm, I'm told. Not much of a match for the combined German counterintelligence forces, what?" He sighed. "But, of course, *D* realizes, as do we, that the situation at Mimoyecques is serious enough to try anything. Take any chances." He turned to Lieutenant Colonel Lamont. "What is the latest intelligence, Colonel?" he asked.

"Nothing really new, sir," Lamont answered. "There is considerably increased activities at the site. Enemy security has been beefed up even more, and the Fifteenth Army is still in place. Local sources indicate that more than five thousand forced laborers are now working around the clock."

"On what, dammit? On *what*?" Baldon exclaimed.

Lamont shrugged. "We do not know," he confessed. "All we know is that more and more workers are arriving almost every day."

Baldon turned to Ramsey. "What about your Brylcreem Boys?" he asked. "Anything?"

Ramsey shook his head. "Air Intelligence has no information."

"Then Misdroy is not just our best bet," Baldon said, "it is our only bet."

The CO looked grim. "Perhaps," he said. "I hope we are not on a losing wicket with Grand Guignol. But just in case we should be, I want a *real* Jedburgh team readied and briefed to try to infiltrate Mimoyecques once more." He turned to Major Roberts. "Get on it at once."

"Yes, sir," Roberts said.

Parnell turned to the others.

"We cannot afford to place our total reliance on three actors, inexperienced in intelligence-gathering, and one Jed, who I understand is a bit of an, ah, inconsistent chap."

He stood up. The meeting was at an end.

"We can only hope for the best," he said.

But there was little conviction in his voice. . . .

They had just left Forbach, where they had filled the tank of the ambulance at a border patrol depot. They'd been on the road for five and a half hours and it was late afternoon. The road sign read: *SAARBRÜCKEN 9 Km.*

Nine kilometers to Germany.

The trip had been uneventful so far. Their first and only scare had come almost immediately after they'd left the alley and started to drive through Paris. At Place de la Republic they had been stopped at a roving checkpoint. But the Feldwebel in charge had only wanted to be helpful. He gave them a motorcycle escort, who piloted them through town, clearing the way for them, and taking them all the way to Noisy on the outskirts of the city, all the way to the main military route over Chalons sur Marne to the German border at the coal mining town of Saarbrücken.

Signs directing traffic to the border checkpoint led them through the old, sometimes French, sometimes German city, which showed the ugly scars of the heavy shelling in 1939 and the later destructive air strikes.

The Grand Guignol team had chosen to enter Germany here at the most conspicuous place and go on to Berlin over Mainz and Frankfurt, Erfurt and Halle. They'd taken the same route, Kevin thought idly, that Napoleon had chosen on his march from Paris to Mainz. Saarbrücken had then been an armament center. Now it was an important checkpoint on the German military route from Paris to Berlin.

A sign at the roadside warned: *GRENZSTELLE 500 m—* BORDERSTATION 500 meters.

At a huge sign with *HALT!* stenciled in black block letters, a border guard waved them to one side. Slowly they drove to the indicated spot and stopped.

Two bored guards came up to Kevin, both of them carrying Schmeisser submachine guns at port arms.

"*Papiere herzeigen!*—show your papers!" one of them ordered. Kevin gave him his clipboard. The guard rifled through the documents. He frowned at them and examined them more closely. He walked to the rear of the ambulance and looked in through the windows, then he came back to Kevin.

"Wait here," he instructed.

He strode to a small building and entered. Kevin and Ted exchanged glances, both desperately trying not to look worried.

But they were. What was wrong?

"Nice day," Kevin said pleasantly to the guard who had remained behind.

The man merely grunted.

Presently the first guard reemerged from the building, followed by a Waffen SS *Obersturmführer*, who held Kevin's clipboard in his hands. The two men marched up to Ted.

"You are *Unterarzt* Dornhoffer?" the officer asked brusquely.

Ted nodded pleasantly. "I am, Lieutenant," he said. "What seems to be the problem?"

The officer nodded at the ambulance. "Your *Krankenwagen*," he said. "Your ambulance. The guards have orders to inspect all vehicles. You will have to open the doors."

Ted stared at the officer. Slowly he shook his head. "I—I regret, *Herr Obersturmführer*," he said, obviously ill at ease. "But I cannot do that."

The officer glared at him. "It is an order—*Sergeant*!"

"The doors are open, *Herr Obersturmführer*," Ted said. "They are not locked. It is—it is just that I—I myself do not want to—to open them. You, of course, may do so."

"You are insufferably insolent, Sergeant," the officer growled angrily. "And you will be reported." He turned on his heel and started for the rear of the ambulance. Ted called after him.

"One moment, *Herr Obersturmführer*!" He climbed from the cab and joined the officer at the rear of the ambulance.

"With the *Herr Obersturmführer*'s permission," he said subserviently, "may I have the *Herr Obersturmführer*'s name and serial number?" He held a pencil poised over a small notebook.

The officer was momentarily taken aback. "Why?" he snapped.

"I beg the *Herr Obersturmführer*'s pardon," Ted said. "But I am under orders to report anyone who enters this quarantined ambulance. It is so *they* can be quarantined if necessary. It is so they will not infect others. I am sure the *Herr Obersturmführer* understands." He held his pencil ready over the booklet. "*Bitte?*"

The officer stared at Ted. He said nothing. Ted fished a cotton face mask from his pocket. "*Bitte*," he said solicitously. "Please. If the *Herr Obersturmführer* will wear this, it may afford *some* protection. And may I respectfully caution the *Herr Obersturmführer* to be most careful in touching anything inside."

The officer turned to the ambulance and peered through the windows in the doors. On the cot inside he saw Mike lying on his back, his eyes closed, his face covered with large red weeping sores. He stirred fitfully. Gaby, wearing a face mask, was gently bathing his feverish forehead.

"The general caught the disease in Africa," Ted said in the half-whisper of awe. "It is a form of virulent leprosy, they believe. Only in Berlin may they know how to treat it. That is why the Chief Medical Officer of *Generalfeldmarschall* von Rundtedt's Army Group himself is anxious to get him there without delay. The patient is a personal friend."

He held up the face mask. "May I help the *Herr Obersturmführer* with this," he asked politely. "And I *will* need the *Herr Obersturmführer*'s identification information," he added apologetically.

The officer brushed him away.

Ted backed off.

"With the *Herr Obersturmführer*'s permission," he said, "I will wait in the cab while the *Herr Obersturmführer* makes his inspection of the ambulance."

The officer turned to him. He slammed the clipboard into Ted's chest.

"*Zum Teufel damit!*—To the devil with it!" he barked. "*Los!* —Be on your way!"

"*Jawohl, Herr Obersturmführer*," Ted cried smartly. "*Sofort, Herr Obersturmführer*!—At once!

He hurried back to the cab. Kevin quickly started the engine, and they drove off. A few minutes later they left the town of Saarbrücken and tooled along the road toward Mainz. The mission of Special Jedburgh Team Grand Guignol had just begun. Ahead of them lay challenges and dangers unknown to them all. And the enigma of the *Tausendfüssler*. . . .

PART TWO

Germany, May 1944

❈ **13** ❈

KEVIN drove the field ambulance at a good clip along the twilight road, the beams from the headlights probing the gray dawn that was just beginning to brighten the darkness. It was 0429 hours. Five days had passed since the dying Nicole had told them about the iron millipede at Misdroy.

It had been a strange, unnerving experience, he thought, driving through a country that was not occupied by an ever-present, highly visible enemy conquerer. No curfew. No checkpoints. No travel restrictions. Here in Germany, they—the four of them—were the enemy, although invisible as such. A state of affairs they all fervently hoped would continue.

They had driven through the night, eating the food Etienne had provided for them. Bread, cheese, some sausage. And as a gift, a small packet of real coffee. But they had had no way of preparing it. Kevin and Ted had taken turns at the wheel, one driving while the other slept; Gaby and Mike had shared cot time in the back.

They had driven through Potsdam, where they once more had filled their tank at an army depot. The darkness had hidden most of the heavy damage the city had suffered from Allied air raids. They had skirted Berlin–Spandau and were coming up on a small town called Bötzow, northwest of the capital.

Ted turned to Kevin. "It'll be daylight soon," he said. "Time we found a place to perform our little metamorphosis." He looked around. They were entering a stretch of the road that ran through a forest with dense underbrush. "Next dirt road," Ted said, "turn off, okay?"

"Okay."

About a quarter of a mile later a rutted, obviously little-traveled dirt road led into the woods on the right. Kevin turned off and inched his way along the narrow lane, winding its way into the still-dark forest. They crossed a trickle of a stream and presently came to a place where the road widened to form a little clearing. Kevin stopped.

Everyone piled out of the ambulance.

"This is where, with regrets in our hearts, we say farewell to General Ludwig Bauernweiss," Ted said with travelogue pomposity, "and commend him for a job well done."

"Good riddance, I say," Mike yawned. He stretched. "Let's get at it. We should be ready to hit the road again by noon."

"Better wait with changing our clothes until we get rid of the meat wagon," Ted suggested, slapping the side of the field ambulance.

The tint of a rosy dawn lay over the little clearing when they were ready to go to work. From the medicine cabinet that had been built into the space under the driver's seat they brought out several gallon cans of quick-drying paint and a sackful of brushes. Gaby tore her ample apron into rags, and as the daylight grew stronger the Grand Guignol team began to transform the field-gray ambulance into an ordinary van, painting it a light-blue color, using the bed sheets from the cot as drop cloths. Under their brushes the big red crosses disappeared, and on the rear doors the quarantine warning was painted out. The warning legends on the two CONTAMINATED WASTE containers were obliterated, and from under the cot to which it had been fastened, a small beat-up, paint-stained extension ladder was hauled out. They all worked under the direction of Kevin, whose knowledge of set-painting, acquired during his do-it-all days as a prop boy, was now paying off.

A few paint splatters in different colors and a new sign on the double doors in the back, half on each door, completed the transformation to the van of a master painter—

> MARCUS LAWETZ
> MALER   MEISTER

—with an address in Berlin–Spandau to go with the new license plates.

The ventilation fan in the roof of the vehicle was removed, and a prefabricated cover plate that had been hidden in the ambulance was secured in place. It contained a clamping device that held the painting ladder in place when it was placed on the roof.

When the paint job was finished and the field ambulance had become a painter's van, they all stood back to admire their work. They were still more than a hundred miles from Misdroy. They still needed fast transportation, but they could, of course, no longer use the ambulance ploy.

The painter's van would take them the rest of the way in style.

They packed the leftover paints and all the painting materials in the van and changed from their now paint-splattered uniforms into their old clothes, which had been stashed in one of the waste containers. Mike, whistling cheerfully, dug a hole into which they threw all the medical paraphernalia from the ambulance, the dismantled ventilation fan, the old *Sanitätsdienst* license plates, their military identification papers, and the discarded uniforms. Carefully, they camouflaged the burial spot with leaves and brush.

No longer were they nurse and patient, driver and doctor of the German Medical Service. They were now Maler-meister Marcus Lawetz; his son Karel, home from the army on medical leave; and his daughter-in-law Gertie, travelling with a neighbor and friend, Theo Hauser, to relatives in Altdamm—a little town near Stettin —after their house in Berlin had been completely destroyed in the terror bombings carried out by the enemy.

"It'll be a few hours before the paint is dry enough to dirty up," Kevin said. "We might as well take it easy."

"We passed a little stream back there," Gaby said. "How about heating some water and using Etienne's coffee?"

"Good idea," Mike said. "I'll build a firepit. You get the coffee, and Kevin, you go get the water," he directed. "Use the water container in the van."

The coffee had been hot, black, and delicious, and they had all enjoyed themselves, luxuriating in the picnic mood of the moment and the peaceful, secluded place.

As soon as the paint had dried, they'd smeared the van with muddy water and wiped it off, leaving just enough drying dirt to take the newly painted look off the vehicle.

It was about 10:00 A.M., the sun was shining, the day was getting warmer. Ford was in his heaven and all was right with the world.

They gathered their things and put them in the van.

———

111

"You two can ride in the back this time," Mike said to Kevin. "Gaby and I'll take the cab. We've spent enough time cooped up back there. I'll drive."

"Just don't get lost," Kevin grinned at his father. "This is not Pigalle!"

They started to get into the van.

"Was machen Sie hier?" The gruff, angry voice thundered in their ears. "What are you doing here?" Startled, they whirled on the sound.

The first thing they saw was the ugly double-barrelled shotgun pointed right at them; the second, was the man holding it at hip's height. In black boots, his knee britches tucked into them, a green jacket with the red Swastica armband slashing across his left sleeve, and a green field cap on his head, the man stood scowling at them, suspicion and animosity flashing from him. At his side, watching them closely and growling softly, a large dog with tightly curled gray-brown hair stood in stiff-legged alertness.

Gaby automatically took a step backward. She stared at the dog, more afraid of it than of the gun. Had she known anything about hunting dogs, she would have recognized it as a *Deutsche Drahthaar*—a German wirehair.

For the span of a few heartbeats, no one spoke.

"Wilddieberei ist strengstens verboten!" the man growled. "Poaching is strictly forbidden! Poachers will be severely punished." He motioned menacingly with his gun. *"Hände hoch—* put your hands up," he ordered harshly.

Kevin quickly sized the man up. He recognized the uniform. The man was a *Staatsförster*—a state forest ranger.

"Please, *Herr Forstmeister*," he flattered. "We are—"

"I am not a Chief Ranger," the man snapped. "Yet."

"—*Herr Förster*," Kevin corrected. "We are not poachers. Not at all. We know that is against the law. We are merely resting here. We have had a long and tiring trip."

The ranger scowled at them. "Put your identification papers on the ground before you and step back," he ordered. "Keep your hands clasped behind your necks. *Los!*"

They obeyed.

"Rolf! *Aufpassen!*" the ranger snapped. At once the dog took a few steps forward and stood glaring at the four people, his teeth bared, a deep growl rumbling in his throat.

"If it pleases the *Herr Förster*," Kevin said respectfully, "My

112

father is *Maler-meister* Lawetz." He pointed to the van. "You can see his name on the doors. We are on our way back home. Back to Spandau where my father has his shop. We come from a visit with my uncle. We only stopped here to rest from the driving and to enjoy a cup of coffee, real coffee my uncle gave me and Gertie for our anniversary." He seemed to have a sudden idea. "Perhaps," he suggested, "perhaps when the *Herr Förster* has searched our van and seen for himself that we have no guns and no stolen game, the *Herr Förster* would join us in having a cup of real coffee. We still have a little of it left."

The ranger was inspecting their papers. He grunted noncommittally. He looked uncertain. His eyes wandered toward the still-glowing embers in the firepit.

"One must be careful when making a fire in the woods," he grumbled. "This is a *Staatsrevier*—a State Forestry District. The rules are strict."

"Yes, of course," Kevin agreed. "As they should be. We were just about to cover the embers with dirt." He paused. "But, now, perhaps we could make another pot of coffee?"

"Rolf! *Zu Fuss!*—Heel!" the ranger called. Unconsciously, he licked his lips. "Something hot to drink would not be unwelcome," he allowed grudgingly. He broke the barrel on his shotgun. "It has been a disagreeable night." He held out their ID papers to Kevin. Kevin took them. He turned to Gaby.

"Gertie, *Schatzi*," he said, "Gertie, darling, why don't you put another pot of our real coffee on the fire? Make it good and strong."

"I will," Gaby said. "Perhaps *Vati*—perhaps Papa—would get some more firewood?"

"Sure," Mike said. He and Ted walked into the woods to look for dead branches.

"Since five this morning I have been on my feet," the ranger complained to Kevin. "All because of that *verdammte*—that damned Hitler Jugend camp over at Bötzow. Only a couple of kilometers down the road." He spat in disgust. "Discipline," he sneered. "Those *Lausbuben*—those young hoodlums—do not know the word. Sometimes they bully the whole town with their arrogant meddling. Finding shirkers and hoarders behind every haystack. They—" He suddenly stopped. He gave Kevin a quick glance. "Of course, they are splendid young men," he protested, a little too fervently. "The Hitler Youth Movement is a credit to the party. And to the Reich. I, myself, always say so."

113

"Of course," Kevin agreed readily. "The cream of our young, with a healthy, rambunctious spirit, as you say."

"Yes, yes, exactly so," the ranger exclaimed with obvious relief.

Mike and Ted returned with some dry branches, and soon the fire once more blazed in the firepit.

While the Grand Guignolers sent a thought of thanks to Etienne, the ranger savored the nearly black brew, downing three cups before he finally picked up his shotgun and stood up.

"You will have to leave here," he said sternly, once again the ranger upholding the law. "It is not permitted to camp in this state forest without permission." He frowned at them.

"I will not report you this time," he said magnanimously, obviously impressed with his own lenience. "But you must leave."

"Of course, *Herr Förster*," Kevin agreed. "We shall leave at once. And thank you, *Herr Förster*, for your kind understanding."

They piled into the van, Mike behind the wheel, and drove away, leaving the ranger and his dog, Rolf, squinting after them in the sun. They retraced their route back along the narrow forest road, across the little stream, toward the main highway. Once there, Kevin banged on the cab for Mike to stop. He did. Kevin jumped out and joined him at the cab.

"Don't go to Bötzow," he said. "I found out from that ranger that there is a Hitler Youth encampment just this side of the village, and the brats are on the rampage looking for trouble."

"Shit!" Mike swore. "That's all we need. Running into a pack of juvenile Nazi hooligans."

"We can bypass the place," Kevin said. He picked up a map and looked at it. "Go back a few miles to that road." He put his finger on the map. "The road to Schwante. We can rejoin the main road at Oranienburg. It's not too much of a detour—and a helluva lot better than tangling with a gang of eager-beaver adolescent thugs."

"Damn right," Mike agreed. He turned the van around.

He sat up with a start. He had been dozing, he realized. The steady drone of a car engine always made him drowsy. He adjusted his tie, pulled down his uniform jacket, and sat up straight as he was passed first through the outer then the inner gate at Misdroy.

Standartenführer Dieter Haupt was suddenly aware of his impatience. The drive from Mimoyecques had taken two days instead of one full twenty-four-hour day. It had, of course, been his

114

decision. He had stopped off in Hannover to put the fear of God and the Armament Ministry into the management of one of the manufacturers of precision instruments in that city, whose schedule of deliveries had become all too lax, and he'd stayed overnight. Hannover had a particularly high-class *Offiziersbordell* run by the SS, one of the best officer brothels in the Reich.

But now he was back and impatient to find out what had happened in his absence. An important test was scheduled in two days, and although he trusted his aide, *Obersturmführer* Stefan Stolitz, he didn't care to trust him with all the intricacies of preparing for a major critical test unsupervised.

The car came to a stop at the building that housed his office. The driver jumped out and held the door open for him. *Obersturmführer* Stolitz met him on the stairs. He was beaming. His hand shot out in the Nazi salute.

"*Heil Hitler!—Herr Brigadeführer!*" he called.

Dieter Haupt stared at him.

"The orders came through just this morning," Stolitz informed him, "from Berlin. The papers promoting you to brigadeführer, signed by the Führer himself, are on your desk. Congratulations!"

Haupt waved a hand at him. "Thank you, Stolitz," he said. "But my promotion is not important. Important is our project— and what has been accomplished while I was away."

Chastised, the aide looked at him. "Of course, Herr Brigadeführer," he said.

Haupt strode into the building. Major General, he thought. At his age, not an inconsequential achievement. He was pleased. Enormously pleased. He silently vowed to prove to the Führer that he was worthy of the honor.

He quickly located the document of promotion on his desk. He held it in his hand. He looked at the strange, slanted signature of the Führer—

Like no other signature he'd ever seen, he thought. But then— the Führer himself was like no other man.

He let his mind go back and savor the memory of his meeting

with Adolf Hitler only two days ago. And Speer. *Reichsminister* Albert Speer.

He frowned.

He had been given some reports by Speer before he left Berlin. He'd studied them on the trip. Intelligence reports and evaluations. There were accounts of an enormous buildup of troops and materiel along the whole of the English Channel coast. A significant increase in radio traffic and espionage activities. From this, and from information obtained from captured enemy agents, it seemed clear that the Allies were in the final stages of planning their invasion of the Continent, and that the initial landing would be in the Calais region. Calais.

And Mimoyecques.

And the day was rapidly drawing nearer. It had become a race, he thought, a real race between their invasion fleet and his Tausendfüssler. Between him and them. And he was determined to win. . . .

The intercom on his desk buzzed. He punched a button. "Yes?"

"*Herr Brigadeführer*," Stolitz's voice rasped over the speaker. "*Generalleutnant* Otto Weigert from OKH, General der Artillerie, is here to see you."

Dieter frowned. What was up? "Ask the *Generalleutnant* to come in," he said. What the devil was a lieutenant general from Army High Command Artillery doing at Misdroy? He rose from his chair and stood before his desk as *Generalleutnant* Weigert was shown in.

"*Heil Hitler!*" Haupt cried.

"*Heil Hitler,*" the general answered perfunctorily. He shook Haupt's hand. "I shall be brief and to the point," he said briskly, taking a seat in one of the chairs standing before the desk without being asked. "I know you must have much to do."

Haupt walked back to his desk and sat down. "What may I do for you?" he asked.

"The OKH—the Army High Command—has been instructed by the Führer to select and appoint an artillery officer of general rank to command the installation now being constructed at Mimoyecques under your supervision," Weigert told him. "Since this officer must be thoroughly briefed on the project," he smiled a thin smile, "*Fleissiges Lieschen*—Busy Lizzie—I understand

---

116

you call it, the man must be selected now so he will be quite ready to take command of the operation when the time comes."

"I understand," Haupt said. "You wish me to brief him?"

"He has not been selected yet," Weigert said. "Before we *do* select him, we want to know exactly what it is he will be commanding." He looked steadily at Haupt. "In other words, General, what *is* Project Busy Lizzie? What is the weapon you call the— the *Tausendfüssler?*"

"The project is top secret," Haupt said slowly. "Eyes only for the Führer and *Reichsminister* Speer. Do you have the authority to be given this information?"

"I do." Weigert pulled a document from his uniform jacket. He handed it to Haupt.

Haupt examined it carefully. It was marked:

STAATSGEHEIMNISS
Geheimhaltungsverpflichtung beachten

STATE SECRET
Observe Obligation to Keep Secret

It was an order from OKH, General der Artillerie, for Generalleutnant Otto Weigert to proceed to *Heeresversuchsstelle*—Army Test Site—Misdroy for the purpose of familiarizing himself with *Unternehmen Fleissiges Lieschen*—Project Busy Lizzie. It was countersigned by Reichsminister Albert Speer.

Haupt handed the document back to Weigert.

"In Ordnung," he said. "In order. I trust you understand my caution in asking you for your authorization."

"You would have been severely remiss in your duties had you not," Weigert countered, "and I would have so stated in my report." He leaned forward. "Now. What is this—this *Tausendfüssler?*"

Haupt looked straight at the OKH staff officer.

"It is a cannon," he said. "An artillery piece. A gun, if you wish. A gun with a barrel that is one hundred and fifty meters long."

Weigert stared at Haupt as if he thought him suddenly gone mad. Incredulously, he shook his head.

"One hundred and fifty meters," he repeated. "That's—that's

117

as long as—as *five* tennis courts placed end to end!" He looked visibly shaken. "A—*gun barrel*??"

Haupt nodded calmly. He was secretly pleased with the officer's reaction. "That is quite correct, General," he said. "We are building two batteries at Mimoyecques, each with twenty-five such guns."

Weigert looked stunned. "But that's—that's impossible!" he said. "To support such a gigantic gun barrel you would have to have a mountain for a base."

"We do, *Herr Generalleutnant*," Haupt smiled. "We do."

Weigert gave Haupt a speculative look. "Perhaps," he said. "Perhaps you had better describe this—this gun to me. In detail."

"Of course," Haupt nodded. "With pleasure."

Weigert sat back to listen.

"*Das Geschütz*—the gun—is in the nature of a *Hochdruck-pumpe*—a high-pressure pump—Herr General," Haupt began. "In fact, that is the official designation for the project: *HDP*."

"And you have a prototype of this gun here at Misdroy?"

"We do."

"I shall wish to inspect it."

"Of course."

Haupt went on. "The one-hundred-and-fifty-meter-long barrel of the gun has thirty-four pairs of booster tubes protruding at a slight angle from its sides, like stubby legs at four-meter intervals for its entire length." He smiled. "That is why the device is called the *Tausendfüssler*—the Millipede. It does resemble such a creature."

"Booster tubes?" Weigert prompted.

"Yes, General. The barrel itself, the main tube, if you wish, is a one-hundred-and-fifty-millimeter smooth bore. The shell is breech-loaded, complete with a propelling charge. When this charge is fired, it propels the projectile up the barrel. As it passes the openings of the first pair of booster tubes, which are loaded with additional charges, these booster charges are automatically fired. This is repeated at each of the booster-tube pairs, as the projectile is accelerated up the main barrel, building up the explosive force behind it until it attains the necessary velocity to reach its distant target as it is shot from the muzzle of the gun." He looked at Weigert. "Am I making myself clear, General?"

"Perfectly."

"The principle is also known as the *Mehrfach-Kammer Geschütz*, Herr General—the manifold-chamber gun."

"And the projectile? What kind of projectile does it fire?"

"The projectile is a little over two meters long. Two point three, four, five, to be exact. It is equipped with rigid stabilizer fins, a four-piece support sabot at the shoulder, and a heavy pusher-piston at the base, designed to fall away at the gun muzzle."

"And the payload?"

"The projectile is capable of carrying sixty-five pounds of high explosives and has a range of one hundred and sixty kilometers. More than enough to reach London and other principal targets in England from the Mimoyecques area."

"The installation at Mimoyecques," Weigert asked, "of what exactly does it consist?"

"We are constructing two main batteries, each with five sub-batteries of five guns each, for a total of fifty guns," Haupt said proudly.

"Describe the layout."

"The code name of the area is WIESE—Meadow. There are two sectors, Anlage Ost—Sector East—and Anlage West.

"Each with five subbatteries?"

"Correct. Each subbattery consists of a shaft dug on an angle into a hill that rises to a height of a hundred and fifty-six meters. Each shaft holds five gun barrels, anchored into the ground and installed with fixed traverse and elevation. In the case of the London guns, fifty-five degrees for optimum effect." He smiled. "As you see, General, the hill, in effect, is our Unterbau—our gun mount."

"I see. Go on."

"The entire emplacement is excavated into the hill and protected by a five-meter-thick concrete roof. It consists of a series of elevator shafts and tunnels at various depths, giving access to the battery shafts; as well as storage chambers, munitions armories, and quarters for the personnel. The lowest level is Level D, where the projectiles are loaded; and the surface is Level A, where the muzzles of the guns emerge through five narrow openings in a seventy-by-thirty-meter cement slab of six meters thickness. These openings can be closed by twenty-centimeter-thick steel doors, making the installation impregnable to enemy bombings."

"How are the logistics handled? Resupply?"

"The entire subterranean complex is serviced by a rail system, with railroad tunnels entering the hill at four points." Haupt looked at Weigert. "Perhaps the General would like to see a recent schematic drawing of the emplacement. It might provide a clearer picture."

Weigert nodded.

Haupt opened a drawer in his desk and brought out a file folder. He opened it, withdrew a document, and handed it to Weigert.

"*Bitte, Herr* General."

Weigert took the single sheet of paper. He studied it.

Weigert looked up at Haupt. "Impressive," he said.

Haupt looked pridefully pleased.

"When the installation is complete," Weigert asked, "what is the estimated fire power?"

"The guns will be capable of firing six hundred projectiles an hour, *Herr* General. One every twelve seconds! Enough to lay down a rain of destruction on every English port on the Channel coast, every enemy troop concentration, and every potential invasion fleet."

He paused.

"And obliterate London itself!"

WOLLIN INSEL

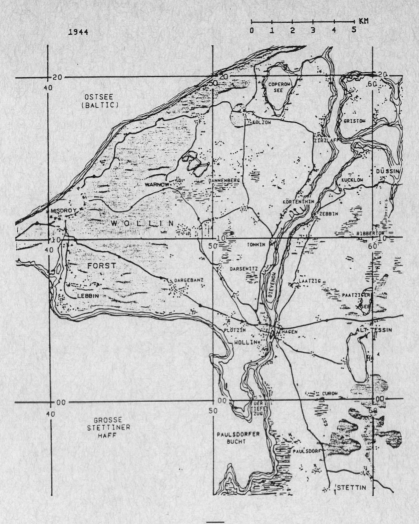

1944

KM
0 1 2 3 4 5

OSTSEE
(BALTIC)

COPEROW
SEE

GRISTOW

KOLZOW

ZIRZLAFF

DÜSSIN

WARNOW

DANNENBERG

KUCKLÖW

KÖRTENTHIN

ZEBBIN

MISDROY

RIBBERTOW

W O L L I N

TONNIN

FORST

DARSEWITZ

DARGEBANZ

LAATZIG

DIEVENOW

LEBBIN

PAATZIGER
SEE

PLÖTZIN

HAGEN

ALT-TESSIN

WOLLIN

CUROW

DER
TIEFE
ZUG

GROSSE
STETTINER
HAFF

PAULSDORFER
BUCHT

PAULSDORF

STETTIN

❖ 14 ❖

"LONDON must look a little like this," Gaby said somberly to Mike as he with difficulty guided the van through the streets of Stettin, the important port city on the Oder River at the terminus of the Berlin–Stettin canal system, some eighty miles north of the capital. With access to the Baltic Sea, the town served as the Port of Berlin.

It was early afternoon, and the streets were filled with drab-looking people drearily going about their tasks. The city had been badly damaged by numerous air raids. Empty ruins pointed their ragged, fire-blackened remnants toward the sky, and heaps of rubble and debris obstructed both pedestrian and vehicular traffic in the streets below. Bomb craters in the roadways had hurriedly and haphazardly been filled and repaired with black asphalt patches; and in the denuded parks, sandbags were ignominiously piled up around statuary of proud German rulers. Signs affixed to buildings and lampposts read, *LUFTSCHUTZKELLER*—Air Raid Shelter—but many of the buildings to which they pointed were gutted and in ruins. On one lone-standing wall a slogan in once-white paint read: *FÜHRER BEFIEHL, WIR FOLGEN!*—Führer Command, We Follow! Shrapnel-scarred and discolored by soot and smoke, it seemed an ill-fated vow. Women were predominant in the streets. They ran the streetcars; they were clearing the rubble; they stood in grim silence in the long lines at food stores. Shortages were apparently severe. *Schlangenstehen*, Gaby had learned they called it, "standing in a snake." The reputation for being one of Germany's most important shipbuilding centers had exacted its toll. Life in Stettin had turned into wretched existence. . . .

The Grand Guignolers were leaving the center of town after

having negotiated the maze of detours and missing street signs. Mike turned to Gaby.

"Okay," he growled. "So I did get lost. I have no idea where the hell we are. Or where to find the damned road to Altdamm."

"Maybe we should ask someone," Gaby ventured.

Mike grunted, not happy at the prospect. Kevin would never let him live it down.

Gaby looked around. Ahead of them, a boy of twelve or thirteen, clad in the brown shirt and short black pants of the Jungvolk, the pre-Hitler youth organization for younger boys, was coming out the front door of a building, headed for a bicycle leaning against the wall.

"Stop by that boy," Gaby said. Mike did. Gaby leaned out the cab window.

"Young man!" she called. "Do you have a minute?"

The boy looked up. He walked over to the van.

"*Bitte?*"

"What is your name?" Gaby asked pleasantly.

"Helmut," the boy answered. "Helmut Krell."

"Helmut, I wonder if you can help us," Gaby said earnestly. "We have to go to Altdamm, but we are lost. Could you tell us which way it is?"

"*Ja, gnädige Frau,*" the boy answered. He pointed. "You go straight ahead for about half a kilometer. Then you come to a fork. You go to the right, and you will be on the road to Altdamm. The bridge is still standing. I was there this morning myself."

"Thank you so much, Helmut," Gaby smiled at the boy. "We are—"

She was abruptly interrupted by the piercing wail of air raid sirens suddenly filling the air.

Helmut started. "Air raid!" he cried. "You had better take cover." He turned away. "I have to get home!" He began to run away, forgetting his bicycle.

Kevin and Ted came running up to the cab. "Come on!" Kevin shouted over the urgent wailing of the sirens. "We've got to get to a shelter. We just drove past one. We can't stay in the open."

Mike and Gaby tumbled from the cab. Together, they all ran for the building that offered shelter, about a block back the way they'd come. The city was filled with urgent alarm.

They joined the crowd of hurrying, jostling people funneling toward the promised haven. In the doorway, an air raid warden valiantly tried to maintain a semblance of order.

Pushing and shoving in grim, determined silence, accompanied by the mournful wails of the sirens, the people pressed forward.

Finally the four Guignolers reached the doorway. The warden was waving his arms in the air.

"*Voll!*" he screamed. "Full! The shelter is full!" he tried to bar the way. "No more!" he shouted. "Go somewhere else! No more!"

A few people fought past him, others turned and ran off to seek another *Luftschutzkeller*. The four Guignolers remained in the doorway, undecided.

"You can stay here in the doorway," the warden puffed, "with me. It is better than out there."

The drone of many planes began to be heard over the noise of the crowd, growing steadily louder.

Distant explosions occasionally drowned out the steadily booming antiaircraft fire.

Ted squinted up at the planes, now visible high in the sky.

"Shit!" he swore under his breath. "B-17's! *Our* guys! We could be wiped out by our own side before we even get started."

Suddenly a terrifying sound intruded itself on their awareness, rapidly increasing in loudness—a sort of swishing whistle, as something monstrous crashed down through the protesting air.

"*Gott im Himmel!*" The warden cringed in terror as he whispered his supplication. "God in Heaven! Phosphorous!"

The giant incendiary bomb struck not a block from where they huddled in the doorway.

It exploded in blinding brilliance, showering its seething contents over the street and buildings. Flaming rivers of inextinguishable fire, glowing luminous-green, splattered over walls and pavement, ran in all-consuming streams. A searing shock wave hit them, immediately followed by a savage gust of turbulent wind that tore at them, threatening to whisk Gaby from Kevin's grip, as masses of cool air rushed to fill the void created by the suddenly super-heated air spewing upward with hurricane velocity. Almost at once, the charring heat returned, scorching their throats and stinging their eyes with scalding tears. They choked on the acrid smoke as they cowered in the doorway, desperately trying to hide from the inferno outside. Through the whirling haze of dust and heat, they watched the hell that had so suddenly been dropped from the skies above.

A violent fire storm raged through the street. Blazing liquid fire seeped inexorably through drains and down stairs to the shelters below. And from the doorways, flaming figures—their mouths wrenched open in screams, unheard in the din of the conflagration, their hair and clothes ablaze—emerged to dance a macabre, frenzied dance of doom before being swept into the holocaust and consumed—grisly marionettes on strings manipulated by a puppeteer gone mad. Every window in every building popped out and shattered, raining shards of glass into the street, and an asphalt patch sizzled and bubbled in the intense heat—little puffs of flame dotting the roiling surface.

Suddenly they saw a small figure, dragging a bicycle, running down the street. It was Helmut. Gone back for his precious bike, he was frantically trying to run away from the fiery nightmare surrounding him. As they watched in shock they saw him run into the street. Wrapped in a cocoon of horror, Gaby stared.

Suddenly the boy fell, his feet stuck in the melting asphalt. His bike flew from his grip. Quickly covered with steaming asphalt, he writhed in agony to free himself from the burning embrace. He struggled to his feet; his arms flailing in slow-motion frenzy at the sticky, searing mass that engulfed him. All at once a little flame licked at him. And another. And in a sudden flash, the struggling figure flared up in fire and collapsed in a spasmodically jerking heap.

Gaby buried her face in Kevin's chest. Her shoulders heaved in great sobs as she clung to him.

Suddenly the noise of another giant explosion slammed into their minds. The world shuddered. The high-explosive bomb had hit a few blocks away, but the force of the blast stunned them.

Unstable ruins began to collapse, toppling bricks and masonry into the street.

Half a block away a wall caved in, in a cloud of mortar dust, burying a light-blue painter's van in a pile of rubble and debris.

And it was over.

Slowly, looking dazed, people began to emerge from the shelters to face the still-raging fires caused by the incendiary bomb.

The four Guignolers ran to their van.

It was covered with crumbled masonry, chunks of brickwork, and splintered wood from the fallen wall.

Ted stared at the debris-buried vehicle. "Damn!" he swore. "The X-35 is inside."

Gaby gave him a quick look. His strong, usually confident face looked waxen with worry. The radio, she thought. It is his lifeline.

Hurriedly they began to clear the van of rubble, and presently it stood stripped before them.

They stared at it.

It was badly dented, the roof all but caved in. Deep scratches were gouged in the sides, the windshield was cracked, and one cab door was sprung and gaped partly open. One front fender hung loose, but all four tires were undamaged.

"See if it'll start," Ted said. "I'll take a look inside." He wrestled one of the back doors open and entered the van. They looked after him. They all knew he would be checking out the irreplaceable X-35.

Mike slid in behind the wheel. "Here goes," he said. "Cross whatever you can cross."

Miraculously the van started up at first try.

Ted joined them.

"I want to take a good look at the radio," he said. "It's been banged around some. But let's get the hell out of here as quickly as we can." He looked up toward the sky. "They may be back."

He started toward the rear of the van.

"Wait!" Kevin called after him. Ted returned.

"We'll have to abandon this junk heap sooner or later," Kevin said. "We won't be able to get gas for it anyway. But we'll need some kind of transportation." He nodded toward the other side of the street. "How about it?"

They all looked.

The building across from them, apparently an office building, had suffered some damage in the blast that had toppled the wall onto the van. Several people were already at work clearing the entrances and stacking rubble. In a small square in front of the building that had served as a bike-parking area, some twenty or thirty bicycles lay scattered, knocked over by the explosion.

"Let's help ourselves," Kevin suggested. "Liberate four good ones. No one will bother us. They'll think we are helping to clean up the mess."

"Sold!" Ted said. "Let's give the bastards a hand."

He started to cross the street.

Gaby stood gazing toward the still-burning street behind them. Kevin took her arm.

"Come on," he said gently.

126

"He was just a boy," she whispered. "Just a boy."

"Don't think about it," Kevin said gently.

She turned to him, her eyes bright with unshed tears.

"How?" she asked.

She turned and started across the street. . . .

It took them close to an hour and a half to cover the less than ten miles to Altdamm. The Stettiner streets in many places had been impassable, and they'd had to zigzag their way to the bridge across the river, and the road to Altdamm. The bridge had been so crowded they'd literally had to inch their way across.

The road out of Altdamm via Gollnow to Wollin, where their contact supposedly lived, was clear. They wheezed along in the beat-up van at a good clip.

Mike glanced at the gas gauge. "Coming up on empty," he said. "Let's stop and find out what Ted wants to do."

He pulled over onto the shoulder and stopped. They were sitting on the crest of a hill; before them stretched a beautiful green and wooded landscape with a sizeable lake on the right.

Ted joined them.

"We've got to dump the van pretty soon," Mike told him. "We're almost out of gas."

Ted nodded. He looked at his watch. "The X-35 is okay," he said. "Contact time with Milton Hall is in about an hour from now. Let's pull off the road and find a little privacy."

At the bottom of the hill, an overgrown path just wide enough for the van led off the road to the left into a little forest. A weathered sign barely readable hung askew from a pole and pointed into the woods: *DAMMSCHER SEE*, it proclaimed—Dammscher Lake. Mike turned off the road and drove down the path.

Half a mile down, they came to the lake. The path ended in a small empty clearing and an old wooden boat pier, with a rotted, half-sunken rowboat lying in the water next to it. There was not a soul in sight.

"This'll do just fine," Ted said. He'd changed places with Kevin and Gaby and was riding in the cab next to Mike. "Pull over here. We can string the antenna between those two trees and use the car battery for power."

In minutes, the antenna wire had been put up and the X-35 hooked up to the battery. Ted again consulted his watch.

"Plenty of time," he said cheerfully, as if deliberately trying to eradicate from their minds the remembered horror they had just witnessed. "Enough to give you all your first lesson in the care and maintenance of the little ol' X-35. Gather round, children."

They gathered around the radio and Ted.

"Okay," he said. He picked up a pencil and held it over a note pad. "School's in session." He looked up at them. "Learn!" he said. "It's damned important that you know how to operate this little devil and how to encode and decode any messages you may have to receive or send." He paused. "Just—in case."

Soberly they nodded.

"Putting your message, called the clear text, into cipher is easy as pie," Ted went on. "All you need is pencil and paper. No need to carry around any fancy, incriminating encoding gadgets. And all you have to remember are two words, called key words. In our case they were made extra easy to remember. Number one is MILTONHALL, number two, GRANDGUIGNOL." He began to write on the pad.

"Now, to encode your message you simply first take key word number one and convert it into a series of numbers by using the numeral *one* for the first letter of the alphabet that appears in the key word, and so on down the line. In that way *A* becomes *one*, and *H*—the next alphabet letter to appear in the key word— becomes *two*, and so on. Like this:

$$\begin{array}{cccccccccc} \text{M} & \text{I} & \text{L} & \text{T} & \text{O} & \text{N} & \text{H} & \text{A} & \text{L} & \text{L} \\ 7 & 3 & 5 & 10 & 9 & 8 & 2 & 1 & 5 & 6 \end{array}$$

"Then you count the number of letters in your clear. The message we want to send now is *STETTIN REACHED OK*." Sixteen letters.

"Not much of a message," Mike commented.

"But enough to let them know we are alive and operational," Ted said. "Always make your messages as short as you can. You'll want to stay on the air the shortest time possible. Don't want to give a monitor truck a chance to pick you up and locate you."

"I see your point," Mike acknowledged.

"Now, we build a grid under the numbered key word," Ted continued, "and write our message in it, including our signature group, TGG, and our security check group. The group is easy to remember. The first letter of each of our given names." He smiled at Gaby. "Ladies first, and then according to age. GMTK." He looked up at them. "Remember always to include this group in the correct order if your transmission is legitimate. Should you be captured, should you be forced to transmit a message by the enemy, all you have to do is change the group, and Milton Hall will know."

He returned to the paper. "Now, we count the letters. We have twenty-three. Since all encoded messages are always sent in groups of five letters, we need to add two letters. They're called nulls. They won't make any difference in the decoded text. We'll use the letter X. So our grid now looks like this:

M	I	L	T	O	N	H	A	L	L
7	3	4	10	9	8	2	1	5	6
S	T	E	T	T	I	N	R	E	A
C	H	E	D	O	K	T	G	G	G
M	T	K	X	X					

"Pretty," Gaby said. "A little like the crossword puzzle in *Paris Soir*."

"But a hell of a lot more difficult to solve once we finish with it," Ted said. "This method is called a double transposition cipher, and it's as safe as they come."

"Double transposition?"

"It simply means that instead of substituting something for the letters or words in the clear text, you transpose the actual letters. Twice."

"That ought to mix them up." Kevin commented.

"What? The letters or the guys who try to break the cipher?" Mike asked.

"Both."

"Okay," Ted continued. "Now we take the second key word, number convert it, and write our message horizontally under it, reading it *down* each line in the grill under the first key word, beginning with the vertical line marked *one*. Like so:

G	R	A	N	D	G	U	I	G	N	O	L
3	11	1	8	2	4	12	6	5	9	10	7
R	G	N	T	T	H	T	E	E	K	E	G
A	G	S	C	M	I	K	T	O	X	T	D
X											

They all stared at the grid. The message had been turned into utter gibberish.

"Easy," Ted said. "Now we copy out the message we'll send, again reading it down, beginning with line *one*, separating it into groups of five letter, and writing it across."

NSTMR AXHIE OETGO
TCKXT TGGTK

"That's it?" Mike said. "From that they'll know we've reached Stettin?"

"They sure will," Ted said. "They've got the same key words at Milton Hall. All they have to do is reverse the procedure we followed—and they'll get the clear message. As you will if you ever receive a message from them."

"Sure. And if I ever get the hang of that damned Morse code," Mike grumbled.

"You will," Ted said. "In a few days you'll know enough to make do in a pinch." He looked up at them. "Which I hope to hell never comes! That goes for all of you. It probably never will," he grinned. "After all, you've got a terrific teacher."

He looked at his watch. "On the button," he said. "They'll be listening for us. We can send them our message."

He turned on the set and put on his earphones.

"First, we establish contact by sending their call letters," he said. Quickly he tapped his key.

RMH—RMH—RMH—

Two minutes later contact had been established and Ted sent the message, which was at once acknowledged. He signed off. He glanced at his watch.

130

"Three minutes, twelve seconds," he said. "Not bad." He turned to Kevin. "Roll up the antenna wire," he said.

They did. Then they removed the four bikes from the van. Each bike had a two-digit number painted in green on the rear mud guard. Some sort of license, they assumed, or permit. Perhaps a parking lot number for the office building where they'd picked up the bikes. They kept a small can of green paint from their painter's supplies, in case they'd have to alter the numbers, and packed it with everything else they needed to take along.

Mike turned to the battered van. He patted the hood. "Time to say bye-bye, old girl," he said affectionately. "You've done your job."

"What are we going to do with it?" Gaby asked. "We can't just leave it here for someone to find."

"We could cover it with branches," Kevin suggested. "Camouflage it."

"That won't really hide it," Ted said. "More likely call attention to it—and to the fact that someone tried to hide it."

"How about finding an old shed or something? A boathouse, maybe. We could hide it there—and it wouldn't be so obvious that it was being clandestinely concealed," Mike suggested.

"We'd have to be damned lucky to find such a place before we run out of gas," Ted said.

"If we do go look," Gaby said. "What if someone sees us?"

Ted turned to her. He gave her a bleak look. "Let's hope no one does," he said grimly. "For their sakes."

Gaby frowned at him. Suddenly she understood what he meant. She looked shocked.

"But—you wouldn't—"

Ted scowled at her. "Exactly," he snapped. "I would. I would have no choice. This is no game, Gaby. This is not Act One of some make-believe play. You must all get that into your heads. And keep it there—at all times. We can leave no one behind who even suspects us. No one!"

Uneasily, the three Guignolers looked at one another. Ted was, of course, right, they realized. This was *not* fun and games. It was deadly serious.

"Well, what the hell do we do with the van?" Mike grumbled. "We can't swallow the damned thing."

Kevin looked quickly at his father. "Out of the mouths of adults," he grinned. "Maybe we can at that." He pointed to the old pier. "How deep do you think the water is off that thing?"

"We can sure find out," Ted said. He grabbed the antenna wire. Quickly he tied a rock to one end of it.

Together they walked to the end of the pier.

Ted lowered the rock on the wire into the water. When the rock hit bottom, he stopped. He marked the spot and hauled the rock back up. He measured it with his arms.

"Better than ten feet," he said. "Deep enough."

Quickly they lined the van up with the pier and wedged the steering wheel in place. Mike started the engine and put the car in gear.

Ted put a heavy rock on the gas pedal.

The van jerked forward, gathered speed, rolled out onto the pier—and off the end. For the span of a heartbeat it seemed to hang suspended in the air—before it plunged into the water with a great splash.

They all walked out on the pier.

In silence, they stood watching the slowly diminishing stream of bubbles that rose to the surface of the lake where the van had gone down.

"Why did you do that?" The voice came from the shore behind them.

Startled, they spun around.

Automatically Ted reached for his gun.

Facing them stood a boy, a homemade fishing rod in his hands, an expression of curiosity on his freckled face.

He could have been no more than eight years old. . . .

❖ 15 ❖

"**H**I!" Gaby said brightly. She walked up to the boy, deliberately placing her body between Ted and the child.

The OSS agent stood staring at the child, his face white and drawn, his eyes terrible. . . .

You are driving a truck, the OSS test problem had stated, *filled with troops along a narrow mountain road just wide enough to accommodate it. On one side is a steeply rising cliff, on the other a deep ravine. As you round a bend you see a child sitting in the middle of the road. There is no time to brake. What do you do?*

The answer had been obvious. You run over the child and save the troops. . . .

And it was equally obvious what he must do now to save his team. And the mission.

He watched Gaby bending down to the boy.

"What are you doing here?" she asked pleasantly.

"Fishing."

"Catch anything?"

The boy shook his head solemnly. "No," he said. "You scared them all away."

"I hope we didn't," Gaby said. "We certainly didn't mean to." She looked questioningly at the boy. "What is your name?"

"Werner."

"Do you live around here, Werner?"

The boy nodded. He pointed. "Over that way," he said. "My father has a farm. He has also a tractor. And a big truck." He looked up into her face. "Why did you drive your automobile into the water?"

For a moment Gaby looked earnestly at him. Her mind raced.

133

What could she do? What could she say? Intuitively, she knew there was no way to be sure the child would keep silent about what he'd seen. She knew the "rules." Eliminate any possibility of being discovered. Any threat. The mission was all-important. Everything, everyone was expendable. Everyone.

They had two choices. They could let the boy go—and hope against hope that he wouldn't talk and alert someone.

Or they could—silence him.

There had to be another way.

There *had* to.

She was aware that the boy was watching her with curiosity. Oh, dear God, what could she do?

Suddenly, she smiled at the child, her eyes on his.

"Is that what you thought you saw?" she asked, surprised. "That we drove an automobile into the water?"

"I did," the boy said emphatically. "I saw you drive your automobile off Müller's pier." He pointed. "Right there!"

"Well," Gaby said. "You saw us drive *something* off the pier."

The boy nodded vigorously. "Yes. A blue automobile."

Gaby knelt down beside him.

"Werner," she said seriously, her tone of voice a conspiratorial whisper. "Can you keep a secret? A real honest-to-goodness secret?"

Wide-eyed, Werner looked at her. He nodded.

"Good. Then maybe I can tell you one. Would you like that?"

Again the boy nodded.

"Well," Gaby said. "What you saw us hide in the water was not an automobile, Werner, it was a *spaceship*! A spaceship *disguised* as an automobile."

Werner gaped at her. "It was—an automobile," he said slowly. But he seemed less certain.

"You go to school, Werner?"

"Yes. I am in my third year already."

"Good. Then you know about the stars, don't you, Werner?" She pointed into the sky. "Way up there?"

Werner nodded.

"And you know there are many other worlds up there, don't you?"

Again the boy nodded. "I know the moon," he said. "And Mars, where the King of War lives." He screwed up his face in thought. "And—and something called the Milk Road, I think."

"My, you know a lot," Gaby said admiringly. "I'm sure you also know that there are people that come from the stars. From other worlds."

Werner nodded sagely. "I have seen such people," he said. "In a film theater in Stettin. Last year, when my cousin took me." He looked superior. "But I knew they were only actors with funny things on their faces."

"But we are not actors," Gaby said earnestly. "We do come from another world. We came here in our spaceship."

Werner looked askew at her. *"Ja?"* he said skeptically. "From where?"

"From Mars."

The boy looked closely at her. "I do not believe you," he said scornfully. "Everyone knows that people from Mars are *green*. I have seen pictures of them in a picture book. They were green, and you are not. So there!"

Gaby sat up. She glanced at the three men standing close by, listening. She called to Mike.

"Find something sharp," she instructed him. "And come back here. I want to prove to Werner that we are really from Mars. That we are really—green."

She looked hard at Mike, willing him to understand her.

Mike stared at her as if she *had* suddenly turned green.

Kevin spoke up. "I'll help," he said. He gave Gaby a little nod, took his father by the arm, and led him off.

"Now, Werner," Gaby continued. "You know who Adolf Hitler is, don't you?"

"Of course." He looked speculatively at her. Perhaps she *was* from another world. *Everyone* knew the Führer. "The Führer," he said.

"Well, Werner," Gaby continued. "We have come to help him against his enemies," she said confidentially. "But no one must know that. It must be a secret. Do you understand?"

The boy nodded.

"It is *very* important, Werner," Gaby said gravely. "It is a *very* important secret."

Mike came back. In his hand he had a small painter's trowel. "That's the best we could find," he said.

"Not very sharp, is it?" Gaby said. "Perhaps Werner has a pen knife. He has been fishing." She turned to the boy. "Do you, Werner?"

The boy nodded. From his pocket he brought out a small paring knife. He handed it to Gaby.

"Thank you," Gaby said. She gave the knife to Mike. "We will show you that we are really from Mars," she said to Werner, "but you must tell no one. You understand that?"

Werner nodded. Wide-eyed, he watched.

"Take hold of your father's arm," Gaby said to Kevin, "and steady it for him."

Kevin took Mike's arm.

"Go ahead," Gaby said to Mike.

Mike plunged the little knife blade deep into his arm. At once green blood oozed out through the hole in his shirt and seeped down his arm.

Werner watched in wide-eyed wonder.

"Wow!" he breathed. Awed, he looked up at Mike. "Does it hurt?"

Mike shook his head. "Naw," he said. "We Martians can stop that sort of pain." He walked away, holding his arm.

Werner looked up at Gaby. "I won't tell," he said. "Not even Heinrich will I tell, and he is my best friend!" He looked after Mike, walking with Kevin toward the bikes.

Gaby walked up to Ted.

"Is he still a menace, Ted?" she asked under her breath. "Who will believe an eight-year-old's tales of spaceships and Martians who have come to help the Führer win the war and who bleed green blood?"

She turned back to the boy.

"Go home, now, Werner," she said kindly. "And remember—it is our secret!"

The boy ran off.

Ted frowned after him. For a moment he stood silent. "Okay," he said, his voice harsh. "Let's get the bloody hell out of here."

He strode toward the bikes. He was aware of feeling as if a huge weight had been lifted from his shoulders—but only part way.

The boy, Werner, was still a loose end.

And loose ends had a habit of gumming up the works. . . .

❖ 16 ❖

To her surprise, Gaby had felt a pang of nostalgia as they bicycled across the bridge over the Dievenow Channel to Wollin, the principal town on the little island of Wollin. Many happy hours had been spent there long ago. For a moment, the horrors she had already witnessed and the certain dangers that lay ahead faded in the light of remembered pleasures of a long ago yesterday, even though she was well aware that the enigma and the threat of Misdroy were only a scant nine miles away.

When she and Kevin had been on Wollin Island five years before, they had not actually been to Misdroy, but she remembered their leisurely bike trips through the heaths and swamps, sand dunes and wooded hills of the island at the mouth of the Oder River, it's ninety-five square miles dotted with tiny lakes.

She had thought the thousand-year-old town of Wollin charming and picturesque. It still was, virtually untouched by the war. And steeped in history; epic tales that had fascinated her. Here once stood the fabled, millenia-old fortress of Jomsborg, built by the Vikings and destroyed a century later by King Magnus Barfod of Norway. The town had been the Pomeranian bishopric; it had been burned and sacked by the Danish King Canute VI and conquered by the Swedes and the Brandenburgers before finally becoming part of the Prussian province of Pomerania.

The twenty-five-mile bike trip from Dammscher See to the village of Hagen on the mainland across from Wollin had been uneventful. They had stuck to the smaller country roads and had only joined the main highway just south of Hagen in time to be overtaken by a large military convoy of heavy supply trucks that lumbered ponderously and evenly spaced down the road, like circus elephants grasping each others' tails. A sobering reminder of the ominous and menacing work going on at Misdroy and the mission of Jed Team Grand Guignol.

They had spent the day following their arrival in Wollin getting settled in a small inn, *"Gasthof Adler"*—Eagle Inn—just north of town, and in making their first tentative attempts to find the man Janusz Keppler. They had been unsuccessful. The only public reference source they could safely use was the telephone book. And Keppler was not listed.

It was noon two days after their arrival, and they were sitting in a Bierstube they had learned was a favorite hangout for those who made their living on the canals. The place was filled with barge workers and boatmen, including many old-timers. One of them was bound to know Janusz Keppler, Gaby thought. In a town of a mere four thousand inhabitants, most everyone would know everyone else—especially in his own field.

"We've been here almost two days," Mike grumbled. And we still don't know where Keppler can be found."

"Or even *if*," Kevin said. He turned to Ted. "Can't Milton Hall help? Give us a clue?"

Ted shook his head. "No dice," he said. He took a swig of his beer. "They don't know anymore than we do."

"Great. We've tried what we could," Kevin went on. "We can't just go around buttonholing people and asking them where to find the man without drawing attention to ourselves. And to him. Too easy to arouse suspicion. Especially in a sensitive area such as this. And that's the last thing we need."

"And we sure can't go around ringing doorbells," Mike grunted.

"Let's not think of what we can't do but what we can," Gaby said. "How about things like registration records?" she suggested. "Licenses? The barge workers' union? That sort of thing. Could we get permission to take a look at them, do you think?"

"Possibly," Ted nodded. "But not without coming up with a damned good reason and a lot of checking. That's out."

"We don't even know what he looks like," Kevin said. "Only that he's in his sixties." He gestured around the room. "Could be any one of these men. For all we know we could be sitting next to him."

"There's got to be a way," Gaby insisted.

"Sure. I could stand up on my chair and shout *Achtung!* and ask if there is a Keppler in the house," Ted said. "But I wouldn't give you a snowball's chance in hell for our getting away with it."

Kevin looked up at him, a sudden gleam in his eyes.

"Snowball!" he said.

Ted gave him a frown. "What did you say?"

"*You* said it. Snowball!" He turned to his father. "Dad," he said excitedly. "*Snowball!* How about it?"

Mike suddenly lit up. "Hey! That's an idea. We can sure give it a try."

They began to talk animatedly between themselves. Ted turned to Gaby.

"What gives?" he asked resentfully. "What the hell are they talking about? Have they gone completely nuts?"

"No, no," Gaby said quickly. "They have an idea. It may work. They—"

"Snowball," Ted interrupted. "Why did Kevin keep saying snowball?"

"It's a play," Gaby explained hurriedly, "from the Grand Guignol called *Snowball*. They used to act in it. Both of them."

"A play?" Ted exclaimed incredulously. "They're discussing a play? Now?"

"Listen," Gaby said, keeping her voice low. "It's a play about a group of skiers cut off by an avalanche and marooned in a lodge in the Alps. An argument begins between two men. Gradually it snowballs and everyone joins in and it becomes a free-for-all that ends in violence and carnage. You'd be surprised how much damage can be done with ski poles. That play had a double ration of stage blood."

"What the hell are they trying to do?" Ted asked, suddenly concerned. Actors! You didn't know *what* they'd do from moment to moment. "Start a bloody riot? How's that going to help?"

"No," Gaby said. "Listen." They turned toward Kevin and Mike.

"You take the part of Petterson," Kevin said. "We can pretty much stick to the lines, with that one exception. "I'll take Rosenfeld." He raised his voice. "His name was Kessler, *du Trottel*—you numbskull!" He spoke with a Berlin accent, in keeping with his cover. "I saw the damned film, and I remember."

"You may have seen it," Mike shot back, obviously exasperated. "But that pea brain of yours isn't big enough to remember anything. His name was *Kentler*!"

"Kessler!" Kevin countered heatedly. *"He* was on the German rowing team. And *he* is the one that became a barge captain here. I know!"

"The Stockholm Olympics was thirty-two years ago. 1912. You weren't even born yet," Mike said derisively. "How would you know? The man's name was *Kentler*, and *he* became a barge captain."

The other guests in the *Bierstube* began to take notice of the argument, turning in their seats to watch Kevin and Mike go at each other.

"You don't know what you're talking about," Kevin snapped angrily, his voice rising in pitch. "You never do. They put a better head than yours on this beer! The man's name is *Kessler!*" He banged the stein down on the table so the beer splashed out.

"Kentler, *du Scheissidiot!*" Mike shouted, his face turning red.

Most of the men in the place were now watching, some with amusement, others in puzzlement. Ted stared at his companions as they continued their antics. He thought he knew what they were doing, at least he hoped so. But who could be sure with actors? In the OSS they'd stressed the importance of an agent's being able to do a little acting. He had to act his cover convincingly. But this was ridiculous.

"—and if ignorance is bliss, you dimwit, you'd be the happiest guy alive!" Kevin yelled at Mike, tapping his finger on his temple.

"Look who's talking!" Mike bellowed back. "Everytime *you* open your mouth it's just to change feet!"

Ted looked in astonishment at Gaby. "Where on earth do they get all those old clichés?" he groaned.

"It's an old play," Gaby whispered.

"Kentler!" Mike shouted.

"Kessler!" Kevin yelled back at him.

Like two fighting cocks they stuck their necks out, glaring at one another in anger. By now they had everyone's attention as they kept going at it.

Suddenly, during a brief pause to catch their breaths, one of the old-time boatmen spoke up.

"You may both be wrong," he pronounced.

They whirled on him.

"Really?" Kevin said sarcastically. "And what makes you think so?"

"There *is* a barge captain living here," the man explained. "But his name is *Keppler*. There is no Kessler. And no Kentler." He frowned. "But I never knew he was in the Olympics." He shrugged. "But then, Keppler is not one for talking much."

"You have a Captain Keppler living right here?" Kevin asked skeptically. "In Wollin? Not a—Kessler?"

The man nodded. "In Darsewitz," he said.

"Darsewitz?"

"It is a little village just north of here. Just three kilometers," the old-timer said. "But Keppler is retired now."

"And you are certain his name is not Kentler?" Mike asked, reluctant to give up.

The man nodded emphatically. "Keppler," he said. "Janusz Keppler."

"Oh, well, we are not talking about the same man then," Kevin said. "The Olympic rower we're talking about was named *Alois* Kessler."

"Kentler," Mike corrected him. "Alois Kentler!"

For a moment Kevin glared at him. He opened his mouth as if to light into Mike again—then broke into a grin.

"Forget it," he said. "Have another beer. Forget about Kessler or Kentler—or Keppler in Darsewitz. . . ."

They leaned their bicycles against the weathered picket fence at the house in Darsewitz that had been pointed out to them as the house of Janusz Keppler, barge skipper, by the first person they'd asked in the tiny village on the bank of the Dievenow Channel. The house itself, a modest, one-story, half-timbered building, stood at the edge of the water.

They walked through the narrow front garden with a yellowing, neglected lawn to the door and knocked.

There was no answer, even after repeated knocking.

"Let's go around to the back," Ted suggested. "Perhaps he's there."

They walked to the rear of the house. A trampled dirt yard lay between the house and the channel. To the right stood a ramshackle shed, and piles of rubble, mostly metal, lay strewn about: empty Diesel oil drums; a rusty anchor; coiled, eroded winch cables; and other discarded machinery parts and repair equipment related to running a barge operation.

At the channel's edge a large broken-down boathouse attached to an oil-discolored pier jutted into the water. A diesel-driven motor barge about a hundred and fifty feet long was moored at the end of the pier. Painted black, with a broad red stripe running along its entire length at the gunwale, it had a two-level pilot house painted gray perched at the stern. Although the paint was badly scuffed and scratched, the barge looked seaworthy.

There was no sign of Keppler.

Mike looked toward the house. "Let's see if the back door is open," he said. He started toward it.

"Mike!" Gaby exclaimed. "You can't just barge in." She giggled when she realized what she'd said.

Mike stopped. He turned to her. "Why not?" he asked. "If the door is unlocked? Keppler will understand." He turned to Ted. "Won't he?"

"I—I suppose so," Ted answered. He seemed uncertain.

Mike walked back to the group. He frowned at Ted. "He will —accept us, won't he?" he asked. "He does know what it's all about?"

"Well—not exactly," Ted said uncomfortably.

"Perhaps you'd better tell us exactly what to expect," Kevin said soberly. "Keppler *is* the man we're supposed to contact, isn't he?"

Ted nodded. "Yes, he is." He hesitated.

"Well?"

"Well, no one has actually alerted him to our coming," he said awkwardly. "In—in fact, no one has been in touch with the man since he helped one of our SOE agents, Jeff, five years ago. At that time Keppler *was* recruited as a sleeper."

Kevin stared at the Jed agent.

"So no one really knows what has happened to him in the interim years?"

"That's the nature of a sleeper agent."

"And he has no idea that we will be contacting him?"

Ted nodded.

"I think we should have been told that. Why weren't we?"

"You had no need to know," Ted said. He looked closely at the Grand Guignolers. "Would it have made a difference?"

For a moment they stood silent. Then Kevin spoke.

"No," he said shortly.

He turned toward the house. "But I think we'd better find out a little about Janusz Keppler before we do approach him."

—

142

Resolutely he started toward the back door. The others followed.

The door was in fact unlocked and easily pushed open. The room in which they found themselves was furnished with sturdy, comfortable furniture. An amateurish painting of a river barge hung on the wall above a massive, scarred eight-foot-long table that served as a desk, and an old-fashioned floor lamp leaned confidentially over an overstuffed easy chair. The floor was without carpet, the floor boards dark and worn with age.

Gaby went over to the desk. Idly she picked up a picture in an ornate, tarnished silver frame and glanced at it.

She stiffened in shock.

Wordlessly she showed it to the others.

It was a black-and-white photograph of a middle-aged man. He wore a dark pea-coat-type jacket, a black leather peaked cap, and a broad smile on his face. On his left sleeve gleamed the Swastica-adorned armband, and his right arm was raised in a stiff Nazi salute. Another man, wearing a sash across his shoulder, stood beaming next to him. A partly faded inscription read:

An mein Freund, Janusz Keppler, Heil Hitler!
Ortsbauernführer Niehman, Wollin, den 24.5.41

Wordlessly they stared at the photograph.

Finally Ted spoke. "A celebration," he said bitterly. "Look at the date. That's the day the *Hood* was sunk by the *Bismarck*."

"What are you doing here?" The deep, harsh voice boomed through the room. "Who are you?"

They whirled on the sound.

In the doorway from the front hall stood a large man in his sixties. The man in the photograph.

Janusz Keppler.

In his ham-sized fist he held the weapon of a Nazi officer. A steel-black Luger pistol.

17

EYEING the Luger in Keppler's hand, Ted took a step forward.

"Please excuse us," he apologized. "We are lost. We were trying to find someone to help us." He nodded toward the back door. "The door was open, and we thought—we do apologize, but finding our way around all these little roads and paths is an enigma which defies us all. Please forgive us."

Keppler glowered at him.

"Put your hands on your heads," he growled. "Turn around and—" He suddenly stopped. "What did you say?" he asked.

"I said that finding our way around is an enigma which defies us all," Ted repeated.

Keppler stared at him. "Enigmas—are—my specialty," he said slowly.

Ted breathed again. It was the right response. He'd been afraid the sleeper had forgotten the recognition code. It *had* been a long time. He sent a thought of appreciation to whoever it was that had decided to incorporate the word *enigma* in the code. A word Keppler was sure to recognize.

Keppler lowered his gun.

"Who are you?" he asked once more. It was somehow a different question this time.

"I am Ted. SOE."

"Took you long enough," Keppler grumbled. "How is Jeff?"

Ted grinned. "Fine. He sends his regards."

Keppler put his gun away.

"We were admiring your photograph," Ted said. "What's the story?"

For the first time a hint of a smile cracked Keppler's weather-

144

beaten face. "The best way to hide among wolves," he said, "is to wear a wolf's skin. I do, and they leave me alone."

He walked into the room. Startled, they noticed that he limped.

"Come," he said. "Sit down. We must talk." He gave a thin little smile. "Although I do not need to ask you why you have come here."

"Why not," Ted asked sharply.

"It is obvious," Keppler shrugged. "The test site at Misdroy." A mocking little smile stretched his lips. "I had expected you to come sooner."

Ted ignored the slight. "We want you to help us," he said. "We have to get onto the site."

"You do?" Keppler snorted. "Your chances of succeeding are a few notches below nil."

Kevin frowned. "There has to be a way."

"If there is, young man," Keppler said tartly, "I am not aware of it. But then, you who have just arrived here can undoubtedly tell me how," he finished sardonically.

Kevin said nothing.

"The *Tausendfüssler* test site," Keppler went on, "is impossible to penetrate. No place has ever been more closely guarded."

"*Tausendfüssler*—millipede," Kevin frowned. "A girl named Nicole kept saying that. Millipede. What does it mean?"

"It is a rumor," Keppler grunted. "It is said that those who have seen whatever it is they are testing say it looks like a giant millipede."

"But—what *is* it," Kevin asked. "What *is* it they're testing at Misdroy?"

Keppler gave him a caustic look. "You know even less than I feared," he said.

"We are here to find out," Kevin snapped.

Keppler spread his huge hands. "*Schon gut!*" he said. "Good enough!" He looked deliberately from one to the other. "It is rumored," he went on, "that it is some kind of a gun. A giant gun. A special gun. A gun with a barrel that is more than one hundred and fifty meters long."

Ted gaped at him. "That's crazy," he exclaimed. "No way. Your informants are out of their minds. No gun in the world could be built with a barrel that long. It's—it's the length of a—of a football field and half. More! That's nuts!"

145

"They'll need that," Keppler said drily, "to fire the huge projectiles they plan for a distance of more than a hundred and fifty kilometers."

"I—don't believe it!" Ted said.

Keppler shrugged. "I don't care if you do—or don't. Those are the rumors."

"If that *is* true," Kevin said, "or even partly true, from the installations being built at Mimoyecques, the Nazis could lay down a barrage of shells on the English Channel coast. On the invasion-staging areas. On London. They could destroy it all!"

"If," Ted said. "*If* it is true. And that's a damned big *if*!"

"Why is it called—Millipede?" Gaby asked.

Keppler shrugged. "They also call the thing *Lizzie. Busy Lizzie.*"

"*Lizzie*? Why?"

"I have no idea. An affectionate nickname, perhaps."

"But—why Millipede?"

"Because of the tubes," Keppler answered her. He glanced at Ted. "My—unreliable, crazy rumor mongers say that there are many pairs of iron tubes, like legs, sticking out of the barrel. They had the—nutty idea that it looked like a millipede."

"Okay, Keppler," Ted said soberly. "Without the crap. What is your honest opinion?"

Keppler took a deep breath. "What I have told you is what I have pieced together from listening to loose tongues in the *Bierstube* down in Wollin. I am retired now. Two years ago I had an accident. One of my legs no longer serves me too well. I spend much time in the Bierstube. Too much time. But—I listen. To the scuttlebutt of military men and German supervisory personnel from Misdroy. They are the only ones allowed outside the test site compound. And they talk when the beer has loosened their tongues. They brag of their importance. Although there are many foreign workers there working on the project, they are isolated and kept under guard. Very strict guard." He looked straight at Ted. "My own opinion is that there is a most dangerous kernel of truth in the rumors, but there is also exaggeration. As there is in all rumors."

"What are the—the legs or tubes for?" Kevin asked. "Stabilization?"

Keppler shrugged. "I have no idea."

146

"And that's exactly why we *must* try to infiltrate the place," Ted said. "However impossible it is." He looked at Keppler. "Will you help?"

Keppler gave him a penetrating look.

"I will help," he said. "What do you propose to do?"

"First, we must inform SOE," Ted said. "They must be told what we have learned. They may consider it important enough, a big enough threat, to mount immediate massive air strikes against both Mimoyecqes and Misdroy." He looked at Keppler. "We won't transmit from here," he said. "We must consider your house as a safe house that in no way can be compromised. I propose we go to the mainland and transmit from there." He looked at his watch. "We have close to three hours before our next scheduled monitoring period. Can you suggest some place from where we can transmit in safety?"

Keppler thought for a while. He nodded. "About a kilometer north of the village of Alt Tessin," he said, "on a little lake called Paatzinger See, there is a small, out-of-the-way power distribution substation. It is unmanned and unguarded. You will know how to tap into the power. You can easily make it there before your transmission time."

Ted nodded. He turned to Mike. "Mike, you and Gaby stay here."

Mike started to protest.

"No arguments," Ted said. It was obvious that he meant just that. "Kevin will come with me." He looked at Mike and Gaby. "Find out as much as you can about the lay of the land here. About the situation. And Misdroy. We'll return here. Let you know what Milton Hall decided."

It was a pleasant ride through the sleepy countryside to the little Paatzinger Lake, and they located the power substation without difficulty. There was no one around.

It was a matter of minutes to string up the antenna and connect the X-35 to the power source.

Ted turned on the set and put on his earphones.

He grimaced. Urgently, he manipulated the dials on the set. Finally he ripped off the headset in disgust.

"Dammit! Jammed!" he announced laconically.

"What do you mean?" Kevin asked.

"The bloody Krauts are blanketing the whole fucking area with interference, that's what I mean," Ted growled angrily. "Nothing comes in. Nothing goes out. All I get is jamming static."

"Could it be the power lines?" Kevin suggested.

"No. This is a deliberate jamming signal. There is no way we'll be able to transmit or receive from anywhere around here!"

It was dusk when Ted and Kevin returned to Keppler's house.

"I did not know," Keppler said, scowling at the floor. "I have no radio." He looked at Ted. "What will you do now?"

"I've got to get outside the jamming zone," Ted said. "I'll have to find a clear spot to transmit from. Wherever the hell that may be. It may be miles away."

"We know it's clear back by that big lake," Gaby said. "Dammscher See, wasn't it?"

Ted nodded gloomily. "I know. But if we have to go all the way back there to send our message, it'll cost us a couple of days each time we have to make contact. Impossible."

"There may be another way," Keppler said slowly. "You would lose time, but only a few hours."

"What?"

Keppler looked at them. "Let me think it through," he said. "Where are you staying?"

"Gasthof Adler."

"Go there. Come back tomorrow, and I may have a solution for you."

They decided to walk back the three kilometers to Wollin pushing their bikes so they could talk.

"Kevin," Ted said. "Go with Mike and Gaby across to the mainland. Find a haystack or something to sack out for the night. I'll stay here."

"Why?" Kevin asked, taken aback.

"Do you trust that guy Keppler?" Ted asked soberly. "Do you believe that wolf's clothing yarn of his? Or that giant gun story?"

"I—I think so," Kevin said slowly.

"Are you sure?" Ted nodded toward Mike and Gaby who walked ahead of them. "Would you gamble their lives on it?"

Kevin frowned, suddenly apprehensive.

"No," he said hesitantly. "I—I guess not."

"Well, neither would I," Ted said. "Nor yours or mine."

"And—you want to make sure of him?"

"I do. Go to the mainland. I'll keep an eye on the Gasthof. If Keppler does turn us in to the local bully boys, they'll come for us tonight."

"What about you?"

"I'll take care of myself."

Kevin gave him a sidelong glance.

"Ted," he said. "If you don't believe Keppler's story about the gun, why inform Milton Hall?"

"They have to know," Ted said grimly, "even rumors. They are the only ones in a position to evaluate information from the field. Any information. They may have other intelligence from other sources that we don't know about. Information that may corroborate or negate our report. But only they can decide."

Kevin nodded. "Makes sense."

"Now," Ted said, "remember the little church we saw in Wollin?"

"There were two of them."

"The one nearest Gasthof Adler. If all goes well tonight, I'll meet you there tomorrow at 0800."

He gave Kevin a long look.

"If I'm not there, get the hell out of here! . . ."

❖ 18 ❖

IT was a gray, overcast day when Kevin, Mike, and Gaby bicycled across the bridge to Wollin Island after having spent an uncomfortable and uneasy night in a drafty feed shack on an outlying grazing field near Laatzig on the mainland. They rode in silence, each preoccupied with his own concerns and uncertainties.

They left the bridge behind and rode through the cobblestoned steets of the town of Wollin.

"Ted said to meet him in the church nearest the Gasthof," Kevin said to Mike. "You take Gaby, go to the other church, and wait there. No use all three of us walking into a possible trap."

"Trap?" Mike said. "We're meeting Ted."

"And what if Ted was taken?" Kevin countered grimly. "Remember what Etienne told him: The Gestapo can make even the walls talk."

Mike fell silent.

They reached the place where they had to turn off for the rendezvous church. They stopped.

Mike took a long, hard look at his son. Then he turned to Gaby. "Come, Gaby," he said. "You come with me." He turned to Kevin. "We will wait for you."

Kevin parked his bike a few houses down the street from the church and walked to it. A few worshippers were entering, and he joined them.

Inside, he took up a position near a pillar to the left of the entrance. He let his eyes get used to the dim light. Under different circumstances, he would have enjoyed the colorful and ornate interior of the little church, but he had only one thought. He searched the pews for Ted.

There was no sign of him.

He glanced at his watch.

It was 0800 hours.

With increasing worry, he scrutinized the worshippers, each one in turn. Was one of them a Gestapo agent waiting to trap him? Were there more than one? Again he looked at his watch.

0801 hours.

Where was Ted?

Suddenly he felt a hand on his shoulder. Startled, he spun around.

"Easy!" Ted whispered. He looked around. "Where are Gaby and Mike?"

Kevin could feel his heart drumming in his throat. He found it difficult to speak. "At—at the other church," he breathed.

Ted gave him a searching look. Then he grinned mirthlessly. "Smart move," he said. "Let's go pick them up. Everything was quiet at the Gasthof last night. Keppler is okay. . . ."

Keppler had made a large pot of coffee, ersatz coffee.

"Tastes like hell," he complained. "But at least it is hot. I thought you might need it."

Gratefully they sipped the scalding, bitter brew.

"Okay, what's the story, Keppler?" Ted asked.

"In a hurry, aren't you?" Keppler remarked sourly. "Did you rise on the wrong side of your bed this morning?"

Ted gave him a suspicious look. What did the old coot mean? "I just want to get on with it," he snapped. "I want to contact my control as quickly as possible."

"I am a riverman," Keppler said. "My plan is of the river. We will go upstream to the Stettiner Haff. On the east side of the lagoon there is a bay, Paulsdorfer Bucht, and a place I know. It is a peaceful spot. There are no people there. It is marshland. The trip will take less than two hours."

"Are you planning to take the barge?" Kevin asked.

"No," Keppler replied. "It is too big. Too difficult to maneuver. And I do not have enough diesel fuel for more than perhaps one trip. I checked. And I can get no more."

"Then what?"

"In the boathouse I have an auxiliary. It also runs on diesel."

"What's an auxiliary?"

"It is a small motorboat. Seven meters. It was used to accompany the barge. For side trips. For supplies. Provisions. Emergencies."

"Sounds good," Ted said. "Let's take a look at it."

"If we do not find a clear spot for your transmission right away," Keppler said, "it will be easy to keep going until we do."

They all trooped out on the oil-blackened pier.

Kevin took a good look at the big barge. Up close he could see it was not in as good a shape as it had appeared from afar. Probably why it had not been pressed into service, he thought. Some of the boards in the pilot house were loose, and wide cracks were visible in the massive sides, above the waterline. The pilot house apparently had living quarters at the deck level and a small wheel house above. A narrow walk ran along both sides of the segmented hatch that stretched the length of the barge from the pilot house at the stern to a small open space in the bow, where a winch and an anchor could be seen.

Keppler opened the door to the boathouse, and they stepped inside.

There was an instant stench of diesel oil, mold, and rotted wood. The light was dim, provided only by a few small openings high above on the walls and a spiderweb of cracks in the planks.

In the gloom, a black-painted motorboat with an inboard motor could be seen tied up to the wharf. Open, it had only a small protected area over the wheel in the bow. A rat scurried along the gunwale, plopped to the floor of the wharf, and darted into the darkness.

The boathouse had apparently been built tall enough to accommodate the mast of a small sailing vessel. The slip was shaped like a horseshoe, with the inside end spacious enough to hold a small machine shop and storage space over which was constructed a half-loft reached by a rickety ladder. The legs of the horseshoe formed broad walkways along the sides of the motorboat lying in the berth, which was closed at the mouth by massive double doors that led to the waterway outside.

They looked around the eerie, somehow sinister place. The boathouse obviously also served as a storehouse. There were a few barrels, presumably diesel fuel, and a jumble of nautical equipment and machinery parts; a fractured ship's wheel and a broken screw; an old lathe, ropes and chains; a couple of blackened kerosene lamps, tackle, buckets and crates. Only the stock nearest to them could be made out, the rest—glimpsed as foreboding shadows—was lost in the gloom.

Scattered around on the walls were sturdy pointed iron hooks, some of which held nautical gear and roping, some of which were empty. Keppler took a kerosene lamp hanging from one of them near the door and lighted it with a match from a large box of kitchen matches lying on a shelf below it.

"How soon can we get underway?" Ted asked.

"At once," Keppler answered. "If you wish."

"I wish."

"Very well." Keppler motioned to a couple of grimy gunny sacks lying on the floor. "Put those on board," he ordered.

Mike and Kevin each took hold of a sack.

"Hell's bells!" Mike puffed. "Damn thing weighs a ton. What's in it? Gold bars?"

"Tools," Keppler said. "Spare parts." He glanced at Ted. "One must have a cover, *ja*? Ours is that we are on the way to a barge that has become disabled in the lagoon. To make emergency repairs." He shrugged. "It is—just in case . . ."

Despite himself, Ted was impressed with the man's thoroughness. "Got another of those sacks," he asked. "for my X-35?"

152

Keppler pointed to a stack of empty sacks. "Help yourself," he said.

"We need not all go," Ted said as he stuffed his radio into an old sack that reeked of oil. "Kevin, you come with me. Mike—"

"Yeah, I know. I stay here with Gaby."

"Wrong. You both go back to the Gasthof. Wait there. If we are picked up, they'll come looking. Here."

Mike nodded. "Got you."

"Give me a hand with the doors," Keppler requested.

He and Mike pushed open the heavy boathouse doors that led to the channel.

Outside, in the gray morning light, lay the waterway that would take them to a clear, safe spot for the vital contact with Milton Hall.

Or to a rendezvous with trouble.

The motorboat chugged noisily but steadily up the channel toward Stettiner Haff. They passed between Wollin on the island and Hagen on the mainland and headed for the stretch of the channel Keppler called *Der Tiefe Zug*—the deep channel—which flowed into the lagoon. The traffic on the waterway was steady, and they passed several large power barges riding low in the water and tugs towing strings of powerless dumb barges, like broods of giant ugly ducklings trailing diminutive mother ducks.

Keppler seemed right in his element. He would shout greetings to other barge skippers and exchange good-natured insults with them in his booming voice.

They were nearing the mouth of the channel, where it narrowed once again, when they became aware that several of the barges had laid to and were dead in the water. As they passed them in midstream with other faster craft they saw why.

Ahead of them a barrier boom had been rigged across the water, guarded by several sleek patrol boats. On the shore of the mainland an inspection station had been established, bristling with armed Waffen SS soldiers.

"*Scheissdreck nochmal!*—Shit and double shit!" Keppler swore under his breath. "That damned checkpoint was not there a couple of days ago. They must be stepping up their security all through the area." He throttled down.

"Can we turn back?" Ted asked.

Keppler shook his head. "They would become suspicious," he said. "I know how they work. They're watching for just such evasive maneuvers. Those patrol boats would be on our tail like sharks."

They watched apprehensively as each boat and each barge was boarded and thoroughly searched from stem to stern before being allowed to sail on. Keppler held his boat steady, keeping his place in line, drawing ever nearer to the barrier.

"We've got to do something!" Ted hissed urgently.

"Junge, Mach dir keinen Fleck," Keppler said calmly. "Don't wet your pants, boy."

"Well, what the hell do we do?"

"Do?" Keppler said. "We do nothing. We let them search us."

"And the X-35?"

"If you don't want them to find it," Keppler said crustily. "You had better heave it overboard."

Ted stared at the barge skipper as if the man had just asked him to cut his own throat.

In a way he had.

He grabbed the sack with the X-35. There was no way he was going to toss it into the sea, he thought fiercely, no way! The radio was his lifeline to the very reason of his being; the umbilical cord to his home base. Without it, he would be lost. None of the information, however vital, that he might dig up could be passed on. Without the radio, the very mission would be meaningless. There was no way he would jettison his X-35!

He watched bleakly as one of the swift patrol boats came speeding toward them.

Slowly, surreptitiously he swung the sack with the X-35 over the side, shielding the action from the approaching security craft with his body.

And he let it slip from his fingers to sink irretrievably to the bottom of the channel.

❈ 19 ❈

"LET'S examine our options," Kevin said grimly, "before we throw in the towel."

They were all sitting in his and Mike's room at Gasthof Adler, where he, Ted, and Keppler had gone after their disastrous sortie to the Stettiner Haff, trying to cope with the knockout blow dealt them with the loss of the X-35. They all realized that Ted had had no course of action open to him other than the one he took. But it was a calamity that all but tossed them out of the ring, and the atmosphere in the little room was one of discouragement and gloom.

"There is, of course, no way of replacing the damned thing. We can't even notify anyone that we've lost it."

"Can we rebuild it?" Mike asked. "From component parts? If we can get them?"

Ted shook his head. "Even if we could round up the kind of radio parts we'd need without arousing suspicion." He looked at Keppler. The skipper shook his head. "Even if we could," Ted continued, "the X-35 could not be reconstructed by us so we could reach Milton Hall. Or anywhere else in England for that matter."

"And this time there is no Underground, no Resistance to contact," Kevin pointed out. "This time we are on our own all the way."

"There *is* a German resistance movement," Ted said. "But it is rudimentary and would be all but impossible to get hold of without a lead. There's no way we could do it."

"How about other Allied agents?" Gaby suggested. "There must be other teams in Germany."

"No way," Ted said emphatically. "Even if by a million to one

155

chance we might locate such a team, which is totally impossible, they would not trust us. They *could* not. We might end up dead."

"We can't just give up," Kevin said stubbornly. "We've got to get the information we do have back to London."

Ted looked at him. "We will," he said. "But we will have to resort to the last-ditch Jedburgh procedure."

"What's that?"

"We will have to bring the information back ourselves. In person."

They all looked at him. "You mean back to Paris? To Etienne? And let his outfit radio it back to London?" Kevin asked.

"Exactly," Ted affirmed. "But there's only one thing. We do not have enough information." He glanced at Keppler. "No offense," he said. "But all we have is your retelling of gossip and rumors. As you said yourself. Before we can report anything definite, we will have to verify those rumors."

"But you were going to radio it to them," Gaby said.

"Yes. Apprising them of the rumors. With the understanding that we were here, ready to verify them. As it is now, we will have to obtain such verification before we leave. And that means, we have to find a way to get onto the test site itself and eyeball the damned millipede."

"How the hell do we do that," Mike protested. "Keppler said that would also be impossible."

"Maybe there is a way," Ted said. He looked at the barge skipper. "What would we need to be able to infiltrate the Misdroy test site?" he asked.

"Proper identification papers," Keppler answered laconically.

"Can they be forged?"

Keppler shook his head. "Not by me. I have no such abilities. Nor is there anywhere else you could possibly turn for such forgeries."

"Then we will have to get hold of the real thing," Kevin said resolutely.

"Kevin's right," Ted said. He looked at Keppler. "If we could get hold of some ID papers that belonged to—to a couple of those privileged German workers you told us about, would they get us into the place?"

"Probably," Keppler nodded. "If you fit the descriptions on them well enough."

156

"Then that's what we'll have to do," Ted said. "Get the papers off a couple of Germans."

"But won't that be dangerous?" Gaby asked, concerned. "If you steal their papers, wouldn't they report it right away? And you'd be caught when you tried to use them."

"We won't steal them," Ted said grimly.

"Then how—?" Gaby suddenly stopped. Her eyes widened. "Oh!" she whispered. "You mean—" She bit her lip. "You would—you would—"

"Look, Gaby," Ted said harshly, "let's get one thing straight once and for all, dammit! When you insisted on going on this mission, you took on all the risks, all the responsibilities, and all the brutalities apt to occur in the execution of it. You are fighting a war. A much more personal war than if you were in the armed forces. And killing the enemy is part of war. There is no damned difference in killing unseen and unknown enemies from a bomber a few thousand feet in the air and killing an enemy face to face down here on the ground. Except you can be more selective—and it's a hell of a lot harder on you. The sooner you get that into your head, the better. You are part of it, dammit! And you will be expected to act accordingly. Is that clear?"

For a moment Gaby stared at the Jedburgh agent, her eyes dark.

"You are right," she whispered. "I *am*—part of it. And I *will* do my part."

Ted turned to Keppler. "Any suggestions?" he asked. "Where can we best get hold of the necessary papers?"

Keppler thought for a while. Then he looked up at Ted. "I would suggest the movie house, Jeff," he said. He stopped. Hell, he was five years in the past. With the Enigma business. With that other agent—Jeff. He hadn't realized how thoroughly he was getting caught up in the whole affair after so long. He marveled, "Ted," he said.

"The movie house?" Kevin asked.

"It is called *KINO*," Keppler said. "It is the only one in Wollin. They play films five nights a week."

"Why the movie theater?"

"The Germans from Misdroy often come down for the show," Keppler explained. "They have little else to do for relaxation. Most of them go back on a truck right after the film is over, but some of them come on their bicycles—it is only fifteen kilometers, less

157

than an hour's ride—and they stay for a few beers at the Bierstube before they bicycle back." He looked at Ted. "If you wait on the road to Misdroy," he said, "you can pick out a couple of likely subjects—and get your papers."

Ted nodded. "Sold," he said. "Is there a performance tonight?"

"There is."

"Good. Here's what we'll do."

He outlined his plan for them. He turned to Keppler.

"Where would be the best spot," he asked.

Keppler frowned; then he brightened. "Two kilometers out of Wollin," he said. "Just past Plötzin. The old Tiemann farm."

"Why there?" Kevin asked.

Keppler eyed him. "Because of Tiemann's Folly," he said drily.

"And what the hell is Tiemann's Folly?" Mike asked.

Keppler told him.

Mike and Ted parked their bikes in a rack outside the KINO motion picture theater. As did the other patrons, they removed their carbide headlights and took them along as they entered the theater.

A ten-year-old film called *"Hans Westmar—Einer Von Vielen"*—"Hans Westmar—One of Many," was playing, with Emil Lohkamp in the title role, and the character actor Paul Wegener as a Bolshevik leader. Mike had groaned when he'd found out what was playing. He'd seen the film in Paris. He'd been curious to see what kind of films the Nazis fed to their people. He'd found out. A piece of Nazi propaganda shit, he'd thought. It was the story of an SA man, aimed at glorifying the Nazi movement. It's theme—"one of many"—was taken from a legend about the Führer's hero, Frederick the Great of Prussia. This legend told that a friend of the King's named Wedel had fallen in battle, and as the King rode among the dead and wounded lying on the battlefield calling his friend's name, one of the fallen soldiers raised himself on his elbow and cried to the King: "Wedel, Your Majesty? Here lie nothing but Wedels!" The propaganda had been so thick, he'd nearly thrown up. And now he had to sit through it again. This damned mission was getting almost too much to take, he grumbled to himself.

After the show, he and Ted mounted their bicycles and rode out of Wollin toward Plötzin and the Tiemann farm, the beams

---

158

from their carbide lamps shining thin lances of light through the darkness.

A few minutes out of town where the road ran through the deserted countryside, they stopped and pushed their bikes off the roadway into the shadows. Ahead of them they could make out a hill on the right side of the road. Below it, according to Keppler's instructions, was the old Tiemann farm.

For a while they lay waiting in silence, hidden from the road, letting their eyes get used to the dark. Ted felt curiously naked. He realized it was because he was without his gun. No guns, Keppler had suggested. Knives. And he had supplied them with two needle-pointed hunting knives.

They let a few groups of three or four bikers go by and a couple of men too old to be impersonated by anyone of the Grand Guignol team.

Finally a pair of bikers came pedalling down the road. They had obviously had a good time at the Bierstube and were laughing and joking in beer-slurred voices. Mike looked at Ted. He nodded. We could take them right here, Mike thought. Right now. But he would follow Ted's scenario. This time.

They let the two Germans pass them, then quickly pushed their bikes back up on the road. They turned on their headlights, shining them down the road after the two bikers and toward the Tiemann farm.

By holding their hands briefly in front of the lamps, they caused the lights to go on and off a few times before they mounted the bicycles and quickly pedalled after the two Germans.

They had almost caught up with them when ahead of them, at the roadside on their right, they saw a girl kneeling at her bicycle which stood upside down on the handlebars. It was Gaby.

The two Germans stopped. They left their bikes lying on the road and walked up to Gaby.

"Trouble, trouble, *kleines Fräulein?*" one of them grinned at her. "Help has arrived. You can put your trust in Max!" He all but leered at her.

"The chain came off," Gaby complained in a small voice. She looked frightened—and it wasn't all acting. "I—I cannot get it back on."

Ted and Mike came riding up. They stopped and dismounted.

159

"What's going on?" Ted asked as he and Mike walked up to the group. "Need any help?"

"Mench!" said one of the Germans unpleasantly. "Don't give us any of your *Berliner Schnauze*—your Berliner lip. Piss off! Max and I can handle this one."

He turned his back on them.

Suddenly Ted's hunting knife was in his hand. In the same instant, his left arm shot around the German's neck in a choking grip from behind. His right arm, holding the knife, swung back, and he jabbed the blade into the man's kidney. At once he ripped it out again and once more stabbed it into the body, sagging in his grip. The man died without a sound, still clutched in Ted's grasp. It was a textbook kill.

Mike had acted the instant he saw Ted attack. But the other German, Max, had a split-second's warning.

It was enough.

Even as Mike grabbed for him, he spun away. Mike stabbed out at him, but the knife blade was deflected by the man's belt and twisted from Mike's hand. With a bellow of rage, the German turned, snatched the knife from the ground, and charged toward Mike.

Gaby, who had followed the attack in shocked silence, suddenly exploded into action. She grabbed her bike and with all her might, she hurled it at the charging German, hitting him in the back of the knees. He toppled backward, entangling himself in the bike.

At once Ted, free of the dead man, leaped at him. With an upward motion, he thrust his knife into the man's abdomen, twisting it fiercely, slicing his life from him.

It was over.

Ashen-faced, Gaby gazed at the dead Germans. Mike watched her solicitously. He had seen that look before. Many times. At Chateau-Thierry. At the Marne. Death, he thought, death is different when read on the faces of the young.

Gaby turned away. She doubled over and vomited.

Mike stared at the dead Germans. "I wonder if one of them is named Wedel," he said. But his voice broke. Ted had been right, he thought bleakly. Always attack from the back if you can. They'd never have been able to take the two Germans if they'd tried it any other way. But—it did make him feel oddly ashamed.

Kevin and Keppler came scrambling across the ditch from the field.

"Get them off the road!" Keppler grunted. "Into the field behind those bushes. Quickly. Before anyone comes."

The four men hurriedly carried the bodies into the dark field while Gaby pushed the bikes after them, one by one.

Ted and Kevin ran back to the road.

"Look for any spots of blood," Ted hissed. "Cover them with dirt. Scuff it into the roadway with your shoes."

There was surprisingly little evidence of the sudden carnage, and Ted and Kevin quickly rejoined the others.

"Where's that Tiemann's Folly of yours?" Ted asked urgently.

Keppler nodded. "Over there," he said. "About fifty meters."

Each pair of men picked up a body. They half ran to the spot pointed out by Keppler. It was marked by a pile of rocks and a few pieces of rotted lumber.

"It is right here," Keppler said. "We will have to look for it."

They spread out and started to search the ground.

"Over here!" Kevin called.

At once they joined him.

He was already on his knees, loosening some dirt-covered, overgrown planks in the ground. They joined him. And soon a Stygian-black hole gaped in the ground.

Tiemann's Folly.

Keppler had told them why the islanders had named it that. Tiemann was a farmer who'd used the field for grazing his cows. Although water was available from a lake less than half a kilometer away, Tiemann had stubbornly insisted on digging a well on the field so he would not have to haul drinking water to his cattle. Against all advice, he had done so. Of course, the water he discovered was so brackish that the animals would have none of it.

"Empty their pockets," Ted ordered harshly. "Take everything they have. And every stitch of clothing. We'll need it. Everything."

Hastily they did.

One by one, the stripped bodies, glowing oddly white in the dark, were thrown down into the abandoned well. Their bicycles followed them.

The planks were carefully replaced, all traces of their having been moved covered up.

The assailants stood back. Curiously spent, they did not look at one another. Finally Ted spoke. He held up one of the identification cards.

"We're in business," he said, his voice subdued. "Tomorrow. Tomorrow first thing we try these things out. . . ."

❧ 20 ❧

"**Y**OU can't just write them off!" Colonel Baldon glared at Brigadier James Hindsmith Parnell. "Give them a chance!"

The brigadier contemplated the U. S. Army officer soberly. The Special Forces command group was gathered in his office. They were all there. The Jedburgh team Grand Guignol control, Major Howard Roberts, and the officer representatives from the British armed forces, Lieutenant Colonel Clifton Hillsbotham Ramsey; the Free French Forces, Lieutenant Colonel Jean-Pierre Lamont; and Colonel Dirk A. Baldon of the United States Army.

"Colonel," Parnell finally said. "It has been three days without any sign of life whatsoever from Jed Team Grand Guignol. Three days with no contact at all." He looked at Major Roberts. "That is correct, Howard?"

Roberts nodded gravely. "Yes, sir, it is."

"We must assume that their mission is blown," Parnell continued. "That the team is either in the hands of the Gestapo or dead. We have no other option."

"After all, Dirk," Lieutenant Colonel Ramsey said. "The team was hardly—eh—professional. Untrained actors, as I remember. Hardly inconceivable that they should have been caught, what?"

"There was a trained Jed agent in charge," Baldon retorted testily.

"Whom I recall you characterized as—eh—inconsistent," Ramsey remarked.

"Inconsistent, not incompetent!" Dirk shot back.

Ramsey shrugged. "Even competent agents get caught."

Dirk ignored him. He turned to the brigadier. "Why not give

them another couple of days?" he tried again. "At least another twenty-four hours. Why not keep up the monitoring that long at any rate?"

The brigadier looked at Major Roberts. "Howard?"

"We need all the operators available to us to monitor active teams," Roberts said. "We are short-handed as it is on experienced people. We are expanding operations very rapidly right now. Some of our operators handle up to three teams. They are overworked already. It is—it is all in anticipation of the invasion. We cannot tie up an operator on an inactive operation. And Grand Guignol must by now be considered inactive. Sorry."

"Twenty-four hours, for crissake!" Dirk exclaimed acrimoniously.

Roberts kept silent.

"Suppose they *have* run into trouble," Dirk persisted. "But suppose they *do* resume transmitting. They'd just be sending into dead air. Taking all the risks of transmitting clandestinely in enemy territory for nothing. Perhaps being tracked down and captured. Or killed. Because *we* wrote them off too damned soon!"

"Sir," Colonel Lamont said to the brigadier. "Could we perhaps not keep the monitoring in effect for twenty-four hours? It is not too long."

For a moment Parnell studied the officers. He made up his mind. It could do no harm. They would learn of it in a few days anyway.

"Gentlemen," he said soberly. "What I am about to tell you is classified top secret. It will not be discussed with anyone, even among yourselves, outside of this room."

Gravely the men nodded.

"The date for the invasion of France, to be designated D-Day, has been decided," he said. "It will be announced to the General Staff by General Eisenhower in one week. The date is June the fifth."

They all stared at him.

"That's—that's in less than four weeks!" Ramsey exclaimed.

"As you can see," Parnell continued, "there is no margin for delays. Every mission in every field of the operations of the Special Forces must be used to the fullest." He looked soberly at the officers. "Everything we can do to ensure the successful execution of the invasion must be done."

"So much more important to find out about those damned

installations at Mimoyecques," Dirk said. "They *may* be a threat to the whole operation. In spades. So much more reason for keeping Grand Guignol alive!"

Parnell nodded. "I agree with you, Baldon, that Mimoyecques is of greater importance than ever. But the answers we seek will not come through Grand Guignol." He turned to Major Roberts. "Howard, what is the status of the new team? Ditto, is it?" Roberts nodded. "How soon can Ditto be sent into the field, to Mimoyecques?" Parnell asked.

"The team is ready now, sir," Roberts said. "It can be dropped tonight. As soon as the order is given."

Parnell turned to Colonel Lamont. "Colonel," he said. "Has the French Resistance organized a reception committee?"

"Yes, sir," Lamont replied. "However, the DZ will be a considerable distance from the target."

"Why?"

"Sir, the whole Fifteenth German Army is still occupying the area around Mimoyecques. A successful drop near the installations could not possibly be made."

Parnell nodded slowly. "I see." He turned to Dirk. He did not relish what he had to do. "I regret, Colonel," he said. "But I have no choice but to declare Jed Team Grand Guignol aborted." He turned to Roberts.

"Order Ditto to be deployed tonight. . . ."

The line moved slowly. There were still about twenty workers ahead of them.

Mike shuffled uneasily. He felt keyed-up as never before. Even the paralyzing stage fright he'd suffered on opening night of his debut performance had been a soothing exercise in tranquility in comparision with the heart-clutching apprehension that held him by the throat.

In a few minutes . . .

He was acutely aware of Ted standing directly behind him. But neither man acknowledged the other.

It had been quite simple, really. There had been no question. The two sets of papers had determined the outcome. Mike could pass for one of the slain Germans; Ted for the other. And that was that.

And now, in the raw elements of an early overcast morning in May, it would be determined how well.

He moved a few steps forward and huddled against the cold breeze that gusted in from the sea. He wondered why it took so long to pass the checkpoint into the first of the two high-security areas. With their German identification papers, they'd had no trouble passing through the first of the three double barbed-wire fences into the nonsensitive outer service area, entering by the outer main gate, where the guards had given their papers only a cursory glance. With the other workers, they'd walked onto the site only to find themselves being herded into line before the second gate.

He shivered. Not from the cold alone. His flesh crawled with the constant thought that he was wearing a dead man's clothing. A man he had helped kill. He had the unreasonable dread that the clothing would tighten up on him and strangle him. And the jagged hole in the front of the shirt, hastily mended by Gaby's shaking hands and now rubbing against his skin, felt like a burning stigmata.

He had an overwhelming impulse to break out of the line and run. He hated standing in line. He knew why. It always brought him back. Back to July 17, 1918 at the Marne. A date he would never forget. His outfit had been brought up to the front to help stem the German tide that was hammering at the Allied positions in Ludendorf's final offensive of the war, his *Friedensturm*—his Peace Drive. He'd been standing in line then, too, at a field kitchen brought up to the front with hot food for the troops. He'd held his mess kit in his left hand while he scratched at a persistent louse on his chest. There had been a sudden, skull-crushing explosion as a German artillery barrage found their position. He had felt nothing, but when he looked for his mess kit, it was gone. And so was part of his arm. He would never forget the sight of the blood spurting from the ragged stump in rhythmic little jets. Ludendorf's Peace Drive had been turned into a rout; Germany had lost the war, and he, Michael Alistair Lavette, had lost an arm—standing in line.

He started as he felt a rough push from behind and heard Ted's voice grumble loudly: "Wake up, you dumb bastard! You're holding up the parade!"

Quickly he took the couple of steps forward that he'd fallen behind. The line was moving.

Exactly as that other line.

He craned his neck to get a good look at the checkpoint to see what the delay was. The gate stood at the apex of a gentle rise. On the left was a wooden guard tower, and on the right, outside the barbed-wire fence, stood a small shack. A troop carrier was parked next to it only a few feet from the men waiting in line. At the gate, half a dozen Waffen SS guards were posted, all carrying Schmeisser submachine guns, and at the gatehouse stood a couple of noncoms.

Mike watched as the next man in line came up to the gate. The worker handed his identification papers to one of the noncoms, who studied it briefly. He, in turn, gave it to the second noncom, who glanced at it, entered the gatehouse, and quickly returned with something in his hand.

Mike felt a chill course through him as he saw the noncom look closely at the worker—and then at what he held in his hand.

It was a photograph.

Each man in line, Mike realized with despair, was carefully being compared to a photograph from a records file. Another security step-up Keppler had not known about.

A step-up that could cost them their lives.

Mike felt stricken. There was no way he and Ted could pull it off now. Within minutes, they would be unmasked.

With a conscious effort, he tried to calm the maelstrom of thoughts that whirled in his mind. He *had* to think clearly. They could not afford to be inspected and compared to photographs at the gate. They had to get out of the line. Leave the compound.

But with a sinking feeling, he knew that, too, would be impossible. It would be a most curious, a most unorthodox thing to do. They would at once become the objects of suspicion and be stopped. And any close scrutiny of their papers could come to only one conclusion.

Discovery. And . . .

He refused to complete the thought. Instead, he mulishly attacked the problem: They could not go on, and they could not go back.

What then? What?

A thought tried to struggle up into his conscious mind. What was it? Dammit! What was it? The theater. The Grand Guignol. A play. A scene in a play at the Grand Guignol. What?

He strained to conjure it up. It would not come.

He stopped.

He knew it wouldn't work. Not that way. He could not force

it. He'd have to let it come gradually. By itself. Without thinking about it. He prayed it would happen in time.

He willed himself to drive it from his mind. He deliberately thought back on that other time he'd stood in line. It was something that came easily to his mind. He visualized the line at the field kitchen; the muddy ground; the itch of the dirty uniform; the smell of the hot food; the shattering explosion; his missing mess kit; and his arm; his—

He suddenly stiffened. His mind was flooded with it. The play. The scene. Nothing at all like the present situation. And yet— he had the answer!

He turned to Ted standing behind him.

"Gotta smoke?" he asked. Ted would be alerted. He knew Mike did not smoke. Mike pulled his collar up around his ears. "Cold enough in this breeze to turn your balls into ice cubes," he grumbled. He leaned toward Ted.

"Photographs!" he whispered. "They compare each man with a photograph."

"Shit!" Ted hissed. "Sure," he said aloud. "Hold on."

He started to fish a pack of cigarettes from his pocket.

"Thanks, *Kamerad*," Mike said aloud. In a whisper he went on. "I have a plan. Follow my lead. Help me. Remember, help me!" He turned away.

"You owe me one," Ted said aloud. He handed Mike a box of matches.

Mike took it. Cupping his hands around the cigarette, he tried to light it. The match went out. He tried again. Again the match blew out.

"Screw this wind," he cursed. He turned to Ted. "Hold my place," he said.

He walked toward the parked troop carrier. He stopped in the lee of the open cab, huddling over his cigarette, his back to the men in line.

Slowly, surreptitiously, his movements hidden, he reached into the cab. He pushed the gear shift to neutral and released the hand brake. Quickly, he lit his cigarette and, puffing, turned to go back in line.

Gradually, at first nearly imperceptibly, the little truck began to roll down the incline.

Mike suddenly noticed the moving vehicle gathering speed, rolling down the incline.

"Hey!" he shouted.

He ran back to the moving truck and trotted alongside it. With his left arm, he reached in to grab the brake in an apparent attempt to stop the car. He slipped. His left arm was caught, and as he fell, there was an audible snap. He screamed as he was being dragged along.

Ted raced to him. By the time some of the other workers had brought the truck to a stop, he'd lifted Mike from the ground and freed his arm.

It hung at an awkward angle for all to see.

Carefully, pain distorting his face and darkening his eyes, Mike gathered his broken arm and cradled it to him.

"I'll help you," Ted said. "Get you to the hospital."

A couple of SS soldiers came running up.

"*Was ist los?*—What's going on?" one of them called gruffly.

"Fellow broke his arm," one of the workers shouted at him.

"He was trying to stop your damned truck," another called.

"Why don't you teach your drivers to set the brake properly?" a third taunted.

"I'll take him down to the hospital," Ted said. He took hold of Mike's elbow. "Easy," he said solicitously. "Can you make it?"

Bravely, Mike nodded.

They started to walk away.

A Volkswagen came driving up. It stopped at Ted and Mike. An SS officer sprang out.

"What's going on here?" he barked.

"*Zu Befehl, Herr Untersturmführer*—at your orders, Lieutenant," Ted said smartly, coming to attention. "This man broke his arm trying to stop a runaway truck. I am taking him to the hospital."

"In the car," the officer ordered. "*Los!*"

"Sir, we can walk. We—"

"In the car!" the SS *Untersturmführer* snapped. "*Sofort!*—At once!"

Without a word, Ted bundled Mike into the Volkswagen. As Mike sat down, he moaned softly. Ted tried to support him. The officer got into the car.

The base hospital was located near the workers' housing bordering on the sea in the service area of the site, inside the fence. The Volkswagen came to a stop at the main entrance. The officer turned to his driver.

"Go with them, Schultz," he said. "See that this man is taken care of."

"*Jawohl, Herr Untersturmführer*," the driver said.

And he followed Ted and Mike as they entered the hospital.

Several people were going about their business in the large reception lounge of the hospital. Ted, Mike, and the driver, stepped inside. Schultz walked up to an ample-bosomed, stern-looking nurse. He spoke briefly to her.

She looked toward Ted and Mike and began to stride purposefully toward them.

Ted glanced at Mike.

We've had it, he thought bleakly. Mike may be a damned good actor. But *that* good he's not.

Dismayed, he watched the forbidding nurse bearing down on them.

❈ 21 ❈

THE Draconian nurse swept up to Ted and Mike, followed by Schultz, the driver. She glanced curtly at Mike's arm, held close to him, the hand tucked into his jacket Napoleon style. She turned to the driver.

"That is all," she said imperiously. "You may go."

Schultz left.

The nurse swung her full-blown chest back toward Ted and Mike.

"Well?" she snapped. "What is wrong?"

"*Bitte, Schwester*," Ted said. "Please, nurse. My friend has broken his arm." He stopped. What the hell else could he say? In a minute it'd be all over.

The nurse gave him a withering look. "I presume your friend can speak for himself!" She bit off the words as if they had been dipped in vinegar.

She reached out for Mike's arm, touching it lightly.

Mike drew back sharply.

"*Auw-wa! Leck mi kreuzweis!*" he exclaimed in his thick Bavarian dialect. "Ouch! Kiss my butt! It hurts!"

The nurse looked at him, startled.

"You are not an *Ausländer*—a foreigner?" she asked. "You are German?" There was some doubt in her voice.

"*Aus Bayern, liawa Schneck*—from Bavaria, my dear lass," Mike acknowledged expansively, his dialect thicker than ever. "From Tegernsee near Munich."

"Let me see your papers," the nurse demanded brusquely.

Mike grinned disarmingly at her. "*Sei net granti, Schwesterle*—don't be nettled, little nursie," he said good-naturedly. With his good hand he fished the stolen identification papers from his pocket. He handed them to the woman. She studied them.

"It says here your home town is Hamburg," she rasped suspiciously. "Hardly Bavarian."

Mike nodded vigorously. "Five years going on six I have lived in Hamburg, *Liebchen*. Working in the shipyards. That is why I have lost my Bavarian accent," he crowed proudly.

A hint of a disdainful smile stretched the woman's face. "We will take a look at your arm," she said.

"*Prima!*—Fine!" Mike beamed. "The quicker I can get out of here, the better I will like it." He winked broadly at the well-endowed nurse. "Not that *you* are the cause of that, *Schatzie*. But I am not one for using a *Potschamperl*—a night potty—for too long!"

"Wait here," the nurse said crustily. "I will send an orderly to take you to an emergency room." She looked pointedly at Mike. "A *doctor* will have a look at you."

Without waiting for any comment, she turned on her heel and sailed off, to disappear down a corridor.

Ted and Mike waited only until she was out of sight before they walked rapidly to the exit.

Mike filed down the last rough edge on his repaired prosthesis. Luckily, only the arm itself had sustained damage; the hand, which was the most intricate part, had escaped the break unscathed. The arm was as good as new, leaving the other spare prosthesis untouched for an emergency.

It was Thursday, May eleventh, two days after the nearly disastrous attempt to infiltrate the Misdroy test site, and they were all gathered in the living room in Keppler's house. It had taken Mike longer than he'd anticipated to repair his prosthesis, using tools and materials borrowed from Keppler. But that was just as well. It had given them all a chance to take stock of their situation and try to come up with a feasible plan of action.

They had proposed and rejected several ploys, which upon discussion and examination had proven unworkable. Infiltrating the site by stealth was patently impossible. The fact remained that in order for any of them to be able to get into the high-security sectors of the test site and take a look at the *Tausendfüssler* itself, their photographs and cover names had to be on file with the security forces.

And that, too, seemed impossible to achieve.

They had discussed the possibility of making contact with someone already on the inside who might be sympathetic to their cause. But that personnel was almost exclusively German, and the odds that such a person would exist were infinitessimal. Finding him, even more miniscule. And winning him over, nonexistent. Keppler had dismissed the idea out of hand. They'd have a better chance of taking the damned place by storm, he'd observed.

Mike blew the file dust off his prosthesis. He stroked it with his good hand. It was smooth. The only damned thing in this stinking job that was, he thought glumly. He looked up at the others.

"Let's face it," he said disconsolately. "What it boils down to is this. One of *us* must get in there and somehow place the photos in the files." He gave the prosthesis a little slap of frustration. "In other words," he went on bitterly, "we've got to *be* there before we can *get* there! And how the hell do we do that?"

Ted stared at him. It did seem impossible. Dammit!—it was. And he, the supposed Jedburgh expert, had not the slightest hint of an answer to the problem. And he couldn't blame their failure on the fact that his teammates were untrained amateurs. He had to admit, however reluctantly, that they'd shown a helluva lot of imagination and plain good old guts.

171

He looked from one to the other of them, sitting in silence, their faces tired and dispirited.

Jed Team Grand Guignol had come to a dead end.

With growing apprehension, *Brigadeführer* Dieter Haupt reread the report that was lying on his desk before him. Perturbed, he frowned in thought at the papers. Then he stabbed a finger at an intercom button.

"*Zu Befehl, Herr Brigadeführer!*" It was the voice of his aide.

"Stolitz," Haupt said. "Come in here and bring your map case."

"Any particular area, *Herr Brigadeführer?*"

"Misdroy and environs."

"*Jawohl, Herr Brigadeführer. Sofort*—at once!"

Haupt returned his attention to the report. What he read obviously disturbed him.

The door opened and *Obersturmführer* Stefan Stolitz entered. Under his arm he carried a large black leather map case. Haupt motioned him over.

"Sit."

Stolitz sat down on one of the chairs before the *Brigadeführer*'s desk. He looked at his commanding officer. The *Brigadeführer* looks worried, he thought. He wondered what was up. He placed the map case on the floor at his feet, leaning it against the chair legs.

"I have received a report that is of some concern," Haupt began. "It pertains to security."

"We have increased all security factors according to your orders, *Herr Brigadeführer*," Stolitz said.

Haupt nodded. "I am aware of that. It is another matter." He picked up the document from his desk. "The report is from Mimoyecques," he said. "It seems they captured a team of enemy saboteurs in the area."

"At Mimoyecques?" Stolitz was startled.

"They were not near the installation," Haupt said. "But that was their target. They were apprehended in the village of Marquise, in what they assumed to be a safe house. It had been under surveillance by us."

"How can they be sure it was Mimoyecques that was the target, *Herr Brigadeführer?*" Stolitz asked. "The Fifteenth Army HQ is in that area. Could that not have been their objective? Or if an

172

Allied invasion is being planned, it probably will come in the Calais area. Could they not have been there to—to prepare? With the French?"

"They could," Haupt said drily. "But they were not."

Stolitz frowned at him, but he kept silent.

"One of the captured agents was—persuaded to talk," Haupt went on. "He confirmed that the target of the team, which was dropped in by parachute, was the installations at Mimoyecques. And he revealed that the code name of the sabotage team was Ditto. Ditto. Not very heroic." He nodded soberly. "They are zeroing in on Lizzie, Stolitz. There is no doubt about that. The batteries at Mimoyecques are close to being at the operational stage. We can afford no interference now. It is only a matter of days. As soon as we have completed our final test here and are able to give them the definitive calculations for the *Seitenkammertreibladungzündungen*—the firing sequence of the booster barrel charges—they will be ready."

"What exactly was the mission of the enemy agents?" Stolitz asked. "Gathering intelligence? Or sabotage?"

Dieter spread his hands. "Unfortunately, we shall never know," he said. "The man died before the—the interrogation could be finished."

"Bunglers," Stolitz said contemptuously. "Obviously they did not know their craft."

"Obviously not," Dieter agreed. "But what disturbs me, Stolitz, is something else that the agent did reveal."

Stolitz raised an eyebrow. "Yes, *Herr Bridageführer*?"

"The man let slip that London also knows about Misdroy. About us. And that we have a *Tausendfüssler* here. Although they have no idea what it is!"

"How much do they know?"

Dieter shrugged. "A dead man could not tell them." He sat up straight. "However," he said determinedly, "we now have no choice but to assume that the enemy will target us as well. May, in fact, already have done so. The test site here undoubtedly is or will be an objective for intelligence gathering—or sabotage. Or both. And we must guard against it."

"Of course, Herr *Brigadeführer*," Stolitz snapped to. "What are the *Herr Brigadeführer*'s orders?"

"First, I shall want all approaches to the test site itself further

---

173

reinforced. Secondly, I want security teams to check all unusual incidents occurring in the area." He pointed to the map case at Stolitz's feet. "Let me take a look at a map. All of Pommern."

Stolitz picked up the case and opened it. He selected a map and spread it out on the general's desk.

Haupt studied it.

"I want you to draw a line with a radius of seventy-five kilometers from Misdroy," he ordered. "That will take in the towns of Anklam to the west, Stettin to the south, and Kolberg to the east. I want detailed reports of all, and I stress *all*, unusual incidents that have happened within that area during the last two weeks, as well as all current incidents. I want reports from all law enforcement organizations, all party leaders, down to every *Ortsbauernführer*—village leader—and every other organization that keeps records. Forest and game wardens; fire brigades; youth camps. Everyone. However insignificant the incidents may seem to them. *I*, and I alone, will be the judge of their significance. Understood?"

"*Jawohl, Herr Brigadeführer.*"

"I want those reports daily until further orders."

"*Jawohl.*"

Haupt pushed the map toward his aide.

"That is all," he said. "Get on it at once!"

"We have no choice," Ted said, a tone of finality in his voice. "We will have to go back without any concrete information."

Dusk was seeping in through the windows in Keppler's house. The barge skipper rose, closed the curtains, and turned on the light. All day he and the Jed team members had been searching for a solution to the problem of how to obtain verification of the Tausendfüssler rumors.

But no solution had presented itself.

"I suggest we split up," Ted continued resignedly. "Mike will go with me. Kevin and Gaby, you go together. The ones who reach Paris first will have Etienne contact London with the little information we do have." He looked in turn at each of his teammates. None of them spoke.

"Kevin," he said, "you've hardly opened your mouth all day. Do you agree?"

Slowly Kevin nodded. "Yes," he said hesitantly. "Unless . . ." He let the sentence die.

"Unless what?"

"I—I have an idea," Kevin said, as if groping for the right words. "I've been thinking on it. A—a plan, if you wish. I haven't quite figured out all the details yet." He looked at the Jed agent. "We may not be super-spies, Ted, but there is one thing we can do and do well."

"What?"

"Act."

"Act? As on the stage?"

Kevin nodded. "Playing a part. I've been thinking of a scheme that might work," he went on. "It is risky. It is audacious. And it will place each one of us in greater danger than ever before. We will all have to agree to carry it out before we implement it." He grinned ruefully at Ted. "And, Ted, it will require acting, so for once *you* will be the amateur."

"What is it?"

"First, a couple of questions," Kevin parried. "A lot will depend on the answers." He turned to Keppler. "Jan," he said, "do you know who is the commandant at Misdroy? The top brass?"

Keppler nodded. "It is an SS officer named Haupt," he said. "Everyone around here knows that. Dieter Haupt. He was just promoted to general a few days ago. He is now *Brigadeführer* Haupt."

"And do you know anything about him?" Kevin asked. "Is he always at Misdroy? Does he travel? Come to Wollin? Anything?"

Keppler pursed his lips. "I have, of course, snooped around a bit," he said. "Old habits are hard to break. And Haupt *is* the local celebrity." He looked at Kevin. "The general does leave Misdroy at times. I presume he goes to that place near Calais you told me about."

"What about local trips?"

"He has never been to the movie house," Keppler said. "Nor the Bierstube." He grinned. "But he does get his—relaxation."

"How?"

"Every Saturday just before dusk he drives to Stettin," Keppler told him. "Some of the German supervisors have had their fun with it. Haupt goes there to spend the night in an officers' brothel. A whorehouse."

"Saturday. That's two days from today."

Keppler nodded.

"How is he guarded?"

175

"Guarded?" Keppler snorted. "This is Germany, young man, not an occupied country. There is no need for guards on the roads here. All he has is his driver."

"Good," Kevin said, obviously satisfied. "That should do it."

"What do you have in mind?" Ted asked. "What are you after?"

"Yeah, what the hell is your plan?" Mike joined in.

"It's a little bit like the scenario for a Grand Guignol one-acter," Kevin said. He looked around.

"It goes like this . . ."

Kevin looked down at her as she lay sleeping in the bed, the thick featherbed thrown off, exposing a naked shoulder and breast. For a while he just watched her and listened to her regular breathing.

It was perhaps their last night. Tomorrow was Saturday. Tomorrow they would carry out his plan. With all its risks. Gaby had listened to him, her eyes never leaving him, as he carefully outlined his plot. She had at once agreed to go through with it, although hers was perhaps the most dangerous role. He was proud of her. And he loved her.

He bent down over her. He let the scent of her hair, spilled out over the pillow, caress his nostrils. Softly he kissed the fragile lids that lay closed over her eyes.

She stirred.

She opened her eyes and looked up into his. Her arms unfolded themselves from beneath the featherbed like delicate butterfly wings from a protecting cocoon. She pushed the heavy cover aside and lay warm and naked beside it. She reached up and ran her fingers through the hair on his chest, gently raking her nails across his skin.

He felt the desire, the love for her, swell in him. He let his hand glide softly across her breasts, thrust up toward him, and felt the darker nipples harden and distend. He kissed them. First one, then the other. And gently he lowered his body over hers, feeling it yielding and open to receive him. He buried his face in the silken, sleep-fragrant nape of her neck.

"Gaby," he whispered. "Gaby . . ."

He felt her stir with anticipation. And he entered her.

He raised his head to gaze into her face, his eyes meeting hers. And he moved. Moved in a slow, deliberate rhythm, like a gentle

176

surf caressing the warm, moist smoothness of a sandy beach, feeling his love for her well up in him.

His eyes never left hers; hers not his. The world existed only in the now of their love.

He felt the irresistible wave of passion gather in him. He saw Gaby's eyes widen and grow to fill his whole awareness, drawing him into their tender depths, and he felt himself plummeting down into her ardor. Her lips parted and her back arched as the gentle surf of his movement suddenly crashed to a crescendo of waves rushing to unite with her impassioned moment of fulfillment.

Together, resting in the glow of afterlove, they lay on the bed in the little room at Gasthof Adler, suddenly transformed into a place of wonder.

Was it worth it? Kevin pondered. Was it all worth perhaps never again to feel this way with Gaby?

Desperately he wanted to say *no*!

But he could not.

❖ 22 ❖

BRIGADEFÜHRER Dieter Haupt squinted at the big red sun setting over the calm waters of the Baltic Sea. It had been a bastard of a day full of minor annoying mishaps, and he had the beginnings of a headache.

Those calm waters should have geysered up in a great upheaval at least a hundred kilometers out. But they had not. Once again they had had to postpone a firing of Lizzie. *Verflucht nochmal*! Damn and double damn! They were still having trouble with the boosters. The charges had to be ignited at exactly the correct position of the projectile as it shot up through the main barrel, literally within a couple of centimeters. And since the time-tolerance for electrical firing of a charge was 0.015 seconds, there was no margin for error. It was a problem they had struggled with from the beginning. It was not impossible to solve, but damn near. Still, he vowed, he would meet his promised deadline, several days ahead. But until they had the answer to the booster charge problem, they dared not fire anything but projectiles loaded with dummy explosives. If a live projectile were to blow up in the main barrel, Lizzie would be set back for months. And, of course, until they had that answer and had tested it thoroughly, the batteries at Mimoyecques could only sit and wait! He rubbed his temples. Damn that headache!

He walked up to a waiting car.

"Put the top down, Kohlman," he said to the driver. "I need some air."

"*Jawohl, Herr Brigadeführer*!" The man at once began to carry out his order.

Dieter Haupt watched him. Perhaps the fresh air would blow his headache away. If not, Helga would take care of it. Already he was beginning to get impatient. And if not Helga, he thought, that little dark-haired *Nutte*. They said she was Italian, but he suspected she was a Jewess, recruited from some camp or other. *Schon gut*. Even a Jew could be good for something. For a while. She *was* a delicious little thing, who would submit to anything, and at least she would be clean. The girls were examined daily. Not much chance of catching *der Tripper*—the clap—at an SS Offiziersbordello.

He glanced impatiently at his driver.

"*Los, Kohlman!*" he snapped. "Let us not take the whole evening."

"*Zu Befehl, Herr Brigadeführer.*" The driver doubled his efforts.

Haupt stepped into the car and the driver took his place behind the wheel. A few minutes later the car left the outer gate of the Misdroy test site and turned left on the road to Wollin and the mainland.

The farmers in the area, up at four, retired early, and the roads were usually quite deserted after 1800 hours. Daylight was reluctantly giving way to dusk as Haupt's car passed the turnoff to the village of Kantreck a couple of kilometers after having crossed the bridge from Wollin Island to the mainland on the way to Stettin.

Haupt was enjoying himself. His headache was gone, and he allowed himself to fantasize a bit about his imminent visit to the brothel.

Helga? Or that little Jew-piece?

The more he thought about it, the more he leaned toward the Jewess. Helga was great—a strapping blonde from Lüneburg, who obviously enjoyed her work. The Jew-girl was different. Passive. Not much more than a girl. But there was something particularly exciting about knowing that whatever he did with her—or to her—was forced on her. Yes. She would be the one. He tried to remember her name. He couldn't.

He was brought out of his pleasant reveries as he noticed that the car was slowing down.

He peered ahead.

Two people could be seen on the road. A young woman walked on the grassy road shoulder along the bushes and brush that lined the road, carrying a battered bundle tied with heavy string. And a man.

It was the man who caused the slowdown.

Obviously blind, wearing dark glasses and tapping his way with a cane, he came walking down the middle of the road right toward the oncoming car. Around his neck hung a sign. Haupt could not read it, but he knew what it would say. *KRIEGSVERWUNDET* —war wounded. There were more and more of them cropping up.

The driver honked his horn.

The blind man started. Instead of moving to the shoulder of the road, he froze in his tracks and stood rooted to the spot, wildly waving his cane in front of him, directly in the path of the car.

The car came to a halt only a few feet in front of the man as the driver swore at him.

"Du Trottel!" he shouted in annoyance. "You imbecile! Get out of the way!"

Dieter leaned forward—and all of a sudden the world around him exploded into a blur of action.

Two men with dark-blue kerchiefs tied over the lower part of their faces, giving them a frightening look, came charging out from behind the bushes on either side of the stalled car. In a span of mere seconds, a flurry of violence erupted.

179

Alarmed, the driver reached to draw his sidearm, but before he could get it halfway out of his holster, one of the kerchiefed men fired at him. Two bullets struck him in the face, instantly killing him.

Before Haupt could act, he found himself staring at a gun pointed at him, held in the steady hands of the blind man—no longer blind. As the first ambusher began to drag the body of the slain driver from the car, the second jumped up on the running board. Firmly grasping a long wicked-looking knife in his left hand, he reached for Haupt with his right.

Terrified, Haupt stared at his assailant.

He knew he had only seconds to live.

All at once a piercing scream rang out. It was the girl, coming up behind the "blind" man holding the gun. Instantly he whirled on her—to be hit a crushing blow in the face with the girl's heavy bundle. Blood spurted from his mouth as he went down, the gun flying from his grip.

Bellowing in rage, the ambusher with the knife collecting himself after his initial shock at the girl's attack, viciously jabbed his knife-wielding arm toward Haupt, his hate-filled eyes burning above the dark kerchief.

Looking death in the face, Haupt shrank back. Time stood still for him, as in horror he watched the gleaming knife blade reach for his throat—an eternal instant, which was abruptly shattered by the sharp reports of gun shots.

Instantly the man's arm holding the long knife exploded in a spray of blood and gore and bits of bone, which splattered Haupt's face with sudden splotches of red.

With a howl of agony, the man dropped the knife and tumbled from the car.

Jolted to the marrow of his bones, Haupt stared. In front of the car stood the girl, wild-faced and trembling, the "blind" man's gun in her hands. She turned—and fired as the other kerchiefed assassin rushed her. Two shots—which hit the man squarely in the chest and sent him crashing to the ground at her feet, as the dum-dum bullets from the gun fired by the girl smashed into him in a spray of blood.

On the other side of the car, the man with the mangled arm stood clutching his bloody stump to him, reeling in pain and shock.

The girl hurled the gun away. She ran to the car.

"Drive!" she shouted as she jumped in. "Drive! Get away!"

Haupt, shaken and white-faced, scrambled from the back of the car into the driver's seat. Out of the corner of his eye, he saw the wounded assailant, blood dripping from his ravaged arm, reach into his belt for a gun; and spurting gravel from the spinning wheels of the car, Haupt screeched the car into a sharp U-turn and careened down the road, back toward the safety of Misdroy, with Gaby at his side.

Behind them, on the road, Mike, Kevin, and Ted stood together in silence, gazing after the disappearing car.

Absentmindedly Mike removed his mangled arm, bloody and mutilated in the best Grand Guignol tradition. The explosive squibs hidden in the hollow prosthesis, which had been stuffed with the remains of a freshly killed chicken and little balloons filled with chicken blood, had gone off right on cue when Gaby fired the blanks at him; as had the squibs planted on Ted's chest.

Ted had acted quickly and decisively, preventing any mishaps from happening, when he killed the driver of the general's car before the man could arm himself. It was a contingency they had anticipated, and Ted had been ready. Kevin had once again used his talent for being "blind" and drooling fake blood.

It had come off, he thought, as effectively as on the stage of the Theatre du Grand Guignol itself. But he was deeply disturbed as he watched the car disappear in the distance.

Gaby . . .

She had insisted in carrying out the ploy. Now it was up to her to make it pay off. She would have to deal with the situation as it developed. Without a script. Alone. And totally vulnerable. A situation that could much too easily cost her her life if the German officer should become suspicious of her.

They had, of course, tipped their hand. It had been a calculated tradeoff. They had alerted the Commanding Officer of the test site to the fact that something was afoot, that someone was out to swat his millipede. But security around the base had already been increased, even more than anticipated. By showing their hand, they had perhaps caused this security to be increased even further, but they had gained the unobtainable factor so absolutely essential to the success of their mission. They had placed someone on the inside. Gaby . . .

Mike's "broken arm" act at the test site gate had given Kevin the idea for the action. Now, he almost regretted it . . .

By the time Haupt turned off the main road fifteen minutes later to enter the Misdroy test site, he had fully regained his composure. He glanced at the girl sitting next to him. Pretty, he thought. Very pretty. And with the courage and daring of a true Aryan woman. They had not spoken since they fled the scene of the ambush. That would come later, he thought. After he had set the machinery in motion to find and apprehend the assassins.

Suddenly the girl spoke.

"Please," she said. "Please stop the car."

Surprised, he looked at her.

"Why?" he asked.

"Please," she said again. "I—I must get out."

Frowning in puzzlement, Haupt pulled over and stopped the car. "Get out?" he repeated incredulously. "You are coming with me, *Fräulein*, to my quarters. I want to talk to you."

The girl looked frightened. She glanced toward the forbidding barbed-wire fence and the looming guard tower at the outer gate. She gave Haupt a fearful look.

"Please, *Herr Offizier*," she pleaded. "Just—just let me go. I—I—" She stopped.

"Why?" Haupt persisted. "You saved my life. I must know more about you. Why do you want to leave?"

Again Gaby looked apprehensively toward the fence. "I—I do not want to—to go in there," she whispered, obviously distressed.

Haupt was genuinely astounded. "Why not?" he asked. "What are you afraid of?"

Gaby looked at him, her eyes wide and somber.

"It is—a prison camp, is it not?" she said haltingly. "I—I have heard of such camps. For—for enemies of the State. I know that—that people die in there."

Haupt threw his head back and laughed.

"That is no prison camp. No one dies in there, I assure you." It was not entirely true, of course, but that was another matter. "It is a government installation," he explained. "A special military base. My headquarters are in there. And that is where we are going."

"Oh," Gaby said in a small voice.

He looked at her. She was extremely appealing, he decided.

With the attraction of both Helga and that little snip Jew-girl. Plus her own personal excitement.

"What is your name?" he asked her. "You risked your life for me, and I do not even know your name."

"Gertie," Gaby said. "Gertie Kerlach." She deliberately did not look at him. It was not lost on him.

"I am *Brigadeführer* Dieter Haupt," he said. "I am the commandant of this base." He smiled at her, a curiously predatory smile. "You will be quite safe with me."

Gaby looked at him in undisguised awe. She nodded.

"Why?" Haupt asked again. "What made you do what you did? What made you fight the men that ambushed me? They could have killed you, too."

Gaby looked shyly down at her hands lying folded in her lap.

"It was your uniform," she whispered.

"My uniform!" Haupt exclaimed, once again taken by surprise. "What about my uniform?"

"It is the uniform of an SS officer, is it not?" Gaby said.

He nodded. "Yes. What about it?"

"I—I know that the SS are special," Gaby continued timidly. "I know such men are trusted by the Führer himself. I—I could not just do nothing when those men were going to kill someone who is special to our Führer." She looked away.

Haupt looked at her. "Gertie," he said. "Why are you afraid of me?"

"I am not," she protested. But it was obvious that she was.

Haupt frowned at her. "Your German," he said. "It is not from around here. I cannot place it. Where do you come from?"

The tears began to brim in Gaby's eyes. "Please," she sobbed, "I beg you. Just let me go. I am nobody. I—I—please, just let me go." She wiped her eyes with her knuckles, a pathetic little gesture.

For the third time Haupt stared at her in utter astonishment. "Who are you?" he asked. "Look, do not be afraid. Let me see your papers. Show me your identity papers, please."

Gaby began to cry. "I—I have no papers," she sniffled. "They were in my luggage. My bundle. I—I left it back there with all I had."

It was a perfectly safe lie. She knew that every trace of the ambush would be long erased before anyone could investigate. The dead driver; the "dead" assailant; her bundle. Everything.

———
183

Haupt looked at her soberly. "Tell me," he said. "Tell me about yourself. Who you are. Where you come from. I promise you, you will not be harmed."

"I—I am not a native German," Gaby began. "That is why my German is not—not perfect."

"What are you?" Haupt asked. He had a sudden, horrifying thought. God forbid the girl should turn out to be a Jew! But—if that *were* the case, all promises were, of course, null and void. It would be a pity, however. . . .

"I am from Alsace," Gaby said. Now that she had begun to talk, the words came easier, it seemed. "My mother was German. From Frankfurt. My father was French, but of German ancestry, as were so many of us. We lived in Haguenau. In Alsace."

"*Elsass*, Gertie," Haupt said. "Elsass is German once again."

Gaby nodded. "Since 1940," she said. "I know."

"Where are your parents?" he asked.

"They are both dead," Gaby said miserably. "They were killed in a terror raid by the enemy planes. Our house was burned. Everything." She blinked the tears away. "I—I had nowhere to go."

She paused, trying to collect herself.

"I knew we had relatives in Stettin," she went on, "so that is where I went. But their house had been bombed and they were gone. I could not find them."

"Where were you going now?" Haupt asked. "Where are your staying? Working?"

Gaby lowered her head. "Nowhere," she whispered. "I—I have no place to go." She looked up at him with tear-filled eyes. "But—I will find some place."

She fell silent. Don't be too eager, Kevin had cautioned her. Play it tough. . . . She had been tough enough. No need to overdo it.

"Nonsense," Haupt said firmly. He smiled down at her. "Do not tell me that my life is of so little value that I owe you nothing for saving it! *I* will give you work. And *I* will give you a place to stay. That is final!"

It was obvious there was to be no further arguments.

"You are from Elsass," Haupt said, his mind already planning for her. "So you speak French, of course."

She nodded.

"Excellent. We have a few French technicians here, and their

German is atrocious. And we have French scientific and technical works. You will be useful."

He started up the car and drove through the guarded gate onto the Misdroy test site.

And at his side sat a member of Jed Team Grand Guignol, accepted as a proven ally.

❈ PART THREE ❈

Germany, May 1944

23

BRIGADEFÜHRER Dieter Haupt glared at his aide.

"Nothing?" he asked acidly. "In twenty-four hours—nothing at all?"

Obersturmführer Stolitz nodded. "That is correct, *Herr Brigadeführer*. As you know, there was absolutely nothing found at the site of the ambush itself, except for a few small glass splinters. Dark-glass splinters. Apparently from a pair of spectacles. Ordinary glass, sir, not prescription. Impossible to trace. We—"

"Yes, yes," Haupt interrupted impatiently. "I know that. The murderers were out to kill me in order to disrupt our test schedule. I am convinced of that. But what else are they planning? What other acts of sabotage? That is what we *must* know." He looked intently at Stolitz. "What about the investigations? In Wollin? In Kantreck? Wietstock? The other villages? Has anything been learned?"

"No, *Herr Brigadeführer*. Nothing. Not by Abwehr III—counterintelligence— nor by our own security forces."

"*Verflucht!*" Haupt swore angrily. "I want all efforts continued. And I am ordering the entire base to remain on full alert, including all special security measures now in force."

"*Jawohl, Herr Brigadeführer*," Stolitz said. He paused. "There is—there is perhaps one thing."

"And that is?"

"Two men, sir. Two crew supervisors from the construction detachment. They have vanished."

"Vanished?"

"Yes, sir. They apparently went to Wollin to go to the cinema last Monday. Six days ago. They never returned."

"Why was I not informed?" Haupt snapped angrily.

"*Herr Brigadeführer,*" Haupt said. "The section chief did not consider it of enough importance to report it at this level. It has happened before. There have been other incidences of—of desertion. It only came to my attention during the ongoing investigations caused by the ambush."

Haupt glared at his aide. But he said nothing. He knew what the lieutenant said was true. He frowned. There could be a connection.

"I want a complete investigation of the two men carried out at once," he ordered. "Their families. Their friends. Look for any connections with anything disloyal to the Reich."

"Understood, *Herr Brigadeführer.*"

"That is all."

Stolitz came to attention and turned to go.

"Wait!" Haupt called to him. "That girl—Fräulein Kerlach?"

"She has been summoned, *Herr Brigadeführer*, as you ordered. She should be on her way here now."

"Excellent. Bring her in when she arrives."

"*Zu Befehl, Herr Brigadeführer.*"

Gaby followed the woman who had come to fetch her as they walked from the German Personnel Housing to the *Kommedantur*—General Haupt's headquarters. The woman was a *Wehrmachthelferinn*—a Women's Auxilliary attached to the HQ staff.

Gaby took note of everything she saw.

She had kept her eyes open the night before as the general had driven her to his quarters after the ambush, and she went over it in her mind. . . .

They had passed through three gates in three separate double barbed-wire fences, and although it had begun to grow dark, she had seen the guard towers and many of the buildings located in the areas all brightly lit by strong floodlights mounted on tall poles.

The general's quarters and the HQ offices were located in the third, or innermost, section of the base, to the right of the third gate, past several low-slung buildings that appeared to house laboratories or research centers. Straight ahead from the gate had been a large area that had been hidden from view. The millipede? Beyond the HQ buildings stood the housing for the German supervisory personnel, and there she had been installed in a room of her own. Some woman had provided her with a few necessities, and she had spent the night trying to plan for events she knew all too well were unpredictable. It was strictly an ad-lib situation, she'd thought. She had missed Kevin. Sleep had been impossible.

The general seemed to have accepted her and her story. The cover that Kevin had concocted for her was perfect; even Ted had been impressed with its thoroughness. The choice of Haguenau as her hometown was ideal. Alsace was a region of bilingual people, which would explain her accent. It was a region that had been shunted back and forth between Germany and France several times, resulting in large population shifts and changes and the wholesale deportation of French inhabitants after Germany took over in 1940. And because the town was an important railroad center on the Paris–Strassbourg–Stuttgart line, it had been extensively bombed by the Allies. She, herself, had been to Haguenau when the Grand Guignol touring company had played Strassbourg, and she knew enough about the town to seem familiar with it, except to someone who might come from there. But it was highly unlikely that she'd run into anyone like that at Misdroy.

There was at least one family in the town of Haguenau by the name of Kerlach. When Mike and his wife had set up housekeeping in Paris after returning from the States to take care of the estate of Genevieve's parents, they had selected a popular pattern of porcelain from Haguenau, which had a well-known china industry, and Mike had at one time corresponded with an Alsatian supplier named Kerlach, in order to get replacement pieces for the set.

Having her "lose" her identification papers in the very act of defending the commandant had really been the master stroke. It effectively eliminated all the risks that forged documents would invite, and under the circumstances, the general could hardly complain about the loss. Moreover, Gaby's apparent reluctance to enter the base had helped to place her above suspicion. Haguenau was far enough away so that it would take a lot of time to check out and verify her story if anyone should decide to do so.

Long enough to get the job done.

Kevin, Ted, and Mike had left Gasthof Adler before the ambush took place and had secretly moved in with Keppler. They had decided to use the little church where they were supposed to have met once before as a place of contact. That is where she would go as soon as she had any news.

But right now, she was on her own.

Dieter Haupt rose as Stolitz ushered Gaby into his office.

"Ah, *Fräulein* Gertie," he said brightly. "Please come in. Have a seat. Have you been comfortable?" He sat down behind his desk.

"Yes, thank you, *Herr Kommandant*," Gaby smiled. "Most comfortable. I—I am grateful."

"No, no, Gertie," Haupt said expansively. "It is *I* who am grateful. And I intend to show my gratitude."

He watched the girl as she walked to the offered chair and sat down. Even prettier than I remembered from yesterday, he thought. Of course I had other matters on my mind. With pleasure he watched the graceful manner in which she sat down. There was something both demure and provocative about her, which excited him. He would have to cultivate their relationship, he thought. Perhaps he could give up his weekly sojourns to Stettin. That would be most convenient. There were few women on the base —all of them in the service and of lower rank. Naturally, he could not have anything to do with them, even though a couple of them were at least passable. But this one. This one was different. This one was a civilian and accessible. He turned to his aide.

"What has been arranged regarding Fräulein Kerlach?"

"*Zu Befehl, Herr Brigadeführer*," Stolitz replied. "Fräulein Kerlach has been assigned living quarters in the German section. Tomorrow, Monday, first thing, she will be introduced to the chief of the library and documents center, who will employ the Fräulein as a translator."

Gaby watched the general as he listened to his aide. Young to hold such high a rank, she thought. He must be a very capable officer. A good-looking man, with the lean build and ramrod bearing of the professional soldier, and steel-blue eyes that seemed to look right to the core of you. He might have been attractive, she thought, had it not been for a strangely predatory air about him, which disturbed her.

"Excellent," Haupt said when Stolitz had finished. He turned to Gaby. "I trust my aide has informed you that I wish the—the incident of yesterday be kept in complete confidence. At this moment only the three of us present in this room and certain

192

investigators have any knowledge of the ambush. I wish it to remain so." He stood up.

"It will," Gaby said. "I shall say nothing about it to anyone."

"Excellent. I hope you will enjoy your stay with us, Gertie."

"Thank you so very much, *Herr Kommandant*," Gaby said. "I shall do my best to be of real service."

Haupt gave a little bow.

"I hope you will be successful," he smiled.

"Oh, so do I, *Herr Kommandant*," Gaby agreed brightly. "So do I. . . ."

Janusz Keppler had few visitors, but to be on the safe side, the three Grand Guignolers had been installed in the attic of his house. Coming up with enough bedding had been a dilemma until Keppler had thought to bring in the slightly musty blankets and mattresses from the living quarters on board the barge.

It was Sunday evening. The four men were sitting in Keppler's living room, the blackout curtains drawn tightly across the windows. It was merely to ensure privacy. Blackout regulations were not enforced on Wollin Island. The area was too remote for routine Allied air raids and—to the Allied Air Forces—too unimportant for special missions. The closest air attack had been on Peenemünde nine months earlier. If Allied planes did approach, there would be plenty of warning and plenty of time to activate blackout procedures.

There was an air of tension in the room. Gaby had been in the enemy camp twenty-four hours. And they had no idea what had happened to her after she drove off with the test site commandant. . . .

"Food is going to be our problem," Ted said. "A sudden tripling of Keppler's buying habits will be sure to raise a few eyebrows. The wrong ones."

"My *Regenbogen* wouldn't go far, anyway," Keppler commented drily.

"*Regenbogen?*," Mike queried. "How the hell does a rainbow enter into it? Looking for a pot of gold at the end of it, Jan? Or a grocery store? What's *Regenbogen?*"

"Ration stamps," Keppler answered. "We have been on ration stamps for almost five years now."

"But—why *Regenbogen?*"

193

"Because of the color of the stamps," Keppler explained. "Blue for meat, green for eggs, yellow for dairy products, orange for bread, pink for cereal, purple for fruit, white for—"

"Okay, I get it," Mike broke in. "So how *do* we round up enough food to keep us going for however long it's going to take?"

"I have a little put away," Keppler said. "Not much. Hoarding is a serious crime in the Third Reich."

"What else?"

"We forage," Keppler said. "The farmers around here have food. They are better off than any city people."

"Okay, so we scrounge," Ted said. "Pretty risky, isn't it?"

Keppler nodded. "There is some risk," he said. "But it will be slight. You will not be the only ones."

"How so?"

"Evacuees," Keppler explained. "There are many people around here who have been evacuated by the government from the heavily bombed cities to the Baltic coast. There is little bombing here. They, too, must scrounge for food."

"Great. Competition yet," Mike grumbled. "And how the hell do we pay?"

"You work," Keppler said. "The farmers are all shorthanded. The young men are all away. You will work a few hours—in the fields, on the farm. They will give you food."

Ted nodded. "Fair enough."

It was Kevin who voiced what was in everyone's mind.

"Tomorrow is Monday," he said. "When do you think we can expect word from Gaby?" He looked at the others.

"Give her time," Ted said. "We'll begin our church watch tomorrow, just in case. But I don't expect any contact for two or three days." He looked soberly at Kevin. "She has a damned difficult task ahead of her. She'll need some time to set it up."

Kevin nodded. He took a deep breath. It had been *his* plan.

The task they had given Gaby was indeed a difficult one, if not impossible.

❈ 24 ❈

WHEN she made her discovery, it came in a totally unexpected way.

Gaby had been put to work in the French section of the research library. There were hundreds of volumes and thousands of documents written in French. Technical books, scientific works covering chemistry, physics, and mathematics; all kinds of technology. Books and papers dealing with electricity, explosives, metallurgy, and the history of science—going back many decades. And much, much more. She had been instructed to familiarize herself with the cataloguing and indexing systems used so that she could locate quickly a specific request for material to be translated into German; and she had been given a long list of specific French words of a technical nature that she could not be expected to know and their translations into German equivalents. She made a list of the German words. If she could get it to Kevin and the others, and take it back to Paris, English scientists might be able to figure something out about the Misdroy project, she thought. There were words like *Hochdruchpumpe* and *Flanschrohr, Gleichdruck* and *Kreuzstück, Schrumpfring* and *Flanschseitenlager*. They meant nothing to her. Making the list was without risk. After all, she had been instructed to learn the words.

Smuggling it out was something else. But that would come later.

Her discovery had startled her. She had been putting away a French book published in 1897. Amazed that so old a book should be part of this ultra-modern library, she had leafed through it and was surprised to see one of the catch words on her list, the French words that translated into *Mehrfachkammergeschütz*—multiple-chambered gun. Curious, she began to read and discovered that if what the Germans were actually testing at Misdroy was a huge gun with an enormously long barrel, it was not of their invention. And more importantly, she found out the function of the mysterious pairs of legs that gave the gun its name, millipede. They were booster barrels containing extra charges of explosives.

Excitedly she filed the information in her memory as she read further in her find.

To her surprise, she learned that the idea for the first such multi-chambered gun—a long gun barrel with additional lateral cartridge chambers that led into the bore of the main barrel at equally spaced intervals so that the plane view of the device resembled a millipede—had first been patented in the 1860s! Designed to give a projectile an extremely high velocity, and therefore great range, it was actually nearly a century old. The projectile, which incorporated a conventional propelling charge, was loaded at the breech of the gun. This charge was fired, starting the projectile up the barrel. And at the exact point when the rate of acceleration ceased to increase, the projectile passed the opening of the first pair of side barrels. As it did, the booster charges in those barrels were fired, generating an additional quantity of propelling gas, which gave the projectile an even greater acceleration; and so on, as each pair of boosters was passed, until the desired velocity was reached at the muzzle of the gun.

The old book was a gold mine of information. She found out that a model of the monster gun, an American design called the Lyman and Haskell Gun, had been fired experimentally in the 1880s, some twenty years later, and discarded when the pressure in the barrel reached alarming figures and threatened to blow the entire device sky-high. And she learned that a version of this multi-chambered gun had been offered to the British Ordnance Board three time since World War I—the last time in 1941—and each time turned down!

There was, of course, no definite proof that that was what the German *Tausendfüssler* actually was. But everything certainly pointed to it.

She was excited. She felt she had made a vital discovery. She was literally bursting with eagerness to get her information to the others as quickly as possible, and she had to remind herself forcefully that her primary mission at the test site had to be accomplished first—that of obtaining two blank test site passes giving access to the innermost sector, and learning how the ID check system using photographs was set up so that photographs of two members of Jedburgh Team Grand Guignol could be placed in the master file. So far, she had no idea how to go about it.

Kevin had not been able to get Gaby out of his mind. Not knowing what had happened to her after she left the scene of the ambush; not knowing what she was doing, what dangers she might be facing; not even knowing if she were still alive—all preyed on his mind. He knew that the more he dwelled on all the things that could have happened to her, the more worried and anxious he would get. But he could not help himself.

He and Keppler had worked for three hours cleaning out an incredibly filthy hen house. The stench had been overpowering, but he'd hardly noticed. His mind had been filled with Gaby.

He was washing the dirt off his hands and arms at the pump in the courtyard of the farm near the village of Düssin on the mainland, some ten kilometers north of Wollin, where the two of them had gone to get food. Three hours of wallowing in chicken dung was worth a dozen eggs, a loaf of homemade bread, and a few vegetables. He couldn't have done much better in Paris, he thought.

Vigorously he scrubbed his hands with the grainy, greenish chunk of "people's soap" that the farmer had given them. It simply melted away and produced hardly any lather. The only noticeable effect of the abrasive stuff the Germans were forced to use in lieu of real soap was a sickening smell of cheap perfume.

He glanced at Keppler. The older man had done a yeoman's job, pushing a heavily laden wheelbarrow to and from the dungheap, located in a corner of the yard, as if taking a baby for a stroll in a lightweight perambulator. The skipper was drying off his muscular arms with a piece of sacking and rolling down his sleeves when he suddenly stopped and looked toward the gate to the farmyard.

Kevin followed his gaze—and froze. Rapidly approaching from the distance was the insistent growl of a motor vehicle, and even as he watched, a motorcycle with sidecar came careening through the gate to come to a stop right inside the yard.

Two Waffen SS soldiers dismounted, one of them a noncom, and strode purposefully over to Kevin and Keppler, submachine guns held at port arms.

Suspiciously the *Unteroffizier* scowled at them while the other soldier covered them.

"You live here?" the noncom asked brusquely.

"No," Keppler answered.

"What are you doing here?"

"Working."

"*Ausweis!*"

Without a word, Keppler gave him his ID papers. The soldier studied them.

"Barge captain," he said. "Retired." He gave the words a contemptuous inflection, as if he had said male prostitute. "You still live in Darsewitz, Keppler?"

Keppler nodded.

"And you work here?" The Unteroffizier sounded skeptical.

"For today," Keppler said. "For a few hours to get some food. That is not illegal."

The noncom looked coldly at him. He glanced around. "Is anyone else here?" he asked.

"No."

"Where is the farmer who owns this farm?"

Keppler shrugged. "In the field," he said. "I do not know where."

The *Unteroffizier* glared hard at him for a few moments. Keppler met his stare. Then the man curtly gave him back his papers. He turned to Kevin.

"Your papers!"

Kevin gave him his identification papers, including his Military Exemption Certificate. The noncom examined them.

"Military exemption," he sneered. He glanced at the certificate. "*Paroxysmal Disorder*?" he asked. "What the devil is *Paroxysmal Disorder*?"

"If it pleases the *Herr Unteroffizier*," Kevin said, mustering up true Teutonic subservience to authority. "I—I have a form of epilepsy. Falling sickness, *Herr Unteroffizier*. I—I have a tendency to—to faint."

The noncom looked at him with contempt. "Faint," he said scornfully. "Like a queer at a shotgun wedding!" he laughed derisively. Again he studied the papers.

"You are from Berlin–Spandau," he said. "What are you doing up here?"

"I was evacuated, *Herr Unteroffizier*," Kevin explained. "The building I lived in was destroyed by the terror bombers."

198

The noncom nodded toward Keppler. "You live with him?" he asked.

Kevin's heart stopped. What should he say? If he said no, the man would want to know where he did live, and he had no answer. If he said yes, he might get Keppler in trouble.

"Yes," he said.

The soldier nodded. "When did you get here?"

"Only a few days ago, *Herr Unteroffizier.*"

The other soldier had stood watching the noncom question Keppler and Kevin. He stepped up to his companion and took him aside. For a brief moment they talked together, then the noncom came back. He turned to Keppler.

"Your papers again. *Los!*" he demanded sharply.

Keppler once more gave him his ID.

The *Unteroffizier* frowned over the papers.

"Keppler," he said deliberately. "Keppler." He looked up and glared at the skipper. "A few days ago someone asked for you," he said. "In the *Bierstube.* Trying to find you." He nodded toward Kevin. "Was this the man?"

"Yes."

"Did you know he was coming?"

"Yes."

"You knew he had been told to report to your house for evacuee quarters?"

"Yes."

"And ask for you?"

"Yes."

"Then how do you explain that he did not know your name?" the noncom shot at him. "How do you explain he did not know where you lived? How do you explain that he thought your name was *Kessler*? And how do you explain that there were three other people with him at the Bierstube? One of them a woman!"

Keppler shrugged. "I don't," he said.

The *Unteroffizier* whirled on Kevin. "Who were the people with you?" he snapped.

Kevin's mind reeled. What the hell *had* they talked about at the *Bierstube*? What *had* they said during their little performance? What could he say now?

"I do not know," he said, his voice unsteady.

"What were their names?"

"I do not know."

"Were they locals? Or were they also refugees?"

"I do not know."

"Where are they now?"

"I do not know."

The soldier glared angrily at him. "What *do* you know?" he asked caustically.

Kevin stood silent.

"*Who* are you?" the noncom barked at him. "Why are you really here?"

"I—I was evacuated, *Herr Unteroffizier*," Kevin said. He knew he sounded frightened. He was. "As I told you."

"Very well," the noncom said bitingly. "You will both come with us. We shall soon find the truth. There are records of these matters in Wollin."

Kevin and Keppler were pedalling down the road toward Wollin, the motorcycle with the two Waffen SS soldiers following behind them. They had just left the village of Kucklow, and the road was skirting a swamp on their left.

Kevin's mind was awhirl with thoughts. They had less than an hour to break away from their captors. Less than an hour to erase their suspicions and avoid being taken to Wollin for any further investigation; investigation they could not possibly survive. They were unarmed and under the guns of two trained German soldiers. Their chances were hardly encouraging, but they *had* to succeed. For themselves. For Ted and Mike. And for Gaby.

But—how?

"Watch it!" he heard Keppler exclaim.

He gave a quick yank on his handlebars. In his preoccupation, he had been crowding the skipper onto the road shoulder, nearly upsetting him. He wobbled on his bike before getting it under control.

He had a sudden idea. It might work.

As he pumped along, he glanced around.

The swamp was still on their left. Little pools of stagnant water and unstable tufts of matted vegetation. Good. A swamp can hide many things.

He let himself drift closer to Keppler once again.

"Jan," he whispered hoarsely. "Follow my lead!"

Keppler nodded.

They rode on for a few minutes, the side-car motorcycle following them.

Suddenly Kevin seemed to lose control of his bike. It swerved across the road toward the swamp and crashed in the sand. Kevin tumbled heavily to the ground. He lay unconscious, jerking slightly.

Keppler at once dismounted and ran to his side. The motorcycle stopped, and the two soldiers, their guns ready, stepped out.

Keppler knelt by the apparently comatose Kevin. Concerned, he turned toward the soldiers. "He's had an attack," he called. "His falling sickness. Out cold!"

He put his arm under Kevin and tried to lift him up. "A little water will bring him to," he called. He nodded toward a pool in the swamp. "Give me a hand."

Uncertainly the two soldiers looked at one another. Then the *Unteroffizier* nodded to his comrade.

The man shouldered his gun and went over to Keppler and Kevin. He grabbed hold of Kevin's feet, and with Keppler struggling with the head and shoulders, they dragged the limp body to the water's edge.

Keppler began to bathe Kevin's forehead with cold water. The soldier bent over them, next to him. He could be taken.

But twenty feet away stood the noncom, covering them all with his submachine gun, alert and watchful.

Keppler bent low over Kevin as if to check his breathing. "Nice try," he whispered. "But no cigar. Only one of them went with us."

Kevin stirred. Groggily he sat up. He wiped his eyes. He looked sheepishly at the soldier standing near him.

"I am sorry," he apologized. "It is my—illness. It happens. I cannot help it."

"Get back on your bicycles!" the *Unteroffizier* called gruffly. He gestured with his gun. "Both of you. *Los!*"

Kevin and Keppler remounted their bikes, and with the motorcycle once again following them, they rode down the deserted road.

Kevin's ploy had failed. And worse, they might have alerted their captors to the fact that the trip was anything but a quiet ride through the countryside. The two Germans would be on guard now for a second try.

If . . . Stubbornly, Kevin clenched his jaws. Not *if*. When. There had to be something they could do. Something, dammit! *Something*. Time was rapidly running out. They had now less than half an hour.

They had passed through the tiny village of Zebbin. Ahead of them the road ran straight at a slight downward incline, and the bikes picked up speed. Speed. That was it! A last chance!

Kevin once more edged close to Keppler.

"Listen, Jan," he said urgently under his breath. "I have an idea."

"Shoot."

In a quick whisper, Kevin told him his plan.

"Got it," Keppler grunted.

They rode for a moment in silence; then Kevin nodded to Keppler. Both men began to pedal furiously, as fast as they could. Their bikes picked up speed and raced down the road. Neither man looked back, but they could hear the motorcycle behind them rev up as it increased its speed to keep up with the racing bikes.

Kevin turned to Keppler.

"Now!" he shouted.

At once the two men stomped hard on their pedal brakes. Screeching, slewing, the bikes skidded to a halt. Even before they had come to rest, Kevin hurled himself from the bike. He was aware that Keppler was doing the same.

In the same instant, there was the squeal of tires skidding on the road and a crash, as the motorcycle, taken by surprise, slammed into the two bikes. Entangled in the jumbled metal, it upended, pinning the two Germans underneath.

Kevin sat up.

Keppler was already on his feet. Kevin saw him run to the upended motorcycle, its wheels spinning ineffectually in the air. The two soldiers lay unconscious in the maze of tangled bikes. Quickly Keppler picked up one of the guns. Holding it by the barrel, with all his might, he smashed the stock down on the head of first one, then the other Nazi soldier.

Kevin came up to him. He looked at the dead Germans. He felt sick.

"Come on!" Keppler said urgently. "We must get them off the road." He began to extricate the motorbike from the warped bicycles.

Together he and Kevin pushed the motorbike into the ditch and dragged the bodies of the Germans to it.

Keppler bashed the gas tank open, and the gasoline drained out to soak both bike and bodies. He fished a box of matches from his pocket, struck one, and threw it on the mangled pile.

Instantly it flared up.

Flames licked the gasoline from the metal pyre in eager gluttony and thrust greedy red tongues of fire into the air. Paint blistered off the bike. The uniforms of the two men caught fire, blackened, and scorched the bodies within them, their limbs jerking grotesquely as the fire consumed them.

Unable to tear his eyes from the macabre inferno blazing under a growing column of black smoke, Kevin stood staring at the burning motorcycle and its riders.

Keppler pulled him by the arm.

"We must get away from here," he said. "Now!"

They picked up their twisted bikes and quickly began to push them down the road.

Kevin looked back.

It was the site of an accident, he thought. Heavy skid marks on the road; lost control—and a fiery crash. Had the riders tried to avoid a stray cow? Or dog?

No matter. The result had obviously been—tragedy.

Back at Keppler's place, the buckled bikes were hidden in his shed.

Mike had been on watch at the church.

There had been no sign of Gaby.

✠ 25 ✠

BRIGADIER James Hindsmith Parnell strode into the room, a surprising bounce to his step.

The eyes of every man present in the large conference room—the top brass of Milton Hall—followed him as he purposefully walked to his place at the head of the long table. He remained standing.

"Gentlemen," he said. "It is official! After a SHAEF meeting yesterday, May fifteenth, at Montgomery's headquarters in St. Paul's School in London, attended by every principal member of the Chiefs of Staff and the War Cabinet, by major Allied generals and admirals, by Prime Minister Churchill, and by His Majesty, King George the Sixth, General Dwight D. Eisenhower has officially set the date for the invasion."

He paused dramatically.

"D-Day will be June fifth—twenty days from today!"

There was a general reaction around the table, but no one spoke. This was a time for listening. Questions and discussion would come later.

Parnell took his seat.

"Gentlemen," he said. "The Neptune phase of Overlord will be the greatest amphibious assault ever attempted. The largest troop concentrations in history are even now being assembled along the Channel coast. The most massive buildup ever of supplies, ammunition, tanks, transportation. An armada of thousands of ships." He looked soberly at the attentive officers. "I need not point out to you," he continued quietly, "the vulnerability of such a concentrated amassment of men and materiél, what?"

"What special security measures are being taken?" Lieutenant Colonel Ramsey asked.

"The whole area of southern England is becoming a vast military encampment," Parnell answered him. "Virtually isolated from the rest of the country. A deadline has been established. No unauthorized persons are allowed to cross it in either direction. In addition, the southernmost camps and staging areas, marshalling yards and seaports—such as Southampton, Portsmouth, and Newhaven—are surrounded by barbed-wire entanglements to keep persons both in and out."

"What about air strikes, sir?" an officer asked. "The Germans will not be unaware of such a mammoth operation."

"Quite," Parnell acknowledged. "But SHAEF is confident that we can contain any air activity by Jerry. The Luftwaffe has been rendered virtually ineffective by our chaps."

"When will the French Resistance be brought into the operation?" Lieutenant Colonel Lamont wanted to know. "What plans have been made?"

Parnell turned to him. "French Underground leaders are even now being alerted to stand by," he said. "We have received orders to put every available Jedburgh team into the field now to work with the Resistance in preparing for the invasion."

"Thank you, Brigadier," Lamont said.

"And Mimoyecques, sir?" It was Colonel Baldon. "We still have no idea what's going on there. We don't know what kind of threat the place may pose. What is being done about Mimoyecques?"

The brigadier looked grim. "Nothing," he said, "at this time. Nothing specific. SHAEF is aware of the unknown emplacements at Mimoyecques. They are aware of the heavy troop concentrations in the area. But we have not been able to supply them with any concrete information. Rebus was—terminated by the Germans. Grand Guignol was a failure, the fate of the team unknown. Ditto was wiped out. In the absence of any hard information, SHAEF must accept the assumption, made by air intelligence reconnaissance and chance ground observations, that the Mimoyecques installation is in the nature of launching pads for the projected, as yet unproven, unmanned flying bombs our intelligence has warned about."

"That assessment is probably correct, sir," another officer ventured. "Such launching installations have been confirmed at Watten, about fifteen miles east of Mimoyecques."

Parnell nodded.

"I am aware of that," he said. "However, SHAEF does not con-

205

sider the installations at Mimoyecques a primary threat to the invasion forces."

"Call me Lutz, and I shall make you look pretty!" the man winked at her.

"Impossible!" Gaby laughed. "All photographs for official documents make you look terrible."

She was perched on an uncomfortable stool in front of the mandatory drab white background in the little makeshift photographic studio adjacent to the test site security office in the HQ building at Misdroy while the photographer, Ludwig Hermann, was setting up his shot.

He walked over to her, limping badly. Instinctively, Gaby's eyes were drawn to his leg. She was suddenly aware that the man noticed her gaze, and self-consciously she looked away.

The photographer smiled at her. "Do not be disconcerted, Fräulein," he said. "*I* stared at your legs. Although, I imagine, for a different reason." He knocked on his right leg. It sounded hollow. "The rest of this one is in Stalingrad," he said cheerfully. "I left it there in forty-three."

He went back to his camera and busied himself with the settings. Gaby watched him. He looked too old to be a wounded war veteran. Middle fifties? He probably was much younger. They said Stalingrad aged everyone by at least ten years.

She squirmed lightly on the hard stool. She had been ordered to the studio to have her photograph taken for her identification papers.

"It must have been terrible at Stalingrad," she said. "The cold. And those Russian barbarians." She shivered. "You are very lucky that you did not die there."

The man gave her a quick glance; his eyes suddenly bleak. "I thought I did," he said softly. Then his face broke into a smile once again. "Sit up a little," he instructed her. He looked through the finder on the camera.

Gaby straightened up. "Were you a photographer before the war, Lutz?" she asked awkwardly, not knowing what to say but not wanting to sit silent.

The man nodded. "And a good one."

"Then you must enjoy your work here." ·

"When I have a pretty face to photograph," Hermann smiled at her, "I certainly do." He made a face. "But that is not often.

Mostly it is a sour-looking *Ziegenbock*—billy goat, long in the tooth, that sits on that stool."

Gaby laughed. She rather liked the man. "And have you photographed billy goats for a long time?"

"It surely seems so," Hermann said. "But it has, in fact, been less than a week since the *Kommandant* gave his order for the new identity procedure with the photographs. Everything was organized very quickly." He motioned around him. "As you can plainly see."

"My!" Gaby said. "You must have been busy photographing everyone on the base. How on earth did you manage that all by yourself?"

Hermann grinned disarmingly. "I am not halfway through yet."

"There must be a lot of disappointed people, then, who cannot leave the base because they have no photograph to go on their papers," Gaby observed. "I am most lucky."

"You are," the photographer agreed. "And so am I to get a welcome respite from billy goats! But everyone who is allowed to leave the base can do so."

"But—I thought—"

"Many have supplied their own photographs for their papers. It was requested that they do so, if possible, to allow the new security routine to go into effect once the *Kommandant* ordered it."

"Well, I shall look forward to having a photograph on *my* identity card taken by you, Lutz," Gaby said.

"But you will not," Hermann said.

Gaby frowned prettily. "But—I thought—" She stopped in confusion.

"That is not the way it works."

"Oh?"

"No one will need to carry his own photograph on his papers," Hermann said. "He has his face. A photograph can be attached to a document that is forged. No one can forge his face!"

"That I can understand," Gaby said. "But the rest—it is all too complicated for me."

"Not complicated at all, *liebes Fräulein*. It is a simple and a foolproof method of checking, the *Kommandant* has devised. Every checkpoint at every gate has a photograph to go with the name of each man's identity paper. This the guards can compare with the man who presents that paper. There can be no mistake. There is a master file in the security office right here in this building. And every day the new photographs that I take are put in envelopes, and one is taken there, one to every checkpoint at every gate. There is no way that someone not allowed here can possibly get in."

Disheartened, Gaby listened to him. He was right. The system did appear impossible to circumvent. And that was exactly what she had to do. Your mission, Kevin had said to her, is to find out how that photograph check procedure works; to get your hands on two blank identity cards and get them to us; and to figure out a way to beat the system. Three almost impossible tasks, one more impossible than the other.

But they had to be done.

"It is most clear," she said, sounding impressed. "And you are certainly an important part of it all."

Favoring his right leg, Hermann positioned himself behind his camera. "Smile, *kleines Fräulein*, at me," he said cheerfully. "And we shall have a *prima* photograph! I shall remember this day, May the sixteenth. The day my camera produced a masterpiece!"

Gaby smiled, and Hermann took the picture.

"Beautiful!" he exclaimed happily. He removed the plate. "By this afternoon, every gate will be graced by your likeness, *liebes Fräulein*."

"Gertie," Gaby said.

"Gertie."

The telephone on Hermann's desk rang. He shuffled over to answer it.

"Hermann," he said crisply. He listened for a moment and glanced toward Gaby. "*Ja, Herr Obersturmführer*," he said. "She is still here." Again he listened. "*Zu Befehl, Herr Obersturmführer*. Heilitla!" he slurred the salutation. He hung up and turned to Gaby.

"You are to report to the commandant's office," he said. "And on the way you are to bring *Obersturmführer* Stolitz his photographs for his new hunting license." He opened a drawer in his desk and took out a small yellow envelope, perhaps eleven by eight centimeters. "He is a brave soldier, the *Herr Obersturmführer*," he said with ill-disguised contempt. "Shooting at game that cannot shoot back." He flung the envelope down on the desk and slammed the drawer shut. "I wonder if he would have enjoyed Stalingrad as much." He started to limp toward a door. "I will get his photographs," he said. "They are in the darkroom. Just finished. All I have to do is cut them to size. I will not be long."

He disappeared into the darkroom.

At once Gaby strode to his desk and opened the drawer. In a quick glance, she took in the contents. There were five oblong cardboard file boxes, fitted in next to one another, each containing several envelopes. The envelopes used by Hermann to distribute the identity photographs. They all had a broad red stripe running diagonally from corner to corner. The envelopes in the first box also were marked with a large red numeral 1; the second box with a 2, and the third with a 3, one for each of the three gates. The envelopes in the next box had *GF* stamped on them. Gaby frowned over it. Then she realized what it had to mean. *Geheime Feldpolizei*—Secret Field Security. They were the envelopes for the photographs that would go into the master file. The remaining box contained unmarked envelopes such as the one Hermann had removed.

For a split moment she stared at the boxes. Almost offhandedly, two of her tasks had been solved. She knew the check system.

And she knew how to beat it!

Quickly she picked out one each of the four marked envelopes and stuffed them down the front of her blouse. She closed the drawer. She glanced around. On the desk stood a large letter basket. Several of the marked envelopes had been tossed into it. New photographs, ready to be distributed, she thought. What else could she learn? She had a sudden thought. What if the photographs had to be stamped with some official stamp? Or identified in some other way?

She glanced toward the darkroom door. Hermann would return any second.

Quickly she picked up one of the envelopes from the basket. With trembling fingers she opened it. She pulled out a photograph and looked at it, turning it over.

It had no markings on it, front or back, except the name of the subject.

There was a ruler lying on the desk. Quickly she measured the photograph. Nine by seven centimeters.

She stuffed the photograph back in the envelope and threw it in the basket just as Hermann emerged from the darkroom carrying a couple of photographs in his hand.

"Always impatient, the *Bonzen*—the big shots," he grumbled.

He walked over to his desk and put two copies of a small picture into the envelope he had picked out. He handed it to Gaby.

"*Bitte*, Gertie," he said. "Give that to the *Herr Oberleutnant* Stolitz."

Gaby took the envelope. "Of course, Lutz," she said sweetly. "And thank you. I have enjoyed being here. And I shall look forward to seeing my photographs, if I may?"

Hermann nodded emphatically.

"*Natürlich*," he said. "You must come back."

He shuffled to the door. He opened it, glanced into the hall outside, and shouted, "Next!"

He stood back to let Gaby pass. Wryly he winked at her.

"Billy goat!" he mumbled under his breath.

As Gaby walked toward the office of *Brigadeführer* Dieter Haupt, she organized and filed away in her mind the information she had unearthed. She was excited and a little proud of herself. She had seen an opportunity, and she had grabbed it at once. Like a real professional.

It had been a profitable photo session. Only one problem remained. It was a crucial one. How to get hold of two blank identification cards?

Obersturmführer Stolitz looked up as Gaby entered his office.

"Ah! *Fräulein* Kerlach," he said. "Thank you for bringing my photographs."

Gaby handed him the envelope. "Not at all, *Herr Obersturmführer*."

Stolitz picked up the interoffice phone.

"*Fräulein* Kerlach is here, *Herr Brigadeführer*," he said. He listened. "Yes, sir." He hung up.

He looked up at Gaby. "Please go right in."

As Gaby walked to the door that led to the commandant's office, she again wondered why she had been summoned. She reviewed her actions after she'd arrived at the test site. She had done nothing to arouse suspicion. Had the commandant become suspicious because of other happenings? Had something occurred to the rest of the team? Were they all right? Captured? No, it couldn't be anything as serious as that or they would have come for her, not just asked her to the commandant's office. What then? Why?

With a sinking feeling, she suspected she knew why. She had

deliberately kept it from her mind. Kevin had warned her about it when he had first revealed his plan. She could still see his gray and solemn face before her as he had put his hands on her shoulders—and warned her. Only warned her. Giving her a chance to decline to take the risk. Giving her no dictates, but letting her know his love, and that whatever she did, whatever she had to do to ensure her safety, he would accept without questions. It would simply not exist. And now, she thought, her decision was upon her.

Brigadeführer Dieter Haupt had summoned her to the inevitable. His demand on her—as a woman. For a moment she hesitated. Then she knocked on the door.

❖ 26 ❖

DIETER Haupt rose from behind his desk as Gaby entered his office.

"Fräulein Gertie," he said, giving her a proprietory smile. "Please come in." He walked from behind his desk toward a low table surrounded by easy chairs covered in a dark-green leather, standing in the far corner of the room. He motioned to one of them. "*Bitte,*" he said. "Please sit down."

"Thank you, *Herr Brigadeführer,*" Gaby said. She sat down. Haupt took a chair next to her. Confidentially, he leaned toward her.

"I wanted to see you for several reasons, Gertie," he said. "First of all, formally to thank you for the not inconsiderable risk you took upon yourself during that—eh, unpleasant terrorist episode a few days ago, and also for accepting a position with us here."

"It is I who thank you, *Herr Brigadeführer,*" Gaby said ingenuously.

Haupt smiled benevolently at her. "Nonsense," he said. He

made the word sound patronizing. "We are happy to have you. Already your section chief has informed me that you are doing valuable work." Again he smiled at her. "You see, I am taking a special interest in you."

"Thank you," Gaby said, giving it an appropriately grateful reading.

"That was the second reason I wanted to see you," Haupt went on. "To compliment you on fitting in so well, and to tell you that I have arranged for you to be allocated more comfortable living quarters."

"But—I am quite comfortable where I am now," Gaby said.

"Of course you are," Haupt said. "But your new quarters will be more—more spacious, with more privacy." He smiled at her conspiratorially.

"I see."

"As a matter of fact—"

The interoffice telephone on his desk suddenly gave a sharp ring. In annoyance he turned to glare at it.

"Please excuse me," he said as he rose and strode to the desk to answer the phone.

"Yes!" he snapped. "What is it?"

For a moment he listened.

"Bring them in," he ordered. He hung up and stood waiting at his desk, drumming his fingers on the top. Almost at once Stolitz entered, carrying a stack of papers.

"The *Herr Brigadeführer* wanted to see these as soon as they were delivered," the aide said as he placed the papers on the desk in front of Haupt. "The first incidents reports from the area you requested be canvassed."

"You may leave them."

"*Jawohl, Herr Brigadeführer*," Stolitz said smartly. He clicked his heels lightly, turned, and left—deliberately keeping his eyes from straying toward Gaby.

Haupt looked at the papers. They were written on all kinds of paper. Some were typed on official forms, others were handwritten on pages from a child's exercise book. Each had a brief typewritten capsule of the report clipped to it. He picked up the top report and began to read it. He glanced toward the girl, sitting quietly at the table. He put the report down. He had other things on his mind right now. Things more pleasant than reading undoubtedly dull reports.

But his curiosity got the better of him. Again he glanced toward the girl. She could wait for a few minutes.

He sat down at the desk and began to read. He was resigned to the fact that he'd have to wade through a raft of ordinary crime reports: burglaries, robberies, fights, and the usual "neighborly" denouncements by informers charging political transgressions. An argument between some refugees in the Wollin Bierstube . . . He was grateful to whomever had written the capsules. They enabled him to skip such trivialities.

But his eye was caught by a few reported incidents.

Item: May 14, Ziegenort. Domicile of one Mestlin, Horst, ransacked and looted. Two male refugees from Hamburg disappeared. Conclusion: Burglary.

Item: May 9, Misdroy. Two skilled workers, German nationals, working at the Misdroy test site, reported missing. Last seen at the Bierstube in Wollin after attending a performance at the KINO theater. Subsequent investigation failed to locate subjects. With them, their bicycles were reported missing. Conclusion: Desertion.

Item: May 9, Misdroy. Unidentified worker suffered broken arm in accident at checkpoint located at Misdroy Gate No. 1. Taken to base hospital by coworker. Both men disappeared before treatment of injury. No explanation. Tentative conclusion: The man was a foreign worker, unwilling to be treated except by his own.

Item: May 11, Kodram. Elderly man found drowned in nearby Fernosfelde marshland. No identification, no valuables on body. Conclusion: Robbery and murder.

Item: May 8, Laatzig. A farmer in Laatzig reported his outlying feed shack broken into, with signs of someone having spent a night or more in the shed. Nothing missing. Conclusion: Refugees seeking shelter.

Item: May 12, Gollnow. Man and woman in their thirties travelling in van with small trailer asking directions to Wollin and asking questions about area. Both spoke with foreign accents. No conclusion.

Item: May 15, Laatzig. Mobile special investigation team assigned to the Zebbin/Kammin region discovered dead in the burned wreck of their motorcycle off the Zebbin–Laatzig road. Conclusion: Accident.

There was one more item. An item which angered him. Either someone was totally moronic—or trying to ridicule his orders.

Item: May 5, Altdamm. Eight-year-old boy, Lippert, Werner, reported seeing blue spaceship landing in Dammscher Lake. Stated he held subsequent conversation with Martians, who showed him their green blood. Conclusion: Child's imagination.

An overimaginative boy's childish prattle, he thought angrily. The youth should have been in the *Jungvolk* instead of running around unsupervised. And making the inane report part of his, Dieter Haupt's, investigation was out-and-out effrontery. He would make it a point to find out who was responsible.

In a fit of anger he tore up the capsule of the report. The report itself was about to follow when he thought better of it. He would need it as evidence in any subsequent disciplinary action. He looked at the reports he had put aside. At first glance there did not seem to be any pattern to them. It would have to be studied.

There was also a report of the travellers who had passed through Wollin and stayed at Gasthof Adler. There had been many during the period. A penalty to be suffered because of the refugee program, he thought. All had had impeccable identification papers. All had since left, but more strangers were still arriving and departing. All would be thoroughly checked out.

And, of course, there had been the ambush.

He frowned over the reports. There had to be a clue somewhere. There had to. . .

Gaby was patiently waiting at the table. She wondered what the reports were that Stolitz had brought. Perhaps the commandant would become so engrossed in them that he would have no time for her, she thought. But she knew it was only wishful thinking. She knew what she would have to cope with.

But she still did not know what she would do when the time for a decision arrived.

With an almost physical ache she thought of Kevin.

She cast a quick glance toward the German officer bent over the reports on his desk.

Could she?

She knew how much depended on her—and on her decision. Lives. Many lives. Perhaps thousands. Perhaps the lives of her friends. And Kevin. Could she—play the part? It would be the most difficult, the most momentous role of her life.

A wave of anxiety suddenly swept over her. If a decision had to be made, let it be now, she thought vehemently. She could agonize over it no longer. The wait was tearing her apart.

Restlessly she stood up. Unconsciously she smoothed her dress. She turned to a wall with a group of several pictures on it. In the center hung an idealized portrait of a stern-looking Adolf Hitler. On each side were smaller framed photographs of what appeared to be important Nazi officers and officials, including one signed, Albert Speer.

Suddenly her eyes stopped their restive roving and remained fixed at one of the pictures.

It was a photograph of Dieter Haupt surrounded by a small group of high-ranking officers and civilians, none of whom she recognized.

Behind them rose the even slope of a wooded hill, and up a cleared path stretched a gigantic iron structure: a large, long, round barrel with numerous pairs of stubby tubes sticking out of it at regular intervals. Like a colossal iron millipede, it crept up the slope, peeking its snout over the crest far up in the distance.

She was gazing at a portrait of Lizzie.

The *Tausendfüssler*!

In a corner, which showed the clear surface of an iron machinery housing marked BERLINER STAHLBAU, the legend *HDP, Misdroy, April 1944* had been written in black ink.

She stared at the photograph.

Keppler had been right. One hundred percent right!

Suddenly she felt the German officer's arms encircle her from behind, his face close to her ear. She stiffened—and at once relaxed. He must not suspect, she thought wildly. He must not suspect.

She felt herself being turned around. She did not resist. She found herself staring up into the face of Dieter Haupt. Roughly he pulled her to him and pressed his lips to hers in a cruel, crushing kiss.

Panic and revulsion cascaded over her—instantly checked. Play the part, she thought. Play the part. Her mind shot back. She had played the part before in a play at the Grand Guignol. She had loathed the actor she had had to kiss passionately. She had loathed his garlic breath. But she had played the part. She had played the part. And she slipped into it. She returned the German's kiss. She could feel his rising excitement as he pressed against her. Play the part . . . Play the part. . . .

He released her. He held her firmly by the shoulders. His eyes bored into her.

"I want you, Gertie," he said hoarsely. "Come to my quarters tonight."

Desperately she tried not to let her growing panic show. If he started to fondle her in earnest, he would find the stolen envelopes.

"Oh, yes!" she heard herself cry. Who was the character she was playing? "Oh, yes, I will." She looked down. "But—it will be so unfair to you, *Herr Kommandant*. To us both."

"Dieter."

"Dieter."

He frowned at her. "Unfair? What do you mean—unfair?"

She made herself blush. "It—it is not a good time of the month, Dieter," she whispered miserably. "I am so sorry."

He scowled at her. *Scheissdreck*! he thought bitterly. Just his damned luck to hit a red-rag day. "How long?" he rasped.

"Not long," Gaby whispered, her voice seductively husky. "Not long. Three days." She looked up at him, eyes wide and moist. "I—I want to come to you fresh and clean, Dieter. Will you wait?"

"I will wait," he agreed reluctantly.

"You are a dear," Gaby said. She kissed him lightly. "Tomorrow I get my identity papers. Tomorrow I will go to Wollin."

He frowned. "To Wollin? Why?"

She looked coyly at him. "Shame on you," she teased him. "There are things a woman needs. And I want to be at my very best. In three days."

He nodded, obviously not happy with the delay.

Gaby turned toward the photograph on the wall. "That is a very handsome picture of you," she said brightly, pointing to the photograph with the *Tausendfüssler*. "I like it."

Haupt smiled at her.

"You are looking at your rival," he said. "Our Lizzie."

Gaby peered at the photograph. "Lizzie?" she said. "She looks very strange, your Lizzie. What will she do?"

"She will pound the Führer's enemies into the dust, Gertie," Haupt said proudly. "She will give him victory. And she will assure the triumph of the Thousand Year Reich!"

Gaby hardly listened to him. She had bought three days. Three days to complete her mission. Or fail.

❧ 27 ❧

As Gaby walked down the corridor in the HQ building, away from the commandant's office, she suddenly realized that even though she had bought herself a little time, she had also given herself an all but impossible deadline to get hold of the blank identification cards.

She had wangled permission to go to Wollin the following day. All she had thought of at the time was that she wanted to make contact with her friends. If it took too long before she showed up at the church, they'd start to worry. And perhaps take foolish chances.

Now she had less than twenty-four hours to carry out her mission, and not the slightest idea of how to go about the problem.

One elaborate, convoluted scheme after another had flitted through her mind, one more hopeless than the next. The problem appeared to be unsolvable. It seemed an impossibility.

A line from a play suddenly popped into her mind: *Impossibilities are only impossibilities because people make them so.* She had always thought it contrived and fatuous. Now it angered her.

Really! What nonsense, she thought. She didn't *make* this situation impossible. It was. Besides, that silly line would mean that everything would be easy if people would just make it so. And that was patently absurd.

Or was it?

She suddenly stopped.

Suppose she just decided to *make* it easy? Would it then be easy? Could she?

She looked down the corridor. Lutz Hermann's studio was a

217

few doors away. A line of people was waiting outside. Across the hallway, a few doors farther down, was the Security Office, where the master file of photographs was kept. And the blank identification cards.

Suppose . . .

She began to walk purposefully down the corridor once again, toward the far office. She had an idea. It was direct. It was brazen. But perhaps that silly line from the play wasn't fatuous after all.

A *Stabsgefreiter*—a corporal—was sitting at a desk. He looked up as Gaby entered the office.

"*Heil Hitler!*" Gaby said. "I am here to pick up my identification card."

"It will be issued to you when it is ready," the corporal informed her tersely.

Gaby frowned prettily. "Oh—I thought . . ." She looked concerned. "I am to go to Wollin tomorrow morning. Lutz Hermann has already taken my photograph. I understood I could pick up my card here today."

"Name?" the *Stabsgefreiter* asked gruffly. This was strictly outside of routine. And it did not please him.

"Kerlach, Gertie," Gaby said.

The man walked to a file cabinet and unlocked a dra er. From it he took a small box. He opened it and searched through it.

"There is no identification card here in the name of Kerlach," he said, pleased to say it. Things out of the accepted routine did not deserve to be rewarded with success.

Gaby bit her lip. "I—I do not understand," she said. "The *Kommandant* himself told me—" She let the rest of the sentence hang. She gazed pleadingly at the corporal, who had not let her mention of the commandant go unnoticed. "Is there—is there anything you can do? I should be most grateful."

The corporal scowled. It was highly irregular. But—the *Kommandant* . . . He glanced toward an open door into an adjoining office. Through it could be glimpsed an officer working at a desk.

"Wait here," the corporal said.

He put down the little file box, walked to the open door, and entered the office.

At once Gaby was at the file. The drawer was still open. She looked. They were there—a tray of identification cards. All of them blank.

Quickly she picked out two of them, and at once they joined the envelopes from the photographer's studio in her blouse. She stepped away from the file cabinet and waited at the desk.

The corporal returned.

"Your photographs are not ready yet, Frülein Kerlach," he informed her. "You may return to get your card before you leave for Wollin tomorrow morning."

"Oh, thank you, Corporal," Gaby beamed at him. "I knew I could count on you."

He nodded. "*Heil Hitler*!" he said.

"*Heil Hitler*!" Gaby responded.

She left the office.

That playwright, she thought admiringly, what a brilliant man he must have been.

She saw him the moment he came into the church. She wanted to run to him and feel his arms around her, but she walked demurely to the pew and took a seat a couple of feet from him. There were perhaps a dozen worshippers in the little church. No one paid them any attention as they bowed their heads in prayer.

"Gaby," Kevin whispered. "Thank God you are safe."

"I am."

"Are you—all right?"

She knew what he meant. "I have three days," she breathed.

"I love you."

"And I love you."

She ached to be close to him, but she did not move.

"We must make this quick," Kevin said in his urgent whisper. "Have you been successful?"

"Yes," she said. "This is how the system with the photographs works."

Quickly she told him.

"And the blank cards?" he asked.

"I have them." She glanced around. No one was watching them. Carefully she removed a small packet of papers from the front of her blouse and placed it in a psalm book. She put it on the seat between them.

"Here," she whispered. "I also copied my own card so you can see how it should be filled out. You will have to forge the signature of the officer who signed it. I traced it for you."

Kevin took the psalm book. He removed the little packet and put it in his pocket.

"When you get the photographs," Gaby said. "You must cut them to nine by seven centimeters in size."

"Exactly?"

"Exactly. It is the size the photographer uses. I measured it. And you must print your name on the back and sign it. Exactly as you have signed the card."

"They don't have to be any special kind of photographs?"

"No, many of the pictures on file were supplied by the people themselves. Any good ones will do. Remember, four of each."

"Fine. Meet me at four this afternoon. Not here again. At the other church. Where we were before. I will have the photos for you then."

"That soon? How is that possible?"

"Jan has an old camera. And he has managed to get everything that's needed. Ted has been taught how to develop the film and make prints."

Gaby ventured a glance at him. "Who—who will go?" she asked.

"Ted and I," he answered.

She had known the answer.

"What about the test site itself?" he asked.

"As I told you, there are three areas and three gates, each with a checkpoint. The Millipede—I saw a photograph of it, and it looks just as Jan said. It is located in the third area."

"What else?"

"I made a sketch of the site. As much as I have seen of it," Gaby told him. She reached to withdraw it from her blouse. "It is—"

Suddenly the solemn stillness of the church was shattered by loud gutteral cries—and the abrupt staccato clatter of a submachine gun coming from outside.

Everyone in the church started, their heads instantly turning toward the massive church doors.

All at once they burst open. A man came staggering into the church, clutching his bloody chest. Wild-eyed, he looked around.

"Sanctuaire!" he cried hoarsely. "Sanctuaire!"

Behind him, through the church doors, three Waffen SS soldiers came running in, their submachine guns on the ready.

The fugitive whirled to face them. He raised both his arms into the air. "Sanctuaire!" he cried again. "Vive la France!"

He pitched forward to lie motionless on the stone floor, a widening pool of red spreading from him.

One of the soldiers, an SS *Rottenführer*, a corporal, walked up to the man. With his hobnailed boot he turned him over. He looked toward the two others.

"*Erledigt,*" he said curtly. "Done for."

He turned to the stunned worshippers watching the grisly drama in horror.

"Everybody!" he shouted. "Up! Up! *Los!*" He gestured with his gun. "Over there! Form a line. *Schnell! Los! Los!*"

The people began to scramble from the pews, crossing themselves as they passed the body, averting their eyes. Deliberately, Kevin and Gaby stayed apart as they hurried to obey the Rottenführer's command.

Gaby found herself near the head of the line. Kevin was one of the last.

The soldiers positioned themselves at the door, and one by one the churchgoers were motioned over to be questioned, their papers examined, before they were let go.

The papers of the man directly ahead of Gaby were being scrutinized by the Rottenführer. He asked the man a sharp question. The man cringed. Gaby perked up. What was going on?

"I—I am sorry," she hear the man stammer, obviously terrified. "It—it is only dirt. It—it got smeared, and I—I tried to wipe it off, and—and the ink . . . There is nothing wrong with it. I swear. Believe me. Please believe me."

The Rottenführer poked him with his gun. "Up!" he ordered gruffly. "Hands in the air. *Los!*"

The man at once obeyed.

One of the other soldiers searched him. Thoroughly. He found nothing suspicious.

The *Rottenführer* threw the papers at the man. "On your way!" he snapped.

The man bowed. "At once, Herr *Rottenführer*," he said. "At once," He literally ran from the church.

Gaby stood frozen. The sketch of the test site at Misdroy! She still had it. If they found it . . . And Kevin. He had the blank cards. And the copy of hers. Could he get rid of them before the soldiers could question him? Bleakly she knew the answer. It would be impossible. The people in line were being closely watched.

"*Sie! Fraülein!*" she heard the *Rottenführer* cry. Startled, she looked at him. "*Los!*" he called to her, motioning her over.

Head held high, she marched up to him. She handed him her identification card.

"I work at Misdroy," she said haughtily, "for *Brigadeführer* Haupt. What is going on?"

The soldier glanced at her card. "A foreign worker, *Fraülein*," he said. "A lousy Frenchman. Somehow he got out of the compound. Tried to escape. Run for home."

Gaby was seething with rage inside. She smiled a superior little smile at the soldier.

"He will not get far now, will he?" she commented.

The soldier grinned at her. "Just as far as hell, I imagine," he said dryly. He handed her card back to her. "*In Ordnung,*" he said with a little bow.

Gaby walked away from the church. Her heart was pounding. Would Kevin get through as well?

In the square before the church was a little fountain set with intricate ironwork. She went over to it. She dipped her handkerchief in the water and gently daubed her forehead. She kept an eye on the church door, where she could see the worshippers, one by one, being questioned—and occasionally searched.

Kevin.

It would soon be his turn. And he had the incriminating cards in his pocket.

She saw him. She saw him give his identification papers to the *Rottenführer.* She saw the soldier look at them—and shoot a curt question at Kevin. She saw Kevin answer. And she saw the soldier poke him with his gun, and Kevin raise his hands. Her heart stood still.

✧ 28 ✧

SHE had to do something. Ad-lib. Now!

She ripped the sketch of the Misdroy test site from its hiding place in her blouse, crumpling it as she did. She saw one of the soldiers begin to pat down Kevin.

"*Herr Rottenführer!*" she cried as loudly as she could. "*Bitte!* Over here!"

Startled by the sudden outcry, the three soldiers looked toward Gaby as she stood by the fountain.

She held up the crumpled sketch in her hand. "You must look at this," she cried. "It may be important."

The Rottenführer handed Kevin's identification papers to the soldier who had been about to search him. With the other soldier, he strode over to Gaby.

"What is it, Fräulein?" he asked brusquely.

"This, *Herr Rottenführer.*" She handed him the sketch, which she had smoothed out. "I found it lying here on the ground. It looks like—like a sketch of where I work. Misdroy. What do you think?"

The *Rottenführer* took the sketch. He frowned over it.

"It may have been dropped, or thrown away, by that foreign worker in there." She nodded toward the church.

Out of the corner of her eye, she saw the soldier with Kevin watching them with curiosity. She saw him glance at the papers in his hand and give them back to Kevin, dismissing him, as he returned his attention to what was going on at the fountain.

And she saw Kevin walk away, disappearing around a corner of the church.

The Rottenführer was studying the sketch.

"Is it of importance?" Gaby asked him.

223

He nodded ponderously. "Yes, *Fräulein*," he answered. "It is of importance."

"It takes someone in authority to recognize such things," Gaby said admiringly. "Someone such as yourself." She smiled at him. "I should not wonder if this *day* is also of importance. To you, *Herr Rottenführer*. Eliminating a dangerous spy and also to be able to provide proof of his guilt. I should not wonder if it would earn you the silver piping of an *Unterscharführer* on your shoulder straps."

"I am only doing my duty, *Fräulein*," the *Rottenführer* said sternly. But the pleased look in his eyes betrayed his gratification.

"You had best go about your business now, Fräulein," he said officiously. "We will take care of matters here."

"Of course, *Herr Rottenführer*," Gaby agreed. "*Heil Hitler!*" And she walked away.

The sun was already low on the horizon, but Dieter Haupt still sat studying the list of suspected reports.

He had placed them chronologically and had added the most recent incident. A foreign worker who was trying to escape was killed in Wollin by a security patrol this very morning. He was carrying with him a rudimentary sketch of the test site. Haupt was fully aware of the grave implications of this latest incident.

He stared at the list. By now he knew it by heart. He itched with frustration. He hated not to be able to control a situation. Much more so, one he could not even get a fix on. He had a nagging feeling that the answer was to be found in that damned list.

But—where?

May 8	Farmer's feed shack on outlying field broken into.
May 9	Two workers, German nationals, reported as deserters.
May 9	Accident at Gate #1; man breaks arms, disappears from hospital.
May 11	Man found drowned in marsh.
May 12	Strangers in van showing exceptional interest in area.
May 13	Ambush.

May 14	Burglary of home by two male refugees.
May 15	Motorcycle security team killed in highway accident.
May 17	Foreign worker, escaped, killed in Wollin, in possession of sensitive sketch.

A vague picture was beginning to emerge in his mind. He had no idea if it was even close to reality.

He had dismissed a couple of the reported incidents, which—although puzzling—did not fit the pattern he had built. The first was the drowned man in the bog. Even though it had happened close to Misdroy, on Wollin Island itself, he could see no connection with the others. The second was the accident at the gate.

And, of course, that ridiculous Martian story.

There was obviously more than one saboteur—at least three. There had been that many at the ambush. There were probably more. And he suspected that they might have inside help from traitors at Misdroy itself. If the enemy *had* mounted an operation against Misdroy, it was undoubtedly a massive one. Certainly the picture he seemed to discern bore that out.

The scenario he had built looked somewhat like this: Two separate teams of saboteurs arrive in the area to carry out a sabotage operation against the *Tausendfüssler*. One team—two men?—temporarily take shelter in a farmer's feed shack (May 8, on mainland east of Misdroy). The other, a man and a woman, arrive in a van (May 12, near Gollnow, southeast of Misdroy). The insider traitor-informers desert to link up and give these enemy agents whatever information they have been able to gather (May 9). It is decided that he, Dieter Haupt, is too formidable an adversary, and the men from the two teams join forces to ambush and kill him. The attempt (May 13) is blocked by unforeseen intervention, leaving one saboteur dead, another incapacitated. The burglary (May 14 at Ziegenort, west of Misdroy) might have been committed by two other accomplices already in place, to "finance" the operation, although that was problematical; and the security team accident (May 15) might not have been an accident at all, but a means to prevent the investigators from reporting information they had unearthed, possibly damaging to the sabotage effort. The foreign worker killed in Wollin, obviously more than just a runaway since he possessed a highly sensitive

225

sketch of the site at Misdroy—was probably part of the internal band of traitors. On second thought, the two workers involved in the accident at Gate No. 1 (May 9) and their subsequent disappearance from the hospital might well have been accomplices, afraid of the questioning a hospital stay would have entailed.

The conclusion would have to be that a concerted, a massive effort to sabotage Operation Lizzie at Misdroy had been mounted by the enemy and was still being carried out by the surviving saboteurs.

If his scenario was even remotely accurate, he realized, there were two paramount things he had to do.

First, strengthen internal security against possible traitors, and secondly, make it not only difficult but totally impossible for any foreign worker to escape the confinement of the base. Meanwhile, the intensive search for the saboteurs would continue, as would all increased security measures.

He was a little awed at the perceived magnitude of the enemy operation, and—secretly—a little proud that his Lizzie was considered important enough to mount a top effort.

But in his analysis of the situation, he could find no indication what their next move would be.

All he knew was—he would crush it.

He realized, of course, why Misdroy had become the focal point of enemy efforts to destroy the *Tausendfüssler* program. The Führer himself, knowing the vital role the Mimoyecques batteries would play in the destruction of the invasion forces, even before they could be deployed, had only recently issued orders to keep the entire Fifteenth Army in the Calais–Mimoyecques area, thereby making enemy infiltration impossible for either sabotage or intelligence-gathering purposes at the HDP batteries at Mimoyecques.

And that left Misdroy.

Misdroy, which was the key to the entire Tausendfüssler operation. There were still a couple of critical calculations to be tested before the Misdroy *Tausendfüssler* would fire her first live projectile armed with a full-load warhead. So far, of course, all firings had been executed with dummy warheads. Just in case of an accident or misfiring. No need to risk blowing up the main barrel. The test firings of live projectiles would commence after all calculations and calibrations had been verified, tested, and retested. The final dummy warhead test firing had been scheduled for May twentieth. The full warhead projectiles would be fired two days later. Both tests would be successful. He had no doubts about that. Mimoyecques was impatiently waiting for the results. No firings could, of course, be undertaken there before Misdroy provided the final answers. After that the batteries at Mimoyecques needed six days to gear up for action. His schedule would give them all the time they needed to get ready to launch a saturation bombardment by June first.

On that day the batteries at Mimoyecques would begin to rain a barrage of projectiles armed with warheads of high explosives on London and on the Channel coast cities from Dover to Bournemouth. The world would not have seen such total destruction before, such annihilation, as his Lizzie would wreak upon the enemy of the Reich!

May twentieth, at 0900 hours, Lizzie would give up her final secrets—and her sisters on the Channel coast would get ready to strike.

He savored the feeling of accomplishment. He'd done it! As he had told Albert Speer he would.

May twentieth. In just three days. He smiled to himself. He would reward himself that night with that delectable little Alsatian, Gertie.

With amusement, he suspected she had used the old bad-time-of-the-month dodge to postpone their tryst. Under different circumstances he would have resented it. He would have done something about it. But he had other matters to contend with. The next few days would be crucial. Besides, it would all enhance the pleasures he planned for the night of the twentieth of May.

He would see to that.

Thoughts of a tryst with *Brigadeführer* Dieter Haupt were the farthest from Gaby's mind as she walked toward the *Kommandantur*.

She had just returned from Wollin. It was late afternoon. She hoped not too late.

The meeting in the second church with Kevin had gone smoothly. Concealed in her blouse, she carried the two sets of photographs he had given her; one set of Ted and one of Kevin, already inserted in their proper envelopes, one for each of the three gates and one for the Security Office. She felt as if she were carrying the collected works of Jules Verne against her chest, and she was astonished that no one seemed to notice.

She took a deep breath—and entered.

Outside Hermann's studio she joined a small group of men still waiting to have their ID photographs taken. It was only a few minutes later when Hermann stuck his head out the door and called, "Next!"

He spied Gaby. He stopped the man about to enter the studio.

"Ah, *Fräulein* Kerlach," he said, obviously pleased to see her, although he tried to sound businesslike. He turned to the man in the door. "Moment, *bitte*," he said. "I must see the *Fräulein* on studio business." He was not a good liar, Gaby thought.

The man grumbled something unintelligible but obviously unpleasant as he stepped aside to let Gaby enter.

Hermann took her hand. He bent over it—his lips not quite touching.

"*Fräulein* Gertie," he said. "I am very happy to see you."

"Thank you, Lutz," Gaby said, retrieving her hand. "I was here in the building, so I thought I would stop by and say hello." She glanced at the desk. The letter basket with the envelopes containing the photographs to be distributed to the gates and the Security Office was full to overflowing. She drew a sigh of relief. She was not too late.

"I am glad you did," Hermann said. He obviously meant it. He looked at her appreciatively. "You must like it here at Misdroy. You look quite radiant."

Gaby laughed. "It is the sea air," she said. "And the bicycle ride back from Wollin." She fixed her eyes on him. "Lutz," she said, "you promised I could see my photo for the ID card. Did you keep a copy for me?"

"Of course," he said. "Of course I did."

"Oh, good," she smiled brightly. "You are a dear."

"I will get it." He started to limp toward his darkroom. Gaby followed him with her eyes, ready to retrieve her envelopes and drop them in the basket as soon as the man left the room.

Suddenly he stopped.

"Whoa!" he exclaimed. "I am a dumbbell. I have it right here. I kept it out for you." He shuffled back to his desk, opened a drawer, and triumphantly brought out a photograph. He gave it to Gaby.

"Here."

Gaby looked at the picture. "Oh, it is excellent," she cried, managing to sound enthusiastic while her thoughts were bleak. If Hermann did not leave her alone in the room, how would she be able to get the envelopes with Ted's and Kevin's photos into the basket?

If she did not, they would both be caught when they tried to enter Misdroy—in the morning.

"How ever did you manage?" she asked admiringly. She looked at the photographer. He was a gentle man, she thought. Perhaps . . .

"Easy, *mein liebes Fräulein*," he smiled at her. "A photographer is only as good as his subject. And I was blessed."

"May I keep it?"

"It is for you," he nodded.

"Thank you, Lutz." She began to unbutton the top button of her blouse. She looked coyly at Hermann. "Lutz," she said demurely, "be a gentleman."

He actually blushed. "Oh," he said, sounding embarrassed. "Of course. Of course." Shuffling on his artificial leg, he turned his back to her.

Quickly she fished the envelopes from her blouse and placed them in the letter basket on the desk. She put her photograph in her blouse and buttoned it up.

"There," she said. "It is safe now."

Hermann turned around.

"A more wonderful safekeeping place I could not dream of," he said. "You—you honor my modest little photograph. And me."

"You deserve it," Gaby asserted. "Both of you." She leaned forward and kissed him on the cheek. "Thank you."

She gave him a bright smile. She found herself liking the man. She even felt a little guilty for duping him, for using him the way she had.

"I had better go," she said. She nodded toward to door to the corridor. "Before those men out there start a riot."

"You will come visit again, Gertie?" Hermann asked her, hope in his voice.

"I will, Lutz," she said. "I will."

She meant it.

She walked toward the door. Behind her in the letter basket rested the ID photographs of Ted and Kevin, duly cut to size and signed. Ready to be distributed that day.

Tomorrow. Tomorrow she would learn if they had done their job.

❈ 29 ❈

THE morning of May 18 was raw and overcast.

Foreboding was the word that came to Kevin's mind as he stood in line at Gate No. 1 to be admitted to the test site at Misdroy. He hoped it wasn't prophetic.

To Ted, who stood a few spaces behind him, there was also something ominous about the scene. It was a creepy feeling of déjà vu, a reminder of misadventure. There was the gate; the checkpoint; the barbed-wire fences and the watchtowers; the armed Waffen SS guards—and even the weapons carrier parked at the shed.

There had, of course, been no way for them to make contact with Gaby, and they did not know if she had been successful in getting their photographs into the files. They could only trust her. They *had* made arrangements for her failure. She was to come to the first gate on some pretext or other so that they could see her. If they did, they would know she had not been able to carry out her mission, and they would have to get away as best they could.

It was a half-assed plan, Kevin realized, but they had not been able to come up with anything better. He craned his neck to catch sight of Gaby, hoping he would not.

And he reached the checkpoint.

Two Waffen SS guards were checking the ID cards. A few more, armed with submachine guns, stood by.

Kevin handed his ID card to one of the guards. The man read off the name on it to his companion who had a file box of photographs before him.

"Lawetz, Karel," he intoned.

"Lawetz, Karel," the second soldier repeated. He searched through the file. He frowned. Once more he looked through the photographs. He scowled at Kevin and motioned the other guard over.

Kevin saw him nod toward him and shake his head. The second guard began to look through the file box.

Kevin stood frozen. Something was wrong. His heart began to hammer. But there was nothing he could do except brazen it out. The thoughts raced through his mind. He was caught. If he ran, he would only get a few feet before he'd be cut down. Fleeing was out of the question. But what if he did try? If he did start to run would Ted be able to get away in the confusion? Could he save Ted? He made up his mind.

He was just about to run when he heard the second guard growl, *"Idiot!"* He glanced toward him and saw him pick up a few envelopes stuck in the back of the file box. "The new ones," he said. *"Blöd bist du!*—stupid!" He opened the envelopes and pulled out the photographs in them. He looked at one of them and at Kevin. He turned it over and read the name on the back.

"Lawetz, Karel," he said.

"He gave the picture back to his companion and turned to Kevin. He returned the ID card to him.

"In Ordnung!" he said, motioning him on.

Kevin moved his legs. They were leaden. He felt as if he were trying to walk in hot tar. He was suddenly uncomfortably aware of the cold sweat that trickled down his sides and of his heart pounding in his throat. But he managed a grin at the guard as he walked through the gate onto the base.

He did not look back. He knew Ted would be along. One of the other new photos had been his.

Their ID cards, faithfully copied from Gaby's authentic one, permitted them access to the third, or innermost, area of the test site, and not until after they successfully had negotiated Gate No. 3 did Kevin and Ted talk to each other.

"Worked like a charm," Ted grinned. "That gal of yours can play on my team anytime."

Kevin nodded. But he was worried. What price had Gaby had to pay to accomplish what she had? He prayed she was all right.

They walked into area three, the area that held the *Tausenfüssler* itself. Ahead of them was a wooded rise, the trees hiding

231

the near slope. They followed a few workers who took a road that led to the rise.

As they rounded a bend in the road, they stopped and stared in awe.

They were face to face with Busy Lizzie.

Like a gigantic iron millipede, it crawled unendingly up the slope. Nicole had been right, Kevin thought. Its massive segmented main barrel did resemble the round, chitinous body of a myriapod, surprisingly delicate because of its enormous length, and the side tubes looked startlingly like stubby legs. In the blink of an eye all the incredible rumors, the unbelievable descriptions, the fantastic claims had been confirmed.

If a battery of such monsters existed at Mimoyecques and were able to go into action, London might well be doomed, the invasion defeated even before it was launched.

At the bottom of the slope, at the breech end of the colossal gun, a platform had been erected, as well as an ammunition hoist constructed with sturdy poles supported by guylines with an adjoining winch.

"Busy yourself for a few minutes," Ted said to Kevin. "I think we've found what we came for—verification, in spades. But I want to take a closer look at the loading mechanism of the thing. Then we'll get the hell out of here and run for home."

Kevin nodded. He glanced toward a shed that stood nearby. He needed some props to look busy. "I'll be over there," he said.

"Right." Ted sauntered over toward the gun.

The door to the shed was open. Kevin glanced inside. No one was there. On a table lay a clipboard with several papers clipped to it. He picked it up and walked outside. He sat down on a low stack of what appeared to be railroad ties and began to study the papers. There were tables of figures, charts, and computations. They made absolutely no sense to him.

One chart that looked like an erratic sales curve presented at a sales convention was marked *Verschusskurve*, which translated into something like "firing curve"; a series of columns of numbers under various headings was marked, *Tabelle: Versuchsdurch—führung, Werte der Abgegebenen Schüsse*—Table of Test Performance, Value of Fired Rounds; and another table was marked, *Geschossgeschwindigkeiten an den Kreuzstücken*—Speed of Projectile at Cross Barrels.

He wondered if he should take them along. He decided against it. The risk was too great. Still, he wondered what the charts and tables meant. He was so engrossed in trying to figure it out that he started when he heard a voice say:

"Have a swig?"

He looked up.

Before him stood a man. He held a bottle of beer toward him.

"No," Kevin said. "No, thank you. It is—it is a little early."

The man took a long pull on his bottle. "*Mench!* Never too early for a beer," he grinned. He glanced around and sat down next to Kevin.

"New here?"

"Yes. I am supposed to replace someone."

"*Na ja,*" the man nodded. "Couple of bastards took off, they say." He spat. "*Scheisskerle!*"

He looked at Kevin. "Name is Günther," he said.

"Karel," Kevin reciprocated.

The man nodded. He leaned forward and peered down the road.

"Gräber is late this morning," he observed. "Big night in town, no doubt." He turned to Kevin. "He is the big wheel at the breech." He shrugged. "I suppose he is getting his final instructions," he said, "for the big day."

"The big day?" Kevin asked.

The man looked at him in astonishment. "Sure," he said. "The final test firings. Where the devil have you been?"

"Oh," Kevin said. Shit! And I'm supposed to be one of them, he thought, disgusted with himself. "I did not realize what you meant."

The man gave him a sidelong glance. "*Na ja.* It is not supposed to be generally known," he said. "But it is. I guess no one got around to telling you."

"I—I had heard something about it," Kevin said. "But no details."

"Details," the man shrugged. "What blasted details? In a couple of days we fire the final test series, and then it is *aus*—finished with the dummies. A salvo or two of live ones, and we can all head for home." He took a long pull on his beer. "I have been here over nine months," he observed. "Long enough for my Else to hatch a kid, and I will kill her if she has! And I am *ready* to go home."

He turned his bottle upside down. It was empty. Again he looked down the road. "No sign of Mr. Big Wheel," he said. "Time enough to get another beer." He turned to Kevin. "Sure you will not have one?"

Kevin shook his head. "Thanks," he said, "Not for me."

The man shrugged. "Your loss," he said. He walked away.

A few moments later Ted joined Kevin.

"Okay," he said, "I've seen enough." He nodded toward the *Tausendfüssler*. "It's a breech load," he said. "From the looks of things, the damned projectiles have got to weigh a couple of hundred pounds and be at least eight feet long."

"Ted—" Kevin began.

Ted interrupted him.

"We've bloody well done it, good buddy," he said. "We can give Milton Hall an eyeball account of the damned thing."

"It's too late," Kevin said.

Ted stared at him.

"Too late?" he repeated. "What the hell are you talking about?"

"The final tests are in two days, Ted," Kevin told him soberly. "Two days! I just found that out. There's no way we can get the information back in time for anyone to act on it."

He looked solemnly at his friend.

"I think we'll have to change our plans," he said. "Our problem has not been solved. It has just gotten a hell of a lot bigger."

❈ 30 ❈

THE air was heavy and tense in Janusz Keppler's blackout-curtained living room. It was past three o'clock in the morning of May nineteenth, and the four men were tired and grim, their faces gray with exhaustion. They'd sat up half the night wrestling with the problem confronting them. It seemed monumental. Unsolvable.

"Okay," Ted said, his voice drained of energy. "Let's summarize."

"Again?" Mike mumbled.

"Yes, again," Ted snapped. "Before we get too damned tired to think at all." He ticked off the points on his fingers. "We agree that we can't possibly make our way back to Paris in time—even if we split up to give ourselves more of a chance. We agree that somehow the final test firings at Misdroy must be made to fail, and we agree that it is up to us to make sure they do fail. We can expect help from no one. And we agree that minor acts of sabotage will be too ineffectual, even if we could carry out enough of them without being caught."

"All of which leaves us with the same impossible conclusion," Kevin said tiredly. "We will have to blow up the whole blasted gun itself. The main barrel."

"And with the same damned question, how?" Mike said.

"Yeah, how?" Ted repeated. "It's a little like asking us to surround the Pentagon and blow up the Combined Chiefs of Staff."

"One thing," Kevin said. "We didn't spend enough time on the base to be able to come up with any ideas. We go back there later today. Take a good look around. Perhaps something will pop up. Some way to get the job done." He looked at his watch. "I suggest we all get some rest and that Ted and I report back at Misdroy at the regular time."

"Only this time *I* go, too," Mike said.

"No way," Ted said firmly.

"And why not?" Mike flared belligerently. "I can carry my own weight. And I want to."

"Why not?" Ted said. "You want to know why not? If we weren't so bloody tired, you'd damned well know why not."

Mike glared at him.

"For one," Ted went on. "That missing arm of yours would be a handicap. What the hell kind of cock-and-bull story would you feed them if they found out? And you can be sure they would find out." He shook his head. "But even if your gift of blarney could get you through that one, have you forgotten about the ID cards? The photos? How the hell would you get around that? There sure isn't enough time to go through that routine again. Let alone asking Gaby to place herself in further danger. And there's—"

"Okay, okay," Mike grumbled. "I get the picture."

"You and Jan can do the most good by staying right here and making sure we have a safe place to return to."

"And be here when Gaby gets back," Kevin said. "We'll have to warn her to get out before we begin our act."

"And what is that?" Mike wanted to know. "What is it you'll be doing to blow that hellish thing to where it belongs?"

"Dad," Kevin said, "I wish I knew."

"Sorry we can't write a script for you," Ted said. "We'll have to, as you say, wing it when we get there. Play our parts by ear."

Silently he wondered. He wondered if all his instruction, all his training received at Milton Hall would help him now. Now, when imagination and "playacting" were the important factors. And he wondered what Milton Hall would do in his spot.

They had only one day to come up with an idea that would work. One day to get ready to cripple the *Tausendfüssler*, to abort the final test firings scheduled for the twentieth.

Tomorrow.

"Thank you, Colonel Baldon."

Brigadier James Hindsmith Parnell leaned back in his chair. He contemplated the American Special Forces officer sitting at ease across the desk from him. A capable sort, he mused.

"I merely wanted to be brought up to date on every detail, what? Tomorrow I am attending the May twentieth high-level conference at SHAEF at oh-eight-thirty hours. I rather imagine they shall ask me for a thorough evaluation."

"Really," Dirk Baldon agreed. "Well, as I said, the efficiency of the Jedburgh teams is tops. The program is an unqualified success. All reports indicate unparalleled cooperation between the Jeds and the Maquis. My gut feeling is that our boys are making a real contribution in paving the way for the invasion."

Parnell nodded. "I shall so inform SHAEF," he said. "Thank you, Colonel."

It was a dismissal.

Baldon remained in his seat.

"There is one other thing I'd like to discuss with you," he said.

Parnell sighed inwardly. He knew what was coming. Again. "What is it, Colonel?" he asked.

"Mimoyecques," Dirk said grimly. "I can't shake the feeling that that place could turn out to be a real bitch." He frowned at the brigadier. "Are there any further air strikes scheduled?" he asked. "Do you know?"

This time Parnell sighed not only inwardly.

"Colonel Baldon," he said patiently. "As you well know, the installations at Mimoyecques were extensively bombed by the Number Two Group Fighter Command in November of last year, and again as recently as in March of this year. By B-seventeens. Post-raid aerial photographs showed the entire area pockmarked with craters. Anything there was probably destroyed or at least badly damaged. In any case, there are at the moment obviously more pressing targets to be taken out." He paused. He looked squarely at Baldon. "I know of no immediate bombing missions scheduled against Mimoyecques."

"And we have no Jeds in the immediate area," Baldon frowned. "Damn it! I don't like it."

"I am certain SHAEF is well aware of the situation."

"I'm sure they are. And I'm sure they're damned pleased that a whole German army, the crack Fifteenth, is still in the Calais and Mimoyecques area instead of at the planned invasion beaches ready to repel our landings." He looked searchingly at Parnell. "But—I wasn't only thinking of an air strike on Mimoyecques," he said. "I was also thinking of suggesting that an air attack be mounted against Misdroy."

"Misdroy?" Parnell raised an eyebrow.

"Exactly. That place may well be the primer that'll make the whole shebang go sky high."

"Are you not making a bit much of this, Colonel?"

"Will you suggest an air strike on Misdroy?"

"It is rather far into Germany, is it not?" Parnell said. It was a statement, not a question. "There are indubitably targets more vital to the invasion than—eh, Misdroy."

"Will you bring it up at SHAEF?" Baldon persisted.

Parnell drew himself up. "I rather think not," he said. "We have no evidence, Colonel, to suggest—"

"That's way off base and you know it!"

Parnell looked icily at his subordinate officer. When he spoke, his voice was arctic. "I rather think, Colonel, that—"

"Oh, come off it!" Dirk exploded. "This thing's too damned serious for that Colonel-sir-Brigadier-sir crap. I want to know what you are going to do about the situation, if anything. I've got a damned good man out there and a bunch of damned loyal volunteers who thought the whole thing important enough to risk their lives over. Perhaps lose them!"

For a moment Parnell sat motionless, glaring coldly at Dirk. Then he relaxed.

"Very well, Dirk," he said calmly. "I understand your concern for your chaps. And I respect it." Slowly he shook his head. "But there has been no word from them. Not a blessed sign of life, what? They have undoubtedly been caught. Or killed."

"But that's exactly it," Baldon exclaimed. "Ted Hawkins was a top agent—despite his individualism. Or because of it. Trained to a T. Too damned good to be caught first day out like a kid with his hand in the cookie jar. Unless. Unless he ran into such an extensive and such a comprehensive security system that he had no way out." He looked closely at the brigadier. "And if Misdroy is protected by that kind of super-security complex, you can bet your ass there's something going on there. Something we'd better find out about. Or—destroy."

For a few moments Parnell sat silent, lost in thought.

"You have a point, Dirk," he finally acknowledged. "The situation is a bit of a sticky wicket." He stood up. This time there was no doubt that it was a dismissal.

"I cannot promise anything, of course," he said gravely. "But I *will* bring the matter up at the SHAEF meeting. Perhaps an air mission can be mounted at a later date. I shall see what I can do tomorrow."

With a flourish, Dieter Haupt signed the final official test-firing sequence scheduled for the following day. He dated the order, Misdroy, 19.5.44. He looked at his watch and added, 0830.

There was something about time, he thought, something that annoyed him. When you were looking forward to something you wanted to happen, time dragged on interminably. But when the desired event finally did happen, the damned time speeded up, cutting your enjoyment to the quick.

And right now he was definitely bogged down in the first stage.

Once more he glanced at the document he had just received. Damn the delays! Incompetence seemed to be on the rise.

Führerbefehl—Führer Order—it read. *Führerhauptquartier den 16.Mai 1944.*

It was stamped *GEHEIM*—SECRET—and *CHEF-SACHE, Nur Durch Offizier*—Command Action, Officer Courier Only.

Once more he read it:

Re. Employment of Long-Range Weapons Against England. The Führer has ordered:

1. The long-range bombardment of England will commence in the beginning of June. The exact date will be set by Commander-in-Chief, West, who will also control the bombardment with the help of LXV Army Corps and 3rd Luftwaffe.

The long-range weapons to be put into action, Haupt knew, were bombers: the Fzg. 76—that pilotless bomb in development— and, prominently, the *Hochdruckpumpe*. His Lizzie.

And the report went on to state:

3. Execution.
   (a) Against the main target, London. The bombardment will open like a thunderclap by night with a sudden long-range artillery attack . . .

He could visualize it. His *Tausendfüssler* batteries opening up and showering the enemy with deadly fragments of hell. He could feel the abject terror of the Engländer as death from the sky rained down upon them. And not knowing. That was the ultimate horror. Not knowing from where that death came. Not knowing how to escape it.

   (b) Orders will be given in due course for switching fire to other targets.

He knew what those other targets were. Targets whose destruction would result in the annihilation of the enemy invasion forces massed along the Channel coast.

And the final entry read:

5. The order for secrecy set forth in Par. 7 of the order of 25. December 1943, No. 663082/43 for Senior Commanders will apply.

And it was signed:
The Chief of the High Command of the Armed Forces,

It was still a thrill for him to read the Führer Order commanding the action of his Lizzie. He felt that he, Dieter Haupt, had made it possible. At least contributed the lion's share toward its successful completion.

And he would be ready.

The Führer's order would change the course of the war. It was about time, he thought bleakly. The enemy had intensified his campaign in Italy on his march toward Rome, begun seven months earlier. He had smashed through the fortified Gustav Line that ran across the boot. The British had thrown a bridgehead across the turbulent Rapido River. And only yesterday, after two months of fighting, the Americans had finally captured the much-contested stronghold of Monte Casino, despite the fact that it had been held by crack paratroops.

Tomorrow, he thought. Tomorrow it will all be over. Tomorrow would at last bring the results everyone so eagerly awaited.

There was, of course, still that annoying business of the sabotage threat. But he could cope with that.

He still was not completely satisfied with his projected scenario regarding the saboteurs, and he had no further significant reports. And somehow that nonsensical story about the Martians kept nagging him. He dismissed it. All he could do was to be unceasingly vigilant.

He had contemplated restricting everyone to the base, but the resentment would have been high, and he needed as much *Korpsgeist*—esprit de corps—as could be mustered to ensure success. And success he would have. At any cost.

❖ 31 ❖

TO Kevin and Ted, there seemed to be more armed guards around and more intense scrutiny of every returning German worker than before, or perhaps they just imagined it because of their own heightened wariness. But there was no mistaking the increased activity on the base, even in the early hours of the morning. They were coming down to the wire at the test site, and it was quite evident that something important was in preparation.

Kevin glanced at his watch. 0837 hours. The final test firings with dummy warheads were scheduled to begin at 0900 hours the next day, they had learned, on May twentieth. They were up against an army of ruthless, vigilant security forces; a gigantic sabotage job they had no idea of how to carry out, in a place that was still virtually unknown to them. And they had less than twenty-five hours to accomplish their mission. Good luck, he thought bleakly.

They were walking briskly into the third, or innermost, area of the test site, where the *Tausendfüssler* itself was located, after having been passed through Gate No. 3, trying to look purposeful.

"We'll split up," Ted said. "You go to Gaby. Warn her to get out. I'll scout around and see what I can find."

Kevin nodded. "Any ideas?"

"We'll take it step by step," Ted said. "Two things first. We'll have to find out how we can get hold of some high explosives. Enough of it to do some real damage. And we'll have to determine the best spot to place the explosives on the gun barrel so the damned thing'll be blown sky-high. We'll only get one shot at it."

"I'll see if Gaby has learned anything more," Kevin nodded. "Where and when do you want to meet?"

241

"Two hours," Ted said. He pointed to a small shack made of corrugated iron. A sign over the door read: *MALWERKSTATT NO. III.* "Over there. By the paintshop."

They parted company. Ted walked to the paintshack; Kevin continued toward the HQ buildings.

Gaby had told them that the Library and the Documents Center, where she worked, were housed in a group of low buildings adjacent to the base HQ. He stopped where the road forked three ways and studied a signpost with several wooden markers pointing in different directions.

A man came walking down the road on his right, from where Gaby had said the German Workers' Quarters were located. He walked slowly, limping badly.

He nodded to Kevin as he came up to him. "*Morgen,*" he said brightly.

"*Morgen,*" Kevin returned the greeting.

"Looking for something?" the man asked.

"Just making sure," Kevin said. "I'm headed for the Documents Center. The French Section."

The man looked at him with sudden interest. "The French Section," he said. "*Fräulein* Gerlach?"

It was a beat before Kevin realized the man was referring to Gaby. "Gerlach?" he said. "Does she run it?" He shrugged. "I do not know anyone there," he said. "Just picking up some papers." He thought the man looked relieved. Odd. The German pointed to a group of buildings on Kevin's left.

"Over there," he said. "The French Section is in the Documents' Center. On the right. It is not to be missed."

"*Danke,*" Kevin said.

"*Bitte,*" the German replied. "You are welcome." He grinned confidentially at Kevin. "Tell *Fräulein* Gerlach that her Lutz gives her his greetings."

"I shall," Kevin said.

The man touched his cap and started toward the HQ buildings. Kevin watched him limp along. Then he turned and began to walk toward the group of buildings pointed out to him.

He did not see the little photographer stop and look back, eyeing him with a speculative frown on his face.

The *Wehrmachthelferinn* seated behind the gray metal desk in the entry hall of the Documents Center looked up as Kevin walked up to her.

242

"Your business?" she inquired briskly.

"I am here to pick up some translations," Kevin told her, "from a *Fräulein* Gerlach in the French Section. They are for the *Herr Doktor* Gautier," he added. It was a name he'd seen on the papers on the clipboard the day before.

"*Ihre Bevollmäcthigung.*" The woman held out her hand.

Kevin stiffened. He hoped he caught himself before the woman noticed. The demand was unexpected. He thought fast.

"The documents are nonsensitive," he said. "They do not require authorization."

"*Every* document requires authorization," the woman snapped unpleasantly. "Dr. Gautier should know better."

"Perhaps—perhaps *Fräulein* Gerlach—"

"Down the corridor. Second door on the left," the woman said acidly. "But if you take any documents out of here, Gerlach will have to sign them out. *Verstanden?*"

"Understood," Kevin agreed.

She was standing at a bookcase when he entered. She turned —and he saw her face begin to light up, immediately checked. She turned back to the shelves.

An older woman with a heavy-featured face came from behind a row of bookcases. She saw Kevin and came up to him.

"*Bitte?*" she inquired. "What do you want?"

"Fräulein Gerlach?" Kevin asked.

The woman shook her head. She nodded toward Gaby. "That is *Fräulein* Gerlach."

"Thank you," Kevin said. He went over to Gaby. "*Fräulein* Gerlach?" he inquired.

Gaby turned to him. Even when her face is totally noncommittal, he thought, she is beautiful. "Yes?" she said to him.

"I have come regarding the translations," he said. "The ones for the *Herr Doktor* Gautier."

"Of course." Gaby at once fell in with his ad-lib. She started toward a far corner of the room. "This way, please. I have the material on my desk."

He followed her to a desk out of sight of the other woman. He ached to take her in his arms. He did not. But as they spoke the meaningless phrases, their eyes spoke a different language.

"The translations are not quite finished yet," Gaby said. "We can't talk here," she added under her breath. And aloud again, "They were promised for tomorrow."

243

"The *Herr Doktor* is aware of that, *Fräulein*," Kevin said. "But as time is growing short, he thought, perhaps, if they were ready . . . in two hours. At paintshop number three," he whispered quickly.

Gaby nodded. "First thing tomorrow morning," she said. "I promise." She sat down at the desk and placed her hand on the stack of papers lying on it. He reached over and covered it with his.

"*Vielen Dank*," he said perfunctorily. "Many thanks."

"*Bittesehr*," she acknowledged.

The words were inconsequential. But they meant—I love you.

Ted strolled over to the paintshack and entered. A man was standing at a sink just inside, cleaning some brushes. He looked up as Ted came in.

"*Heil Hitler*!" Ted said cheerfully. "Where is the black paint?"

The man glared at him. "What the devil do you want with the black paint?" he asked. "Who are you?"

"Replacement," Ted said. "Understand some fellow broke his arm a couple of days ago. Didn't you know?"

"Heard about it," the man grumbled. "Damned fool." He frowned at Ted. "What do you want with black paint?"

"I'm supposed to touch up the distance markers," Ted said, "along the *Tausendfüssler*." He had noticed the markers when they first saw the huge gun. Seemed like a good excuse to get close to the damned thing.

"Who the devil told you to do that?"

Ted shrugged. "Big fellow," he said. "Don't remember his name. Seemed to be someone in authority."

The man eyed him suspiciously. "Was it—Schunzel?" he asked.

"Could be. Sounds like it."

"*Verflucht!*" The man spat on the floor. "Dammit! Sticking his stinking nose in matters that do not concern him, that *Scheissidiot! I* am supposed to be in charge of scheduling paint jobs. Not that damned Schunzel! Just because he works at the *Arbeitsbureau*—at the Work Office doesn't make him the Führer's right hand."

"Don't jump on me," Ted said plaintively. He met the angry man's stare. "Where else but the Work Office would I go to get assigned?" he asked pointedly. "Where is the black paint?"

"The hell with it!" the man snapped. "I have not scheduled any marker touchup."

Ted shrugged elaborately. *"Ist mir gleich,"* he said airily. "It's all the same to me. When tomorrow the *Kommandant* complains that he cannot see the cruddy things, I will just explain to him that the *Werkmeister*—the foreman—at paintshop number three ordered me not to fix them up." He turned to leave. *"Heil Hitler—Herr Werkmeister,"* he said.

"Piss on you!" the foreman snarled angrily. "The damned black paint is over there." He pointed. "You can damned well clean your own damned brush!"

The millipede barrel was even more mind-boggling close up. Ted, carrying a bucket of black paint and a paintbrush, began to climb the wooden steps erected next to the gigantic barrel. To the right of it, placed at every twenty-five meters, a square wooden sign with black numerals on a yellow field marked the distance up the barrel.

Ted walked up to the first of the six markers and began to touch up the numbers. He took a good look around. The massive barrel of the *Tausendfüssler* with its numerous pairs of side chambers ran up through the middle of a broad swath cut through the woods on the hillside. The branches on the remaining trees at the edges of the strip had been cut back to leave a clear space of about fifteen feet on each side of the barrel.

And as he looked, he realized the impossibility of his plan.

Every twenty-five feet along the huge gun, at each of the distance markers, stood two armed sentries, one on each side. It was obvious that there was no conceivable way that any unauthorized person could even get close to the damned thing. Let alone plant an explosive charge.

He walked the length of the barrel, touching up all the signs. He saw no possible way to circumvent the guards; no possible way of sabotaging Lizzie herself.

The paper airplane sailed past Gaby, dipped in flight, and caught itself briefly before nosing into a scraggly bush.

The trio sitting on some wooden boxes pulled from a stack of empty packing crates near paintshop number three looked no different from several other small groups of workers relaxing during the half hour allowed them for a lunch break.

But their conversation was far from being the small talk exchanged in the other groups.

Kevin carefully began to fold another plane from a piece of scrap paper. It was a fancy kind, with wings and a tail, not the usual flying wedge.

"If we can't blow up Lizzie herself," Gaby said disconsolately, "what can we do?"

"There can't be an *if*," Ted grimly refuted her. "We know that we can't destroy the damned thing by setting conventional charges, that's all. We'll have to find some other way."

"Isn't there a saying—easier said than done?" Gaby commented bitterly.

"Everything's easy, if you know how," Ted said. "We will just have to figure out *how*." He frowned. "We'll need more information."

"All right," Kevin agreed. "But let's see what we already do know." He looked at Ted. "You have determined that there's no way for us to get close to Lizzie herself. She's guarded too well." He turned to Gaby. "Gaby," he said. "What do you know? Anything you haven't told us about yet? Anything at all?"

Gaby shook her head. "I do not think there is anything I have not mentioned. I cannot think of a thing."

"You've been around here for a few days," Ted said. "You may still know something that could be of use to us without realizing it."

"Yes," Kevin said. "What about tomorrow? What do you know about the tests? What have you heard?"

"Only that they are planning to fire twelve yellows," Gaby answered, "beginning at nine o'clock in the morning."

"Yellows?" Ted picked up.

"Dummies," Gaby explained. "Projectiles with dummy warheads. They are painted yellow. The ones with live warheads are red."

"Anything else?" Kevin pressed. "Anything you might have seen when you did your translations? Any document you might have read?"

Gaby frowned in thought. She shook her head. "I—I can think of nothing."

"What about previous tests?" Ted asked. "What kinds of problems did they run into? Do you know anything about that?"

"There were a lot a problems, I understand. Development problems," Gaby said. "But they were all more or less minor ones. And they were all solved."

"Any major mishaps? Any—serious accidents?"

Gaby nodded. "There were a few accidents," she said. "But nothing really major." She bit her lip. "Except—"

"Except what?"

"Well, early in the development process there was a serious accident. A whole section of the main barrel blew out. The project was crippled for many months. I read about it in an old report. She looked earnestly at the two men. "But that—that was long ago. Months and months. And whatever the problem was, it has long since been corrected."

"What was it?"

"I—I am not sure," Gaby answered hesitantly. "They'd had some problems with the projectiles. They were apparently unstable in flight. And there was something about—they called it abnormal, sporadic high-pressure waves that—that ruptured the barrel."

"Was that the accident?"

"No. No, that was something else. That was not that disastrous. The big accident was they were testing a live projectile—and it blew up in the main barrel. Lizzie was out of commission for a long time after that." She looked at Ted. "But the report also stated that the problem had been located and solved. And that was long ago."

"Did they say what the problem was?"

Gaby shook her head. "I—I can't remember that."

Ted looked intently at her. "Gaby," he said. "Try to remember. Did the report state why exactly the projectile detonated prematurely? Think!"

Gaby knit her brow in concentration.

"What exploded?" Ted pressed. "The warhead? Or was the problem with the propelling charge? The booster charges? Did the report say anything about it?"

Gaby shook her head. She looked miserable. "I—I do not remember," she said. "It was an old report. And I did not read it all. I—I never thought it would be important."

"There was no way you could have known," Ted said. "Can you get to that report now?"

Again Gaby shook her head. "No," she answered wretchedly. "It is locked away. I only saw it that once, because I had to copy out and translate a small section of it for a French scientist. Nothing we can use."

Ted thought for a while. "Gaby," he said. "Do you know where the projectiles are stored?"

She shook her head.

"I think I do," Kevin said.

They looked at him.

"Where?" Ted asked.

"Right here," Kevin replied. "Right here in the innermost security area. Just to the right before you leave through Gate Number Three there are a few buildings. Pretty sturdy buildings. They look like they might be storage hangars."

"What makes you think the projectiles are kept there?" Ted asked.

"Outside the largest building there stood a couple of dollies," Kevin explained. "The kind of low-slung trailers the bomber crews use to transport their bombs to the planes. I noticed them this morning. They were long and had heavy rubber-tired wheels. I'm sure they were designed to carry the projectiles from the storage area to Lizzie. And there was an armed sentry at the door."

Ted suddenly was briskly alert. He turned to Gaby.

"At night," he said. "What're the conditions at the base? Everything shut down?"

"Oh, no. Most everything is, of course, but there are many necessary jobs that still have to be done."

"Then—there are people about?"

"Yes."

"What about security?"

"There are patrols. Some on foot. Some in cars. They roam the base. That's only been the last few days, they say." She watched Ted with concern. "Anyone may be stopped. And questioned," she added.

"Okay," Ted said resolutely. He looked from one to the other of his companions. He turned to Gaby. "Go back to work, Gaby," he said. "We'll meet you here again. At 2330 hours. That's eleven thirty tonight. Can do?"

She nodded.

Ted gave them a determined grin. "There're more ways than one to squash a bug," he said. "I think I have an idea how to blow our dear Lizzie to hell and back!"

Kevin let his finished paper plane go. It flew only a few feet—then nose-dived straight into the ground. . . .

❈ 32 ❈

THE night was overcast; there was no moon or stars to be seen in the black sky. The test site itself was an expanse of oppressive darkness pockmarked by pools of brightness under each of the many light poles planted throughout the area.

Kevin, peering from a small dirty window in paintshop number three almost missed Gaby as she came walking rapidly down the road from the HQ compound. He turned to Ted.

"Here she comes," he said.

Ted opened the door. He struck a match and immediately blew it out as Gaby walked over to the shack. Quickly she entered, and Ted closed the door behind her.

Kevin drew the heavy, stained, and paint-splattered blackout curtain across the window and turned on a small lamp. He took Gaby by the shoulders and kissed her on each cheek.

"Gaby," Ted said urgently. "We haven't got much time. We've already put everything we need together, and we're ready to get going." He pointed to some clothing lying on a table. "There's a pair of overalls and a shirt over there. And a cap. Put them on. While you do, I'll give you a brief rundown of what we'll be doing."

Gaby walked over to the table. On it stood several cans of paint, an open cardboard box with padlocks packed in individual cartons, and a box of hinges, as well as a pan with clean but used paint-brushes. A folded, paint-splotched dropcloth lay next to the pan and the clothing. Gaby picked up the soiled overalls and at once began to change.

"Here's the poop," Ted said quickly. "We've timed it, and the guards at the various posts are standing four-hour tours of duty. Next change of sentries is at midnight. We'll have to be near the projectile hangar by then, so we've got to hurry."

"Why?" Gaby asked as she was stepping out of her skirt.

"We want to see exactly how the changeover is handled." Ted answered. "What the routine is. As soon as the new guard has taken his post and is alone at the hangar, he will be—eliminated, and—"

Gaby started. She looked at Kevin.

"*I* will do it," Ted said, catching her look. "That's the sort of thing I've been trained to do."

Gaby looked at him. She steeled herself. This was not the time to be squeamish. She wanted them to know she could handle herself. And—whatever had to be done.

"How," she asked. "You can't shoot him. With—with a knife?"

Ted shook his head. "No," he said, his voice flat. "No knife. The bastard would bleed. The uniform would be stained. We can't afford that. I'll use this." He held up a length of steel wire firmly tied to a short piece of wood at each end. "A garrote," he said.

Involuntarily Gaby shivered.

"It is necessary that the man's uniform be spotless," Ted explained. "Kevin will have to wear it when—"

"Kevin!" Gaby exclaimed.

"We can't let the guard post at the hangar be unmanned," Kevin said. "They may check. I will take the man's place, wearing his uniform, while you and Ted work inside. Ted knows what to do, and I will have no trouble playing a guard—not the most demanding role."

"And he'll stay on after you and I have finished and gone and let himself be relieved at the next change of guards," Ted added. "That's why we have to know exactly how the bloody relief change is carried out."

"But, that means Kevin will have to—he'll have to go with the German soldiers," Gaby said, alarmed. "With the relief detail. You can't—"

"I can pull it off, Gaby," Kevin said quietly. "And there is no other way. There's got to be a guard on duty at the hangar when they come to relieve him or they will know at once that something is wrong. I am sure I can pull it off."

Gaby was almost finished changing. She'd put the shirt on over her blouse and tucked her rolled-up skirt into her overalls. She put the cap on her head and pushed her hair under it. She looked worried.

"Ready?" Ted asked her.

She nodded.

Ted picked up a basket with several cans of paint and a bunch of brushes; Kevin, the folded dropcloth.

"Got the lock?" Ted asked him.

"Got it."

Gaby turned to Ted. "What are *we* going to do while Kevin stands guard?" she asked.

"I'll tell you on the way," Ted said. "We've got to get going." He turned off the lamp.

They had walked past the cordoned-off *Tausendfüssler* area on their right and Gate No. 3 on their left and were within a couple of hundred feet from the hangar when they stopped dead in their tracks, imprisoned in the glare of the suddenly turned on beams from the headlights of a vehicle that was parked on the side road that led to a guard tower at the barbed-wire fence. The vehicle started up and began to drive slowly toward them. As the beams turned away from them, they saw it was a patrol car, an open Volkswagen with two armed soldiers and a driver.

"Stay here!" Ted hissed at Kevin and Gaby. "Let me handle it." He hailed the approaching patrol vehicle.

"*Holla!*" he cried. "*Moment mal!*" He walked over to meet the oncoming Volkswagen. It stopped. The soldiers regarded him suspiciously.

"Gotta match?" he asked, pulling out a pack of cigarettes. "I ran out." He nodded back toward Kevin and Gaby. "And those two idiots do not smoke." He held up the pack of cigarettes. "French," he said. "*Gauloise.*" He removed one cigarette and offered the pack. "Help yourselves for later."

The three men each took a cigarette. One of them gave Ted a box of matches. Another—a corporal—was about to say something when Ted went on.

"Wish that *Arschloch*—that asshole Schunzel at the *Arbeitsbureau* knew what he was doing," he complained. He lit up. He mimicked a whining voice. "Sorry, I forgot about the street barricades, he says. Sorry, they need a fresh coat of paint, he says. Sorry, they have to be done by tomorrow, first thing, he says. Sorry, but there is no one else to do the job, he says. *Scheissdreck nochmal!* Thinks he is a real big shot! In the middle of the *verschissene* night! While he, no doubt, is sharpening his pencil with

251

some *Nutte*—some chippy—in Wollin! *Na ja*—we all get it in the neck." He touched his cap and threw the box to the guard. "Thanks," he said. "Don't get lost! Heilitla!"

And he turned and started to walk back toward Kevin and Gaby.

The soldiers in the Volkswagen watched him leave—and drove off.

"Took a helluva chance, didn't you?" Kevin remarked as they continued on their way.

Ted shrugged. "Bigger risk if they seek you out," he said. "We'd already been seen. We were already at a disadvantage, and I am a firm believer in turning disadvantages into advantages if at all possible. This time it was." He grinned. "Human nature," he said. "If you ask for it, they won't give it to you. If you want to hide, make yourself conspicuous, become a nuisance—and they can't dismiss you quickly enough."

There were two buildings separated by a narrow road, each of them approximately ninety by thirty-five feet. The one nearest to the gate was a machine shop, the other was the storage hangar for Lizzie's projectiles. That was the one they had to get into.

At the far end of the machine shop building, several pieces of rusty, discarded heavy machinery had been dumped, along with other damaged equipment and a wagon with a broken wheel. The area was in the dark, and the jumbled shapes of the machine shop junk offered an excellent hiding place with a clear view of the large sliding door to the hangar in the center of the hangar building, some fifty feet away. A smaller door was set into the big slider, and there an armed sentry stood guard.

It was four minutes to midnight when the three Grand Guignolers silently crept into place among the twisted, jagged metal of the makeshift junkyard.

Kevin peered intently at the guard. The man stood outside the door in a pool of bright light. There was not the slightest bit of cover on either side of him for the length of the entire hangar building.

"Shit!" Kevin whispered. "How the hell are you going to get close enough to the bastard to—take him out?"

"First things first," Ted breathed grimly. "We'll figure a way. First—let's take a look at the changing of the guard. Keep your eyes open. Both of you. And remember."

Even as he spoke, the faint sound of men marching reached

252

them from the distance, and presently a small detail of soldiers turned from the main road into the narrow one between the two buildings, headed for the sentry at the hangar door.

There were eight men marching in two rows, led by an *SS-Unterscharführer*—a sergeant. All except the sergeant carried MP 35/1 guns, the standard Waffen SS submachine guns. Unorthodox for guard duty, Ted thought, where a rifle is the usual weapon carried.

As the detail drew even with the sentry, who stood at attention with his gun at port arms on his post at the hangar door, the sergeant called out: *"Wache—halt!"*

The guard detail came to a halt.

"Rechts—um!" the sergeant barked.

The detail executed a smart right turn.

"Richt—euch!"

Looking to the left and using quick, small shuffling steps, the men straightened their lines.

"Augen gerade—aus!"

The men snapped their heads to the front and stared straight ahead.

The sergeant walked over to the door. Vigorously he tested the big padlock that secured it. He returned to his column.

"Ablösung zur Wache—wegtreten!" he commanded.

The first soldier in the front line of the detail took two steps forward, as did the sentry on post.

"Beide Wachen—rechts—um!"

Both the guards turned right.

"Beide Wachen—marsch!"

The two men walked forward until they had changed places.

"Beide Wachen—halt!

They stopped.

"Rechts, links—um!"

The sentry being relieved turned right toward the relief detail and the new guard turned left, toward the building.

"Neue Wache—wegtreten!"

The new guard took up his position at the post, and the old guard joined the rear of the front row of the relief column, the others moving up.

"Links—um!" the sergeant ordered, and the detail turned left.

"Vorwärtz—marsch!"

The column moved off, leaving the new guard at the post. Not until they had disappeared around the corner of the hangar opposite the machine shop junk pile did Kevin speak.

"Quite a production," he said.

"Can you remember it?" Ted asked. "Can you do it?"

Kevin nodded. "Can't miss," he grinned. "The stage directions are being called out at every turn!"

They returned their attention to the guard at the hangar.

Holding his submachine gun firmly at port arms, he stood rock solid in the middle of the brightly lighted area outside the door.

"We don't have any time to lose," Ted said tensely. He looked at his watch. It was an automatic gesture—he didn't notice the time. "We have to get rid of that guard as quickly as possible. It's unlikely there will be a sentry check right after the change of guard; we'll have to take advantage of that. And the sooner we can get in, the better. We'll need two or three hours in there, at least, and we have to finish and get out while Kevin is still on the post or we're cooked." He peered worriedly at the conspicuous sentry standing in full view at the door. "Damn it!" he swore. "The bastard might as well be standing in the middle of Times Square."

"What can we do?" Gaby asked. She looked at Kevin. "Kevin?"

"How about the roof," he suggested. He turned to Ted. "If you could get up on the roof, you could jump him."

"I could," Ted agreed. "But probably not before he could get off at least one shot and alert the whole damned hornets' nest."

For a while they thought in silence. How?

"Could you pull a—a bluff?" Gaby ventured. "Could you just go up to him under some pretext or other? And—and—"

"I probably could get close to the bastard," Ted acknowledged. "But I'd have lost the element of surprise. Any wrong movement on my part, any menacing or suspicious gesture, and the guy would either call for the sergeant of the guard—or shoot me." He shook his head. "No go. Remember, the kill has got to be silent. Completely silent. No outcry. No alarm. The post is within earshot of the gate. Or the guard tower. Or perhaps another post."

He surveyed the bare area around the sentry, empty of all cover. "I've got to be able to get to the man without him seeing me," he said. "Short of making myself invisible, I'm damned if I know how."

They all stared at the exposed sentry, their concern and frustration growing.

Time was running out.

Fast.

"*Killjoy!*" Gaby suddenly said.

Kevin gave her a quick look. "Yeah," he said. "Might work . . . Wait! Better still, *Lovers' Quarrel*."

"That's it," Gaby said. "That's perfect."

"What the hell are you jabbering about," Ted asked in annoyance. He suddenly stopped. "Oh," he said. "Don't tell me. Another one of your Grand Guignol plays."

"Right," Kevin said crisply. "I think we have a way for you to get to that guard without him seeing you." He turned to Gaby. "Get ready," he said.

Gaby had already removed her cap and shaken out her hair. She was stepping out of her overalls.

"What are you going to do?" Ted asked.

Kevin told him.

The narrow road between the machine shop and the hangar building was quiet and deserted. The sentry at the hangar door stood immobile at his post.

Suddenly the night stillness was disturbed by the sound of rapidly approaching footsteps crunching on the gravel of the main road, and almost at once a young woman came into view, hurrying along the road. She glanced apprehensively over her shoulder and quickened her steps.

It was Gaby.

As she came to the narrower side street she hesitated for a second, then—resolutely—she turned into it, walking toward the sentry.

At once alert, the guard turned to watch her approach, his weapon ready at port arms. Suddenly another figure, a man, came hurrying around the corner after the young woman.

It was Kevin.

Quickly he caught up with the girl. He grabbed her by the arm and spun her around to face him. The guard watched with curiosity. The two young people talked in low, urgent voices, too faint to be understood. But they were obviously quarrelling angrily.

The sentry shifted his position to face the two people. In his stance his indecision could be read. Should he interfere? He would

255

have to leave his post to do so, and that was, of course, impossible. Should he alert someone? The sergeant of the guard? Why? The young man and the young woman posed no threat. Their quarrel was their own affair, not his. He watched.

He did not notice that behind him the figure of a man quickly and silently crossed the roadway to hug the wall of the hangar building.

Suddenly the young man grabbed the woman, pulled her to him, and kissed her soundly. As the sentry watched in fascination, she at first fought the young man, but soon she yielded and her arms stole around his neck.

The sentry was engrossed in the spectacle, so much so that he did not hear nor sense the furtive figure that silently approached him from behind. Closer and closer. Ted's hands were gripping the wooden pegs of the garrote so tightly that his knuckles showed white. He moved slowly, without making the slightest sound.

Only ten more steps . . .

The young woman suddenly pushed the man away from her. She turned her back to him. He reached out to touch her—but hesitated. The sentry watched. What would the *Kerl* do? What would happen next?

Three more steps . . .

The sentry was still engrossed in the mini-drama being played out before him.

Ted crossed his hands, making the lethal loop with the wire as he'd been taught at Milton Hall.

One more step . . .

He whipped the wire loop down over the unaware sentry's head and pulled on the wooden grips with all his might. At once the wire grew tight and bit sharply into the man's flesh, to disappear in a thin red groove around his throat, instantly blocking the flow of blood in both of his jugular veins and choking his windpipe, cutting off even the sound of a whimper.

The German's eyes bulged in abject terror with the shock of the sudden knowledge that he was doomed. He spent his last two seconds of life digging his nails into his flesh in a desperate but futile effort to loosen the stranglehold of the killer wire that encircled his throat.

His mouth wrenched open in a silent scream as he jerked convulsively and went limp, sagging lifelessly in Ted's deadly grip.

Kevin and Gaby were at his side.

"The basket, Gaby," Ted rasped quickly. "Get it!"

Without a word Gaby ran for the junk pile. Ted unwrapped the garrote from the dead sentry's neck. "Break the lock, Kevin," he ordered. "Use the barrel of his gun. Move!"

Kevin grabbed the guard's submachine gun. He ran to the door, inserted the tip of the barrel through the loop of the padlock, and wrenched down on the gun with as much force as he could. At his second try the lock flew apart. He had opened the door by the time Ted had dragged the body of the sentry over and Gaby had come running with the basket.

At once they pulled the German into the building and closed the door. Kevin immediately began to take off his clothes as Ted hurriedly removed the guard's uniform, which Kevin put on. He picked up the submachine gun as Ted handed him a new padlock he'd fished out from a pocket in Kevin's jacket.

"Quick check," he said. "Remember the change of guard routine?"

"Yes."

"You have the new padlock key?"

Kevin patted his pocket. "Got it."

"Good. Don't forget to substitute it for the old one on the board in the guard room."

"I won't."

"Rendezvous?"

"0600 hours at the paintshop."

Ted gave him a searching look. "Good luck," he said quietly.

"You, too," Kevin replied. He gave Gaby a quick embrace; and donning the dead sentry's helmet, he quickly went outside. He snapped the new padlock in place, locking Ted and Gaby inside the building, and took up the German sentry's post.

Dieter Haupt reached over and turned on the light. It was no use. He was too keyed up to sleep. Tomorrow was an important day. That was what was keeping him awake.

He frowned in irritation. He knew it was a lie. It was something else. It was a nagging, unsettling feeling that he was missing something. Something obvious. Something important. It was a disturbingly foreboding feeling of—of some threat hanging over him. Some—disaster building and about to erupt.

But what?

It lurked just below the surface of his mind—mocking and elusive.

Was it something contained in the latest incidents reports that he'd gone over earlier in the day? He wracked his brain. What? Nothing had stood out. Nothing had alerted him.

And yet . . .

He looked at the clock on the nightstand next to his bed. Almost one o'clock in the morning. He might as well get up.

Perhaps he should take another look at those reports. . . .

The HQ building, although not deserted, was strangely quiet as Haupt sat at his desk in his office, poring over the latest reports.

Trivial, he thought disgustedly. All of them. Inconsequential. Certainly not alarming.

He picked up a report from the Channel Patrol Command. He remembered. That was what had bothered him. A motor launch had been stopped and searched at the Stettiner Haff checkpoint. Two men on board, one a barge captain. Nothing found. Only tools. The barge captain had stated that they were on their way to repair a disabled cargo barge in the Haff. Not unusual. Happened all the time. But—there had been no report of any disabled barge on that day. By itself, that meant nothing. Either someone had not thought it important enough to report, or it had been deleted as routine from the reports forwarded to him. What had troubled him about the report was the fact that it was dated May 18, and the incident had taken place on May 8. That was ten days. A delay of ten days before the matter had been brought to his attention. That could, of course, be because the Patrol Command only now had learned about the conflicting reports. Or—there could be some other reason. Was that what was needling him?

He turned the thought over in his mind.

There was something else . . .

He dug out the previous reports dating back to the very first ones. Slowly he reread them all. Both the ones he had pulled out as possibly significant and the ones he had discarded as inconsequential.

Suddenly he chilled.

It was that unmistakable chill of discovery he had learned to respect. It always happened to him when he was onto something. Carefully he reread the old report that had caught his attention, fully alert now.

In the *Bierstube* in Wollin, an argument had taken place between some refugees, strangers to the town. Three men and a woman . . . *Three men and a woman!* The number of saboteurs in his scenario. The argument concerned a retired barge captain by name of Kessler or Kentler or Keppler. A *barge captain!*

Abruptly he rose from his chair. He hurried to the outer office. Where did Stolitz keep the damned population rolls? There!

He flipped the pages.

Keiner—Kellerman—Kempf—Kenburg—

KEPPLER!

Keppler, Janusz. Barge Captain, retired. Darsewitz.

Mesmerized, he stared at the name. Here was the possible link to the saboteurs. The tingling sensation coursing through him convinced him he was right.

He picked up the phone. He stabbed at a button. The sleepy voice of *Obersturmführer* Stolitz answered.

"Stolitz!" Haupt barked. "Get my car and my driver. Report here at the *Kommandantur* at once. Armed!"

He had trouble keeping his voice from sounding triumphant.

"We have a job to do!"

❈ 33 ❈

TED looked around the huge ammunition hangar in dismay. The place seemed much bigger on the inside than it had appeared from the outside. The job was going to be more difficult than he'd anticipated. Half a dozen work lights were burning in the hall. The accumulated light was dim, but enough to work by, he decided. Quickly he took stock.

Immediately facing the large sliding door with the smaller door through which they had entered set into it stood twelve long, low-slung trailers, each with a yellow projectile strapped to it.

They were obviously the shells scheduled to be fired later in the day. The area of the hall to the left of him was occupied by four rows of three-tiered steel racks with large cradlelike double shelves, most of them holding long blunt-nosed projectiles, all of them painted red. They were the shells with the live warheads. At the other end stood at least twice as many storage racks, with projectiles all painted yellow and with cone-pointed noses. The dummies.

Ted walked over to the yellow shells on the trailers. About eight feet long, he estimated. He unstrapped one of them and strained to lift one end. "Not going to be easy," he muttered. "Bloody thing must weigh a couple of hundred pounds."

"What can I do?" Gaby asked.

"Get out the paints," Ted answered her. "Both the red and the yellow. Stir them so they're ready to use."

Gaby at once set to her task. Ted looked around. On a row of sturdy shelves placed against the back wall stood several cone-shaped metal objects about a foot high, protected from falling off by a small railing running along the shelf. At once he walked over to them. He picked up one of the cones and examined it.

"We're in!" he said excitedly. "These are the nose fuzes for the live warheads. And they're point-detonating." He turned toward Gaby. "Gaby," he said tautly. "This is extremely important. I *have* to know more about that report you saw."

Gaby looked stricken. "But—I—"

"Wait," Ted interrupted her. "Let me finish. I'm going to tell you exactly what I have in mind. It may trigger something for you. Some recollection."

She nodded solemnly. "I will try."

"Okay," he said. He pointed to the cone-shaped objects on the shelves. "These are the fuses for the live shells," he explained. "They'll be fixed onto the noses of the warheads just prior to firing. That's SOP. The dummies have prefixed, inert dummy fuse bodies already attached." He picked up one of the fuses. "They are what's called superquicks," he said. "They'll detonate on impact. Some are so sensitive they'll explode even when hitting the skin of a barrage balloon. It's a matter of certain adjustments. This is the way it works. The fuse is a percussion type. That means that a blow or a given amount of pressure, depending on adjustments or pressure on the closing cap at the tip of the fuse, will activate a striker in the primer detonator mechanism, which in turn will set off the full, high-explosives load in the warhead itself.''

He locked his eyes upon hers. ''Now listen, Gaby. This is of the utmost importance. In that report you saw, do you remember any mention of barrel pressure? Any discussion of the fuses? The accident? Think!''

Gaby knit her brow in concentration. She tried to visualize the document pages she had skimmed. The charts. Terminology.

''They—they talked about premature detonation,'' she said slowly. ''The warhead on a live shell exploded in the barrel. . . . There—there were some charts. One said: *GASDRUCK IN ATMOSPHÄREN*—Gas Pressure in Atmospheres. It was pretty uneven, with high peaks. I think it mentioned sporadic high pressures occurring in the barrel.'' She stopped, frowning to remember.

''Go on,'' Ted urged.

''There was a—a later section,'' she went on. ''I—I did not read through it. All I remember is it discussed something like sensitivity adjustments, but—''

''That's it!'' Ted exclaimed. ''Their trouble was the sensitivity factor of the nose fuse! The pressure in the barrel became so great as the projectile was shot up the length of it, that it set off the fuse. It literally ran into a wall of air and detonated. They had to make adjustments. Sensitivity adjustments!''

He looked at the shelf of fuses.

''Hell, if *they* can adjust the damned things to withstand the high-pressure points in the barrel, *I* can adjust them to go off if a butterfly breathes on them!''

He turned to Gaby. ''Okay,'' he said resolutely. ''Here's what we have to do. We'll substitute as many of the yellows with reds as we can and repaint them. We should be able to do three or four. You paint the reds we'll place on the trailers with the yellow paint. Make them look like the dummies. And the yellows we take off, you'll paint red. We'll have to put them on the racks in place of the ones we remove. In case they make any kind of count. Be sure to use the dropcloth.''

He looked around.

''It won't be easy, Gaby,'' he said. ''The bloody things weigh a ton. A pretty hefty load for the two of us.''

''I will manage,'' Gaby said.

Ted nodded. He had no doubts that she would. He glanced up at the ceiling. ''There's a hoist up there,'' he said. ''But we dare not use it. I don't know how noisy the bloody thing is. We'll have to roll the trailers as close to the racks as we can. That way we only have to make a transfer."

He tugged at one of the trailers. It moved easily. "As soon as we've made the change—let's do three—as soon as we've replaced them, you start painting. And I'll work on the fuzes. Make them as sensitive as a baby's ass!"

They set to work.

They'd made the transfer of one of the projectiles when Ted suddenly stiffened. Quickly he motioned for Gaby to be quiet.

He listened.

From far away, the sound of a speeding car approaching could be heard.

They both stood frozen, listening tensely, as the racing motor sounds came closer and closer.

It stopped. And immediately started up again—gradually fading into the distance.

Ted nodded at Gaby in relief.

"False alarm," he said.

Dieter Haupt sat stiffly in the back seat of his staff car, bracing himself as the driver took the turn from the road to the Misdroy test site onto the highway that led to Wollin with a speed that just allowed the car to stay on the tarmac.

He checked his Luger. Loaded and on safety. Extra magazines in his tunic pockets. Stolitz, who sat next to the driver, was armed with a submachine gun. They would be in Darsewitz in less than twenty minutes. At the home of one Janusz Keppler, barge captain.

The more he thought about the connection between the man Keppler and the saboteurs, the more certain he was that he was on the right track. He felt exhilarated, keyed-up, flushed with the excitement of the chase, a chase he had no doubts could have only one outcome.

He looked at his watch. 0147 hours. In seven hours and thirteen minutes his Lizzie would face her final tests. He did not have much time.

Neither did the saboteurs.

Mike was lying in the attic darkness of Keppler's home, not asleep—his concern for his son and the others had kept him from sound sleep for the last few nights—and not awake, his eyes were closed, his breathing deep and regular. He was dozing in a discarnate twilight existence.

A sudden blast on a horn from a vessel on the channel outside startled him. It produced a burst of brilliant, intricate purple patterns on the inside of his eyelids. He sat up. He had always wondered why a sudden sound while you were in a state of half-sleep—a door slam, a car horn—would produce a flash of visual splendor, one more brilliant and kaleidoscopic than the other. He had once decided that it was because the sensitive nerve ends in his eyes were startled by the sudden sound, and the only way they had to express their shock was visual, so that's what they did.

He looked at his watch lying on a small table next to his cot. It was a few minutes before two o'clock in the morning. He tried to go back to sleep. It was no go. Perhaps a little fresh air; the attic was stuffy.

He got dressed and quietly made his way down the steep steps. As he passed Keppler's room he could hear the deep, peaceful snoring of the man. Silently he made his way to the back door and went outside.

The night was cool and dark. The lights from a few houses along the channel pointed long silver fingers across the black water, and only a few boats displaying their navigational lights could be seen chugging through the darkness, looking like eerie luminous fish swimming in the inky depth of the deepest ocean.

He went out on the pier all the way to the old barge tied up at the end. He was enjoying the cool breeze that came in from the sea; it soothed his fretfulness, and he began to feel less on edge.

Suddenly he tensed. The sound of an approaching car intruded upon the stillness of the night, coming steadily closer and closer. He strained to see the road up above. Glimpsed through the shrubbery obscuring it, he could make out the headlights of the car, leapfrogging the silhouetted bushes. It stopped at Keppler's house. Although the car was hidden from view by the house, he instinctively melted into the shadows of the old boathouse.

Haupt leaped from the car before it had come to a complete stop.

"Stolitz!" he ordered. "Take the back. *Los!* You!" He turned to his driver, "Come with me."

Drawing his Luger and followed by the driver clutching a sub-machine gun, he marched up to the front door of Keppler's house while Stolitz ran for the back. With the tip of his boot, he kicked noisily at the door.

"*Aufmachen!*" he bellowed. "Open up! Security!"

He gun-motioned to his driver. The man banged on the door with the butt of his gun.

"*Aufmachen!*" Haupt shouted again. "*Sofort!* At once!"

The door opened, and Keppler, clad only in a long nightshirt, peered out at the two men with sleep-gummed eyes. "What the devil?" he exclaimed angrily. "Who in hell—"

"Shut up, old man!" Haupt snapped at him. "Put your hands up. *Up!* Now!"

Keppler obeyed.

Roughly Haupt pushed him into the room. "Stolitz!" he called loudly.

There was a splintering crash from the rear of the house as Stolitz kicked in the back door. Startled, Keppler turned around.

"Hold it!" Haupt glared at him. "Stand perfectly still. Keep your hands high and don't move a hair." He smiled a highly unpleasant smile at the man, more like a cat licking his chops before pouncing. "You and I are going to have a little talk, Kep-pler," he said with silken menace. "It will unfortunately be the last one you will ever have. But it is entirely up to you if it will be a pleasant one—" He smiled again.

"Or an extremely unpleasant one."

Horrorstruck, Mike had watched the figure of a man carrying a weapon come running around the house to take up position at the back door. Crouched in the darkness, he had heard the commotion at the front of the house and had seen the armed man kick in the back door and enter the house.

They had been betrayed!

How?

Icy thoughts whirled through his horrified mind. Had Kevin been caught? Gaby? All of them? Had they been made to talk? Unbidden, the dire words of Etienne—the Resistance leader—came to his mind: *The Germans, they can make the walls talk.* . . . He tried to deny the images of horror that rose in his mind to eclipse all else. He was only partly successful.

And Jan?

His friend was in the hands of the enemy—and there was nothing he, Mike, could do to help him. Nothing. He was unarmed. All he could do was to watch impotently from his shadowy hiding place on the pier—or get himself killed. And that would do no one any good. If there were even the slightest hint of a chance that he could help the others or Jan later on, he would have to stay alive.

He felt a sharp pang of guilt. Had it not been for the fact that he couldn't sleep and had wanted some fresh air, he would now be with Jan and the Germans in the house. But here he was. Safe.

For now . . .

Janusz Keppler stared at the officer standing before him, booted legs slightly apart, Luger in hand. He looked at the man's insignia. An SS general, no less. His friends must really have become thorns in the sides of the Nazis. What had happened? How had this general found out about him? He at once abandoned that train of thought. It would become apparent soon enough. Had his friends been captured? Killed? That, too, he would learn soon enough. Before he died. And die he would. He was certain of that. It was only a matter of *how*.

Pleasantly or unpleasantly, as the SS general had said.

The general turned to his aide. "Search the house," he ordered. "Round up anyone else here. *Los!*"

The young officer at once left the room. The general turned back to Keppler.

"I am *Brigadeführer* Dieter Haupt," he introduced himself. "Kommandant of Misdroy *Heeresversuchsstelle*. I believe you and I have a common interest, Captain Keppler. The *Tausendfüssler*. Am I correct?"

Keppler stood silent, his hands high in the air. The draft from the broken back door made his bare legs cold. That, he thought with dark humor, would be the least of his discomforts.

The general nodded to the other soldier with him. "Cover him," he snapped. "If he moves, shoot him. But do not kill him. Just shatter his knees."

"*Jawohl, Herr Kommandant*," the man barked. He leveled his submachine gun at Keppler.

Haupt holstered his Luger. With mocking eyes, he gazed at Keppler. "You look quite ridiculous in that absurd nightgown, old man," he scoffed. "You must feel absolutely ludicrous." He brightened. "There is no need to make you have to feel that way, is there?" His voice suddenly grew steely. "Take it off! Now!"

Keppler glared at him. Without a word, he shrugged out of his nightgown and let it fall at his feet. Naked, his hands in the air, he confronted Haupt, meeting the officer's mocking eyes coldly.

Derisively Haupt looked him up and down. Inwardly he gloated. It had been a textbook opportunity handed to him unexpectedly: Make your subject as uncomfortable as possible; make him feel as inferior to you as possible.

"Not a bad body for an old man," he mocked his captive. "Well muscled. Well hung. Must be the hardy life on the channel." He measured Keppler appraisingly with his eyes, obviously enjoying himself. "Pity to mar it too badly before it is dumped on your next of kin." He made a show of brightening. "On the other hand, you may be quite a challenge," he observed. "Your—stamina is probably high. Your defiance most certainly appears to be."

Keppler stood silent. Haupt began to pace before him in a curious manner of mixed anticipation and impatience; an eager ballet of death.

"I know a good deal about you, Keppler," he went on, his tone of voice deceptively conversational. "About you—and about your fellow traitors. There are three of them and one woman, am I correct?" He obviously did not expect an answer. "And I know you are planning to sabotage the Misdroy *Tausendfüssler*. You will not succeed, of course."

He stopped directly in front of Keppler. "I have three questions to ask you, Keppler. Only three. I am certain you will answer them for me. Eventually." His icy eyes bored into his victim. "The questions are *One*—who are your accomplices? *Two*—where are they now? And, *Three*—what are their exact plans?

Keppler did not move a muscle. But he exulted! The damned Nazi knew nothing! Kevin, Ted, and Gaby were still safe. He wondered about Mike, who was asleep in the attic. Any moment the young officer would be bringing him down. Fleetingly he wondered how Mike would bear up under the—the questioning that was certain to come.

"No ready answers, Keppler?" Haupt commented. He shrugged. "I had not expected it. Not yet, that is. But as I said—eventually." He resumed his curious pacing. He stopped to peer at the naked man.

"I once read a book, Keppler, about torture," he said. "Fascinating. Absolutely fascinating. A history of the art." He gave Keppler a quick, mirthless smile. "For it *is* an art, Keppler. Believe me, it *is* an art."

He settled himself on the edge of Keppler's table–desk.

"In view of what may be facing you, Herr Keppler," he said pleasantly, "perhaps you would like to hear a little of what I read in that history of torture. One of the earlier cases, described in minute detail, was originally related in biblical Apocrypha. It was the story of the torture to the death of the seven Maccabee brothers. You may have heard of them, Keppler. The youngest was a mere child. All, while the mother watched. It was the work of King Antiochus the Fourth who ruled Syria, oh, a couple of centuries before Christ. He was effective, of course, but without much finesse. The boys were scourged, their limbs were pierced, dislocated, broken, and ultimately torn off; they were skinned, disemboweled, and slowly roasted alive; heated spears were driven into their entrails until they cooked, and they were boiled and burned alive." He shrugged. "All well and good—but without real finesse, do you not agree?"

He gave the silent barge skipper a quick glance. If his tales of horror and the implications of telling them had any effect on the man, he did not betray it. Tough, Haupt thought. Tough enough? No one was.

"Now, the Inquisition did produce a few—eh, interrogators who showed finesse. Real finesse." He raised an eyebrow at Keppler. "What do I mean by finesse?" he asked. "Well, there was a sixteenth-century fellow named Schmidt, Franz Schmidt of Nürnberg. He was an excellent craftsman who could gauge human suffering and tolerance of excrutiating pain with great accuracy. He never applied too much, never too little, to achieve the desired result. And, he showed imagination, Keppler." He was warming to his subject, his face showing an agitated flush. "Once he had a recalcitrant woman strapped down and a tin box containing mice clamped down on her naked belly. Then he heated the tin box red hot, and in their agony the mice gnawed their way into the woman's body, their only way of escape!" Triumphantly he looked at Keppler. "Now that, Keppler, is what I mean by finesse. I am sure you will agree?"

Still Keppler stood silent. He knew exactly what the Nazi was doing. The horrors that his mind would conjure up listening to his gruesome recounts were supposed to terrify him. Soften him.

Make him ready to talk. To betray his friends in order to save himself. And he did let his mind dwell on the nightmare images created by the Nazi officer. He could do nothing else. They were much like the stage horrors at the Grand Guignol theater that his teammates had told him about. And he forced himself to think of them as such. Deliberately he subjugated reality for make-believe. He did not allow the perception of real torture to reach him. It was—theater. . . .

"A fascinating book, Keppler," Haupt went on. "An admirably thorough study of the subject matter; all the way from the dawn of history to the present times. From the Christian martyrs in Rome to witch hunts in America. From thumbscrews that could be tightened so fiercely that blood squirted from under the fingernails to the water torture that usually burst a man's entrails. And much, much more, Keppler. Much more."

He stood up and walked over to stand in front of his victim.

"But I can do better, Keppler. Much better. Right here. Right now."

Despite all his efforts to deny the horrors that clawed at his mind, Keppler felt his flesh crawl. That would not be apparent to the Nazi, he thought. But the cold sweat that was beginning to trickle down his sides would. He wished he could stop it.

He looked up as the German officer who had been sent to search the house reappeared. Alone. The general whirled on him.

"Well?"

"No one, *Herr Brigadeführer*," the officer reported. "No other persons in the house. However—"

"Yes?"

"In the attic, *Herr Brigadeführer*, there are sleeping places for three. And the bedding on one cot is still slightly warm."

Thoughts flashed through Haupt. Warm? Then the occupant would have left it only a short while ago. If he were not in the house, he might still be close by. Should he send Stolitz to search for him? He at once dismissed the thought. It was dark outside. Impossible to find anyone who wanted to stay hidden. And if he did pick up someone, how could he be certain it was the saboteur? No—he would concentrate on the bird in hand.

Keppler stared at the man. Mike? Where was Mike? Had he managed to hide himself somewhere? For a fleeting moment he allowed himself the glimmer of hope. Then he dismissed it. He knew there was none. But he was puzzled. Where was Mike?

Haupt turned back to Keppler. With a slight frown, he contemplated the man. "It seems your friends are not here," he said slowly. "Would you know where they are and what they are up to?" He nodded to himself. "I am certain you would. The question is, will you tell me? Without a little prompting?"

Keppler did not look at the Nazi. He fixed his eyes on a spot in the distance above the man's shoulder. He said nothing.

Haupt shrugged elaborately. "I thought not," he said. "Then—we may as well begin our little chat in earnest, *nicht wahr?*—is that not so?" He looked around the room. "First, however, we will have to make things a little more comfortable." He smiled at his victim. "For me, Keppler, not for you. Unfortunately."

He walked over to the long table that served as Keppler's desk. With a sweeping gesture, he brushed it clean of everything, including the silver-framed photograph of Keppler with the village Nazi leader. He gestured to his driver.

"Upend it," he ordered.

The driver struggled with the heavy table and soon it stood upended, all of eight feet tall. Haupt nodded approvingly at it.

"*Gut,*" he said. "*Sehr gut.*" He pointed to two large books of bound charts lying on a shelf of a bookcase. "Those," he said to the driver. "Both of them. Place them on top of each other at the foot of the table."

The driver did. Haupt turned to Keppler.

"Up, Keppler!" he ordered. "Step up on the books. Move!"

Stolitz gun-prodded the skipper over to the table. Keppler stepped up on the books, his hands still held high.

"Now," Haupt said. "We need some rope. I am certain there will be some rope available in the house of a barge captain. Or perhaps outside." He looked around. "But we need not look for it." He pointed to some slender but sturdy braided pull ropes attached to the blackout curtains. "They will do admirably." He snapped his fingers. "Stolitz!"

Using a bone-handled hunting knife that had been swept to the floor from the table by Haupt, his aide cut a couple of lengths of rope.

"Tie him," Haupt ordered. "One hand to each table leg. Make it tight." He smiled. "We would not want Herr Keppler to fall and injure himself, would we?" He drew his Luger from its holster and leveled it at Keppler's midriff. "No grandiose ideas, Keppler," he said. "You can live a long time with a bullet through your guts."

The two men each grabbed one of Keppler's arms. They reached just above the edge of the upended table. Cruelly the men forced the skipper's wrists over the sharp edge and tied them securely to the table legs.

Haupt nodded approvingly. "*Prima*!" he exclaimed. "First rate! Our own version of the popular medieval *strappado*." He looked politely at Keppler. "Are you familiar with the strappado, Herr Keppler?" he asked. He walked over to the barge captain suspended against the upright table top. Suddenly he kicked the two big books away from under Keppler's feet. The body of the man jerked down heavily, the sharp top edge of the table cutting into his wrists. He could barely reach the floor with the tips of his big toes.

Haupt contemplated him amiably. He pulled up the big over-stuffed chair and sat down in it opposite Keppler, making himself comfortable.

"Let me tell you a little about the strappado," he said. "I am sure it will interest you. Under the circumstances. It was a favorite of the interrogators during the Inquisition because it had so many applications. Usually the subject's hands were tied behind him and he was suspended from an upright rack, much like our table here, Herr Keppler." He leaned forward and knocked on the massive table top. "Sometimes, with just the tips of his toes touching the floor. After a while, of course, the poor fellow's arms were gradually, and extremely painfully I might add, dislocated from his shoulders, and the inquisitors of old undoubtedly found much amusement in observing their subject's desperate struggle to reach the floor with his toes to obtain even a little relief from the agony." He made a show of inspecting the ceiling. "Of course," he mused. "When time was of the essence, the subject was hoisted into the air and suddenly allowed to drop. It produced the same dislocating effect so much quicker." He contemplated Keppler hanging from the upended table. "As you can see, Keppler, I have not been quite as—as pitiless with you. Yet." He sighed. "Although time is, of course, of the essence."

He stood up. "However, I do have a few other methods of—of persuasion in mind." Again he looked around the room. "We shall, of course, need a few—eh, tools of the trade, you might say.

270

Unfortunately," he continued, "we did not come prepared. But every home is usually well equipped with, shall we say, instruments of persuasion. Torture, if you insist." He indicated the big hunting knife Stolitz had used to cut the rope. "That, for instance, will come in handy, I should think. What else can we find, do you suppose?" He walked to the fireplace and picked up a poker. "This, too," he said. He slapped it into the palm of his hand a few times. "Has a nice heft to it," he observed. He handed it to Stolitz. He opened the lid of a wooden box that stood on the floor.

"Ah!" he said, obviously pleased with what he found. "You are a fisherman as well, Captain Keppler," he observed. He picked up a piece of cardboard with several fishhooks attached. "Excellent!" He turned to Keppler and held up the fishhooks. "These little commonplace barbs have been and can be used in an intriguing improvement on the rather boring common flogging," he explained. "In the Orient, robbers were often flogged with a whip to which several fishhooks had been tied. After every blow, the hooks stuck in the flesh, and—amusingly enough—the withdrawal of the whip was infinitely more painful than the laying on." He smiled his thin, humorless smile at Keppler. "Perhaps we shall experiment with it? Try it out?" he suggested. "A little later?"

He nodded pensively. "Perhaps even with the Chinese refinement. In case you are curious, Keppler, the Chinese refinement consists of heating the fishhooks until they are red hot. I understand that if you let the hooks cool while embedded in the flesh, you can actually see a reddish steam rise. The flesh is said, literally, to bubble and close over the imbedded hooks, adding a special little fillip to the act of withdrawing the whip." He nodded, engrossed in thought. "I have often wondered if that is actually so," he mused. "Perhaps I shall find out."

He peered into the tackle box and brought out a pair of pliers. "These, too, may prove useful," he observed.

He suddenly reached down and pulled the electric cord out of the floor lamp, exposing the naked wires.

"And, of course, electricity. The good old Gestapo standby." He chuckled. "I have seen it used quite often on the most intimate parts of a man's anatomy, with astonishing results."

He turned to Stolitz. "We seem to have enough tools to make a respectable beginning," he said. "What do you think, Stolitz?"

"I agree, *Herr Kommandant*."

271

Haupt nodded. "Excellent!" He walked over to stand directly in front of Keppler.

"Now, Herr Flussschiff Kapitän Keppler. Question number one: *Who are your accomplices?*"

❈ 34 ❈

GABY peered at the little red drop of paint collected at the underside of the projectile. Red, she thought. Such an insistent color. The color of danger, of warning, and anger. But also the color of life. She smoothed the spot with her brush. She inspected the dummy missile lying on the rack. With its new coat of red paint it looked as dangerous as its lethal mates.

She carefully folded the dropcloth spread out under the rack and scrutinized the floor minutely. Not even the smallest drop of paint could be left behind to betray their tampering.

She walked over to Ted, who was working on a live projectile that had been transferred to one of the dummy trailers.

"Number one is finished," he said. "We're ready for the next one."

He pointed to where he had screwed the sensitivity-adjusted fuze onto the live shell, now sporting a bright yellow. "It'll need a little touchup," he said.

Gaby spread the dropcloth out under the nose of the repainted projectile and opened her can of yellow paint. She was just about to dip her brush into the paint—when she stiffened.

Faintly, in the distance, the sound of a car could be heard approaching. Quickly she looked up at Ted. Automatically he held up his hand in an unnecessary gesture of silence. He cocked his head to listen.

The car was coming closer.

Standing in frozen alarm, they both listened intently as the car came to a stop outside.

Straining their ears, they could hear barely audible voices—and suddenly the lock on the door rattled loudly.

They glanced at one another—not daring even to breathe.

There was the short exchange of muffled words, the slam of a car door—and the vehicle drove off.

Without realizing it, they both drew a deep breath of relief. It had been a guard check. And Kevin had passed his first test with flying colors.

"Okay," Ted said briskly, perhaps a little too briskly. Despite himself, he knew he had been shaken. "On to number two."

He looked at his watch.

It was 0239 hours.

Dieter Haupt stood back and contemplated the naked man hanging awkwardly from the makeshift strappado. He glanced at an old carved-wood clock on the wall behind him. Past three in the morning. The stubborn old idiot had endured his—his questioning for over half an hour. Fool! Did he not realize it was all for nothing? Ultimately he *would* talk. There was no doubt about that. It irritated Haupt that the old man couldn't see that. It was a waste of time. And energy.

Haupt watched his subject's face closely for any sign of weakening. There was none. Drawn, pained, and streaked with blood, yes. But no surrender. Pensively he followed with his eyes a drop of bright-red blood as it slowly ran from a cut on the man's forehead down onto the bridge of his nose. Blood, he thought. Nothing quite as brightly red as fresh blood. He had, of course, been careful not to spill too much of it. A subject weakened by the loss of blood is not quite as aware of the various methods of persuasion used on him as is one still in full strength.

Curiously he looked at the man's wrists. The skin on them had been peeled back by the tight bonds and bunched up around the heels of his hands. One wrist was bent back over the table edge in a strange angle. Probably broken, he thought idly. The slightest movement as the man was suspended from it would have to be agony. And yet, the old riverman had remained obstinately silent. He had uttered not a word. Not a cry. He had spat once. In annoyance, Haupt had thought it more in defiance than merely to spit out the teeth broken from his gums to expose the nerves.

Haupt glanced at his driver, who stood gaping at the naked, blood-seared man hanging on the upended table.

"You!" he snapped at him, angered that the man was witnessing his lack of success. "Search the house. Go through it top to bottom. See what you can find. Anything unusual, anything out-of-place, you bring it to me. *Verstanden?*"

The man came to attention. "*Jawohl, Herr Brigadeführer,*" he said smartly. "Understood." Quickly he walked off.

Haupt returned his attention to Keppler. The damned bastard had to be made to talk. He *had* to. It was becoming a matter of of pride. Almost absentmindedly he picked with the tip of the sharp hunting knife at the already tattered flesh around his victim's nipples.

Almost imperceptibly Keppler twitched. It wasn't that he did not feel the pain; that he was not aware of what was being done to him. But a long time ago he had learned how to cope with pain. It was simply a matter of priorities. He willed his mind to devote itself completely to another crisis—literally blocking the full force of the pain inflicted on him from reaching his awareness. As long as he concentrated fully on the present priority concern—that of protecting his friends and his own integrity—he relegated the pain to a secondary position of importance in his mind. It was as if he put it on hold. It was there. It was clamoring to be acknowledged. He was fully aware of its existence. But he kept it in abeyance . . .

He had been fifteen years old when he had first discovered that he, to some extent, could control pain. A few kilometers from his home had been a field with an old abandoned windmill. Because the mill was ramshackle and unsafe, his father had forbidden him to play there. He had, of course, disobeyed, and one day when he was climbing the rickety stairs to the mill loft, the rotten wood gave way and he fell. In the fall he broke a leg; a bad compound fracture. For hours he'd lain at the bottom of the stairs in agony, shouting for help, and finally a passing farmer had heard his cries. The man had taken him in his spring-less cart over the extremely bumpy field road to his home, and every bump in the road had produced an excruciating pain in his leg. But young Jan had discovered that when he dwelled on the forthcoming anger and certain punishment by his father that awaited him, the pain in his leg was hardly felt. A matter of priorities. The leg had been

somewhat unreliable ever since, but over the years Jan unconsciously had perfected this ability to select one exigency to shut
out another from his awareness. It was a form of self-hypnosis.
He did not think of it as such; he only knew it worked for him.

He felt a sharp lance of fire knife through him as Haupt probed
a little deeper. He blinked away the blood that trickled down into
his eyes from the cut on his forehead and stared steadily and
terribly at his tormentor.

"Very well, Keppler," Haupt said coldly. "Since you do not seem
to be able to recall the answer to my first question, we will proceed
to the second, and considerably more—eh, disagreeable stage of
our little, so far one-sided, talk."

He placed the tip of the hunting knife under Keppler's right
eye, dimpling the soft flesh.

"My second question, Keppler." He narrowed his eyes and looked
straight into the skipper's face. And spacing every word he asked:
"Where are your accomplices now?"

Ted stood back and stared critically at the three live projectiles
lying strapped onto three of the missile trailers. Repainted bright
yellow and armed with sensitive fuzes, they were indistinguish-
able from the harmless dummies.

"That's it," he said. "First one of those babies the Krauts load,
Busy Lizzie is through being busy!"

"How do we know they'll fire them?" Gaby asked, suddenly
worried.

"There are twelve dummy shells scheduled to be fired during
the test," Ted said. "You confirmed that yourself. And if the
Germans schedule twelve projectiles to be fired, you can be damned
sure they'll fire twelve. And even if they don't pick one of the
Grand Guignol specials until there are only three left—it'll be
goodbye Lizzie."

He glanced at his watch. "Less than twenty minutes to the
change of guards," he said. "We've got to get the hell out of here.
Pronto!" He looked at the basket at Gaby's feet. "Everything
picked up?"

She nodded. "I have checked and checked again," she said. "We
have left nothing behind. No sign that we have been here."

"Okay, let's go."

Gaby frowned. "What—what about him?" she asked. She nod-

275

ded toward the dead German soldier lying in his underwear sprawled against the wall next to the door.

"We take him along," Ted said. "Even if we could find a place to stash him here, we can't take the chance of them finding him."

He strode to the door. For a moment he listened, then he rapped sharply on it. Almost at once the small door opened and Kevin peered into the hangar.

"Cutting it close," he said, his voice taut. "All done?"

"All done," Gaby answered him.

"Give me a hand with the Kraut," Ted said. "Heave him up on my shoulders. We'll take him with us to the junk pile. We can hide him there. I'm sure he won't be found in time to raise an alarm."

"Will do." Kevin grabbed hold of the dead sentry. The man was heavy. Surprisingly so. Heavier than he looked to be. Dead weight, he thought. It really is. And as Ted and Gaby ran for the concealment of the junk pile, he locked the hangar door and took up his post.

The plan is working, he thought with excitement. The script is turning out beautifully. Ted and Gaby had had their moment. Now it was up to him to take center stage.

He pulled himself erect and stood ramrod straight in true Teutonic fashion, waiting for his relief . . .

Ted was shoving the dead sentry under what appeared to be the cracked, rusty metal hood from a forge. He crammed the basket with the paint supplies and the soiled overalls in with him, keeping Kevin's clothes out, and covered it all with rubble and debris.

Gaby was bundling up Kevin's clothes when Ted put his hand on her arm. In silence, they lay immobile among the junk as from the main road at the far end of the building the guard relief column came into view and started to march down the street toward Kevin.

Ted strained to see. It seemed to him that it was a different noncom in charge of the detail, but he couldn't be sure. He prayed it was. It would mean that much less of a chance of Kevin's being unmasked. They were counting on the fact that with the recent influx of Waffen SS reinforcements, there would be a lot of unfamiliar faces around. Ironic, he thought. The very fact that the Kraut commandant almost doubled his guard forces for extra safety might actually work against him. He fervently hoped it would.

The relief detail drew even with Kevin, who stood at attention at his post.

"*Wache—halt!*" they heard the noncom command.

And with hearts pounding, they watched the whole routine of the changing of the guard.

Kevin went through it as if he'd done it all his life. He always was a quick study, Gaby thought proudly, as they watched the guard detail march off, Kevin bringing up the rear.

"What now?" she whispered to Ted.

"We wait," he whispered back, "until it's time to meet Kevin at the paintshack. Then we hightail it back to Mike and Jan." He looked at her. "I think we've done it, Gaby," he said soberly. "Only one thing can go wrong now."

"What?"

"If they find out that there is something wrong—and call off the damned test!"

Dieter Haupt was taut with anger, impatience, and frustration. The old bastard refused to be broken, despite everything that had been done to him. He studied the man's mutilated face with curiosity. What was it that enabled him to hold out? In silence, his subject returned his tormentor's gaze. Defiance and contempt still blazed at the Nazi from his one remaining eye.

Time, Dieter thought bitterly. It was always time that softened up an interrogation subject so that he would respond to the various methods of prodding to make him talk. And time was the only thing he did not have. Time.

He had a sudden chilling thought. He whirled to face his aide.

"Stolitz!" he snapped. "Have you seen a telephone here?"

"Yes, *Herr Kommandant*," his aide answered. "In a small room." He pointed. "Through that door."

Haupt at once strode into the little room. It seemed to be a den. On a table in a corner stood a telephone. It was an old-fashioned square instrument, with the receiver lying in a twin-forked cradle, and with a handle to crank.

He picked up the receiver and turned the handle vigorously. In a few seconds a woman's voice answered.

"Central Wollin."

"Get me *Heeresversuchsstelle* Misdroy," he barked. "*Sofort!* Military priority."

"At once."

He waited for another few seconds. Then—

"*Heeresversuchsstelle* Misdroy." The female voice was clear and efficient.

"This is *Kommandant* Haupt," he said crisply. "Put me through to the HDP Test Director. Immediately!"

"At once, *Herr Kommandant*."

There was a series of clicks, and a phone began to ring. To Haupt it seemed an age before a man's sleepy voice answered. "Baumeister here."

"Baumeister. This is Haupt. What is the situation at the test site?"

"At the test site, *Herr Kommandant*?" The man's voice sounded puzzled. "Why—all is quiet. The test firings are not scheduled to begin for—for three and a half hours. It's only—"

"I know what time it is, Baumeister," Haupt snapped impatiently. "Has anything happened at the base? Anywhere? Anything unusual?"

"No, nothing."

"And *Fleissiges Lieschen* herself? Has anyone been near her? Or tried to get near her?"

"No one, *Herr Kommandant*. Besides, it would have been impossible. There are armed guards stationed every ten meters along the entire length of the barrel. As per your own orders. And the area itself is well lit and heavily guarded."

"And elsewhere?"

"All has been quiet. All *is* quiet." There was a slight pause. "Is anything wrong?"

"No, nothing is wrong. I am merely checking."

"I—see." The test director sounded puzzled. "Any changes in orders, *Herr Kommandant*?" he asked. "The test firings are still to be carried out as scheduled, are they not?"

For a split second Haupt contemplated postponing the test until all the saboteurs were caught. He at once decided against it. It would not look good on his record of efficiency if in the last minute he failed to deliver as promised. Besides, the saboteurs obviously had been unable to carry out any action against his project.

"Of course," he said curtly.

"Will you attend the test, *Herr Kommandant*?"

"I will be there," Haupt answered. He glanced at the old phone. In a little square window, a faded number could be made out.

"Meanwhile, Baumeister, if anything should happen. Anything at all. Anything—out of routine, you are to call me at once. I am at Darsewitz 57. Is that clear?"

"Yes, *Herr Kommandant*. I shall advance my personal schedule and go to the HDP site at once."

"Excellent," Haupt said. "I shall see you there at 0900 hours."

He hung up.

He felt better. Obviously Keppler's cohorts had been unable to penetrate his security screen. If they had tried. And he felt certain they had. Just as he felt certain they would again. Perhaps another day.

He had to get the old man to talk. He had to know who the man's accomplices were—and what they were planning.

He returned to the living room. Malevolently he glared at Keppler.

"Now, mein lieber Herr Kapitän Keppler, my third and last question. He placed himself directly in front of the cruelly mangled body of the man suspended from the now blood-smeared table.

"What are the plans of your accomplices?"

Mike was racked with indecision and uncertainty as he crouched at the far end of the Keppler pier in the shadows of the old boathouse. Apprehension enflamed his mind, and his body was beginning to cramp from the contorted position, but he dared not move. His head was bursting with anxiety, with questions and doubts.

What was going on in the Keppler house?

It had been hours since he had seen and heard the car arrive— and the armed soldier break down the back door to the house. What were they doing in there? They must have surprised Keppler. He had been asleep only minutes before they burst in. He had seen him in his room. He must be a prisoner now. But—what was happening?

He had heard not a sound from the house.

Were they questioning Jan? Were they roughing him up to make him talk? If so, would he not have heard some kind of outcry? Or was Keppler talking freely? Spilling everything he knew? Delivering Kevin and Gaby and Ted into enemy hands. Was he?

He refused to believe so. Jan would not betray his friends. He tried to dismiss the thought from his mind. But he was not completely successful. After all, how well did they know the man?

279

And why had he heard nothing? Not a sound. Nothing at all. For so long.

Were they still in there? They had to be. He would have heard the car again if it had started up and driven away. As he did when it arrived. Even though it was now hidden from view by the house, he was certain it was still there. He would have seen the headlights again if the car had driven off. Or he would have *heard* it if for some reason they would have left without turning on the lights. He was sure of it.

They were still in there. Whoever they were. He was certain of it.

They—and Jan Keppler.

He was suddenly aware of the fact that it was beginning to grow lighter. Already the far horizon across the water in back of him was turning pale pink. In a short time it would be light enough for him to be fully visible from the house to anyone who might look out. He had to find better cover before it was entirely too late. And that meant he had to move. Now.

He looked around. Behind him lay the old barge. It would afford cover—but to reach that cover he would have to climb up over the gunwale. He would be silhouetted against the brightening sky. It would be only for a few seconds, but that might be enough. In front of him was the door to the boathouse. He might reach it if he sidled along the wall, staying as much as possible in the shadows and moving slowly. That was the only way.

Or should he try to slip down to the house? Find out what was going on? Perhaps do something?

What? Was there anything he could do to help? If, in fact, Keppler was being held prisoner?

He was unarmed against an unknown number of German soldiers armed with automatic weapons. Even the element of surprise would not be enough to keep him from getting killed. And if he were to be of any help at all to any of his friends at any time, he had to stay alive.

As long as the Nazis were still in Keppler's house, Kevin and the others would be safe. He suddenly stiffened. Would they? A disturbing thought struck him. If Keppler *had* talked, perhaps the Germans had contacted the Misdroy base by telephone! Perhaps Kevin and his teammates had already been caught!

Did Keppler have a phone? He racked his brain to remember. He could not. He could not recall having seen one, but that meant nothing. He was not in the phonebook, they'd already ascertained that. But that, too, was meaningless. His number could be unlisted. And it was impossible for him to see if Keppler's house was connected to the telephone lines that ran along the street.

He agonized over what to do—and made up his mind. He would take cover in the boathouse, hoping he could get there without being discovered. Every second he waited to move would place him in greater danger of that. Once safely in hiding, he would decide on a course of action.

Slowly he began to inch along the wooden boathouse wall. He was in full view of the Keppler house. And the Germans in it . . .

It was almost 0600 hours when Kevin slipped in the door to paintshop number three.

Ted closed the door behind him. Gaby threw her arms around him.

"Any problems?" Ted asked.

"None," Kevin answered. "The key is on the rack. When they use it on the lock on the hangar door, it will fit."

He began to shrug out of the German uniform. "But if I ever have to play a German soldier again, I hope to hell it will be before a different audience."

Gaby handed him his clothes. "I was worried, cheri," she said. "But—I am proud of you."

"So am I," Ted grinned. "You looked like a real tin soldier out there." He turned to Gaby.

"It's time we thought of getting the hell out of here," he said. "Of getting back to Mike and Jan. That pass of yours will still get us a car from the motor pool, right?"

Gaby nodded. "I am sure it will." She bit her lip. "But—we must wait, I think."

"Wait? Why?"

"It is early yet. It—it might look suspicious if we went there now and requisitioned a car."

"Gaby is right, Ted," Kevin said. "Let's wait until the base gets to be a little busier. It's much easier to lose yourself in a crowd than in the middle of an empty soccer field."

Ted nodded. "You have a point. We wait two hours. To about 0800. By that time, only an hour before the test begins, the joint should be jumping."

"Will we be safe here?" Gaby asked.

"I think so. We won't lock the door. If anyone comes by, look busy. Confer over some papers. Anything. Ad-lib, as you theater-types say. Just make it look good. And let me do the talking. I'm an old hand at this paintshop talk by now."

"You're the doctor," Kevin nodded, "as you American-types say!"

"So we sit pretty," Ted acknowledged, "for two hours." He shrugged.

"It'll be a damned long two hours."

Haupt glanced at the ornate clock on the wall of Keppler's living room. It was already a few minutes before eight. And he had gotten nowhere. He cursed under his breath. One more try, he thought. One more. And then he would have to leave for Misdroy if he wanted to be there for the crucial test firings. And he did.

He watched the man strapped to the rack. He was obviously getting weaker. For the first time his head hung listlessly down on his chest. This time. Perhaps this time.

He frowned. He had to be careful. He could not afford to have the man die on him before he had told him what he wanted to know. If he had to leave before that was accomplished—and it was becoming more and more apparent that he would—damn the stubborn *Drecksau!*—the man would have to be kept alive for further . . . interrogation.

Until he cracked.

He turned to the little table that had been placed before the strappado and on which the various instruments of persuasion that had been collected were laid out.

He picked up the hunting knife just as his driver came hurrying into the room. In one hand he carried a Luger, in the other a curious, misshapen object.

"*Zu Befehl, Herr Kommandant,*" he reported. "I found these things in the attic behind a pile of junk." He placed the Luger on the table. "It is fully loaded, *Herr Kommandant,*" he pointed out. He placed the object next to the gun and stood back.

Haupt picked up the object. Curiously he examined it, turning it over in his hands. It appeared to be an artificial limb. A lower left arm without the hand. And it had been badly damaged; at one time crushed at the elbow, perforated with a jagged cut near the wrist and peppered throughout with smaller holes, all of which had been crudely repaired. He stared at it.

And as if illuminated by a blinding photo-flash, everything suddenly became searingly clear in his mind.

One of the saboteurs was a one-armed man!

The man whose arm had been broken in the accident at the gate and who had disappeared! And the Martian incident. That ridiculous, inane fairy tale he so cavalierly had dismissed!

He whirled on Stolitz.

"Stolitz," he asked hoarsely. "That report about the Martians. The boy who said they bled green blood. Do you recall it?"

"Yes, *Herr Kommandant*, I do."

"Did you read the whole report?"

"I did."

Haupt stared at him, his eyes boring into the man. "How?" he rasped. "How did he bleed?" He knew the answer, but he had to hear it spoken.

"One of them made a cut on his arm, sir," Stolitz said, "with the boy's own knife. When he bled, the boy said, the blood was green."

Violently Haupt slammed the prosthesis against the edge of the table top strappado. It splintered. He broke it open. The inside of it was coated with green paint splotches and streaked with dark-red stains.

The ambush!

The hand that had held a knife to his, Dieter Haupt's, throat as he sat in his car that fateful day had been on the end of that shattered abomination he held before him. It had been into that foul, artificial contrivance that the bullets had slammed. He felt a blinding rage swell in him. There had been three men.

And a woman!

The woman who called herself Gertie Kerlach. A woman he, himself, had placed in a trusted position on the base. A woman who with her fellow saboteurs even at this moment would be plotting to destroy his Lizzie.

He had been played for a fool. And that was the greatest sin of all. Mounting fury threatened to choke him. He stalked to the little den with the telephone. Savagely he cranked the handle.

"Central Wollin," the operator answered.

"*Heeresversuchsstelle* Misdroy! *Sofort*! Military emergency!" he shouted into the receiver.

He waited impatiently. After a few seconds the operator came back.

"I am sorry, sir," she said. "All the lines are in use."

Damn it! he thought. They would be. It was close to test time. They would be in contact with all the surrounding military installations and spotting centers, apprising them of the test. It was SOP.

"Break in!" he ordered.

"I am sorry, sir," the operator said. "That is impossible. We are not allowed to monitor or interrupt classified military communications."

He slammed the receiver down. He stormed from the room.

"Start the car!" he snapped at his driver. "We leave for Misdroy at once!" He turned to Stolitz. "Finish him!" He nodded toward Keppler.

Stolitz moved to obey.

"No, wait!"

Haupt walked over to the strappado. He glared hatefully at the broken, mutilated body that had been Janusz Keppler. It was no longer a man who was hanging from the jury-rigged torture rack. Haupt looked at the disfigured, blood-streaked face. He could not decide which was more terrible to look at. The remaining eye that stared back at him with mocking contempt—or the gore-smeared empty socket that glistened in crimson horror next to it.

"Damn you!" he grated. "Damn you to hell!"

He picked up the mangled prosthesis and hurled it at Jan. It struck him full in the face.

"It would be too easy for you if I killed you now, old man," he snarled. "You are already dead. But I hope the hell it will take you a long time to realize it."

Abruptly he turned on his heel and stalked from the room.

He glanced at his watch. 0831 hours. He would be in Misdroy before the tests began.

Gaby walked up to the motor pool sergeant who stood at a guard shed just inside the gate to the motor pool. With slightly haughty confidence, she handed him her pass.

"I shall need a car at once," she said in a tone of voice that invited no contradiction. She nodded curtly toward Ted and Kevin who stood waiting respectfully a short distance away. "Those two men will accompany me," she went on. "We will be picking up some crates of special material at the main library in Stettin. Important material."

The noncom frowned over the pass, taking his time examining it.

"Be quick about it, Sergeant," Gaby snapped impatiently. "Can you not see the authorization is signed by the Kommandant himself?"

A car drove up to the guard shed. The driver tried to get the sergeant's attention. The noncom glanced at him. The place was getting busy. He sighed.

"*Jawohl, gnädiges Fräulein*," he said. He motioned to a soldier who was tinkering with a car near one of the garages. He raised his voice.

"Ernst!" he shouted. "Bring K-3 over here!"

He took a clipboard from a nail on the guard shed wall behind him and fished a stubby pencil from his tunic pocket. He peered at the forms clipped to the board with a couple of carbons between them.

"Destination—Stettin," he read as he filled in the proper spaces on the form.

"Purpose—library business. Authority—Haupt, Kommandant . . . Vehicle number—K-3 . . . Return—" He looked at Gaby.

"We will be back this afternoon," she said. "Late this afternoon."

"1800 hours?"

"That is fine. 1800 hours."

"1800 hours," the man wrote. He handed the clipboard to Gaby. "Sign there." He pointed to the appropriate spot and gave Gaby his pencil. She signed the form and returned the clipboard to the noncom. He countersigned it, tore off a copy, and gave it to Gaby.

"*Bitte Fräulein*," he said. "This is your trip ticket. It will get you to Stettin and back. And it will authorize you to draw any needed Benzin at any military depot on the way."

"Thank you, Sergeant, *Heil Hitler*!

"*Heil Hitler*!"

The vehicle that the motor pool soldier drove up to the guard shed was a sparkling-clean staff car. With amusement, Gaby noticed that it was one of the cars used by *Brigadeführer* Dieter Haupt himself. On the front fenders were the little rods that would hold his personal pennant when he was in the car.

With Ted and Kevin she got into the car, and with Kevin behind the wheel, they drove off.

It was 0842 hours when they passed through the last checkpoint and headed for Darsewitz and the home of Janusz Keppler.

The sudden sound of the car starting up had startled him. In the gloom of the tightly closed-up boathouse, he had moved to a small grime-caked window in the wall facing the main house and the road, careful not to make any noise by bumping into the diverse pieces of equipment and stowage scattered about the place. And in a few minutes he had seen the car drive away.

The Nazi soldiers had left.

And Jan?

He peered through the window. Although overcast, it was bright daylight outside. But he saw no movement at all. He made up his mind. He would chance it.

Carefully he picked his way back to the door. For a moment he hesitated, then he quickly opened it and raced for the back door, hanging broken from its hinges. Again he stopped and listened. He could hear nothing.

Slowly, noiselessly he stole into the house. Cautiously he peered into the living room—and stiffened in shock, a cry of anguish escaping him.

In abject horror, he stared at Dieter Haupt's improvised strappado and the bloody, mutilated tangle of lacerated flesh and broken bones that were hanging from it.

He was suddenly and brutally catapulted back for an instant to the most gruesome, the most gory and ghastly scenes they had staged at the Grand Guignol: The savaged lighthouse keeper. The scalping of Lisette. Blinded Emil. They were like mild pastel dreams . . .

This was his friend. This was reality. And it was terrifying.

Jan.

Jan, who must have suffered the agonies of hell itself while he, Michael, had been sitting in safety out on the damned pier without lifting a finger to help.

He was overcome with guilt and self-reproach, with shame and remorse for ever having doubted his friend. His friend, still alive, but no longer a human being.

Janusz Keppler slowly raised his head. His single pain-ridden eye fixed itself on Mike. A blood-crusted slit in his face opened and moved grotesquely, mouthing one word—

"Mike . . ."

Instantly Mike was at his side. Desperately he searched about, his eyes blurred with burning tears. He spied the big hunting knife and at once cut the blood-soaked bonds that tied Jan to the table legs. With infinite tenderness he lowered the broken body of his friend to the floor.

Jan gasped with the agony of the movement. He stared up at Mike.

"I—said—nothing, " he breathed laboriously, the words that gurgled from his lacerated lips barely understandable.

"Lie still, Jan," Mike said. He spoke in a whisper, not trusting his voice. "Lie still. We will get help. We—"

"No." Jan looked up at his friend, his eyes pleading. "There is—no help. Only—more—pain." He gasped with the effort of talking. "Finish me," he begged. "Please, Mike, finish me. . . ."

With terrible eyes, Mike stared down into the imploring face of his friend.

"The—Luger," Jan breathed, "on—the table."

Mike looked up. Automatically he took the gun. He stared at it. It felt heavy and obscene in his hand.

"Please . . ."

Mike held the gun in both his hands. His mind was awhirl with emotions that came so fast that none had time to register. He looked down at his friend. The sight of the monstrous effects of Dieter Haupt's interrogation seared itself on his mind. He knew his friend must be suffering indescribable agonies. And he knew he would never live to be a man again.

But—this was Jan.

This was the man who had let himself be torn to pieces, who had endured an orgy of agony, all to ensure the safety of Kevin and Gaby and Ted and himself.

Tear-blinded, he gazed down into the grisly, disfeatured face of his friend.

He could not kill him. He could not. He pulled the trigger.

Dieter Haupt could taste his anger. It coated the inside of his mouth with a bitter taint of acerbity until he felt he would gag on it.

That bitch! That damned little *Luder!*—that damned little whore! He had once lusted for her. He had once wanted her. He still did. But for a vastly different reason. That stubborn old fool in Darsewitz had paid the price for defying him. His would merely be an *Erntedankfesttanz*—a Thanksgiving Dance—in comparison to what he had in mind for the Alsatian whore.

He glanced at his aide who sat stolidly erect in the seat next to him, staring straight ahead, as the staff car hurtled along the road to Misdroy. They had left Wollin behind, sped through the village of Plötzin, past the place the islanders called Tiemann's Folly, and through Dargebanz. In a few minutes they would be at the turnoff to the base.

Only a few minutes—and he would get his hands on that two-faced woman who called herself Gertie Kerlach and lock her safely away for later while he witnessed Lizzie's final test firings.

He braced himself to keep from lurching against his aide as the car swerved to make room for another vehicle that came racing down the road in the opposite direction.

Idly he noticed it was a military vehicle. A staff car. Almost subliminally he glimpsed the occupants. Two men and a woman.

He suddenly felt lightheaded as the blood rushed from his brain in chilling shock. Something else? Realization exploded in his mind. The staff car. It had been one of *his*! He had caught an instant's glimpse of the two little rods on the front fenders of the vehicle that were meant to hold his own pennants, as did the ones on the car he was even now riding.

And the woman. *The Alsatian whore!* And her two cohorts. There could be no doubt.

At once he leaned forward.

"Stop!" he screamed at the driver. "Stop the car! Turn around at once! Hurry! Hurry!"

Startled, the driver stomped on the brakes. The car slewed to a halt.

"Back the way we came!" Haupt shouted at the man. *"Los!* As fast as you can drive!"

And as the car gathered speed, careening down the road, he sat back in his seat. He would miss the test at Misdroy. No matter. He would not be needed. And it was vastly more important that he apprehend the enemy saboteurs before they could try again to cripple his Lizzie. And he would have to act at once—or the terrorists would be long gone.

And he had to get his hands on the girl.

He knew exactly where the saboteurs were headed. He just came from there himself—the house of Janusz Keppler.

Mike did not know how long he had been kneeling on the floor gazing at his dead friend. Seconds? Minutes? Hours?

He was suddenly aware of the Luger still clutched in his hands. He hurled it away from him as far as he could.

He stood up and looked around. Over the back of a chair a folded blanket had been placed. He took it and unfolded it. Gently he wrapped the broken body of Janusz Keppler in it.

He glared at the blood-stained table standing on end in the middle of the room. In sudden grief-stricken rage he kicked it. It toppled off its end to stand on the floor like a huge freshly used butcher's block.

Something lying on the floor, revealed when the big table had settled down, caught his eye. Something twisted and crushed, but he still recognized it. It was his discarded prosthesis. The one he had worn at the ambush and at the incident at the gate.

The Germans had discovered it! And they would have put two and two together. He was sure of it. That is why they left without getting any information from Jan. They no longer needed it!

In horror, he realized that they would now know. They would know the ambush was a fake. They would know that Gaby was a plant. And they would seize her. And Ted. And Kevin . . .

Suddenly he started. Outside on the road a car could be heard coming to a skidding stop.

He ran to the window. Through the shrubbery he could make out the vehicle. It was a German staff car. The Nazis had returned! He was caught. But this time he would fight. He ran to the corner of the room where he had thrown the Luger. He would take as many of them with him as he could—before turning the gun on himself. He would not end up as Jan.

He heard a car door slam.

Where was that gun? He found it. He grabbed it. And as the door flew open he fell to one knee and whirled toward it.

In the open doorway stood Kevin. It was too late for Mike to stay the pressure of his finger on the trigger. He fired.

But in the split-second of recognition, he'd wrenched the gun a hair's breadth aside and the shot went wild.

289

He let the Luger fall from his hands. He ran to his son and enfolded him in his arms.

"Kevin," he sobbed. "Kevin. Kevin . . ."

Kevin returned his father's hug. "Dad," he whispered. It was all that needed to be said. Affectionately he pushed Mike away from him. He held him by the shoulders and looked into his face. "Some reception," he grinned. "Gun salute and all."

"You idiot," Mike grumbled. "How the hell was I to know it was you?" Gaby and Ted joined them. Mike looked from one to the other, his face grim. "Thank God you are alive," he said quietly.

Kevin picked up on his father's somber spirit. "Dad," he asked. "What's wrong?"

"The Germans," Mike said heavily. "They were here."

"Jan?" Gaby suddenly exclaimed. "Where is Jan?" She looked around the room and saw the blanket-wrapped form. Her face went white. She started toward the bundle.

"No, Gaby," Mike restrained her. "Don't. There is not enough left of him to be called a man."

"What—happened?" Gaby was deeply shaken.

"The Germans—questioned him," Mike answered, his throat tight. "They were here a long time."

"The commandant!" Gaby cried. "I thought it was his car we passed. Only—only minutes ago. He was here!"

"He never gave you away," Mike said, staring bleakly at the blanket-shrouded form. "He never talked. And they—they—" His voice broke.

"What happened, Dad?" Kevin asked. "How was Jan caught? How—"

"It is a long story, son, and not an easy one to tell," Mike interrupted him. "I will tell you, but not now. Now we must get away from here. The Germans found my old prosthesis. The one with the bullet holes in it." He looked soberly at Gaby. "I am certain they know about you now," he said.

"If Dieter Haupt himself was here," Gaby said quietly, "he will know."

"That is why we have no time," Mike repeated urgently. He had a sudden thought. "Misdroy?" he asked. "The Tausendfüssler? What—"

"I'll tell you all about that, Dad, later," Kevin said. "We've got it fixed. We hope."

290

"But—we cannot just leave without taking care of—of Jan," Gaby cried.

They all turned to gaze at the blanket cover that held the body of their friend.

"We won't," Ted said. "We'll take him along. Our trip ticket will take us as far as Stettin. We'll stop on the way and bury him on the bank of the waterway he made his life for so long. I think he would have wanted that." He looked up. "But Mike is right. We'd better get the hell out of here."

He turned away—just as the front door to the house was flung violently open to slam against the wall.

In shock, they all whirled toward the crash.

Three men stood just inside the door. Three men in SS uniforms, the blood-red swastika armbands encircling their left arms, the silver death heads gleaming on their caps.

Brigadeführer Dieter Haupt, a steel-black Luger held firmly in his hand, stood smiling coldly at them, flanked by his aide and his driver, each with a submachine gun trained on Jedburgh Team Grand Guignol. . . .

❈ 35 ❈

FOR a taut, eternal moment they all stood frozen, staring at one another. The very air in the room was charged with tension. Then Haupt spoke, his voice deceptively calm.

"Raise your hands," he ordered. "All of you."

He turned to Gaby and made a small clipped bow to her. "*Fraülein* Gertie," he said with exaggerated politeness. "How very nice to see you again."

Gaby stood silent. Drained. It was over. And she knew it. Out of the corners of her eyes she could see the Luger that Mike had dropped. It was lying near the body of Jan. Too far. She made a conscious effort not to look at it directly, even though she realized that there was no way any of them could reach it in time. There was no way out.

Haupt turned his attention to the three men who stood impotently with their hands high in the air. "And these gentlemen," he said, almost conversationally. "They must be your fellow saboteurs. British? American? Perhaps French?" He smiled pleasantly. He was enjoying himself immensely. He had won. "We shall see," he said.

He fixed his eyes with curiosity on Mike. "You must be the one with the artificial arm, is that not so? You fit the description given by the nurse whom you so discourteously ran out on." He made a show of studying Mike with mock interest. "Let me see," he mused, "I believe it is your—your left arm. Am I correct?"

Mike said nothing. He only glared at the German officer, his eyes filled with hate and loathing. He knew he was looking at Jan's tormentor.

Suddenly Haupt brought up his Luger and fired one shot. It tore through Mike's prosthesis just below the elbow.

Gaby started violently. The men all stood silent. Mike did not move.

"Ah! Yes, I was correct." Haupt said with self-satisfaction. "I am pleased I did not injure your good arm," he said. "We shall get to that one later."

He turned back toward Gaby. Suddenly his eyes shone with hatred. "But first," he said, his voice all at once harsh with malice. "First there is another matter." His cold eyes bored into Gaby. "You and I, *gnädiges Fräulein*, you and I have some—unfinished business to conduct." He glared at her, a thin smile stretching his lips. "Perhaps a few, eh, preliminaries can be attended to now. Then we can spend a more substantial period of time together back at the base." He shrugged regretfully. "Perhaps not quite in the way I had envisioned it, but it should prove interesting all the same." He smiled at her, a grimace more menace than mirth, a foreboding promise of vengeance. "And when you and I have finished with our little—talk, I have a base full of foreign workers out there, some of them compatriots of yours, I believe, all of them starved for—for female companionship. I am certain you can find a way to pleasure them. If they will want you."

Abruptly he gun-gestured to the three men. "You! Step away from her!" he ordered curtly. He turned back to Gaby and took a step toward her. "She and I—"

Suddenly the booming, roaring thunderclap and the force of a shockwave from a gigantic, distant explosion struck the house with a fist of pure sound and power.

Haupt flinched in shock.

He did not see the tremendous blast that ripped the huge barrel of his *Tausendfüssler* asunder, shooting chunks of jagged, red-hot iron into the air, showering the surrounding woods with a hail of fiery devastation. . . . He did not see the booster barrels explode in a lightning chain reaction, adding their destruction to the holocaust. . . . He did not see the enormous billowing fireball that erupted and engulfed the burrow of the Misdroy Millipede.

He did not have to. It was vivid in his mind's eye.

Lizzie!

His distraction lasted only for a split second. It was enough.

Kevin threw himself at the Nazi, even as Haupt spun around and fired. Kevin felt a feathery tap on his left shoulder as the bullet grazed him—and he crashed into the German. The impact sent Haupt's gun flying from his hand before he had a chance to fire again. It skidded across the bare floor to disappear under a massive armoire, out of reach.

In the same instant, Ted hurled himself in a low tackle at *Obersturmführer* Stolitz, hitting him hard at the knees and sending them both sprawling. The burst from the officer's submachine gun singed Ted's hair over his right ear and slammed harmlessly into the ceiling. And Mike, with a roar of rage, charged headlong at the driver.

He grabbed the man's submachine gun by the barrel before he could recover completely from his shock and pushed it up—even as the driver fired. The heat from the bullets being shot through the barrel forced Mike to let go. With his right fist he swung a haymaker at the man's belly. He connected, and with a grunt the German doubled over in agony. Mike struck him viciously across the neck, but in collapsing, the man managed to grab Mike's legs, and the two men went down together.

Gaby dived for the Luger dropped by Mike as Haupt broke free from Kevin's onslaught. Wildly he looked around for something with which to defend himself. His eyes fell on the heavy poker lying on the little table. At once he grabbed it. He raised it high to bring it down on Kevin's head as he was struggling to get up from the floor—when Gaby fired.

Holding the gun with both hands, shaking with determination and fear, she emptied the gun at Haupt.

One of the bullets grazed the arm held high with the poker, and Haupt dropped it. He gave the girl a murderous glance. In two steps he was at her side, as she stood petrified, the Luger still extended in front of her, clutched in both her hands. He grabbed the empty gun and struck the girl a violent blow across her chest. She dropped.

He ignored her. He had a gun, a Luger, and he had a spare magazine in his tunic pocket. Feverishly he brought it out, just as Kevin regained his feet.

In a glance, Kevin took in what had happened. He saw the German eject the spent magazine from his gun, and he heard the sharp click as the man slapped the full one in place.

Instantly he knew what he had to do.

He ran.

Haupt watched him disappear out the back door. He cursed. He could not afford to let the enemy agent escape. He had to follow him at once. Before the bastard had a chance to lose himself. He had to go after him.

Kevin prayed he would. If the Nazi stayed behind, armed now with a gun, Ted and Mike would be no match for him. And Gaby . . .

There was only one choice, and he took it. Draw the officer away.

He ran across the Keppler backyard. He glanced back over his shoulder.

The SS officer came tearing out of the door, Luger in hand, and pounded after him.

He felt a surge of relief. He had heard no shots from the house. The Nazi was saving the bullets for him.

He was on his own. Unarmed against a ruthless enemy armed with an automatic pistol, pressing in close pursuit. He ran on. The frenzy of the fight totally consumed him and galvanized him to even greater speed. Like the others, the fate of Janusz Keppler was vivid in his mind. Like them, he acted with the desperation of knowing that whatever happened, none of them must face that fate. One all-consuming thought possessed him and drove him on. Elude the German officer. Defeat him. And kill him.

Only in the back recesses of his mind was he aware of the more rational and imperative reason for having to kill the man. The German could not be allowed to be left alive to spearhead an operation to catch them, if they were to get away. He knew too much about them. With his death and that of his subordinates, there would be no one to raise the alarm against them; no one who could identify them; no one to mount a hunt and endanger their return home.

The SS general had to die.

As he sped along, he plotted how. The incongruity of his thoughts never entered his mind. He needed to equalize the odds against him. How? His eyes flew about as he ran.

The boathouse!

It was dark in there. The German and he would be at an equal footing. Neither would be able to see well. And he knew there were tools in there. Something he could use as a weapon. Something sharp. An ax. A crowbar. A knife . . .

He reached the pier and sprinted headlong for the door to the boathouse, every split-second expecting a bullet to rip into his back.

He flung the door open and leaped inside.

The gloom struck him like a dank, tangible shroud. For a moment he could see nothing. He stopped just inside the door to let his eyes get used to the darkness before he tried to find a hiding place. And a weapon.

His mind screamed at him to move, but he stood still while his eyes gradually adjusted to the murkiness. His pursuer would have to do the same. He tried to stay his labored breathing so he could listen. He heard the running footsteps, hollow on the wooden pier, slow down and stop. The Nazi was cautious. Good. It would give him a little extra time.

Quickly he was able to see enough to get around. At once he ran for the machine shop. First—the weapon.

On a greasy workbench lay a big rusty wrench. It would do. He grabbed it.

Now—a place to hide.

The half-loft.

From there he would be able to see every move the German made below. And from there he might be able to jump him.

He scrambled out from under the half-loft; the ladder was on the other side. As he stumbled over a pile of cans and buckets in his way, he upset a small barrel. A viscous dark liquid spilled out to form a slick pool on the floor. Old oil. He narrowly missed getting it all over his feet.

He ran to the ladder and scurried up the rickety rungs. He looked around. At the other end a few empty crates were stacked. They would provide cover. He made a dash for them.

Suddenly he almost lost his balance. A loose board in the flooring gave way as he stepped on it. Teetering at the edge of the loft, he barely managed to grab hold of a strut with his free hand and steady himself before he heard the faint sound of the German entering the place below.

Stealthily, silently he crept to the cover of the crates.

Dimly, below, he could see the man, pressed against the wall just inside the door, his gun held at the ready before him, waiting for his eyes to get used to the darkness.

And time oozed by.

Suddenly there was the blinding flash of a match being struck, and presently a lamp blazed up.

Kevin swore under his breath. He had forgotten. He had forgotten the kerosene lamp on the hook at the door and the box of matches on the shelf just beside it. Dammit! The German had found them.

Once again he held the upper hand.

He knew that he, Kevin, was unarmed. He need not fear any sudden gunfire. He could take his time to search for him and find him. And ultimately he would. The door was the only way out.

Kevin had trapped himself.

He watched the German search methodically below. The walkways, every stack of equipment, every dark corner. He watched him go through the motorboat, and he heard him rummage through the machine shop directly under his hiding place and comb through the storage space.

In a few minutes he would turn his attention to the loft. And to his hiding place.

Kevin's eyes flew about the gloomy spot. The stack of crates afforded the only cover. The German would know at once that he would be hiding there.

That was it.

That was his only chance!

Quietly, slowly, he crept away from the crates toward the far inside corner of the loft area, careful not to make the slightest noise. He inched his way across the loft, waiting before moving for the sound of the Nazi pushing around boxes and pieces of junk to cover any possible creaks made by the planks that formed the flooring of the landing.

He was there.

Two or three empty sacks had been thrown there. From his pocket he fished out a small coin and noiselessly cradled down in the dark corner, covering himself with one of the sacks, leaving only a tiny spot to peek out.

Almost at once he heard the creaking of the old ladder as the German cautiously mounted it to reach the loft.

He saw the man's head warily rise above the floor level and stop. He saw him slowly and awkwardly climb up to the landing, holding the lamp in one hand, the Luger in the other. He saw him letting his eyes search about and come to rest on the stack of crates.

With infinite care not to make the slightest sound, Kevin freed one of his arms—and threw the coin at the crates.

There was a small clinking sound as it struck.

At once the German froze.

Then, totally intent on the stack of crates, he began to inch his way toward them.

Like a silent whirlwind, Kevin broke cover. He knew he could never reach his enemy to use his wrench before he was heard, but within a split-second he was at the loose board in the floor. With all his weight he jumped on it.

At the other end the board flew up. It struck the German officer a numbing blow on the side, even as he turned to fire. His hand with the Luger flew up, a shot rang out, and in his effort not to fall, he dropped the lamp, which lay burning on the floor at the edge of the loft, illuminating the eerie scene.

The German fought desperately to keep his balance. But with a bellow of rage, he pitched from the loft.

He never reached the floor.

One of the big sharp iron hooks on the wall embedded itself in the back of his tunic as he plunged down. It ripped through the uniform to hook itself deeply into the flesh on the man's back.

Haupt screamed.

Flailing his arms wildly and kicking his legs in a horrifying *danse macabre* performed by a giant, grotesque Grand Guignolish jumping-jack, he hung in agony on the hook on the wall, unable to free himself.

His violent struggling shook the whole ramshackle structure, and suddenly the burning kerosene lamp, dropped by him, toppled from its precarious perch on the edge of the loft landing and fell to the floor below. It landed directly below Haupt in the dark pool of oil spilled by Kevin.

There was a dull whoosh, and instantly the inflammable fluid flared up in a blaze, and Dieter Haupt's kicking feet were licked by greedy flames which quickly grew to a fountain of fire as the old paint and grease in the containers ignited.

Horrified, mesmerized, Kevin watched.

Within seconds the screaming German's clothes were smoking. Little flames erupted from the cloth of his uniform as the man writhed and shrieked in terror and agony, trying to tear himself from the relentless grip of the hook.

Suddenly his hair flared up in a burst of flames, and his clothes exploded in a blaze of fire, the flames peeling the scorched skin from his face.

Kevin turned away from the twisting human torch. Shaken, he climbed down the ladder. He ran for the house.

Behind him the roar of the fire grew louder, and the conflagration shot tongues of flames through the wooden roof of the old boathouse.

At the door to the house he was met by Mike. For the second time in the span of less than an hour, Mike threw his arms around his son.

"Kevin!" he cried. "I heard a shot. I thought—"

"I'm okay, Dad." He looked searchingly at his father. "Gaby? Ted?"

"They're fine."

"And the Germans?"

"Dead."

Kevin nodded soberly toward the blazing boathouse. "So is the general," he said.

They went into the house.

Gaby was sitting on the little table. Her blouse had been removed and Ted was taping her up with a roll of masking tape. She saw Kevin and started to jump off the table to run to him. Firmly Ted pushed her back. "Sit still," he ordered.

Kevin was at Gaby's side. "Gaby," he cried in alarm. "What happened?"

With radiant eyes she looked at him. "I am all right, cheri," she said. Her eyes grew bright with tears. "Oh—Kevin," she whispered.

"She may have cracked a rib or two," Ted said. "That Nazi bastard hit her pretty hard." He tore off the tape. "This'll hold her until we can arrange for something better."

With Kevin's help, Gaby put her blouse back on.

"Let's get the hell out of here," Ted said. "We'll have company pretty damned soon. Just throw a few essentials in the car." He glanced toward the blanket that covered the body of Janusz Keppler. "Kevin," he said. "Give me a hand with Jan."

As the two of them carried the body to the car, Mike looked around. He picked up the discarded and mangled prosthesis. They'd take it along. Nothing must be left behind that could possibly point to them. From the big armoire he grabbed an armful of clothes—and ran to join the others at the car.

As they drove away, they could hear the mournful wail from the horns of approaching fire engines.

Suddenly there was a loud explosion.

Gaby started.

"The motorboat," Kevin said. "The fire must have reached the fuel tank."

Dutifully they gave way as two fire trucks came barrelling down the road from Wollin toward the Keppler house. They drove across the bridge to the mainland and stopped. They looked back.

Towering twin columns of thick smoke, stained red by blazing flames, rose behind them. One from the test site of Misdroy on the horizon, where Lizzie—in her death throes—lay shattered in a crater of fiery destruction; one from the closer village of Darsewitz, where on his boathouse funeral pyre *Brigadeführer* Dieter Haupt, her tenacious champion, was being consumed in the truest Grand Guignol fashion.

For a while they sat watching, each with his own thoughts. Then, in silence, they once again started up the car and continued on their way to Stettin.

And home.

❈ EPILOGUE ❈

Paris, May 1945

Kevin forced his victim down across the rough wooden bench, the man's screaming head hanging over the end of it mere feet from the footlights and the front row of the audience. Kevin's "blind" eyes shone with sightless madness, and Emile—his hapless victim—howled in blood-curdling terror. It was the climax of *The Asylum*.

Kevin's eyes, burning with insanity, looked out over the audience. Full house. Great.

Once again the auditorium was packed with men in uniform —American, this time. Perhaps not as resplendent as the Nazi regalia, but a hell of a lot more desirable.

Much had happened in the year gone by. As he struggled in make-believe on the stage to keep the frantic Emile down, the actual events of the past year cascaded through his mind in a kaleidoscope of remembrances. . . .

Their moving farewell to Janusz Keppler when they buried him at the spot on Paulsdorfer Bucht that he had mentioned with such fondness . . . Their long and arduous trek from Stettin after the destruction of the *Tausendfüssler* at Misdroy and the death of *Brigadeführer* Dieter Haupt, through the wartime chaos of a Germany going down to defeat . . . Their return to Paris and the Theatre du Grand Guignol and to Etienne and to Lisette. . . . It had taken him a little while once again to get used to the sham carnage on the stage without feeling the horror of the reality. But he had put it behind him. . . . The excitement of D-Day and the invasion, carried out without the deadly interference of the millipedes of Mimoyecques . . . The triumphant liberation of Paris, and the overrunning of the Mimoyecques installations by the

303

Canadian First Army, who reportedly used fifty tons of high explosives to blow up the gigantic guns . . .

Ted had been exfiltrated to London as soon as they got back to Paris so he could make a complete first-hand report directly to Milton Hall; a plane had picked him up at a field on the farm of François Marot. But he had returned for the happy day when Kevin and Gaby were married. He had been the best man. The baby was due in five months now. It would, of course, be a boy, Mike had assured them, so he and Gaby had decided to name him Jan. . . .

Emile's lusty screams brought Kevin back to things at hand. Gleefully he jabbed his gleaming screwdriver into Emile's eye socket, broke the little pouch with synthetic blood, and pried out the glass eye so it slid down the man's forehead to plop on the stage floor.

As he groped for his prize in the special Grand Guignol gore on the floor, his eyes met those of an American army officer sitting front row center. A general. With four stars gleaming on his shoulders.

Kevin knew who he was. His name was George S. Patton. They called him "Blood and Guts," he knew. What could be more appropriate for a patron of the Grand Guignol?

The general grinned broadly at him—and winked.

Kevin could not help himself. All was well with the world. Dropping out of character just a little couldn't hurt.

He winked back.

❈ Author's Notes ❈

I.

Theatre du Grand Guignol

The Theatre du Grand Guignol that flourished in Paris for nearly six decades was truly a unique theatrical phenomenon that has left its indelible mark on dramatic performances everywhere in the world. The information about the Grand Guignol and the descriptions recounted on the introductory pages and in the text of this book are factual and authentic.

The little theater at 20 bis, Rue Chaptal in Montmartre, a former chapel and later artist's studio, opened its doors in 1896 under the management of Maurice Magnier, who was succeeded as director by the Paris impresario Oscar Metenier a year later. In 1898, a third director, Max Maurey, took over. And after his highly successful production of Edgar Allen Poe's *The Tell-Tale Heart*, the Grand Guignol blossomed forth as a theater dedicated to horror and blood-soaked realism—the gorier the better. It became the undisputed master of this macabre and grotesque form of theater until it finally closed its doors permanently in 1962, unable to compete with the violence and mayhem presented on the motion picture screens—and on television news programs.

Thus, it is also fact that *Reichsmarschall* Hermann Goering and General George S. Patton, Jr., both were among the prominent patrons of the theater, and a Paris newspaper actually headlined *"Blood and Guts* at the *Grand Guignol"* after Patton's attendance. Among the many other celebrities who became Grand Guignol aficionados was Alexander Woolcott, who is said to have liberally sampled the brandy kept on hand in the house infirmary.

Madame Eva Berkson, a comedienne born of English parents,

who had lived all of her life in France, took over the theater in 1939 from the director at the time, Monsieur Camille Choisy, when he decided to let it go. But after the Nazis occupied Paris on June 14, 1940, triumphantly marching down the Champs Elysees, and Madame Berkson produced her famous Nazi atrocity play at the Grand Guignol and had to flee the country, the Germans reinstated Monsieur Choisy, who ran the theater during the Nazi occupation. Camille Choisy died a few years later, just before the French Committee of Liberation got around to trying him for collaborating with the Nazis. After V-E day, Madame Berkson once again took over the management of the theater. She was now Mrs. Dundas, having married an RAF pilot, a former British film actor named Alexander Dundas, while she was in England serving in the RAF Women's Auxiliary.

Although a typical performance at Theatre du Grand Guignol consisted of two one-act horror plays and two farces of the broadest kind, it was the horror plays that made the theater internationally famous.

Titles such as *The Horrible Experiment*, *The Kiss of Blood*, and *The Last Torture*; *A Crime in a Madhouse*, *The Hand of Death*, and *The Butcher of Babies* clued theatergoers to what they were about to see, and they would indeed watch the actors on the little stage chop off each other's limbs, gouge out their eyes, and sear the flesh from their faces with gruesome, gory reality. The stage was at times awash with the Grand Guignol special, ultra-secret formula stage blood.

In order to portray this realistic carnage, many of the actors were indeed crippled in some way, possessed of those "special endowments" such as missing limbs or eyes, or certain grotesque deformities. One actor had had a shattered lower jaw replaced with a removable prosthesis. Imagine the audience reaction to seeing him stagger from behind a door through which a shotgun blast had just been fired—the lower part of his face hanging in tatters, dripping realistic blood and gore.

This was the Grand Guignol at its most devastating, and the scene brought at least half a dozen patrons to the little infirmary in the back of the auditorium.

This constant carnage sometimes took its toll on the actors and actresses. One seasoned performer, Mademoiselle Maxa, who was justifiably famous for her blood-curdling screams, so frayed her vocal cords that she could no longer speak her normal lines above a hoarse whisper; and the actor Jean Goujet, who possessed one of the most diabolic and sinister faces that ever frightened an audience, fell dead prematurely—burned out by his stage brutality and violence.

The author of *Code Name: Grand Guignol*, who in 1937 and 1938, at the height of Theatre du Grand Guignol's popularity, was himself an actor and stage manager with a British theatrical company, The English Players, that had its own theater in Paris, Theatre de L'Oeuvre on Rue de Clichy, was acquainted with the stage manager of long standing at the Theatre du Grand Guignol and spent many an evening backstage, learning the company's secrets. Although never the formula for the famous Grand Guignol blood, a secret that perished with the theater itself . . .

Project HDP—The *Tausendfüssler*

However fantastic and incredible Project HDP—the *Hochdruckpumpe* (the high-pressure pump)—may seem, it is no figment of a runaway imagination.

The giant guns with their 492-foot-long barrels did exist, and the history and description of them given in the text of this book are authentic.

The *Hochdruckpumpe* was known under many names and designations other than the *Tausendfüssler* (the Millipede) and *Fleissiges Lieschen* (Busy Lizzie). It was also at various times and by various agencies called the *Gleichdruckrohr* (the straight-pressure barrel), the *Mehrfachkammer-Geschütz* (the multiple-chamber gun), the London Gun, and V-3. It was indeed a weapon that defied imagination, one of the most extraordinary weapons of World War II. The sketch that accompanies the text of *Code Name: Grand Guignol* was drawn from sketches and photographs available at the German Militärarchiv, Bundesarchiv in Freiburg i. Br. in West Germany and in the Imperial War Museum in London.

The *Tausendfüssler* project was actually one of Adolf Hitler's favorite projects. In January 1944, he ordered the project at Misdroy to proceed to completion "with all vigor and under all circumstances," and the Führer Order mentioned in the book is a shortened version of such a war directive ordering the bombardment of London by the giant guns, actually issued by Hitler on May 16, 1944.

Although the Allies—despite extensive aerial photographic

missions and intelligence operations—did not know the nature of the activities and construction taking place at Mimoyecques, the installation was bombed several times. Damage was done, but due to the extraordinary protection of the batteries, it was relatively minor; and although one battery ultimately was abandoned, the other was ready to go operational.

The story of *Code Name: Grand Guignol* is, of course, fiction—fiction based on factual background material. But the fact is that the test firings at Misdroy were beset with mishaps, some explainable, some not, and the *Tausendfüssler* constructed there did sustain a major accident in May 1944.

Mimoyesques was bombed on May 21, 1944—the day after the action of *Code Name: Grand Guignol* comes to an end—by forty B-17 bombers that dropped 189 thousand-pound bombs on the area. It was the twelfth attack on the installation, but only surface damage was inflicted.

Busy Lizzie at Misdroy was reconstructed after her May accident and placed back on a test-firing schedule—much too late, of course, to interfere with any D-Day operations. But Secret Report #V/Bb. Nr. 1595/449, dated *den 19. Dez. 1944*, for example, states: "On 13. 12. at Misdroy, 19 rounds were fired. No mishaps with the device occurred, 60% of the projectiles flew well."

In September 1944, the installation at Mimoyecques was finally overrun by elements of the First Canadian Army, without having fired a single projectile. And in May 1945, after exhaustive examination and documentation, the incredible *Tausendfüssler* batteries at Mimoyecques were blown up with tons of high explosives. Today, only the half-destroyed tunnel entrances to the batteries remain.

Two smaller versions of Busy Lizzie, however, were brought into action against United States forces.

One of these guns, which had barrels of "only" 197 feet long, was employed against Antwerp, the other against Luxembourg. This author, while serving with the U.S. Army Counter Intelligence Corps, was himself in Luxembourg City in December 1944 during the Battle of the Bulge, when the city was the target of this bombardment. The big gun was firing from an emplacement on a hillside near Hermeskeil in Germany, a distance of over sixty kilometers away. At the time, the source of this bombardment was a complete mystery to us. One of the rounds hit a church tower, others fell in the railroad yards. These two mini-Lizzies were destroyed by the Germans when the guns were in danger of being overrun by the Allied advance.

And today, Busy Lizzie exists only as a memory and a collection of documents and strange, incredible photographs. . . .

Special Forces and the Jedburgh Teams

"Set Europe Ablaze!" Winston Churchill had charged the leaders of the newly established SOE in November 1940, and this became the motto of the Special Operations Executive, an organization developed to conduct espionage and sabotage and to encourage, to direct, and to supply Resistance forces in countries occupied by the Nazis. It was called "the gangster school" by the Germans. Originally, the SOE was placed under the direction of Dr. Hugh Dalton, Minister of Economic Warfare. There were several executive chiefs—code-named *D*—until the organization in 1943 was stabilized under Major General Colin McVean Gubbins, a native of the Hebrides. The SOE by then had offices in various locations in London around Baker Street, between Oxford and Marlybone.

Modeled after this organization, the American counterpart, the Office of Strategic Services, was organized—the brainchild of the maverick officer Colonel William Joseph "Wild Bill" Donovan, a World War I Congressional Medal of Honor recipient and a personal friend and confidant of President Franklin Delano Roosevelt. The OSS was founded in July 1942, the first spy and sabotage organization formed in the United States. The operations of the two organizations quickly became closely integrated, and in 1943 a combined Anglo-American unit, called Special Forces, was formed.

Largely due to the efforts of a 35-year-old West Point officer, Colonel John Haskell, an Army Intelligence Officer put in charge of the OSS forces in England by Donovan, now a major-general, a new and imaginative operational scheme, code-named Jedburgh and designed to be an international intelligence service, came into being. The original idea was to team one American OSS officer or one British SOE officer with one French officer and an enlisted man radio operator, usually an American. The Jed teams would be parachuted into France to aid Resistance groups and to prepare for the invasion. Later, these activities were expanded to include other special missions.

The code name for the operation, according to some British

intelligence sources, was picked at random from a schoolbook atlas, while others claim it came from the place in Scotland where the teams were trained. Either way, the Jedburgh teams were highly effective.

After World War II came to an end, General Donovan was not successful in persuading President Harry S Truman that the OSS had a place in peacetime America, so—on October 1, 1945, the OSS ceased to exist. . . .

❈ Bibliography ❈

In addition to several European books and periodicals, as well as programs from the Theatre du Grand Guignol in Paris, the following English-language publications have furnished factual information for *Code Name: Grand Guignol*.

Asprey, Robert B., *War in the Shadows: The Guerilla in History*, Doubleday, New York, 1975.

Blumenson, Martin, *Liberation*, Time–Life Books, New York, 1978.

Bradley, Omar N., & Clay Blair, *A General's Life*, Simon & Schuster, New York, 1983.

Brown, Anthony Cave, *Bodyguard of Lies*, Harper & Row, New York, 1975.

Eisenhower, Dwight D., *Crusade in Europe*, Doubleday & Co., New York, 1948.

Haswell, Jack, *D-Day*, Times Books, New York, 1979.

Hine, Al, *D-Day. The Invasion of Europe*, American Heritage Publishing Co., New York, 1962.

Hogg, Ian V., *German Artillery in World War II*, Hippocrene Books, New York, 1975.

———. *German Secret Weapons of World War II*, Arco Publishing Co., New York, 1970.

Hyde, H. Montgomery, *Secret Intelligence Agent*, St. Martin's Press, New York, 1982.

Hymoff, Edward, *The OSS in World War War II*, Ballantine Books, New York, 1972.

King, J. B., & John Batchelor, *Infantry At War, 1939–1945*, Marshall Cavendish, USA, n.d.

Kobler, John, *Afternoon in the Attic*, Dodd, Mead & Co., New York, 1949.

Mannix, Daniel P., *The History of Torture*, Dell Publishing Co., New York, 1983.

McCombs, Dan, & Fred L. Worth, *World War II: Strange and Fascinating Facts*, Greenwich House/Crown, New York, 1983.

Palmer, Raymond, *The Making of a Spy*, Crescent Books, New York, 1977.

Perrault, Giller, *The Secret of D-Day*, Little, Brown & Co., Boston, 1965.

Pia, Jack, *SS Regalia*, Ballantine Books, New York, 1974.

Peikalkiewicz, Janusz, *Secret Agents, Spies & Saboteurs*, William Morris & Co./Südwest Verlag GmbH & Co., Munich, 1969.

Pryce-Jones, David, *Paris in the Third Reich*, Holt, Rinehart and Winston, New York, 1981.

Roosevelt, Kermit, *War Report of the OSS*, Walker & Co., New York, 1976.

Schoenbrun, David, *Soldiers of the Night. The Story of the French Resistance*, E. P. Dutton, New York, 1980.

Smith, R. Harris, *OSS*, University of California Press, Los Angeles, 1972.

Thompson, R. W., *D-Day: Spearhead of Invasion*, Bookthrift, New York, 1968.

Trevor-Roper, H. R., ed., *Blitzkrieg to Defeat: Hitler's War Directives 1939–1945*, Holt, Rinehart and Winston, London, 1964.

Whiting, Charles, *The Home Front: Germany*, Time–Life Books, New York, 1979.

About the Author

IB MELCHIOR, as well as being a best-selling author, is a motion picture writer-producer-director in Hollywood, with twelve feature films and numerous TV shows and documentaries to his credit.

He was born and educated in Denmark, majoring in literature and languages, and he graduated from the University of Copenhagen. He then joined a British theatrical company, The English Players, with headquarters in Paris, France, as an actor. He toured Europe with this troupe, becoming stage manager and co-director of the company. Just prior to the outbreak of World War II, he came to the United States with this company to do a Broadway show. Then followed a stint in the stage managing departments of Radio City Music Hall and the Center Theater Ice Shows in New York. When Pearl Harbor was attacked, he volunteered his services to the U.S. Armed Forces. He served with the "cloak-and-dagger" OSS for a while and was then transferred to the U.S. Military Intelligence Service. He spent two years in the European Theater of Operations as a Military Intelligence Investigator attached to the Counter Intelligence Corps. For his work in the ETO, he was decorated by the U.S. Army, as well as by the King of Denmark, and he was subsequently awarded the Knight Commander Cross of the Militant Order of St. Brigitte of Sweden.

After the war, he became active in television and also began his writing career. He has directed some 500 TV shows, both live and filmed, ranging from the musical *The Perry Como Show* on CBS-TV, on which he served for three and a half years, to the dramatic documentary series *The March of Medicine*, on NBC-TV. He has also served as a director or in a production capacity on eight motion picture features in Hollywood, including AIP's

[American International Pictures] unusual *The Time Travelers*, which he also wrote.

Besides this extensive career as a director, Ib Melchior's background as an author and writer includes more than a million words published in story and article form in many national magazines, including *Life*, as well as in several European periodicals, some of which have been included in international anthologies. He has also written a couple of legitimate plays for the stage, one being *Hour of Vengeance*, a dramatization of the ancient Amlet legend that was the original source for *Hamlet*. This play was produced at the Globe Theater in Los Angeles, and Melchior was honored with the Shakespeare Society of America's Hamlet Award for Excellence in Playwriting, 1982.

He has also won several national awards for TV and documentary film shorts that he wrote, directed, and produced. He has written several scripts for various television series, including *Men Into Space* and *The Outer Limits*. Among his feature films are *Ambush Bay*, a motion picture with a World War II background, filmed for United Artists; the notable *Robinson Crusoe on Mars* for Paramount; and several other films with a science fiction theme. In 1976, he was awarded the Golden Scroll for best writing by the Academy of Science Fiction.

Ib Melchior is the author of the best-selling, critically acclaimed novels based on his own experiences as a CIC agent: *Order of Battle*, *Sleeper Agent*, and *The Haigerloch Project*; as well as *The Watchdogs of Abaddon* and *The Marcus Device*, all published by Harper & Row; *The Tombstone Cipher*, published by Bantam; and *Eva* and *V-3*, published by Dodd, Mead & Company. Melchior's novels have now been published in twenty-five countries.

Ib Melchior lives in the Hollywood Hills. He is an avid collector of military miniatures and historical documents. He is married to the prominent designer Cleo Baldon and has two sons. His father was the late Wagnerian tenor Lauritz Melchior.